Waiting for Summer

A life without love is like a year without summer

~Swedish Proverb

G.G. Lourie

This book is a work of fiction. Names, characters, places, and incidents are the product of the author's imagination or are used fictitiously. Any resemblance to actual events, locales, or persons, living or dead, is coincidental.

ISBN: 1491246332
ISBN 13: 9781491246337

Dear reader,

This book was inspired by the Seaside Heights and Seaside Park we all knew and loved before Hurricane Sandy targeted our beloved coast. My children, and I'm sure many of yours, looked forward all school year to a summer vacation at the Jersey Shore. From our home in north Jersey, the drive took less than two hours, the excitement in the car irrepressible as we travelled the Parkway south, eagerly counting down the exits to #82. *The crabs are in!* We hoped to see welcoming us as we crossed over Barnegat Bay. You'd think we were on the way to paradise.

For adults, a vacation at the shore is a break from the daily grind—it's family time, it's party time, it's the good times. For teens, it's late-night fun on the boardwalk feeding quarters into the claw and holding on for dear life on a fast ride under the moon. For the little ones, it's the freedom to run back and forth from beach blanket to surf's edge, just for the simple joy it brings. It's endless photos of brilliant smiles under sun-kissed noses, and it's packing up and leaving all too soon. It's a quiet ride home while we reflect on wonderful memories made with siblings, cousins, and new-found friends. Those memories remain with us forever tied to boardwalk souvenirs and sand pails now home to treasured seashells.

To Seaside, thanks for the memories…May you rise once again to provide summer fun in the sun to the countless children yet to enjoy you.

This book was in the editing process while Sandy was ravaging New Jersey's beautiful shoreline. To those who fell victim, my heart and the hearts of my family go out to you.

Acknowledgements

Many thanks...

To my husband and best friend, Eric: Your love and encouragement mean everything to me, and I thank God every day for our wonderful life and beautiful family.

To my daughter, Brianna: You are the wind beneath my wings. You gave me the confidence to see this through, and I know I would never have been so brave without your support. To my sons, Eric and Frankie: You make it easy for me to write about men with big hearts and true character. The three of you make me laugh and make me so proud each day. I am truly blessed to be your mother.

To my friend, Cathy Mindel: A special thank you for being my biggest fan and always lifting me up just when I need a boost. You understand the stuff dreams are made of, and I am so grateful to have had you with me on this journey.

To those of you who read *Waiting for Summer* (my debut novel) when it was still a work in progress, your positive feedback led me here and it's because of you that I persevered.

A big thank you to Laurie Wells for your editorial guidance and C.J. McDaniel of Adazing for the beautiful cover.

To my amazing Mother and all of my wonderful family and friends who've supported me through the years: As you are all well aware, this book has taken many detours to the finish line but it's been the ride of my life and a true labor of love.

Chapter 1

"Hey boss, if you want to know what happened to the twins this morning, check out the patio over at Paradise Pub. Looks like they took a wrong turn."

The information, tossed lightly at Mick Leighton's back, sunk like a knife between his shoulder blades. Memorial weekend was never easy to gauge when it came to figuring out the number of employees to put on the schedule. It was Sunday morning of the three-day holiday, the big season opener at the Jersey Shore.

Prom kids were packed like sardines into nearby motels but they were more likely to grab a bagel from the corner market than waste good beer money on an elaborate brunch. With school still in session, weeklong renters hadn't hit in full force yet. Day-trippers generally packed a cooler and headed straight for the beach. His regulars were year-round residents and second homeowners down for the weekend. He could always count on a swarm of them after church service.

Above all, Mick considered the forecast. Fair weather was a good indicator The Cove would be busy, period. He'd made up the weekend schedule according to the series of sunbursts lined up across the five-day outlook. For a business owner in a coastal hot spot that promised *fun in the sun*, you couldn't ask for more than a perfect stretch of weather like that. Too bad he had about as much faith in that forecast as he did in his summer employees. Case in point, this morning he'd received a weather alert warning of an afternoon thunderstorm, and he'd had two call-outs and four no-shows counting the twins.

Most of his new hires were college kids. The ones who were raised with a good work ethic and honored their commitment—some a little bleary-eyed from a rowdy Saturday night and no doubt regretting they hadn't slept in like their lazy counterparts—weren't happy to hear he needed them to kick it up a notch. Mick couldn't blame them, and with a packed house and a long wait list, he knew the potential for problems increased as the day progressed and his employees' patience wore thin.

To avoid any unpleasant situations, Michael Shane Leighton III, better known as Mick from the day of his birth, had been strolling his restaurant's three connecting rooms, doing what needed to be done to compensate. Jack, his manager, was away on personal business so it was up to him to keep a close eye on things. At the moment, everyone seemed to be pulling together and working as a team. Satisfied with the way things were going after a rough start, Mick was beginning to settle into a better frame of mind when Dylan came up behind him with news on the twins.

Long seconds passed before the knife settled, finding a home among a host of others. Mick gave his chest a rub where old scars shifted to make room for the new. Over the years, they'd all joined together to form a chronic condition called heartsick. He'd learned to live with it and found the easiest way to combat the agony was to think of Tanya Reese Morgan as nothing more than a royal pain in his ass. Damn her, the season had barely begun and she was already up to her old tricks. So much for his better frame of mind, he thought, turning to the employee that just ruined his day.

Dylan's eyes widened as he took a step back in the interest of self-preservation. From the look on his boss's face, the information he'd delivered struck a raw nerve and then some. It kind of made him wish he'd kept the sighting to himself. This was his second summer working at The Cove in Seaside Heights, and he liked his job. From the start, he'd found the owner to be fair-minded and reasonable. Mick didn't tolerate any slackers and ran a pretty tight ship, but he was easy to talk to when a problem developed, work related or otherwise. Even so, nice as he was, Dylan got the feeling that now might not be the best time to share that he was disappointed too that the twins dissed him for another job. He had seen the girls after their interview last week and thought it would be pretty cool working with them this summer. One had a silver stud in her nose, and the other had a tattoo of a long-stemmed purple flower behind her right ear, otherwise Dylan didn't know how anyone was going to tell them apart. Not that it mattered now, since they didn't show up for training. All morning, he'd been feeling kind of bummed about it when he happened to look up after serving drinks to a four-top on the terrace, and there they were, wiping tables and setting up placemats at the restaurant next door.

"Don't kill the messenger boss," Dylan laughed out loud, hoping to lighten the mood. Not getting the desired response, he stepped wide to the side and made a hasty getaway.

With a set to his jaw that had more servers scurrying out of his path, Mick worked his way across The Cove's main dining room and walked through the terrace doors he had opened earlier to the warm May morning. Looking out across the landscaped courtyard, he had a clear view of the recently constructed patio of the newly named Paradise Pub, previously known as Morgan's Bar & Grill. Customers dined at round garden tables under lime green market umbrellas but his focus was on the employees bustling around in their tropical shirts and khaki shorts. Sure enough, he spotted one twin, then the other.

Son of a— retracing his steps through the dining room, he rounded the bar and headed for the front entrance. It was standing room only in the vestibule. On any other day that would have been a good thing but for the mission he had in mind, he cursed anything that stood in his path.

Mick nodded to familiar faces, excusing himself as he slowed his pace to weave through his customers. Once he made his way through the wide double doors, it was clear-sailing around the corner to the other end of the block.

The first Sunday brunch at the new Paradise Pub surpassed all expectations. The doors opened at ten a.m. Within thirty minutes, every table was occupied. By twelve noon, the wait-time for one of those tables was close to an hour. Call-ahead seating, normally available for any number of people, was restricted to parties of eight or more. It was all they could

.andle the crowd trailing from the bar to the reception area to the .ewalk. The kitchen staff was in a frenzy preparing food and refilling buffet trays as quickly as possible. Individual meals could also be ordered off the special brunch menu. All servers lengthened their stride to shorten the time it took to hustle from point A to point B.

Assistant manager, Dana Barnes, opened the door for customers leaving the pub and took the opportunity to ask them how they enjoyed their meal. So far, all replies had been favorable. A few people specifically praised the deep-dish blueberry french toast and lemon pie bars, but the big hit of the morning seemed to be the frittatas. She made a mental note to inform Tanya and chef.

When the hectic pace began to ebb, Dana shooed the hostess, Melanie, off for a well-earned break. Filling in until her return, she began to tidy up the area when suddenly a loud clatter coming from the patio made her lose her train of thought and miss the end of a favorite song she'd been humming along with. Hastily, she stepped closer to one side of the open french doors to gain the new busboy's attention.

"Easy Colin, easy," she urged lowly, making a motion with her hands to lighten the volume and hopefully save some dishes in the process. Muttering beneath her breath about common sense and the apparent lack of it in sixteen-year-old boys, she returned to the hostess station with a poise portraying confidence and efficiency.

Now co-assistant manager, along with her fiancé Stephan, Dana counted this summer number seven working for the Morgans. They were both hired by Tanya's father when the gold etched wooden sign hanging above the rather medieval looking door read *Morgan's Bar and Grill, Proper Attire Required (No Bathing Suits or Bare Feet).*

The building's once Tudor facade had always reminded her of an English pub with its steeply pitched entry roof, rough stucco walls and dark diagonal beams. The interior followed suit, lined with high-backed pine booths and Tiffany lampshades. Cozy for sure, but Dana had always thought the ambiance better suited to the countryside than the seashore, and crocks of hot soup rather than frozen margaritas.

At the pub's re-opening gala earlier in the month, she and Stephan had been in awe of the transformation. The exterior boasted a facelift with smooth stucco walls blushing a pale conch shell pink. Arched windows sparkled behind black ornamental antique grills. *Paradise Pub* was emblazoned in a flourish across the building's brow, along with a rather artsy looking palm tree designed to symbolize an exclamation point. The script and symbol were also black, creatively backlit after dark.

Inside, large terracotta tiles paved the way between watercolor walls and a center archway. Tall palms in gorgeous Talavera pots graced two pair of black lacquered french doors that opened from both ends of the dining room onto a large garden patio. Water trickled over smooth rocks into a small lily pool in the corner of the reception area while dark banana leaf fan blades whirred high overhead.

It was the general consensus the evening of the gala that the new Paradise Pub now suited a beach locale perfectly, beautiful and airy with a contemporary yet Casablanca feel. *Check your worries at the door* was now the only stipulation for entry.

Over the course of her seven summers, Dana spent two working the hostess station. Although years had passed since then, it was still a matter of routine for her to reach for menus at the swooshing sound of the door. Half a dozen or so were tucked in the crook of her arm while she double-checked the chart for open seating. She knew Colin had finished bussing the six-top on the patio and the table was currently being reset but there seemed to be nothing available inside at the moment.

Not that it was going to matter, she soon discovered as her gaze came full circle and landed on the man who had entered. Immediately, her actions stilled and her warm *Welcome to Paradise* smile leveled with a sour twist. For just a millisecond, she had an urge to say, "*Table for one sir?*" Dana thought that would have been hysterical, albeit only to her. Mick Leighton wouldn't have been the least bit amused. By the look of him, he was hanging on to common courtesy by the grit of his teeth. It never boded well for Tanya when he walked in the door.

Mick took a quick look around when he entered the pub but there was no sign of the sneaky, conniving witch. The two minute walk from his place to hers hadn't cooled him down. If anything, he became even more incensed seeing the twins again through the fence as he walked by the patio.

"Where is she?" he asked the girl standing behind the hostess station. He didn't know the employee by name but he'd seen her before, and he imagined the reverse would likely be true. She had to have seen his snarling face over here enough times to realize he hadn't come for a meal and a Mai Tai.

Hoping to save her boss from whatever grief the man was about to bestow this time, Dana considered telling him a little white lie—that Tanya hadn't come in yet—when he suddenly swept past her and headed into the restaurant. Pivoting in his wake, Dana spotted Tanya as Mick obviously had, hips swaying in her pretty calypso skirt as she walked by the buffet table. Too late. Poor Tanya, she thought, watching her take the short hallway and disappear into her office—unaware her nemesis was in hot pursuit.

Dana exchanged a knowing look with Stephan who'd been assisting behind the bar during the morning rush. With the front quiet for the moment, she walked over to him. "Well, call the paramedics, they are at it again," she leaned in to whisper. There was no one within earshot but better to be safe than sorry. Gossiping about their boss was certainly no way to go about setting a professional example for the rest of the staff, especially now that she and Stephan held positions of authority. Tanya had even surprised them with a bonus that morning, a sort of congrats on your degrees and your engagement, and thanks for returning for one more summer. She warmly added how she and her father valued their loyalty through the years and attributed the success of their establishment to employees such as themselves.

The Morgans had always been kind and generous employers. Over time, they'd become like family. Dana was protective of the people she cared about and took her responsibilities very seriously. She had no idea why her boss and Mick Leighton were at constant loggerheads but if there was an enemy in their camp, Dana felt it her duty to keep an eye on him. It wasn't easy, the way he was dodging buffet pedestrians but when his path opened up and he barged into Tanya's office, she sputtered in disbelief.

"Of all the nerve. Do you believe that Steph? He didn't even bother to knock. Maybe you should go and listen at the door and see what he's up to."

Figuring his *no way* scowl should suffice, Stephan continued with what he was doing and slid a glass stem between the rungs above his head. Being tall, lanky and long-armed worked to his advantage behind a bar, but he valued his physical attributes much more on a basketball court. He slid one more glass along the wooden track before his gaze, still bearing remnants of the scowl, shifted to the right and lowered onto Dana's honey blond bangs. "You are joking," he remarked, certain she had to be.

She looked up, unsure of his meaning but damn sure of her own. "No, I am not joking. Mick is riled up about something, just like every other time he comes over here, and Tanya might need one of us to run interference. What on earth is up with those two? Have you ever seen them be civil to each other? "*Where is she?*" she mimicked deeply, imitating Mick's arrogant demand.

Clearly less concerned, Stephan grinned while he polished another glass. He raised the stemware to the light for a water spot inspection. Tanya was very fussy about that, as she should be. He slid the glass into place then paused for a moment to calm his little firebrand with his undivided attention. Arms braced on each side of the sink he worked at, his eyes bored into hers, sending a message that finally began to register.

"What?" Revelation came slowly but when understanding dawned, she gasped in quiet surprise. "Oh, my gosh. Do you know something I don't know?"

"C'mon Dana. Think about it. You can't be that naïve." Completing the task at hand, he ran a towel over the gooseneck faucet and the sink's perimeter.

"Ah, excuse me?" Dana wrapped her knuckles on the bar, wishing she had access to his head. *Hello?* Was she not famous among her friends and family for her matchmaking skills, and were they not scheduled to attend one of the happy couples' nuptials in just a few weeks time? "It seems you've forgotten who you're speaking to? Please state my favorite holiday for the record."

"Valentine's Day."

She smiled sweetly while her eyelids took a satisfied glide. "Thank you very much. I rest my case." Smoothing her hand along the bar's glossy surface, Dana shook her head with certainty. "No Steph, unless you have some evidence to the contrary, I'm convinced those two practically hate each other."

"No argument there but you know what they say about the fine line between love and hate."

"Mmm, well anything is possible I suppose, but my instincts tell me otherwise."

Stephan cocked his head smiling at his future bride with his own brand of charm. Bending forward, he wiped his towel over a water spot on the bar and while in her personal space murmured, "Care to make a little wager that we'll see a change in the wind this summer?" Wagers happened to be their little thing, a way of reaching a decision when they disagreed. It was more fun than endless arguing or tossing a coin.

Returning his challenging gaze, Dana made a thoughtful moue of her lips. "Honeymoon destination?"

"Whew, that's a big one but you are on. If nothing happens between Mick and Tanya by the end of summer, we honeymoon in Hawaii, but if they do get together by then, you my lovely lady are off to Italia."

Finding his confidence a little too cocky, her eyes narrowed playfully. "Hmm, well don't start counting your euros just yet. Did you know they've known each other since they were kids? If it's taking them this long to cross that line, I doubt there is anything fine about it."

Tanya Reese Morgan set her coffee mug and brunch plate on her desk, kicked off her sandals and tucked both sides of her calf-length skirt between her thighs. Curling one leg beneath her, she sat down in her newly delivered, deep blue, executive-style chair with an appreciative sigh and crossed right leg over left knee. The hem of her skirt wound up edging her kneecap, leaving one shapely limb to dangle, bare and golden smooth. Grateful for the plush comfort of her chair after being on her feet for the last four hours, she reached for the plate and placed it in her lap just as her office door swung wide. Mick Leighton closed it behind him and walked steadily towards her void of expression or sound.

Watching him advance, Tanya saw her life flash before her eyes, unfortunately in frames that included him. She didn't resume breathing until he stopped on the other side of her desk and slid his hands in his pockets, instead of around her throat where she thought they might be headed. Surprised, to say the least, by his appearance, she searched her memory trying to recall if she had set any traps for him recently. If so, she should have been expecting him, armored up and ready with her lines.

Her six-step *get even* process actually began several years ago, by accident, sort of, with his precious Jaguar. Step 1 - she'd do something to upset him, like having said Jaguar towed from the alley. Step 2 - he'd come looking for her in a similar fashion, full of fire and fury. Step 3 - she'd feign ignorance. Step 4 - she'd smile innocently at his face. Step 5 - she'd smile smugly behind his back, and last but not least, Step 6 - she'd check off another point on her scorecard.

Getting even with Michael Shane Leighton III had become her primary objective in life. When an opportunity presented itself, there was nothing she relished more. But this morning, his appearance was completely unexpected, and if the fat was in the fire, and apparently it was, well she was hardly to blame.

With her mind spinning with myriad thoughts and her heart racing as it always did just from the very sight of him, Tanya waited for the upheaval of emotion to subside. Full recovery in his presence was never an option but she'd learned how to adjust through pretense. She had nothing but contempt for Mick Leighton. Reminding herself helped steady her nerves—like advice from an acting coach, she would imagine.

Well, ready or not, *Showtime,* she thought, giving her chestnut waves a toss along with her greeting. "Morning Mick, try the buffet won't you? Victor's frittatas are out of this world." Taunting him with the mention of his ex-chef was mean. Tanya reached for her coffee mug, hiding her smile behind its rim.

Other than a sardonic twist of his lips at her audacity, which he'd come to expect by now, Mick chose to ignore the crack about Victor. It was all part of the head game she played, like pulling two employees out from under him on one of the busiest weekends of the season.

"I hired two waitresses to start this morning, Tanya, and they didn't show. I look out over the courtyard and what do you know, there they are, working for you." Saying it out loud triggered a fresh wave of anger. Flattening his palms on the edge of her desk, his hardened features closed in. "Exactly what the hell are you up to now?"

Tanya pressed a little deeper into her chair, wishing she had bought the desk with a bit more bulk and depth instead of this delicate strip of cherry that offered about as much protection as—well, absolutely nothing since he looked mad enough to whip it aside one-handed.

Just let him try, she thought, meeting his accusing glare with a wide-eyed innocent stare. This was her favorite part of their battles. She couldn't care less about his problems and making that crystal clear gave her a rush of satisfaction. A little sexual tease on the side never hurt her cause either. She might not have orchestrated this particular battle, but since fate had stepped in to lend a hand, there was no reason not to take advantage.

Tanya's midnight blue eyes continued to hold Mick's captive. His were a deep olive green and presently shimmering with the heat of his temper. Maintaining control in spite of their effect, she picked up a strawberry from her plate and took a nibble from the tip. Her motive shamelessly evident, she made the movement of her jaw appear as provocative as the slow tilt of her head which sent a cape of luxurious hair sliding across one shoulder. Her visual stroll down the front of his shirt paused on his belt buckle.

Certain that all of her salvos hit their mark, and she had his thoughts precisely where she wanted them, Tanya dropped the performance as if he bored her beyond measure. "I have absolutely no idea what you're talking about," she finally returned. Her tone carried a blatant disregard for his dilemma. Her expression, *cry me a river.*

Mick laughed gruffly in disbelief of her nerve and shoved off from the desk as if he didn't trust himself within arms reach of her. Thinking the faster he got out of there the better, he turned back and said bitingly, "The twins with the spiky blond hair. Are you going to tell me you had two new employees start this morning, identical twins no less, and you don't know anything about it?"

Gone went all pretense and out came the defense. Tanya's chin lifted, her eyes flashed. She'd play a role when it suited her but she worked long hard hours to make the pub a success. There wasn't a crumb swept or an egg cracked without her knowledge or stamp of approval, never mind a new employee hired, and she wasn't about to let him think otherwise. "Katie and Kirsten Kramer. I know my employees, Mick. What I don't know is why you think they should be yours."

His inner sigh carried the weight of a never-ending frustration with her, which seemed to have become his lot in life. "Because I hired them on Tuesday," he began to explain in a tone that might have passed for patient, if it wasn't riddled with sarcasm. "After I heard the forecast for Memorial weekend, I knew it was going to be busy. A few of my regulars requested off, which was going to leave me short staffed. Jack was out of the office when the twins happened to walk in off the street and ask if I was hiring. They filled out an application. I interviewed them. I hired them, and I told them to start at eight a.m. this morning. That is why I know—not think—but know, they should be mine. Now I repeat, how did they end up over here working for you?"

"Oh for heaven's sake." Tanya practically tossed the plate onto her desk along with a balled up napkin. So much for her breakfast and a moment's peace. Untangling her legs she stood up then plopped her bottom back down on the chair in order to swivel and face her computer. She typed in one of the twin's names to bring up her file. She thought it was Thursday when they walked into the pub and asked if there were any openings available, but since Mick looked ready to throttle someone over this, namely her, she wanted to be absolutely sure.

Just as she thought. "Look, see." Tanya angled her monitor towards him and tapped her nail against the screen. "You hired them Tuesday. I hired them Thursday. They must have had a change of heart because I certainly didn't snatch them off your doorstep with promises of higher pay or better tips or tell them you turn into a werewolf during a full moon. They asked for a job and since there's no law in this town that says I need your approval first, I gave them one."

Mick wasn't convinced. Even with the blinking cursor pointing out the evidence right before his eyes, he still didn't trust she was telling the truth. He would have gone as far as betting The Cove on the fact that the twins were working at her place instead of his due to some vengeful plot she'd concocted for the sole purpose of twisting the knife she'd buried in his back eight years ago.

Debating how far to go to prove it, Mick dropped his gaze from the computer screen and refocused on the woman now wallowing in self-satisfaction in her *fit for a queen* chair. Legs crossed, she swayed languidly from side to side, as if her cares were nil and his were insignificant. Knowing the consequences would only add to his pain and suffering, he'd been resisting the view beyond her magnificent eyes, which was torture enough. He was trying. God, how he was trying but what was the use. Without focusing directly on her mouth, he'd still been aware of her pink tongue sweeping a pair of lips that had been haunting his dreams long before it was legal. Without looking directly at her breasts, the fullness behind the soft drape of her blouse fit perfectly within the scope of his vision. Without zeroing in, like he wanted to, on that one sexy leg on display when he walked in the door, it was now branded in his mind's eye like so many other images in his memory, of her, of them. The familiar scent she wore drifted towards him with each sway of the chair and as always, he wanted to sink straight into her bones and die there—and that just served to piss him off even more. To hell with her, he thought, sick of her moods and head games. He'd die wanting her, and for reasons known only to her, she reveled in the fact.

Mick's hands returned to his pockets where they curled into tight fists. His posture was straight but unsettled, his thoughts in a quandary. Then, a smile emerged. A smile his dimples denounced. It held no trace of humor, only a self-disgust that seemed to deepen each time he found himself here, chewing her out over some mischief she'd caused, and still walking out feeling like crap warmed over. He knew that's what he should be doing now, turning around, walking out. But something was stopping him, something brewing inside him that wasn't willing to let her off easy this time.

"You're enjoying this aren't you, Tanya?" Mick asked her, the idea suddenly occurring to him for the first time. Not really expecting an admission, he continued in the same vein. "Do you think I don't see what's going on here? Do you think for one minute I believe it's been just a coincidence that my misfortune somehow ends up to be your gain?"

"Don't be ridiculous," she scoffed, but on a weak burst of laughter that lent it a false ring. Knowing this was headed in a bad direction, Tanya picked up the silver letter opener lying on her desk. She tapped the blade against her palm, threaded it between her fingers. What a fine weapon it would make should the need arise. Mick on a stick. The thought tickled her and helped keep her focused.

"As I said before, I have absolutely no idea what you're talking about." There, that sounded sincere enough, she thought until she saw one of his brows spike and his lips smirk. The expression basically calling her a liar.

"Why don't I refresh your memory then," he stated, crossing his arms and shifting his legs to an *at ease* stance, a term contradicted by the rigidity of every muscle in his body. "Let's see, you get chummy with Victor's wife and steal my head chef away. You disrupt my business with your renovations over here and completely disregard my repeated requests for a few small concessions that would have minimized some of the noise and dust. I checked with the crew you had working here. They said you never discussed it with them. Instead of calling me and asking me to move my car out of the alley one night, you call a tow truck. The kid scratches the hell out of it and claims the damage was already there. Never mind that I assume it was stolen and spend half the night at the police station filing a report.

"Now here we go, starting another season, and I find out you're already butting your nose in where it doesn't belong and badgering old Tony about what he's planting and where. Apparently, he should be planting taller, vibrant flowers against the fence and he should plant high grasses below the terrace, or whatever it was you said to rile him up. He is a very sensitive man, Tanya. He considers his gardens a work of art. You add on a patio to border my courtyard, and there's nothing I can do about it, but you damn well aren't going to have a say in the way it looks. I'll tear down that fence and turn it into a parking lot if I want, and there isn't a damn thing you can do about it. Now here we are again today. I have two new hires on the schedule this morning and somehow they find their way to your place instead of mine."

Tanya continued her to and fro, feigning an indifference she was far from feeling. Inside, more pieces of her heart succumbed. He'd never spoken to her this way before. There was something different about his behavior this time—as if he could no longer tolerate her interference in his life—as if he were growing to hate her as much as she hated him. The thought seemed to paralyze her voice, which left a gap open for him to continue.

"Is this how you get your kicks, Tanya? What do you do, stay up at night thinking of new ways to twist the knife?"

His question, delivered with a clench of his jaw and a bitter reference to their past, was the slap in the face she needed to remind herself that she was the one first betrayed here, not him. The knife he claimed she'd buried in his back, was the one she'd pulled out of her own. With a burst of emotion, she was up on her feet.

"I think you're becoming paranoid, Mick. Believe me, I have much better things to do with my nights than to lay awake thinking about you. First of all, Victor and Connie decided it was time for a change. Yours is a full-scale restaurant open ten months of the year. We're half the size and only open eight. That's the main reason Victor is working for me and not you. Connie was concerned for his health. He'd begun to stress easily and has a family history of heart disease. I had your precious Jaguar towed because it was blocking a delivery truck that arrived late that night due to the weather. It was pitch black and pouring and the car was in my way. You never park there, so it never crossed my mind it was yours.

"Let's see, what other horrendously evil crimes have I committed against you? Oh yes, how dare I bring Tony a glass of iced tea while he's out there baking in the sun, and how dare I strike up a friendly conversation and mention planting red cannas in the corner because, yes, in my opinion, they really would look more striking against the black fence than that weeping thing he's planted there. I do hope I haven't damaged his ego too much and he can find it in his heart to forgive me.

"And oh, about the twins, Mick—did you ever stop to think they might have left you a message that you never received? Or hey, here's a thought, maybe it's exactly as it appears—they neglected to give you a courtesy call to tell you they changed their minds." Tanya's thighs pressed deep into the edge of her desk as she leaned forward to deliver her closing with all the Jersey girl attitude she could muster. "Not my fault. Not my problem."

In the heat of the moment, it was only that strip of polished cherry that kept their noses from touching as Mick met her halfway across, white teeth bared, lips curled in scorn. "You have turned into a royal bitch."

"And a first-rate bastard would be a step up for you." Tempted to use it, Tanya released her death grip on the letter opener and tossed it aside. "Now that we've finally reached the bottom line, have a nice day."

Trembling from head to toe, Tanya fell back into her chair as though pushed by an invisible hand. She closed her eyes, drawing in deep shuddering breaths. He had thrown two words back at her before shutting the door behind him and it wasn't *you too.* So this is what it's come to, she thought, with a sadness so profound she felt grief stricken. Name-calling, abusive language—how much lower could they sink?

Her eyes stung fiercely from fighting back the tears. Tanya absolutely forbid them to fall. Full of purpose, she drew in her chair and looked around her desk for something, anything, requiring her attention. Shuffling papers with one hand, she picked up her fork with the other and stabbed a chunk of melon. She put it in her mouth only to find the ache in her heart had spread upwards into her throat and jaw muscles. She could barely chew or swallow.

She reached for a pen and notepad with the intention of writing her daily *to do* list. The silver barrel of the pen beat a staccato on the paper as she tried to think, think, think. Closing her eyes, the heel of her hand pressed against her forehead, as if it could aid in the effort. Finally forcing the fruit down, her knuckles covered her lips to stop them from quivering. One by one, the tears began to descend, and while her left hand started swiping them away, her right hand began the list with *picnic @ Lisa's.* That was as far as she got before the dam gave way and the flood burst forth.

Five minutes later, she padded swiftly across moon-pale carpet to her private powder room in the front corner of her office. It was a tiny room with only enough square feet to accommodate a commode and a pedestal sink, but she was glad she had the forethought to include it when designing her new office. Especially now, when she desperately needed a place away from prying eyes to collect herself.

One look into the oval mirror had her heaving a deep sigh. God, she was a mess. Her mascara was smudged, her complexion blotchy. If anyone had walked into her office and seen her like this, she would have been mortified.

Tanya opened the doors to the narrow cabinet above the commode and searched for some help. Great, she'd thought to install a bathroom but she didn't have the sense to stock it with anything other than a few basics. There was antibacterial soap, toilet paper, a few fingertip towels and, oh thank goodness, hand moisturizer. She used that and a few squares of toilet tissue to remove the makeup from her cheeks then splashed her face with cool water and patted it dry.

Her breathing was still short and choppy as she walked back to her desk. She might have stemmed the tears but it was temporary. An emotional geyser was still bubbling inside. She'd been here before and knew that when the tight reign on her self-control gave way, regaining it was often a long process. She was going to have to leave quickly, or run the risk of making an utter fool of herself. She was just slipping into her sandals and collecting her purse from the desk drawer when someone rapped on the door.

Dana poked her head inside. "Are you okay?" she asked.

It felt like there were weights on her lips holding her smile down. "Still in one piece," Tanya quipped, and hoped to leave it at that. It would have been pointless to pretend she didn't know what Dana was talking about. Her assistant manager was obviously aware of Mick's visit or she wouldn't be asking about her well-being.

Dana decided she wasn't going to leave it at that. Partly out of concern for Tanya, who, by the sound of her voice, revealed just how *not ok* she really was—and partly because curiosity was getting the best of her since Stephan's enlightening comment.

Dana thought back seven years to her first summer here. Tanya had been a student at Boston University, working in the family business during breaks. Tanya had trained her, Stephan and most of the seasonal staff. Dana couldn't deny being more than a little envious of the owner's daughter. She seemed to have it all; exceptional looks and figure, a certain confidence and sophistication beyond her years, not to mention brains. Jim Morgan took great pride in bragging about his daughter's academic achievements to his regular patrons over the years, although Tanya would become livid with him for doing so. Unspoiled and unselfish, genuinely kind and hard working—those were the qualities Dana was pleasantly surprised to find beneath the physical perfection.

Her admiration for Tanya grew steadily over the years, starting from day one when Tanya took her under her wing, showing a young, nervous newbie the ropes with boundless patience and understanding of first-job jitters. Now a college grad herself, Dana had the utmost respect for Tanya. Though they'd never exactly become best friends or confidantes, more importantly, Dana considered her a mentor. If Tanya needed a shoulder, she would look no further than her faithful employee.

"Thank God you're okay. I was ready to send Stephan in," Dana persisted on a trolling for information note as she crossed the threshold into Tanya's office. Unsure of her welcome, she inched her way across the carpet. She veered a little to the right, tilting her head forward in an attempt to view her boss's features hidden behind a waterfall of hair. Tanya was standing at an angle behind her desk. Her head was bowed. Her glossy waves were acting as a shield for her profile. By design, Dana suspected. "I could tell Mick was upset about something, and when he was in here for so long, I got worried."

"No worries. Everything's fine," Tanya assured her, again hoping to curb Dana's curiosity with another casual comeback as she searched the well of her purse. She knew her sunglasses were in there somewhere. Her eyes were pink-rimmed and puffy, and she wanted to get them on before having to face Dana or anyone else.

"You know the twins that started this morning?"

The subject matter grabbed Tanya by the jugular, forcing her head up against her will. "Yes, what about them?"

Dana nearly gasped. If eyes were the windows to the soul, Tanya was clearly wrought with complete and utter despair. After an awkward pause during which they both seemed to read the other's thoughts, Dana went on to say, "Well, um, Mick came out of your office and walked straight out of the pub. Then all of a sudden he was back and talking to both of them. They looked a little anxious and—"

Listening intently, Tanya's jaw began to drop. "I don't believe this," she interrupted. "Did he cause a scene out there?"

"Well, no. Not really," Dana rushed to clarify, not wanting to mislead. "They were talking quietly, up front, just inside the french doors. You know, off to the side by the palm tree. I couldn't actually hear what they were saying but by the end of their conversation, the twins were looking pretty uncomfortable. Why?" she frowned. "Did Mick's visit have something to do with them?"

Tanya rubbed her brow, her head beginning to pound. "He thinks I lured them from The Cove."

Dana chuckled. "You're kidding. Why on earth would he think that?"

Back to rummaging through her purse, Tanya elaborated, but only briefly. "Apparently, he also hired them to start this morning and well, you know men, Dana, when something goes wrong they find a woman to blame."

"Mmm," the other girl agreed just to be supportive. Fortunately she was never given a reason to draw such a conclusion. It wasn't like Tanya to form cynical judgments either. Dana chalked it up to the emotional stress she appeared to be under.

In any case, Dana's thoughts were already turning to a second conversation she witnessed. This one near the front entrance as Mick was leaving. She hesitated mentioning it. Tanya was obviously shaken by whatever happened here, and if Stephan was right about the two of them, it would be tantamount to rubbing salt in her wounds. Still, Dana felt compelled to let her know and perhaps the privacy of her office would be the best place for her to find out.

"Did you know Mick is dating Melanie?"

Bullseye. Tanya's hand rushed to the aid of her heart while it struggled to keep beating. Even though it was too late to check the reaction, she made an attempt by fussing with the neckline of her top. Her head shook slightly. "No…I…I had no idea. How did you come by this information?" If she'd known her voice was going to sound so frail, she wouldn't have asked.

Dana grimaced sympathetically, mostly for Tanya's sake and just a tad for her own. Stephan was going to enjoy serving her crow for dinner. "Actually, Mick stopped to talk to Melanie on his way out. I was standing next to her. I heard him say that he would pick her up at seven. I think they're going somewhere for dinner then out on his boat to watch the fireworks." Uncertain, she shrugged. "Melanie happened to mention that after...well, it was after he...after Mick left." Dana's words began to falter as a little voice inside her head began screaming—*Stop talking you idiot! Can't you see she's crumbling before your eyes? Some shoulder you are.*

"I see," Tanya murmured, and wondering if this day could get any worse, she felt blindly for the arms of her chair before her legs buckled. Oh God, her feelings were too raw to handle this on top of the harsh words she and Mick had exchanged. Afraid she was going to fall apart again, she shoved the dark glasses she'd finally found onto her nose.

Melanie Harris, Tanya thought. A young woman she'd hired last month for the hostess position. She seemed like a lovely person, around the same age as herself. Pretty. Of course, they were always pretty. Mick and Melanie. Even their names sounded poetic together. He'd probably had dozens of women since the summer they spent together. Tanya hoped after all this time she would have built up some immunity to news like that. Apparently eight years wasn't enough.

"Dana, I think I'm going to go home for a little while. I'm not feeling very well." Tanya's voice had weakened to a hoarse whisper. Pride, however, had always been her strong suit, and her head remained high in an attempt to salvage what remained of her dignity. Hooking her bag over her shoulder, she stood and reached for her brunch dishes on the desk.

But Dana was already there, gathering up her coffee mug and plate. "I'll bring them to the kitchen, Tanya, and let Victor know you're leaving," she assured her, communicating compassion in her soft voice and demeanor. "I'll shut your computer down and lock up the office. Stephan and I will take care of everything."

"Thank you, Dana. I'll be back. I just need to..."

"Go," Dana insisted gently. "You're only a phone call away if we need you."

Chapter 2

Tanya didn't know how long she sat on her living room sofa, fingers plowed into her mop of hair as she stared down at the floor through eyes that felt like they'd been open during a sand storm. An hour or more, she imagined. Long enough for her body to feel that if it didn't start moving soon, it might actually petrify in this pathetic position. When her cell phone chimed for what seemed like the fifth time, the irritation spurred her into action. Dragging her purse closer, she retrieved it from an inside pocket and looked at the screen with a complete lack of interest.

It was Lisa. Tanya expected her to be calling to see if she was going to make the picnic this afternoon. Answering was out of the question. Her friend would know instantly by the sound of her voice that something was wrong. Then she would pry—pry, pry, pry until the only way to make her stop was to hang up on her or threaten to tell her husband, John, that she did not purchase her new Fendi bag at an outlet but indeed paid full price at the mall—which of course Tanya would never do no matter what. Lisa was her very best friend and she loved her like a sister but, oh no, the Malone's traditional Memorial weekend picnic was definitely off limits today.

The pressure of sitting with her head bowed for so long after crying her eyes out earlier left her skin feeling all tight and itchy. Falling back against the couch pillows, Tanya scrubbed her hands over her face. Her fingers continued up into her scalp, raking her hair back and away, twisting it all into a free-formed knot that began to loosen the moment she stood up and started walking. By the time her bare feet stepped from hardwood to ceramic tile, the dark tumbling cascade had returned to the middle of her back.

The kitchen received minimal sunlight with the blinds lowered over the glass sliding doors and the window over the sink facing north. As a result, the floor tiles were refreshingly cool against the pads of her feet. Tanya opened one of the lower cabinet doors and removed a tall bottle. Straightening, she drew a deep, reachable breath and realized the post-hysterics numbness was finally starting to wear off. Time for some serious thinking, she decided. But first, a little panacea from Jose Cuervo.

Standing at the counter, she threw back a shot, wincing as it slid down her throat, sighing as it bled through her system. Up in her bedroom, feeling a little less likely to repeat her pitiful performance at the pub, she changed into shorts and a t-shirt. Out on the deck, she lay down on a lounge chair and began her self-help assignment for the afternoon—*How to Let Go of the Past and Start a New Life by Tanya Reese Morgan.*

She fidgeted at first. She wasn't used to being home in the middle of the day and the guilt was making her restless. At least it was quiet. Blessedly quiet. Thankfully none of her neighbors were hosting picnics. Tanya didn't think she could bear the sounds of merriment with her own mood at rock bottom. The sun was a comfort, sprinkling its warm rays through the new spring leaves above her head.

Spring, she mused…a time for new beginnings. Yes, why not, she thought. She would take her cue from the season and try opening her mind to the possibilities of change. Lord knows it couldn't hurt. Clearly, the past eight years had gained her nothing but more misery, the way she was handling things.

Tanya pictured herself thirty years from now, alone and bitter, checking off another point on her ridiculous imaginary scorecard—as if anything she did to him could possibly compare to the suffering he'd caused her. For the past few years, she'd been trying, no doubt about that. And in the beginning, she derived at least some measure of satisfaction. In the heat of their verbal battles, it was usually she who prevailed, but the final victory would always belong to Mick. It was high time she accepted that fact.

She should have moved to Florida with her parents. That would have been the smart thing to do. By now her new life would have been in full swing. New job, new friends, maybe a lover—a faithful one. But she just couldn't bear cutting her lifeline with the Jersey Shore.

No, if she were completely honest, she couldn't bear severing all ties with Mick. Instead, she dug in her heels, refused to leave and persuaded her father to hand over the reins to Morgan's Bar and Grill and what remained of his boardwalk property. Tanya knew she was young for so much responsibility but felt perfectly capable or wouldn't have suggested it. Since college, her father had been grooming her to take over anyway, just not so soon. Her strongest argument had been that their business was seasonal and their move to Florida a temporary arrangement, only a few months to get her grandfather's affairs in order since his demise and find someone trustworthy to manage the golf course for Nan. Little did they know they would come to love the warmer climate, become avid golf enthusiasts and choose to make Naples their permanent home.

Even if her father had said no, she'd been nearing twenty-five at the time and ready for independence. Sell the house and the business then, she'd told them. Her decision was final. She was not moving to Florida. Finally, her father agreed but only on the condition she spend the winter months with them in the sunshine state. That was two years ago now, and she hadn't let him down, though the tight spots she'd gotten into in the beginning would go with her to her grave.

Her guard was down, thanks to Jose, the sun's comfort and her peaceful surroundings. As a result, she could feel the memories creeping in. Like fog under a closed door they came. As usual, for the sake of her sanity, she tried steering her thoughts in another direction. The memories were too painful, at least in the end, but not the beginning. Oh no, those were beautiful and precious and a part of her life she would never wish to have been different.

Helpless to stop them and thinking it may be cathartic and necessary for the new beginning she so desperately craved, Tanya opened the door and welcomed them in for one final farewell. No longer was she going to let the past rule the future. After today's showdown with Mick, finding some way to resolve her feelings was obviously a matter of emotional survival and imperative to any happiness she hoped to find one day with someone else. Falling under his spell, as thoughts alone of him possessed magic, Tanya reached out and took his hand. Back in time they went, far back, to childhood, where long summer days were filled with sunshine and laughter, innocent awakenings and her best buddy, Mick.

The Leighton's resided in Seaside Park, the Morgan's in nearby Lavallette, but on the Seaside Heights boardwalk stretching between the two coastal towns, the two families were practically neighbors. Business neighbors, that is. Mick's grandfather owned a souvenir shop along the famous mile-long stretch. Jim Morgan, three nearby amusement stands.

Before her father bought the bar on the Boulevard, he spent most weekdays on the boardwalk in his office behind the music stand. She and her mother would often join him there for lunch. Afterwards, they would linger on one of the park benches, finishing their lemonade, enjoying the summer day. Usually at some point, this boy everyone called *Mick*, then his grandfather's sidekick, would come over to say hello.

Her first clear memory of him was around the age of five. He would have been ten or eleven. On this particular day, with her mother trailing behind, Mick had taken her by the hand and led her into his grandfather's shop. Stopping at a grab bag barrel, he smiled down at her and told her to choose one of the toy filled bags. She remembered staring up at him, fascinated with the funny grooves in his cheeks, then looking to her mother, she'd asked her for some money.

"*This one's on me squirt*," he'd said to her, and inside the bag she chose was a small silver heart suspended from a chain. Mick knelt down and fastened it around her neck, saying something about making a *good choice*. Tanya could still see herself thanking him with a quick bashful kiss.

Dampness gathered at the corners of her eyes now. She still had that damn heart. The chain she'd lost long ago, but eventually the heart became her most treasured possession. With the passing of time, its sentimental value grew along with her feelings for Mick. Graduating the charm accordingly, Tanya had upgraded it from a stockpile of juvenile trinkets to her first satin-lined jewelry box. Then, one September night, she frantically wrestled it from its secret compartment in the far corner of her lingerie drawer with the intention of heaving it out the window. Instead she had clutched it in her fist and cried herself to sleep.

Tanya wasn't ready to face that devastating moment of her life, though. Not yet, at least. If this was going to be the big heartbreak finale, the day she finally buried the past for good, she wanted, no, she actually needed to remember everything one last time. A new summer was about to begin. This one, she promised herself, would start with a clean slate.

The gap in their ages set them apart when school was in session but each summer on the boardwalk, their friendship would renew and the bond between them strengthen. At age twelve, after much persuasion, she was finally allowed to start helping her father at the amusement stands.

It was her mother who opposed the idea, fearing too much exposure to such an earthy environment would be an unhealthy influence on a curious adolescent. Her mother did her best to dissuade her, but Tanya was growing up and therefore growing bored with her usual mundane pastimes. She was also eager to start earning her own spending money. What better place, she beseeched her mother, than under her father's supervision.

Tanya loved the boardwalk atmosphere—the smell of popcorn and pizza, the spinning and twirling of the rides on the pier, the spectacular view of the Atlantic, but most of all, being near Mick. She could always count on him calling her squirt and pulling her baseball cap down over her eyes. Often, he'd buy her vanilla custard or challenge her to a game of skee ball.

Otherwise, he too would be busy working for his grandfather or socializing with girls his own age—which did nothing more than stir her curiosity. She could only assume he knew lots of jokes since his girlfriends always seemed to be giggling. Tanya was sure she had never giggled in her entire life and hoped if she ever behaved in such a ridiculous manner, someone would cuff her upside the head. At that point in her life, only two people she knew aroused pangs of jealousy: Cassy Lambert for her poker straight hair that looked so much easier to braid than her own curling mass, and Seth Pritchard for his superior spelling abilities. That cocky little twerp beat her out every time at the annual spelling bee and took home the trophy. As far as Mick was concerned, she considered him her buddy. As long as he made time for her, the older girls could giggle and wiggle to their hearts content.

Over the next few years, however, hormones entered the picture and all thoughts, feelings and emotions took a sharp teenage turn. Her body began to develop, Abercrombie & Fitch became her two favorite words and unlike her equally blossoming girlfriends, high school boys left her completely unmoved.

Mick joined the Marines. It was from eavesdropping on the tail end of a rather strange argument between her mother and father that she discovered he'd left home, angry and bitter over his parents' divorce. She saw him only once during his four-year tour of service. She'd taken her ten speed out one morning for an early ride on the boardwalk and turning a corner to exit one of the ramps, she'd run her front tire directly between his legs.

Half dozing now, Tanya chuckled, recalling the pained look on his face. She had been thoroughly embarrassed, mumbled some apology, inched the tire out of his crotch and sped away, pretending not to hear him when he called out her name. For months after, she would go to sleep thinking of the way his arms looked when he reached out to grab her handlebars. They looked different than she remembered, so muscular and strong, with their hard ridges and hair.

In fact, if it hadn't been for his distinctive olive green eyes, she might not have recognized him. He had only a half-inch of hair, darker with most of the sun-streaked layers shaved off, but the short cut only enhanced his good looks, emphasizing his hard, high cheekbones and the lean contours of his face. A face that had matured into one so heart-throbbing handsome, she was sure after time she must have remembered incorrectly and her memory was simply serving her an image from every young girl's dream.

Not a day went by that Mick didn't cross her mind, but at least the four-year high school whirlwind kept lingering thoughts of him at bay. She would never forget, though, the summer he returned home for good. Neither her heart nor her body had ever been the same. She and Lisa were on their lunch break, both working full time for her father at

Morgan's Music stand. They were strolling down the boardwalk, bound for a slice of their favorite Three Brothers pizza when she felt a single tug on her long braid. She'd tossed a look over her shoulder, expecting to see one of several boys she knew from school. It wasn't a boy.

"Hey squirt," he'd said to her. "You just walked right by me. What, you can't say hello to an old friend?"

Tanya remembered stopping, turning, staring. She waited, as he did, for even the simplest of greetings to roll off her tongue. The news hadn't reached her that he was home, and the shock had rendered her speechless. Aside from her heart, which felt like it was jumping for joy beneath her t- shirt, only her eyes were capable of movement. They traveled uncontrollably from his sexy sunglasses, down the straight bridge of his nose, across the breadth of his shoulders that seemed to be blocking her view of the entire beach, and before they could travel any farther, Mick had placed his index finger under her chin and pressed upwards to close her mouth.

"She's always been shy," he said to Lisa with a flash of his dimples.

Thankfully, Lisa had countered with a...*her?...shy?* Brief though it was, the interlude had given Tanya the moment she needed to pull herself together and unwittingly do something that would set her on a new and wondrous path. In an attempt to prove she was much more mature than her behavior obviously portrayed, she took one bold step forward. Her hands slid up his shirt and around his neck. She'd aimed for his cheek, but the welcome home kiss landed closer to the corner of his lips than she'd intended.

Tanya would never be sure whose body jolted first or what was said in parting but when she and Lisa continued on their way, Tanya could think of nothing save the powerful sensations that flooded her body when it pressed against his. One minute she was innocent and carefree, laughing with her BFF and hungry for pizza. The next, a delicious craving had taken up residence inside of her and refused to budge. She was sixteen and knew some of her friends were already having sex. At that life changing moment, it was her turn to discover precisely why.

It was a discovery that plagued her the entire summer. Mick was too old for her. She knew that and was sure he knew it too, but there was something happening between them that kept her awake at night, tossing and turning, both excited and fearful. The sexual undercurrents when they spoke, walked side by side, or caught each other in a certain look, were crystal clear. One day, when she noticed his fixation with the way she was licking her custard cone, it slipped through her fingers and plopped between their feet on the boardwalk. She avoided him for weeks after that, needing a reprieve from the exhilarating rush of feelings he was awakening inside of her.

Nothing could have prepared her for her parents' reaction. It was a year later, the day following her high school graduation that Mick finally asked her out on an official date. He'd been adorably offhanded, making the invitation sound as if it would be no big deal if she said no. His eyes told her the time had come and she had damn well better say yes.

For the first time, Tanya understood the expression and knew what it felt like to have wings on her feet. She'd flown through the front door of her house and raced up the stairs, calling out to her mother that she had a date and to count her out for dinner.

Tanya had been socially active throughout her high school years, always dashing here and there. Her precipitous plans were, on most occasions, accepted with an indulgent sigh. In truth, Jim and Carol Morgan enjoyed their daughter's outgoing nature and were pleased with her selection of friends. And if, at times, her mood became stubborn or rebellious, they assured themselves it was just a stage or the good ol' Morgan genes. Tanya had graduated from high school with honors and had been accepted into a prestigious university. They'd congratulated themselves on raising such a smart, beautiful, well-rounded child.

It wasn't until she came back down the stairs that her mother stepped from the kitchen to inquire about her date. Mick Leighton, she'd announced, nearly breathless with anticipation. Tanya remembered pausing on the bottom step after catching sight of her father in the front entryway. Her first thought was to draw her sweater draped arm closer to her body to cover her peeking midriff and hide the bellybutton ring she'd been keeping a secret.

In fact, for a moment, she was afraid she hadn't been quick enough and that was the reason for the horrified looks on their faces. She'd known they weren't going to be happy about it and was even set to begin the argument she'd prepared, until she realized they hadn't seen her pierced naval. They were reacting to what she'd just told them, that she was going on a date with Mick Leighton.

Her mother had covered her face with her hands, leaving little doubt as to the expression behind them. Her father's face filled with color as he first subjected her mother to a burning glare before turning it on his daughter.

"What?" Tanya had cried. "Why are you acting this way? Please Daddy, you've known Mick his whole life," she'd implored.

To this day, Tanya could still hear the fury in her father's voice. Mick Leighton was a player, a skirt chaser. He only wanted one thing from her and she was deluding herself to think otherwise. Never had she seen her father so upset. He proclaimed the issue non-negotiable. The subject, closed. He was never to catch her with Mick Leighton or heads would roll, first hers, then his. Teary eyed, she'd appealed to her mother for support. She thought her mother had always liked Mick. But with a rather strange look of regret, her mother had dashed from the room.

By the time her father finished his tirade, punctuating each claim and demand with the thrust of his index finger all but two inches from her nose, Tanya had made the decision to defy her parents. Nothing was going to keep her from being with Mick, not after she'd waited so long.

However, bringing Mick around to her way of thinking had not been easy. He was adamantly opposed to the idea of dating behind her parents' back. But then she hadn't been entirely honest with him. To protect his feelings, she had given him the impression that her father's main concern was the difference in their ages and only skated gingerly over his disapproval of her dating a man with a love'em and leave'em reputation—which would have been putting it mildly.

None of which concerned her anyway. She knew something wonderful had been growing between them over the years. Nothing else mattered. Nevertheless, it was an awkward discussion, with Mick suggesting he speak with her parents, and the memory of her father's hateful remarks ringing in her ears. Mick thought he might be able to turn their decision around. Tanya knew it was carved in stone.

And so her summer of secrets began on one beautiful, magical night in late June. Regardless of the way it ended, she had no regrets. How could she possibly regret the most wonderful time of her life? She often wondered though, if they had become lovers, if things might have turned out differently. Surprisingly, it was Mick who called a halt each time their make-out sessions soared out of control. He'd take her halfway to the moon, to the point of pleading, then set her away.

Tanya knew exactly who to thank for her virginal status. Her father. Knowing Jim Morgan didn't trust him or his intentions weighed heavily on Mick's shoulders, and he seemed determined to prove her dad wrong—even though she hadn't made it easy for Mick. By word and by deed, she let it be known that she was ready, willing and eager to go all the way. Still his conscience wouldn't budge. Finding him in bed with someone else, Tanya could only assume he grew weary of the responsibility of dating a minor and the frustration of holding himself in check.

This was the heart-wrenching part. Tanya tossed and turned for a while, resisting the memory that took such staunch control of her life. She'd relived that September night in her mind for years afterwards, and so often during those first few months that it nearly consumed her every waking moment. One more time. She would remember one last time and promised her heart she would bury the memory forever.

As the end of August drew near, everything began to change, and not for the better. Summer had flown and she was preparing to leave for college. The thought of spending months apart was unimaginable, and though they tried to meet as often as possible, life outside their stolen moments began to monopolize their time and attention.

Tanya knew Mick's grandfather's health had been sliding for months. What she didn't know and was quick to discover was the scope of their business beyond the souvenir shop. There were summer rentals in South Seaside Park, two fix-and-flips in progress in Ortley Beach and a fifty-percent investment in a struggling restaurant down the street from her father's bar and grill. They'd recently acquired a piece of property across from the boardwalk and were in the process of tearing down the small condemned building. The plan was to turn the half-acre of land into a parking lot.

The company was called Leighton Holdings LLC, an equal partnership between Michael Sr. and his grandson. Mick was already working long hours and now, with his grandfather unable to share the responsibilities and continue at his usual energetic pace, it was necessary for Mick to devote even more time and attention to the business. The company employed half a dozen people, but they were either administrative or cashiers at the shop. None possessed the necessary knowledge or level of experience to be of much help.

It wasn't any different for Tanya. Eight hours a day, six days a week, she worked in her family business as well. In addition, there were two out-of-state family trips planned, one for a cousin's wedding and the other for her great Aunt Loretta's 80th birthday. Between those events, she'd scheduled doctor and dentist appointments. She had to shop for dorm necessities. Her car needed servicing and new tires or her parents weren't going to let her take it to Boston. She wanted to reach out to her roommate before school began. So much to do her head spun.

It wasn't long before they found themselves down to one last evening before she was due to leave for college. On that foggy day with a fine mist falling, she'd parked her car and jumped into his at their usual meeting place. "Where are we going?" she'd asked him, studying the outline of his profile. He didn't answer immediately. He just continued to stare through the windshield, appearing deep in thought. Wondering about those thoughts on this last night together, she was committing his face to memory and wishing the next few hours could last forever when he suddenly turned, gave her features a slow perusal, then cupped the back of her neck.

"My house," he finally replied as his lips drew near.

Tanya knew hers had parted on a small gasp of surprise. All summer, he'd refused to take her there, knowing what would happen if he did. After the kiss, a potent preview of things to come, he'd drawn only far enough away to look into her eyes. His own were dark with meaning. "Any objections?" he'd asked her deeply, and her response had been an unhesitant and already husky with desire, "No."

That night was the closest they came to making love. Mick had barely shut the front door, and he was backing her against the foyer wall. His mouth had come down hard and hungry for her own. It had been a fight to see whose tongue could delve deepest, which one could make the other want more. The oversized shirt she'd worn open over a pale blue camisole was pushed off her shoulders. Bunched halfway down her arms, he'd held it there and stepped back to look his fill of her body. He'd closed his eyes groaning something unintelligible.

She'd worn the cami deliberately, bought it especially for their last night together. His reaction had been all she'd hoped for. He'd watched his own hands weigh the underside fullness of her breasts while two of his fingers worked on gathering the fabric and sliding it up her torso. He'd stretched the pale silk high, cursing lowly as he filled his hands with her softness.

She'd thought that her body was going to spin like a twister over Kansas. Either that or she was going to faint. When his mouth lowered to the tip of one breast, she'd clung to his shirtsleeves and prayed he wouldn't stop this time. Determined not to let him, she held nothing back.

Restless for something she knew was on its way, she swung her hips against him until he began to control the rhythm by pressing his muscled thigh between her own. Soon, a cry started deep in her belly, working its way up until it tore from her lips with the most excruciating, inconceivable level of pleasure she'd ever known. She'd heard his voice in her hair, urging her into the unknown. It was the moment his fingers returned to her nipples and his tongue once again joined her own that she slipped beneath the surface of conscious thought and drowned in pure emotion. Her bones seemed to liquefy. Her nails bit into his shoulders, clung to them, then raked his chest in sweet surrender. Gloriously, she'd taken her first rise and fall.

When it was over she'd burrowed against him not wanting him to see the tears. He'd hugged her close, bowing his head to kiss the top of hers. "Come upstairs with me," he'd whispered. "I swear I want you so bad I'll go crazy if we don't do this before you go."

That was when the phone rang for the first time. He ignored it as he led her by the hand up the staircase. The ringing stopped, only to start again as they entered his bedroom. With the loud interference spoiling the moment and the mood, Mick had grabbed the receiver with a snarling, "*What?*" It was the local police calling to say his grandfather had suffered a stroke on the boardwalk, and the rescue squad was taking him to the hospital.

The next day was their last chance to say goodbye. Mick spent most of it at the hospital but would be able to meet her for a short time later that evening. But Tanya was imprisoned inside her house. Her parents had planned a special going-away dinner and afterward, the fabricated excuse of running out for last minute toiletries had her mother tagging along. The following morning, two cars weighed down with Tanya's belongings, crossed the bay bridge and headed north to Boston.

That first week at the university had been the longest of her life. Looking back, Tanya was sure if it hadn't been for her feelings for Mick, she would have met the adventure head on and, like any typical college freshman, she would have been celebrating her independence with all the fervor of her youth. Instead, her love for Mick and those precious final moments stolen from them was all she could think of, robbing her of any other interest, social or academic.

She'd called him the next day, as soon as her parents left Boston, only to hear that his grandfather's condition continued to worsen. She and Mick spoke each day until that final call came from Mick telling her that his grandfather had passed away. Her heart ached for him. He needed her, she was sure, and there was simply nothing else to do but go back home.

That decision came easier as soon as she remembered the upcoming Mardi Gras weekend in Seaside, the end of summer celebration. It was all she needed, a viable excuse to give her parents for making the seven-hour trip back home. No doubt they weren't going to be happy, since they weren't expecting to see her until Thanksgiving, but they knew it was her favorite of all weekends and she counted on her newfound acting ability to pull the wool over their eyes one more time.

Had the scene been filmed for a motion picture, Tanya was sure her performance would have earned an Oscar nod. Nevertheless, what she hadn't anticipated were her visiting relatives from Maryland—or her father exacting punishment for what he called her senseless and irresponsible behavior by making her stay at the house and babysit her young cousins while the adults went out to enjoy the festivities in town. He accused her of being foolish for pulling such a stunt and by much later that night, Tanya had begun to think he was right.

It was after midnight by the time she was able to sneak out of the house and drive to Mick's. By that time she was nearly sick with the need to see him, hold him. Parked cars lined both sides of his street and she had no choice but to find a spot on the next block. Rounding the corner, she heard AC/DC playing before the house even came into view. When it did, she saw groups of people milling about the yard, the porch, standing out on the street by their cars.

Feeling a little self-conscious, she'd walked up the sidewalk and climbed the porch steps. She thought she heard her name mentioned by one of the smokers gathered along the rail. Since none of them looked familiar, she ignored their curious stares and walked through the open front door. Her only thought was to find Mick. She searched the rooms that formed a circle around the staircase, but there was no sign of him. She recognized a few people from the area but most of them were Mick's age. Certain he had to be in the house somewhere, she thought she would ask one of them only as a last resort.

The man who finally appeared in front of her wasn't Mick, but Tanya had often seen them together. He was tall and slim with black hair pulled back and tied at the base of his neck. He wore a t-shirt with a skull graphic and above it the words *Rock On* were spelled out in orange flames. His left arm was covered in tattoos. His lashes dipped low over his jet dark eyes as he studied her with a lazy, *Does your daddy know where you are?* amusement. Tanya got the feeling he was keeping an eye out for troublemakers, like a friendly watchdog. Friendly, as long as no one stepped out of line. There was no bulk to him, but she sensed a whipcord strength that would be a mistake to test.

He carried two open bottles of beer and offered her one. She took it to calm her nerves and have something to do with her hands. "Looking for Mick?" He'd asked her in a surprisingly rich and beautiful baritone voice. He hadn't waited for her reply but went on to say simply, "He's not here."

"Not here?" She'd parroted, trying not to sound as frantic as she felt. "What do you mean he's not here? I don't understand, why would he leave his own house, especially with—"

In his unhurried way, she saw one corner of his lips slide up beneath his thick black mustache. "Yeah right, especially with a houseful of people. Half of them I doubt he even knows."

"Do you know where he went?" she'd asked him. "His car is in the driveway. Did he go for a walk somewhere?" This couldn't be happening, she'd thought, ready to scream with frustration.

He took a swig of his beer then, not taking his veiled eyes from her face. It was at that point she should have realized he was lying. Maybe subconsciously she had. He'd taken too long to answer, no doubt trying to come up with something believable.

"All I know is he borrowed some wheels and took off about an hour ago. It's been a rough week for him with his grandfather and all. This thing just sort of happened. Mardi Gras weekend you know." He'd shrugged, as if that should explain it. "Guess he just needed to get away from everybody."

Tanya had set the bottle of beer on the porch on her way out and nearly reached her car before she remembered his boat was docked behind his house. Determined to find him, she turned around and retraced her steps but this time veered off through the side yard. A floodlight illuminated the rear of the house and the walkway leading to the dock. Two girls were sitting cross-legged on the boards, conversing quietly, but other than that there was no one around. Tanya could see the hulking white body of the boat rocking gently and hear the water lapping against the hull, but she sensed it was as deserted as it looked.

Turning to leave, she noticed the double deck attached to the back of the house. She'd seen the lower one when she'd past it the first time, but the staircase leading to the second story was hidden by a shadow, and she hadn't realized it was there. With high hopes, she ran lightly up the steps to the first level and walked across to the second flight. She was sure it led up to the bedroom he'd taken her to just weeks before.

Halfway up and out of the blue, the thought struck her like a two by four that he might not be alone. Hope was instantly replaced by a nauseating fear. She'd paused, hugging the railing, thinking she might vomit over the side. Moments later, with her faith and courage restored by assuring herself that her fears were unworthy of Mick and the past few months they spent together, that they were a couple now and that Mick would never do such a thing, she continued up the stairs.

Just as she reached the top, the music paused. Into that dark, suspended silence came feminine cries of pleasure. Tanya gasped and raised a trembling hand to her mouth. Her eyes welled up with tears as she fought the sudden weakness that made her want to sink to her knees. She wanted to turn and run and even started to but knew she would always wonder if she didn't see for herself whether it was him.

Approaching the door, she hesitated when a strong breeze caused the inside drape to billow into the room. Seconds later it fell back into place and the sheer panel was sucked against the screen. Heart pounding, poised to take her next step but terrified to do so, she prayed with all her might and lifted her shaking hand to the handle. As slowly as she possibly could, she pushed the screen across the track. The bed was on the other side of the room with the headboard against the opposite wall. In order to see who was there, she knew she was going to have to step inside. She did so, coordinating her entrance at a moment when the song currently playing was at its loudest.

There was a couple on the bed, intimately entwined. They were moving to an unmistakable rhythm. As the man's body shifted slightly and his head reared back, Tanya could clearly see Mick's shoulder and profile outlined by the faint light spilling into the room. The vision was branded into her mind forever.

Chapter 3

It was another beautiful morning, Tanya's favorite time of day. A canopy of milky blue arched high above her head. Beneath her Nikes, the gray weathered boards stretched as far as the eye could see. On her left lay a wide, white sand beach. To her right, a string of surf shops, eateries, arcades and games of chance. With the advent of summer only a few weeks away, some of the connected buildings boasted new awnings and modern facelifts. Others wore the nostalgic look of yesteryear and were garishly painted to promote a sense of fun. Seaside Heights wasn't exactly everyone's favorite vacation spot along the Garden State coastline, but if you were Jersey born and bred, you'd made a memory or two here over the course of your life and would return one day to remember the good times.

A half mile later, the sun grew warmer and climbed higher in the sky. Tanya removed the jacket that matched her black workout capris and tied it around her waist. Bikers and joggers passed by her on both sides, taking advantage of all the wide open space before the boardwalk became a maize of activity. She smiled at familiar faces and waved to shop owners and their employees, many of whom she'd been acquainted with most of her life. She even turned up her smile for a flock of seagulls hovering over the beach. Squawking, they searched the sand then, spotting something the beach sweepers left behind, swooped down for breakfast.

She felt different this morning, lighthearted, just as she hoped. There was a new spring in her step and an uplifted sense of well-being. She was glad she decided to park her jeep at the north end of town and walk the boards. After lying around the house most of yesterday, her muscles were screaming for activity.

It was late afternoon when she spoke to Stephan to let him know she'd be coming back in. He'd told her the day had been busy but manageable, and he expected the evening to be the same. He assured her that he and Dana had everything under control. It wasn't necessary for her to return and, yes, they would call with any questions or concerns.

Since she was still feeling emotionally drained, she gave in gracefully, then wondered what she was going to do with herself for the remainder of the night. Making a salad seemed like a good way to pass the time, however she'd barely begun to enjoy it when she made the mistake of glancing up at the clock. It was nearly seven. She thought of Mick picking up Melanie, dumped the salad, went up to her room and cried out the last of her tears. Exhausted, she'd slept, then woke hours later with the feeling that she had risen to a new plateau, but not without the lingering sadness of having left something precious behind. Mick. It was over and done. Fini. Time to let go. By clinging to the memories all these years, she'd only prolonged the healing process. Perhaps, she thought, just perhaps, if she could work up the nerve, it was also time to mend their friendship.

The braid it seemed had become her trademark, and giving it a yank, apparently impossible to resist. Tanya looked over her shoulder to see who the culprit was this time and saw the word *Lifeguard* stamped in bold white letters across the front of a red tank top.

"Good God woman, what's your hurry? I've been trying to catch up with you for two blocks."

"I actually can't believe you're admitting that, Ty. I guess it just goes to show you who's in better shape." Her gaze swung upward with a teasing twinkle. She patted his rock hard abs. "Slacking off on the workouts lately?"

Ty Harding was a Phys Ed teacher at the local middle school. His summer months were spent lifeguarding the Seaside Heights beach. California blond, baby blues, tall, tan and tons of muscle, he worshipped the golden image he saw in his mirror each day, and every other surface he could find to reflect it. Tanya counted it a major turn-off but still found him likeable enough for an occasional date.

"Just the opposite in fact," he answered her, though he knew she'd only been sassing him. "Think I may be overdoing it a little. I had a charley horse last night that damn near brought tears to my eyes. I'm just trying to walk it out this morning."

Tanya commiserated. "Mmm, I know what you mean. Cramps can be brutal. I took a pilates class with my mom over the winter and had a similar problem for awhile."

"Pilates, huh?" he grinned. Tilting his head, he eyed her from head to toe. "They offer that at my gym. I'd be happy to take you as my guest sometime if you promise to wear this hot little number."

Swinging her gaze out to sea, Tanya groaned inwardly. Oh yeah, and there it was. Another one of his stupid chauvinistic comments, or maybe it was just because it was coming from him. Dragging her gaze back in again, those thoughts were evident in her eyes. "They're called athletic coordinates, Ty. It's just a plain tank top and a pair of yoga pants or whatever. I'm hardly workin' the boardwalk here."

"Okay, okay." He could hear the censure in her tone and knew she had taken offense. Hoping to sooth her ruffled feathers with an explanation, he stated, "That very well may be but not everybody looks quite like you do in athletic coordinates, Tanya. It was just a compliment, honey. No need to jump all over me. Though you are always welcome to you know, jump all over me that is."

Despite his incorrigible ways, Tanya began to laugh. "All right, all right, enough!" she cried and he chuckled along with her.

Reaching Morgan's Music stand, she sorted through the bevy of keys hanging from the lanyard around her neck and unlocked the wide metal door that pulled down to meet the betting counter. Ty helped her push it up the track into the overhead hanger. They chatted about the warm sunny weekend drawing in the crowds. He told her about the young girl he'd rescued from the strong undertow the previous day.

"Good morning, Brian." Tanya spotted the approaching teenager. She looked down at his half eaten chocolate donut and can of root beer.

"Miss Morgan," he returned. Dropping the hand that was holding the donut down at his side, he looked up at Ty with an uneasy smile. "Morning, Coach."

Tanya hadn't considered the fact that Brian had been one of Ty's students. The boy was clearly embarrassed being caught eating sweets for breakfast. Poor kid. Good health and fitness was usually Ty's main topic of conversation during their occasional dates. She could only imagine how he was with his students.

Brian found her early in the season putting displays together at the stand. He inquired about employment in such an endearing way, he managed to bend her better judgment and persuade her to hire a sixteen-year-old for the first time. She'd offered him a bussing position at the pub where he'd be under closer supervision, but he had his heart set on working on the boardwalk, he'd told her. In a sincere and very serious manner, he had promised her he would work very hard, and be honest and punctual. Since that was precisely what she was looking for, she decided to give him a try. For the past four weekends, he'd been true to his word. As soon as the school year ended, he'd be working some weekdays as well. She had to admit, she had a soft spot for him.

Tanya listened in on Brian and Ty's conversation and was frankly surprised Ty wasn't giving him a lecture on the importance of good nutrition. They were talking sports.

Brian set down the donut and soft drink as though he were glad to be rid of it and hopped over the counter. Tanya watched him sort through a pile of CDs he kept tucked in the corner. Boom Boom Pow came blaring through the speakers. Tanya motioned with her hand to lower the volume. "It's a little early for the Black Eyed Peas," she chided him gently.

"That was nice of you," she told Ty, as they strolled a few feet away from the music to say their goodbyes.

"What, ignore that garbage he's putting in his system? Believe me, it wasn't easy, but I hate to come down on him. The kids got some family problems right now. I have his younger brother in my class this year, and there's definitely something going on at home. I believe their father lost his job and their mom always seems to be sick. They've fallen on some pretty hard times. Anyway, I always liked Brian. He's a good kid. Respectful. And God knows there are a lot worse habits kids can pick up these days besides junk food."

Tanya crossed her arms at her waist, tilting her head a bit as she listened and wondered about the changes she was noticing in Ty. Her expression must have given her away.

"What?" he asked her, frowning. "I'm capable of being a nice guy, you know. You just don't give me enough chances to prove it."

Tanya laughed, affronted. "I never said you weren't a nice guy."

His brow unfolded, leaving one thoughtful crease behind. Ty reached for her braid and brought it over the front of her shoulder. "Not exactly, but you say no just as often as you say yes. What am I supposed to think?"

Uh oh. Tanya realized she was giving him the wrong impression. She liked things just the way they were, nice and iffy. "Well," she shrugged, "I guess you're supposed to think exactly what I keep telling you. I'm very busy most of the time. You know it's nothing personal. I just don't date much as a rule."

"What about this doctor I saw you with a few days ago? Is he the reason you turned me down last time? Does he have a problem with sharing?" Ty ran the pad of his thumb down her thick braid, enjoying the smooth silky texture and the way the sunlight defined all the twisting colors.

When Tanya felt his knuckles bump into her breast, she took the braid away from him and tossed it back where it belonged. Boy, give him an inch, she thought and ignored his knowing grin. "How did you know he was a doctor?" she asked him, curious.

"I've seen him at the hospital. We had quite a few injuries during football season last year, unfortunately. I was at the ER pretty regularly."

"That's too bad," she replied tonelessly, thinking back to his previous comment. She didn't exactly appreciate his use of the word, *sharing*. The comment was typical of him—so was the sneaky intimate touch. "Charles and I are just friends," she told him, though it was certainly none of his business. "I'm not in the market for a serious relationship, Ty. I prefer to keep things pretty casual for the time being."

Ty chuckled at the breezy brush off as he gazed out over the empty beach. "Honey, I wonder if you have any idea just how many guys in this town are dangling on that casual string of yours."

"That's ridiculous," she half laughed, knowing the statement to be completely false and at the same time wondering where he could possibly be getting such information. She estimated seeing about five or six guys from the area over the past few years. Some just weren't her type, and she'd turned them down the next time they called. The others stopped calling her, eventually, and it didn't require a dating expert to help her figure out why. A few dates, a few dinners, a few drinks, a few kisses and that's where it always ended. Her decision. Not that she hadn't tried to go further a few times, but Mick's image always seemed to be hovering in her mind, getting in the way. She'd made that horrendous mistake once and wasn't about to repeat it.

"If you're getting your information from the local grapevine Ty, they must be pretty hard up for gossip. I can assure you, none of the guys I've dated are losing any sleep over me."

Tanya heard her cell ring and reached into her jacket pocket. It was Dana. Excusing herself, she answered and since Ty appeared willing to wait, she turned slightly away while conversing.

Ty didn't mind the interruption. It probably saved him from saying something foolish like, *you're looking at one honey*. Waiting for her to finish, he studied the woman who stood less than an arms-length away, yet would forever remain beyond his reach. He supposed there was no harm in enjoying the view. At least he had that. It was hard to say which was her best feature. She had the long, dark eyes of a seductress, by day blue as ink, by night black as pitch. Her straight, pretty nose hooked ever so slightly at the tip. Coupled with a pair of full-blown, naturally rosy lips, her features possessed an exotic sensuality that could make a man sit up and beg, especially when she looked at you a certain way. He thought it would help if he could find some inner flaw, but her personality was that of a sweet tempered angel garnished with the spunk to razz him down off his high horse. All that and a brain to go with it. Twenty-six and she was running Paradise like a seasoned pro. A local critic had given it a five-star rating and a glowing critique.

Remembering the tickets he had to see Rascal Flatts at the PNC Bank Arts Center the following weekend, he was tempted to ask her to join him. But what was the use, he thought, changing his mind. Nothing was ever going to come of it, especially with Leighton in the picture.

Ty was pretty sure Tanya hadn't noticed Mick watching them from the other side of the boards. He'd been there all along, leaning against the rail talking to one of the beach attendants. Talk about local grapevine. Mick and Tanya had the market cornered there. *Is-they-or-ain't-they* rumors had been buzzing around the boardwalk for years. Ty had no idea if they were based on fact or fantasy, but at the moment, he had an uncanny suspicion he was being targeted for fire.

"Sorry Ty, um, where were we?" Tanya asked, pocketing her phone and looking up at him.

Regrettably, he shook his head. "We were nowhere kid." Just to make mischief, he lifted her chin and planted a kiss on those scrumptious lips. "Give me a call if you ever get lonely."

Mick figured there came a time in every man's life when murder crossed his mind. If Tanya hadn't put a stop to Ty Harding's attempt at copping a little feel, he would have taken great pleasure in kicking his ass to the ends of the earth. Backed up against the boardwalk guardrail, arms widespread and hands circling the steel bar, it was a relaxed pose until he saw Tanya come walking along with Ty.

Now Mick's hands gripped the rail as if he was counting on it to hold him back. Standing there with his grandfather's friend, Sophie, he projected an image of composure, unless one looked close. Sophie didn't. She rambled on, reminiscing about his grandfather and the good ol' days when taxes were lower, tourists were friendlier and kids had respect for their elders. Mick listened with half an ear while he watched the couple across the boards.

He wanted to know what they were talking about, what Harding was saying to make her laugh like that. He wanted to know what touching her braid would feel like again, and if making contact with her breast would still make him feel as lightheaded as giving blood. He wondered if Harding was asking her out, if Tanya was saying yes, if they were sleeping together. He wanted not to care when he saw them kiss so his heart wouldn't sink into his gut and a lump wouldn't rise to his throat. He'd do just as well crying for the moon. Behind the cover of his Oakleys, Mick watched the man strut across the boardwalk and head down the ramp to lifeguard.

The clock struck nine a.m. The beach officially opened and all attendants were instructed by the droning phantom of the boardwalk loudspeaker to report to their ticket booths. Mick said goodbye to Sophie and walked the half block that separated Morgan's from Leighton's. He moved in a lazy, hands in pockets stride. Seeing Tanya with another man always left him feeling deflated, empty, except for his right arm. There, the nerves kicked with energy, aching with the need to strike something. Mick curbed the impulse since his wrist was finally getting back to normal.

Several years back, Mick divided his grandfather's souvenir shop in half. One side he'd turned into a seafood bar and the other side into a game stand. He contracted a company to build him a wheel of chance with a custom designed sports theme. Floor to ceiling display shelves along the inner wall contained a variety of quality prizes for the lucky winners to choose from; sporting goods and team apparel, as well as tailgating accessories and stadium seats. On schedule as always, Garrett Ames was there opening up for business. The man was first and foremost a friend, an employee second to none.

Spotting Mick's approach, Garrett turned and stood waiting for him under the signature red *Leighton's* awning. "Well, well," he drawled, "a little early for you isn't it? What happened, no luck with Melanie last night?"

Mick leaned back against the counter and stared beyond the beach into the blue horizon. "Did it look like I was trying?"

One corner of Garrett's lips tucked under his black mustache. "It looked like it always does, like you could give a damn."

"That's about the size of it," Mick replied, and meant that in more ways than one.

"Why'd you ask her out then?" Garrett wanted to know.

"Beats the hell out of me," came the flat response.

In the silence that followed, Garrett shifted his weight to one side. Rubbing his twice-punctured earlobe, he studied the toes of his Doc Martens. Mick was his usual uncommunicative self this morning, but Garrett knew him well enough to see something in particular was eating him. It wasn't hard to figure out what. He saw Tanya Morgan getting cozy with Ty Harding.

As usual, Garrett played dumb and shifted to a comfortable balance on the worn down heels of his favorite boots. Folding his arms, he braced his narrow hips against the counter. Like his longtime friend beside him, his gaze reached far out over the ocean where the Atlantic touched the sky. While Mick looked bleakly into his future, Garrett looked thoughtfully into their past.

It had been more than twenty years now since Mick helped him dig a hole in his backyard after his dog ran under the wheels of a delivery truck. Garrett had been inconsolable, cried so hard he made himself sick, but Mick hadn't made him feel like a sissy about it. He had given him some space, found himself a pickax and headed for the straggly pine tree in the neighboring yard. He'd routed it up with a vengeance, taking out Rusty's death on the stunted tree the lame brain dog insisted on peeing on no matter how many times he got the paper for it. Later that day, when Garrett found the strength to let Rusty go, he and Mick buried him in the grave and re-planted the tree along with him.

Mick had stayed with Garrett that night, there on the ground beside Rusty. They didn't say a word to each other. They just lay there in their sleeping bags, staring up at the stars, hurting. They were typical ten-year-old boys at the time, enjoying summer vacation, playing ball, riding bikes and helping out at Pop's souvenir shop. Until that day, they knew squat about life and the way it could turn on you when you least expect it, leaving you with a hole in your heart that never fully heals. Garrett would never forget how Mick stuck by him. He didn't shed a tear that Garrett was aware of, but he felt his pain and sorrow just as sure as his own. That experience had cemented their friendship and turned it into something more as they grew older. Blood brothers, he would have said, had they actually performed the ritual. They never spoke of their closeness. It was just something each felt and he knew that as well as his own name.

That day would always mean the most, Garrett thought. Even more than the day Mick was a pallbearer at his father's funeral, and the damp April day he stood beside him at his wedding. Mick's gift had been a reception at The Cove. He'd spared no expense.

After their high school years, when he and Mick opted to enlist in different branches of the service, their furloughs home overlapped only once, but until they were both back to stay, their letters circled the globe. About eight years ago, on a sunny September day, Garrett carried Mick's grandfather's casket. Ever since, when some demon inside Mick becomes too much to bear, Garrett will find him drowning his sorrows in a bottle of whiskey.

Through the years, they'd shared a lot of laughs, plenty of sorrow, and on one rowdy night when their brains skipped town, a couple of joints and the easy Passerini sisters, but not once during all that time had Mick ever brought up the subject of Tanya Morgan. Garrett knew they started seeing each other years ago, but something had gone wrong, and whatever it was had been tearing Mick apart ever since.

"You going to the Memorial service this morning?" Garrett asked him. They'd talked about it the previous night. Mick was going to confirm the time.

"Yeah, it starts at ten over at the municipal building."

Garrett checked his watch. "Did you bring the t-shirts and baseball caps?" he wondered, following up on another topic they'd discussed during their double date the previous night. Mick had spent more time talking to him than he did his date. Maggie had come to the rescue and kept Melanie from feeling ignored. It wasn't the first time and probably not the last.

Mentally and physically, Mick gave himself a push. "Yeah, they're in the van. We'll unload when we get back."

Two hours later Mick rested on a wooden crate in the back storage room. He was tired from lack of sleep. Yesterday and through most of the night he thought of the argument he'd had with Tanya in her office. He kept trying to make sense of it all but couldn't. In the first place, she'd been telling the truth about the twins. He supposed he owed her an apology for that.

With a soundless chuckle, Mick rolled his spine against the wall. Crossing his arms, he stretched out his legs and overlapped his ankles. Yeah, he could just see himself going to her with the proverbial hat in his hands. She'd only have a field day ramming it down his throat.

He'd called her a bitch. A royal bitch to be exact, and as far as he was concerned it was a pretty apt description. The question was, *Why*?

Why did she only play the bitch for him? According to everyone else in town, the sun rose and set on Tanya Morgan. It was almost as if she had some vendetta against him and for the life of him, he had no idea why.

The summer they started seeing each other ended in disaster. But afterwards, when he'd pulled himself together over the loss of his grandfather and came to terms with the possibility of losing her to some college jock, she suddenly wanted nothing more to do with him. Ever since, her complete reversal of feelings had him baffled.

When he hadn't heard from her by mid-September of that year, he started calling her cell. He left umpteen messages, all unreturned. Finally suspecting she was screening, he'd called her from a borrowed phone. He'd been right. She'd answered, and it had been like talking to a stranger, as if they'd shared nothing more in life than a passing acquaintance.

Baloney. They'd never had intercourse but he'd had his tongue down her throat, her bare breasts in his hands and managed to give her an orgasm without even taking her pants off. She'd gone off like a rocket. Didn't that account for something? Apparently not. She'd given him the brush off that night on the phone with all the aplomb of a hooker telling her John his time was up. During her Thanksgiving break, he happened to see her walking into the drugstore. He'd followed her in and tried again. That was when she told him she'd met somebody else. Over the next few years, he lived in fear she was going to marry the guy and come back to the island to raise a family. Instead she returned with some weird compulsion to drive him nuts.

She was doing a damned fine job of it too. Absently Mick massaged his wrist, a habit he'd adopted ever since the break. It never bothered him much anymore but he found himself rubbing it every time he thought of Tanya. Since she was forever on his mind, he was surprised he hadn't worked the skin through to the bone by now. The injury took place the first time he found her moving within his circle of friends.

It was the year she graduated from college and long, lonely months since the last time he'd caught a glimpse of her. He was accustomed to seeing her around town by late May each year but rumor had it she and some friends had taken a trip abroad after graduation.

It had been a Saturday night near the end of June, the pretty summer evening reminiscent of their first date four years prior. A retirement barbeque was given in honor of the town's Chief of Police. Mick had been dating Laura Petersen at the time, a local real estate agent, and had asked her to go along.

He remembered as if it were yesterday. A made-to-order sunset spreading across the bay sky, a soft breeze ruffling the white canopy over the buffet table, background sounds of smooth jazz and quiet conversation, flaming torches adding atmosphere and light—and Tanya Reese Morgan walking into the host's backyard looking more sophisticated and more beautiful than he'd ever seen her. She'd been on the arm of local police officer Richie Messina, his Friday morning racquetball partner.

The shock of seeing her in a social setting with one of his friends to boot was just about more than he could handle. He'd suffered in silence through the entire evening and for most of it had been unable to tear his eyes away. Tanya managed to avoid getting anywhere near him and other than a nod from a short distance, Mick managed to avoid his friend. Tanya's gaze locked with his only once that night. She hadn't looked away but rather through him, as if he didn't exist, as if he were invisible, or a complete stranger rather than a lifelong friend, and at one time so much more.

Laura was forgotten and ignored for the majority of the evening and entertained herself by conversing with the other guests at their table. It wasn't long before his brooding silence caught her attention and had her wondering why. Simply connecting the dots led her to the reason. She began asking questions about the girl he kept staring at, none of which he answered. By then he had nothing, no clever excuses to keep her happy and not enough interest in her to care. He was only too willing to oblige when Laura demanded he take her home.

God only knows why he tried getting back on her good side in the car. He'd pulled up in front of her house, turned off the engine and tried turning her on. It worked for a few minutes then with a slap to his face she was off and running. Later he'd pulled into his driveway, got out of the car and tried putting his fist through the driver side window.

Mick sat up rubbing his eyes, thinking he must have dozed off. He wasn't sure if someone called out his name or if he'd been dreaming. Listening, he cocked his head towards the curtained doorway that separated the back storeroom from the front display.

Garrett came through. "Did you hear me? I said Tanya's out here looking for you."

The scowl Mick woke up with deepened. "Who?" Now he knew he had to be dreaming. Tanya never came looking for him. Not anymore.

"Tanya. Tanya Morgan. You know from…"

"I know who she is for chrissakes."

"Then I repeat, she's out here and wants to talk to you." Garrett slid two fingers along his mustache to help tone down his grin. He watched Mick rise and comb his fingers through his hair. "Make yourself pretty now."

"Go to hell."

He took the street exit from the storage room rather than follow Garrett out to the front display. Consequently, he walked up the boardwalk ramp and came up behind her. "Looking for me?"

Startled, Tanya spun around. Her hand flattened against her *Mick-activated* heart. She was nervous enough as it was and should have known he might come from the other direction. She was so busy rehearsing what she was going to say, which for openers was, "Hi." It came out a little breathless, no doubt from the start he'd given her.

Hi? Mick thought, taken aback. What the hell was this? They hadn't exchanged a friendly greeting since she dumped him, which seemed like a hundred years ago. Just yesterday he called her a bitch, she called him a bastard and he'd even taken it down to the f/u level. He'd been sick to his stomach over that ever since. Obviously, she hadn't lost any sleep over it though.

Okay, he'd play along. "Hi," he returned with false levity, mocking whatever game she'd cooked up this time.

Tanya expected some initial attitude from him until she was able to convey her good intentions. For the moment, she didn't let it bother her. "Can I talk to you about something?" she asked him pleasantly.

"I'm listening," he answered, this time without inflection.

The boardwalk was getting busy. A few skateboarders barreled by and tried going around them to reach the exit ramp before they got into trouble for riding them after designated hours. One of them flipped his board, lost his balance and accidentally bumped into Tanya, causing her to lurch forward. Mick caught her upper arms while the boy whipped his head around with a quick *sorry*. Simultaneously, Mick released her as if he'd touched fire and Tanya jerked back as if burned.

"Let's move over here," he told her, cursing under his breath as he turned to lead the way.

Tanya followed him around the corner of the building, suffering the consequences of his unexpected touch. She thought the back of his thumb might have grazed the side of her breast when he grabbed her by the arms. Tanya could only hope and pray there was another man out there in the world who would be able to turn her insides into a molten lava puddle of pure aching sexual need with nothing more than the slightest graze from the back of his thumb.

Taking a bracing breath before he turned back around, she shooed away all thoughts save the one that brought her here. She knew full well how difficult this was going to be. Nevertheless, it was her first giant step to a new beginning between them and the peace of mind she wanted back so desperately. When Brian handed her the perfect opportunity, she knew she had to act on it.

"I was just wondering if you still need help at The Cove?" she asked him once they were face to face again.

"Why?"

"I know someone who might be interested."

"Go on."

"Brian works our stand, at least on weekends he does right now until school is out. Do you know him?"

"No."

"Oh, well anyway he has a sister who really needs a job. Apparently she's worked as a waitress before—Denny's or Perkins, he couldn't remember. They're not exactly fine dining establishments but at least she has some experience. I don't know," she shrugged. "I can't really recommend her. I don't know her personally. What I do know is that she needs a job and if she's anything like her brother, you won't be sorry. If you're still looking for someone, I'll let Brian know that she should come in to The Cove and fill out an application."

Mick tried following along but had trouble keeping up. He was mesmerized by the visual, soaking in the sound. She was either a figment of his imagination or for the moment anyway, the Tanya he once knew. He had to wonder what had changed overnight? What reason could she possibly have for coming to see him this morning and talking to him in a civilized manner after all this time? A job for the sister of one of her employees? It didn't make sense.

He wasn't saying anything. He just kept staring down at her. Tanya grew restless waiting for his response because silence led to thoughts, thoughts led to feelings, and right now her feelings really wanted to focus on all pleasure points and savor their secret reaction to his touch—and that, she could not allow.

Damn it, couldn't he see she was extending the olive branch or waving the white flag, or whatever could possibly apply to this situation? Her blood began to boil, which was a relief. She could handle him much better with her back up.

"Well, yes or no? You seemed to be in a bind yesterday." Tapping one of her Nikes, she crossed her arms.

"Feel free to tell anyone you want to come in and fill out an application, but I'm not going to make any promises until after the interview." He knew that probably didn't come out the way he wanted but his brain was still processing the past five minutes starting with that sweet'n sexy "*hi*" and hadn't caught up yet. He knew he was going to lose her if he didn't say something soon, but what the hell did she think he was going to say, *Your wish is my command*? He had eight years of bitterness churning inside of him and a hard time suppressing it.

He was being uncooperative. In his place, she might have said the same thing but it was difficult to be objective where Mick was concerned. No matter how hard she tried, she imagined she'd always be programmed to find the beast in him. She didn't know why his answer ticked her off. Yes she did, and couldn't help the sneer that began to spread along with her line of thinking.

"What you mean is you won't make any promises until you see for yourself that she's a what, an 8, 9 or hopefully a 10 in the looks department? Isn't that right, Mick? Your waitresses don't really need to know beets from broccoli do they, as long as they look hot in their tight black pants and fill out their starched white shirts?" Surrounding himself with pretty waitresses had just been another reason to hate him all these years. God, her father had been so right about him. "Just forget it," she muttered disgustedly and turned to leave.

"Whoa whoa whoa." Mick caught hold of her elbow before she could get away. "For your information, Jack does all the hiring at The Cove now," he clarified, referring to his manager. "Almost half the staff are guys, not girls, and personally, I don't care if they all look like pit bulls as long as they're reliable and willing to work." Mick paused there, searching for the answer in her eyes before the question even crossed his lips. "And what the hell do you care anyway?"

"I don't care, Mick, not in the least. What I do care about is giving all job applicants a fair and level playing field. Otherwise it's called discrimination. You might have heard of it? What are you doing over there anyway, running a restaurant or trying to revive the Playboy Bunny Club?"Tanya could feel her face flushing, her breath rushing. Biting her lip, she looked in the opposite direction. Her eyes slammed shut. Shit. Damn. What the hell was she doing? She looked back quickly to prove she was still in control of the conversation—and as far as she was concerned, it was over.

"Look, I'll just tell her to come in and fill out an application. Whatever you do makes no difference to me." Turning away from him and taking a step forward, she wasn't surprised to feel her arm still locked in his grasp. Too late. She'd come off sounding jealous. God, could she have made it more obvious?

Tanya felt him closing in, turning around as he switched hands and repositioned his hold from the inside of her elbow to the back of her upper arm. He didn't speak. Didn't have to. He'd always been a man of few words with an unnerving knack of communicating his thoughts and feelings with his eyes, his touch, his actions.

"Let go of me, Mick," she uttered lowly, knowing he was up to something.

"Not for a million bucks," he vowed deeply. There was something happening here. He wasn't exactly sure what it was but he wasn't about to see it end until he got some answers. There were too many people around. At anytime someone could come up to them and break the emotional momentum he had going. She'd flee and he'd be back to square one. He wasn't about to let that happen. "You're coming with me," he told her, and began ushering her down the ramp.

"No," she insisted. "Mick no! I am not going anywhere with you!" Tanya dug in her heels every few feet, but there seemed to be no stopping him. Like it or not she was swept along at his side. "Mick, let me go! What are you doing? Please!" As they rounded the corner, she saw his company van parked at the curb.

Holding on to her with one hand, Mick reached into his pocket for his keys and pressed unlock. As he opened the passenger door, he saw her lean her free arm on the side of the van and collapse against it. The arm he was gripping went from a persistent tug to limp.

"I swear I'll scream if you don't let me go."

Her threat, if it could be called that, came out soft and slurred. Still, Mick was afraid to trust her and thought she might be faking to throw him off guard. Because of that, there was a noticeable lack of concern in his tone when he asked her what was wrong.

"I don't know. Hurry, please. I need to sit down." Tanya let him give her a lift up and onto the bucket seat. She immediately leaned over and dropped her head on her knees.

Mick shut the door, walked swiftly around the vehicle, climbed in beside her and started the engine. With one eye fixed on his passenger, he adjusted the temperature to cool down the interior. She'd come up on her elbows but her head was still cradled in her hands. He cursed himself for getting carried away and roughing her up. However, finesse would have gotten him nowhere. It seemed he was always caught in a no-win situation.

After a moment, she straightened and rested against the back of the seat. "Are you okay?" He wanted to touch her in a comforting way, but doubted she'd welcome it.

"I just felt lightheaded. I skipped breakfast this morning. I imagine that's the problem. I'm sure I'll feel better after I eat something."

Mick sighed, relieved to hear it may be something as simple as that. Slipping on his sunglasses, he faced forward and reached for his seatbelt. "That's easy enough to take care of."

Tanya reached for her own seatbelt. "My jeep is parked up past the Palace. If you'll drive me there, I'll just go home and get something."

Feeling a little better, out of the sun and off her feet, she looked over at Mick and found it hard to believe she was actually sitting beside him inside his van. She never intended for things to go this far. Approaching him about a job for Brian's sister was supposed to have been an icebreaker, a simple experiment to see if opening the doors of every day, casual communication could eventually help her deal with the past. She'd gotten testy with him though and had to shoot off her big mouth. Now look where it landed her, practically in his lap. This, she was not ready for.

Mick dodged the holiday traffic on Ocean Terrace. Turning down one of the side streets, he said, "Why don't I take you for some breakfast or an early lunch. When you're feeling better, I'll drop you off wherever you want." He didn't pose it as a question. Whether she liked it or not, that's what he was doing.

Sit across from him? Share a meal with him? Tanya found the idea almost laughable—and impossible, of course, absolutely impossible. "No, no. That's not necessary. I'll just—"

"Yes, damn it. It is necessary."

She blanched at his clipped response and turned her head, feigning interest in the view outside her window. Since he was in control of the vehicle, arguing would only be futile and she wasn't about to risk life and limb by jumping from a moving van. Accepting her fate, a resigned sigh pushed its way through her lips in one long steady stream. There was only one way to get through it. Time for her chameleon act.

"How about here," he stated, pulling up in front of a small luncheonette on the Boulevard.

Switching her view to the windshield, Tanya gave the canopied entrance a bored look and shrugged. "It's your party."

If he didn't ignore the wisecrack, they'd just start fighting again. Obviously, she'd regained some stamina and he'd lost the edge he had on the boardwalk. Still, he'd have her undivided attention for a while. That was a breakthrough at least.

The hour fell between mealtimes. Tanya assumed that was the reason the place was nearly empty. It was pretty inside with a coastal décor. The hostess greeted them, suggested they sit wherever they please, and followed them with menus in hand. She didn't have far to go. Since Tanya was in the lead, she chose the first booth right next to the door. It would make for a quick exit.

Her stomach cartwheeled when Mick bent his body and slid in across from her. It dawned on her suddenly that after all the years they'd known each other, aside from the boardwalk, this was their first time together in a local, public place. She felt trapped, vulnerable, and worst of all, completely unprepared. He was going to try to expose all her secrets. What she didn't understand was, *Why*? Why bother? He had Melanie now and practically any other woman he crooked his finger at. If he still had that much interest in her, it was a safe bet he'd been storing it behind his zipper.

"It's been a long time."

Sex. It was all she could think of when he spoke like that. Tanya wasn't sure if it was the reference to their past or the bedroom pitch of his voice. Either way, she could only hope and pray there was another man out there in the world who would be able to turn her insides into a molten lava puddle of pure aching sexual need with nothing more than the pitch of his voice. She was in trouble, big trouble. She had to get her mind off bedrooms and zippers. Ignoring the comment, she studied the menu as though she were seriously considering any one of the 3,000-calorie breakfast selections.

"Are you going to give me the silent treatment now?" Mick asked her, eyeing her down-bent head.

Tanya stared at the Memorial Day dinner special stapled inside the menu. They were having meatloaf, mashed potatoes, green beans with dinner rolls and a choice of garden or caesar salad. Feeling her stomach beg and plead, she scratched her nose and tucked a wayward strand of hair behind her ear. After uncrossing and re-crossing her legs for the second time, there really wasn't anything left to do and she realized she was being silly, and making much too much of the situation. Isn't this what she wanted after all—to restore their friendship, or at least some measure of it? It couldn't possibly be that hard to just sit and chat with him and exchange pleasantries. *So how've you been? What's new? Do you believe another summer is almost here? Oh, by the way, who was that slut you were screw...*

Tanya brought that thought to a screeching halt and bravely tore her eyes away from the comfort of the menu. Trying to get her vocal cords to cooperate, her gaze bounced from one object to the next— the condiments at the end of the table, Mick's left hand, the charming starfish curtains, his nose, a hanging basket of white geraniums, his lips, the empty booth across the isle, his beautiful, smoldering eyes.

"Okay, now what will you people be having this morning?"

Sex please. Tanya's eyes widened and jumped from Mick to the waitress and back again. For a moment she thought she had said it out loud.

"Tanya." Watching her curiously, Mick invited her to go first.

"Oh, umm. I'll just have wheat toast and a small glass of orange juice." She handed her menu to the waitress. "Thank you."

Mick ordered coffee.

"Well, that was easy enough," the woman commented smiling.

"Mmm." Tanya half smiled in return wishing she could trade places with the waitress when she disappeared. She didn't know what was happening to her. She felt strange on this new plateau, adrift. Maybe it was just low blood sugar or something making her so susceptible to his nakedness. *Nearness, nearness*, she meant to think. Food, she needed food. Sustenance. God, no. Who was she kidding? What she really needed was to have sex. Lots and lots of sex!

Again Tanya made a concentrated effort to look at him, open her mouth, say something, anything. But her larynx felt clogged. Her gaze got all tangled up in his chest hair. Like Ty Harding, he was wearing a tank top, only Mick's was a muddy color green that turned his eyes to velvet. How different men could be, she thought. He wasn't as pumped up as Ty. Mick's muscles were leaner, yet appeared hard as apples, large golden delicious apples. They sloped gracefully, one into the other, symmetrically proportioned outside the V-like structure of his upper torso. There was a smooth sheen of light maple flesh encasing them, from his nicely broad shoulders right down to where the hair growth began on his forearms. She didn't particularly care for hairy men. Mick had the perfect amount set in perfect patterns. He had wonderful hands too. She knew full well the strength in them, the tenderness. They knew full well how to drive a girl crazy and make her feel safe. One word, she thought. Just one word and she could have those hands wherever she wanted them to be.

There was no hope for it. She had to leave. Pressing her palms on the table and her toes to the floor, she started to slide out of the booth.

Mick knocked her feet out from under her with his foot and stretched his arms across the table to grasp her wrists. "You are not going anywhere!"

"Yes I am! I have to leave!"

"No!"

"Yes!"

"Why?"

"Because!" Tanya felt a whimper coming on. Breaking one arm free, she tucked in her chin, shielding her face with her hand.

"Because why?"

"Because I don't want to be here with you!"

"Why?" Why can't you sit here and talk to me, even look at me?"

Tanya threw back her head, eyes bright slits of blue in a mask of tension. "Because I don't want to and that's all there is to it!" she hissed.

"Here we are," the waitress announced cheerfully and immediately discovered she had come upon a private moment. Her eyes swerved back and forth between the couple. Patiently, she waited for the man to remove two of his limbs from the table.

Mick let go of Tanya's other wrist. Drawing his arms in, he straightened his shoulders, giving the waitress room to set his coffee down. He placed one hand on his thigh, kneading the tight muscle there. His eyes didn't stray from the woman across from him. If she bolted, he'd be right behind her. It put him at ease when she began buttering her toast.

"You're holding something against me. I'd like to know what it is." There was no other explanation for her behavior. He'd begun to suspect and the last few minutes seemed to confirm it. Here all this time he'd bought the story of another guy—but it had been something else. All along, maybe it had been something else.

"Don't flatter yourself, Mick. I have better things—"

"Will you knock off that crap!" He nearly jumped out of his seat with the exclamation but thanks to the emotion gripping his jaw, his voice didn't carry beyond the space between them. This was definitely not a discussion he wanted to have in public but neither was he about to pass up the opportunity. Running an unsteady hand around the back of his neck, he filled his lungs to tide him over for the next round.

Tanya went back to hiding her face with her hand. It was trembling so badly, she transferred it to her juice. Wrapping her fingers around the glass, she considered tossing the drink in his face and making a run for it.

Mick stirred one packet of sugar in his coffee and kept a close eye on her glass. Sometimes she was so transparent, other times he didn't know what hit him. "If you're not going to tell me straight up, then why don't I throw out some ideas and you can let me know if I'm right or wrong, hot or cold, whatever." He didn't have a clue what he might have done to deserve the way she'd been treating him, but if she was going to make this as difficult as pulling teeth, he was going to have to start somewhere. Something told him he didn't have much time.

"That's silly, Mick. You're blowing this whole thing out of proportion." It was an effort but Tanya found a way to exhale and rest her shoulder blades against the booth. "You want to know what's wrong with me? PMS."

The heat lighting up her cheeks was on par with the way this whole, *Let's be friends again,* plan was going. How humiliating. She'd pulled PMS'ing out of thin air—not that she'd ever prepared a multiple choice of lies to pick from if this moment ever arrived. But please, her menstrual cycle? That was the best she could do?

Mick fought back a laugh. "Do you have PMS every time I see you?"

"No, of course not," she answered, tearing off a piece of toast.

"Then why are you always so cold and indifferent, or nasty, or whiney or bitchy every time we have two words to say to each other? I've seen you give a pile of seaweed a friendlier look than you give me."

"I don't whine. I never whine." She was very clear on that.

Mick sighed, raising his eyes to the small slice of heaven he could see outside the window. "Can we stick to the subject please?"

"I didn't know there was a subject." Tanya finished her juice and toast, her energy restored along with her usual spunk. Thank God it had only been a need for food. "Well, I'm ready," she said, wiping her mouth and hands on her napkin. She caught the waitress's eye and motioned.

"Can I get you anything else?" the woman asked, pulling her pad and pen from her apron pocket.

Tanya took charge. "No thank you, just the check please. Oh, and where is the restroom?"

"Back left corner, door on your right," the waitress answered and began clearing their dishes from the table.

"Thanks." Tanya slipped out of the booth, rounded the cashier and walked out the canopied entrance.

Chapter 4

It rained most of the following week. According to Doppler radar, a front stalled along the northeast coastline bringing low-lying clouds, occasional downpours, temps below norm and rough surf. Mother Nature had been a tease with her warm pre-summer weather over the recent holiday weekend, but New Jerseyans were all too familiar with her unpredictable ways. Tank tops and shorts might have made their season debut, but jeans and jackets were always on standby.

For Tanya, a change in wardrobe was the least of her worries. The inclement weather was not only bad for business, it seemed to spark a streak of bad luck. Victor came down with the flu, the new roof over Paradise sprung a leak, one of the toilets overflowed in the ladies room and the battery in her Jeep Cherokee died at the worst possible time. Tanya was certain one of those gloomy gray clouds had singled her out for sabotage and was dogging her every move. Either that, or Mick had put a hex on her.

Since the morning she ran out on him at the luncheonette, they had one brief encounter. It was Thursday night on the boardwalk and though the soupy sea air was as icky as being cloaked in a wet blanket, it was thankfully between downpours when she'd pulled into a primo parking spot that had her thinking maybe her luck was on the upswing. She'd come along just as someone was backing out of one of the few cut-ins along Ocean Terrace where about half a dozen spots butted right up against the boardwalk ramp. There was even fifty minutes on the meter, allowing plenty of time for her to take care of business.

With several employees coming down with the change-of-season flu, she'd asked Brian to work a few evenings at the music stand. She was there to close early and drive him home. Boardwalk traffic had been sluggish all day and she decided there was no point in staying open and getting Brian home late on a school night. The kid was becoming a lifesaver. Seeing Mick standing there talking to him, she would have reversed her steps but Brian spotted her too quickly to switch gears.

"Hey, Miss Morgan, Mr. Leighton hired my sister to work at The Cove," he'd told her with unbridled enthusiasm, and Tanya could tell he was proud to have played some part.

"Well, well, how nice of Mr. Leighton," she'd replied, sprinkling extra sugar on her already sweetened response. And you said I wasn't kind, she conveyed with her eyes as she hiked her fanny onto the betting counter.

Except for the street-side delivery entrance, climbing over was the only way to get on the other side. It was the same for most of the game stands along the boardwalk. Too late, she realized there wasn't enough room to swing her legs over with Mick standing in her way. "Would you mind moving over? Please?" Again she spoke to him very kindly, proving she was magnanimous enough to raise his status above a pile of seaweed.

He didn't oblige though, at least not in the way she'd requested, or expected. The only thing he moved was his right hand, from his jacket pocket to the back of her calf, high up behind her knee.

She'd been wearing jeans but even through denim, she could feel the warmth of his palm and the gentle pressure of his fingers as he squeezed her leg.

She'd gasped, first in surprise then again from the sensations his touch instantly aroused. Even though his actions were carried out just below the counter, hidden from Brian's view, she had thrown a look over her shoulder to see if the boy was watching. But, Brian had his back to them, busy at some task.

Tanya and Mick were nearly nose to nose, thanks to her perch on the betting counter. "What do you think you're doing?" she'd whispered heatedly.

There was another squeeze, warm and gentle and a penetrating look into her eyes that was almost spellbinding. "I just miss you, that's all," he'd said deeply, and in a caressing manner, he slid his hand lower to the curve of her calf before slipping it back into his pocket. "See you around Brian," he'd called out, holding onto her gaze and as Brian bid him a goodnight, Mick walked away.

She expected him to look back. She watched him go, waited with bated breath, sure that he would, sure he would want to see if there'd been more to her reaction after the words had time to sink in. But he just kept walking. It was for the best, Tanya decided, because if he had looked back, she would have been helpless to hide the longing mirrored in her own eyes—the longing that would have revealed just how much she missed him too.

Her office had grown dark outside the pool of light shed by the desk lamp. Within the spotlight, a stack of invoices sat center stage, long forgotten. Music played via satellite throughout the pub and unless she turned off the switch to her office, it played through speakers above her head as well.

She'd chosen something contemporary but light for the Saturday evening diners and always kept the volume at a moderate level, allowing the music to enhance the ambience for her customers, not intrude upon it. Although it never took much, the love song recently aired turned her thoughts to Mick and the night he'd caressed her leg on the boardwalk.

Soon her chair was angled and rocked to a slight recline. Her body was melting into the plush velour, and the focal point for her musings was the small window high up on the opposite wall. It was raining, again, and water ran in glistening rivulets over and over down the short glass pane.

He was a wizard. A simple touch, through fabric and behind her knee of all places, combined with the words, *I miss you*—that's all it took and she'd pulled into her driveway that night via cloud nine, barely having any recollection of driving Brian home. She'd had trouble falling asleep, trying so hard not to think about Mick and wanting nothing more than to do just that. She'd tossed and turned, forcing her mind in directions it had no interest in going. Finally she'd rolled onto her side and cupped her hand around the back of her knee. The sensation his touch aroused came back to her in a warm surge of need that flooded the core of her body. Unable to resist, she'd drifted off to sleep reliving another time, another night, eight years prior. The night he'd taken her to his house and against the foyer wall…

"Hellooooo, earth to Tanya. Come in Tanya."

She jumped hearing a live voice crooning to her from the other side of her desk. "Oh my gosh! Lisa! I didn't even hear you come in."

"No kidding." Dark eyes pinned her with a comical glare. "I knock. I open the door. I peek in. I call your name." Lisa regarded her friend closely as she walked around the desk. Her arms opened for a hug. "Where in heavens name were you, and next time, please take me with you."

Tanya shook her head as much to deny she'd been anywhere *that* good as to banish the erotic vision in her mind. In the process, she swayed slightly and had to touch her fingers to the desktop for balance. "I was just deep in thought, that's all." The smile was a mistake. It had guilt written all over it.

Lisa took hold of her shoulders and held her at arms length. She examined her face. "Uh huh, you were deep into something all right. Look at you, you walked around the desk like you've had one too many tonight." Leaning in, she took a sniff just to make sure. "You're all flushed and drowsy. Your eyes are at half mast and black as Midnight," she stated, actually referring to her beloved cat, not the witching hour. "Out with it. Who is he?"

She'd been caught red-handed, fantasizing about Mick and all but smacking her lips after that deliciously satiating foyer wall replay. Her friend's unexpected appearance might be sobering as a splash of ice water, but fantasies of Mick came with a force hard to shake. Withdrawal required some intense concentration. When she finally got there, a frown was quick to form. "Who's who?"

Lisa's sigh was full length. Find Tanya a lover was written daily in her daily planner. Their September birthdays were five days apart. This year number twenty-seven. Lisa found it mind-boggling that Tanya never even had a boyfriend. She could have had her pick in high school. Guys practically swooned when she walked by. But no, nada, zippo. When necessary, a platonic escort for a prom or special event, otherwise the girl could not have cared less.

Undoubtedly, it was the same for her at college. Over the years, she'd come to the conclusion that Tanya was just very selective. Too selective, which made her own job of finding her a man that much harder. After the second blind date she talked her into went absolutely nowhere, Lisa told her she was just going to have to be a little more flexible. Hopefully, she'd finally taken her advice.

"You were thinking about a guy," Lisa stated, involving her round shoulders and her Jersey Italiano, Soprano's influenced inflection. "It's as plain as the nose on your face."

Tanya tried looking down at her nose, which made them both chuckle and accomplish what it was meant to—throw Lisa from her one-way track. Back on steadier ground, having booted all thoughts of Mick to the moon where they belonged anyway, she was quick to take control of the conversation while she had the chance. She knew the best defense with Lisa was offense. Attack or be attacked.

"Speaking of guys, did you bring yours? Is Jennifer here too? What are you even doing out on a miserable night like this? You know it's only supposed to get worse."

"Please, I'm growing old waiting for this rain to end." Lisa punctuated that comment with a flip of her hand.

Tanya grinned at the hand gesture she'd often seen used by members of Lisa's family. With her leftover baby weight, Lisa was also beginning to resemble her hot Italian mama more than she would ever in a million years want to know, even though it would be a compliment.

Tanya slipped away, marveling about that while her friend continued to talk. Absently, she touched her own cheek, wondering if she was beginning to resemble her own mother as well. Yes, she and Lisa were both growing older. Pushing thirty. When had that happened? Lisa with a child, she ensconced in work, day in, day out. The hefty dose of reality came out of left field, churning up some deep, thought provoking emotions while she stood there half listening.

Lisa tucked her straight raven hair behind her ears. "So, Jennifer is with her Nonna for the night. Her first sleepover." She could barely contain her excitement and reached out for Tanya's hand in guilty pleasure. "Seriously, Tan, I miss her already, but John and I were so desperate for some alone time. He's been working long hours and Jenny and I have been stuck in the house all week thanks to this wretched weather. We were going cuckoo. Thankfully, my mother came to the rescue and picked her up this morning and will keep her until tomorrow afternoon. And guess what? You're not going to believe this, but I was able to get a last minute appointment at Christopher's today."

Tanya gasped. Well, at least Lisa liked to think it was a gasp, and a well-deserved one at that. You needed to call months in advance for an appointment at Christopher's. "Look at me. I had thee best facial ever, my hair cut and styled. Look how it swings. I even had a mani/pedi," she continued, showing off ten crimson nails. "Now all I need to do is lose twenty pounds and I'll be my old self again."

Tanya chuckled. "And you look marvelous darling." Then on a more serious note because she was. "I mean it, Lisa. You do. You look wonderful."

"Don't I? How about the dress, huh? Check out this cleavage." She cupped her breasts and gave them a lift. "I finally look like you. Of course you get to keep yours. I have to pump half of mine out when I go home."

"Ow." Getting a visual, Tanya made a face.

"Na, you get used to it. In fact I'm in the process of weaning her off. Enough is enough, you know what I'm saying?"

"I suppose I will someday. Well, I'm honored you chose to spend your evening here but aren't you forgetting someone? Where did you leave poor John, at the bar? C'mon, I'll walk out with you. He's probably starving."

"Oh no, I'm sure he's fine. We've already been seated and he's happy to have time to read the menu without me tapping my foot. You'll join us, right Tan?"

"I'm certainly not going to intrude on your romantic evening, but I will sit and have one drink with you."

"Good, because I want to talk to you about missing our picnic Memorial weekend. You'd better have a good excuse."

Tanya winced, knowing Lisa would get around to that sooner or later. "Um, actually I was having a really bad day. I'm sorry, Lis. It was rude of me not to call." As they exited her office, Tanya closed the door behind her and hoped the subject was closed as well. No such luck.

Her friend turned her head to talk as they walked. "I was worried. I kept trying to reach you. I said to my mother, she would call if she wasn't coming." Lisa stopped short in the middle of the hallway and with a sudden hand on Tanya's arm turned her to face the suspicion squinting between her silky black lashes. "You were having man trouble weren't you? You little devil, you do have a guy."

"I don't!" Tanya insisted but was helpless to control the hint of a smile that caused Lisa's hands to grip her hips and practically turn her newly waxed brows into question marks. It was an all-too-familiar pose. One that silently demanded an explanation.

"Okay, my bad day was caused by a guy but it's not what you're thinking. How do you do that anyway? How do you always know these things?"

"My great aunt Annalisa. Supposedly, she had *The Gift*." Lisa raised both hands to mime quotes then airing the flat of her palms, she shook her head as if to say, don't even ask. "My mother claims I look just like her. Unfortunately, she also had a rump the size of a VW. Time will tell I suppose. It begins after your first-born and now suddenly I have this thing I do. I read people's minds. Next thing you know, I'll be opening up on the boardwalk. What can I tell ya. It's spooky. John, Tanya's having man problems. So who is this creep, Tan? Do I know him?"

As usual, Tanya could barely keep up with her. Glad to have a third party now as a buffer, she ignored that last query and turned her attention to the man sitting in the booth munching on the complimentary nachos. "Hello, John, welcome to Paradise." He'd missed the grand opening gala the previous month. Lisa had come with her parents.

Ever the gentleman, John rose and kissed her on the cheek. "I bet you love saying that," he teased.

"Of course. Why do you think I chose that name?"

They seated themselves, Tanya sliding in beside Lisa. She signaled Ethan, the waiter assigned to their section, and asked him to bring her a glass of Chardonnay. She saw the Malone's drinks had already been served.

"Lisa raved about this place after the opening last month," John told Tanya, glancing around. "She tried to describe it, but I still thought I would come here and see some resemblance to Morgan's. It looks like you knocked down the entire building and started from scratch."

"That's not far from the truth," Tanya answered with a wry smile. "I talked my father into it while I was in Florida over the holidays. Just some minor renovations, I told him. The contractor he called was a good friend of his. When the two of us put our heads together, we just started coming up with all of these ideas and voila—Paradise." Seeing the wine glass being placed before her, Tanya looked up and thanked the waiter. "Anyway, I'm sure my dad is still cursing me out. I went a tiny bit over budget."

John grinned, his gaze lighting on the fantastic new bar, the raised ceiling, the terracotta tiled floor. "How's business?" A financial advisor by profession, his focus was on the gain.

"Oh, definitely improved. Now the ambience, along with the new menu, appeals to a younger demographic…which was the whole idea. It was time," she shrugged.

"Has your dad been up to see it?" he wondered.

"No, he's only seen pictures. He and my mom are coming up in August."

John raised his mug of beer. "Well, I can't imagine your father having any complaints. I've heard nothing but high praise. You've done a remarkable job, Tanya. Best of luck with Paradise." Three glasses met and chimed over the center of the table.

"Thank you, John. Hopefully, the weather will clear up soon and we can open the patio again. Oh Lisa, I forgot to tell you, I strung those fairy lights through the trees as you suggested and they look so pretty at night."

"You did?" Pleased to have made some contribution, she turned her head to look out the window but there was nothing to see but dreary dark gray through the rain splattered glass. "Oh darn, I wish we'd come on a nicer evening."

"Mmm, I had them lower the umbrellas and turn off all the lights out there before the wind gets any worse." Tanya took a sip of her wine then nudged her friend with her elbow. "You know, we do have highchairs, Lisa. You guys should come more often and just bring Jennifer with you."

As if on cue, husband and wife looked at each other, their thoughts in sync. "Easy for you to say." Lisa returned Tanya's nudge and added a grimace. "Been there, done that, not fun."

Ethan returned at that moment to take their order. Lisa decided on the chicken fiesta and Tanya assured John he would love the grilled salmon. She then began her well wishes so they could relax and enjoy each other's company before their dinner arrived.

"Not so fast, missy." Lisa linked arms with her before she could get away. "You're not leaving until you tell me who this guy is. Don't tell me it's your ol' pal, ol' buddy, Mick Leighton."

With one foot poised to exit the booth, Tanya froze. Her feelings for Mick and the summer they spent together were probably the only secrets she'd ever kept from Lisa. Tanya looked back over her shoulder. "Where in the world did you ever get that idea?"

Equally stunned, Lisa stared back. "I don't know. His name just popped into my head. Am I right? Good God, I am right," she exclaimed, since no denial was forthcoming, and Tanya appeared at a loss for words. "You know, I always knew you two had the hots for each other," she went on excitedly. "Remember that day you kissed him on the boardwalk? I swear I saw steam rising. He's what, six or seven years older than us? You were jailbait, kiddo. I swear he could have been arrested just for the way he looked at you. What have you two been pining away for each other? Is he married now? Is that the problem?"

"Which question do you want her to answer first, hon?" John laughed, scooping up the last of the salsa.

Tanya bowed her head. Supporting her brow with her fingertips, she closed her eyes as Lisa continued to fire. One question in particular rang out loud and disturbing. It wasn't as if the possibility never entered her mind, but to hear the thought spoken aloud hit her like a sucker punch. God, was she ever going to get over him?

Tanya threw back her head. "Lisa, please. Before you get carried away, it's not what you think—and by the way, he is *not* married. The only thing Mick and I have is sort of an awkward business relationship, I guess you could say. With The Cove right next door..."

"What does he have to do with The Cove?" Lisa asked, diving down on the straw of her frozen daiquiri.

"He owns it." Both John and Tanya spoke in unison.

Anxious to speak, Lisa rushed her swallow. Her frown jumped back and forth between her husband and best friend. "Mick Leighton *owns*

The Cove? This Cove, right here?" Her hand waved towards the window and down the block. "How did I not know this? You never mentioned it," she accused Tanya. "We've eaten there with John's parents a few times, haven't we John? No offense, Tan, but the food there is really good. Not that yours isn't. I'm just saying."

"He actually owns quite a bit of property in the area," John inserted and at the same time felt his phone vibrate against his hip. Reaching into his pocket, he gave both girls a second glance, realizing he had gained their undivided attention with that statement. "Mick comes into the office occasionally. He works with J.T., one of my associates," was added for Tanya's benefit, since unlike Lisa, she obviously wasn't familiar with the staff at Braun and Chadwick's, the financial firm in Toms River where he was employed.

"Hot diggity!" Lisa gave Tanya a thumbs up as if to say, *reel him in!* Then, as John seemed to drop the subject in favor of his message, she hunkered down and leaned in close for a little private chick chat. "I'm surprised I never ran into Mick at The Cove, but you know I did see him a few months ago at the DMV. I don't know if he really knew who I was but there was like that split second of recognition. You know what I mean? He didn't say anything, and I certainly didn't." Her expertly shadowed lids lowered as she shook her head in heavenly recollection. "I gotta tell ya though, Tan, that is one yummy dude."

As her peripheral vision spotted her husband putting his phone away, Lisa straightened and resumed her position in front of her daiquiri. She gave it a stir with the straw and drew a quick sip before wrapping up her thoughts. "I just assumed Mick was married by now, Tan, or I would have put him on my list for you. But you must see him all the time if he's right next door, no? Hey, maybe that's why he bought the place, to be closer to you, stir something up again. Ya think?"

She really wished Lisa would stop saying Mick and married in the same sentence. It was seriously getting on her nerves. Tanya managed a thin smile and shook her head. "Mick's grandfather was a silent partner in The Cove years ago. I don't know the details. I'm guessing Mick inherited it and bought the others out. I've never eaten there but I know it's now considered one of the best restaurants around. And no, I don't see him *all* the time. Sometimes yes, but often, no. As John said, he has other interests so I'm sure he doesn't spend all day and night at The Cove. But honestly Lisa, there is nothing going on between us and nor will there ever be. In fact, he's actually dating one of my employees. Melanie. She's a hostess here, but she's off tonight."

Lisa reared back. Relaying an unsubtle message, her gaze narrowed all the way down to thin, spiky slits. "You don't say? Dating one of *your* employees? Hmm, I smell a rat trying to make you jealous. What do you think, John?"

Sighing, her husband shook his head. His eyes rounded and rolled towards Tanya with a plea for help. "I've really got to get her out of the house more. I think she's getting hooked on reality TV."

"She's all yours, John," Tanya chuckled, making her getaway.

"Hey, I know there's something you're not telling me," Lisa called after her in a loud whisper. "And you'd better answer your phone tomorrow missy because I want the full scoop!"

"Thanks for the warning. Byyye."

On the way back to her office, Tanya stopped to have a word with Ethan. "Dinner and drinks are on the house for the couple I was sitting with. Could you please let them know when they ask for the check and just bring it to my office before you leave tonight?"

Tanya had been home approximately thirty minutes during which time she turned on the air conditioning, sorted her damp mail, pinched two yellow leaves off the philodendron in the kitchen window, turned on her bedroom TV to the eleven o'clock news, took off her skirt and blouse, exchanged her bra for a white Jockey tank, went to the bathroom, and exfoliated and moisturized her face. Next up on her bedtime routine, flossing and brushing. Two minutes later, standing at the vanity, absently gazing at her reflection in the mirror and wishing she could erase the words *yummy dude* from her mind, the house went black and scary movie silent.

Tanya emitted a foamy curse. Rather than feel around for the glass she normally used and probably break it in the process, she cupped her hand under the cold tap water and slurped. Hurriedly, she rinsed, spit and reached for a nearby towel.

Terrific! Just terrific! She knew this was going to happen. The storm had been intensifying all day and along with it, a nagging fear that before it was over she was going to lose power either here or at the restaurant, or both. Thankfully the emergency generator would kick on automatically at the pub. One less thing to worry about at least.

A second, more colorful, curse split the air when she stubbed her toe on the door jam in her haste to exit the bathroom and get to a flashlight. She paused to rub the pain away then proceeded with more care and a slight limp into her connecting bedroom. The pearl gray carpet underfoot was luxuriously soft and well worth the investment, she decided when she felt how it cushioned her little toe and made it feel better. Her queen size pillow-top bed was equally inviting and if it weren't for the freaking storm, she'd be climbing into it right about now.

Frustration practically oozed out of her pores. Up until John and Lisa's visit, it had been a long, arduous day that started at about six a.m. and she was feeling the effects, both mentally and physically. She was tired, just plain tired of everything and wanted nothing more than to climb between those cool, smooth, butter-soft sheets, watch a little mind-numbing TV and drift into dreamland. Was that too much to ask?

Apparently so. *Breathe it out, Tanya. Breathe it out.* It could be worse, she reminded herself aloud, finding small comfort in the sound of her own voice. Fortunately this wasn't the first time she found herself alone late at night in the pitch dark, and thanks to the first time, she was better prepared.

Destination, the tall wicker armoire across from her bed that housed her TV, Tanya felt along the wall until she bumped into it. So much for catching up on the news and unwinding with a little SNL. Inching her way around to the front of the cabinet, she bent down and opened the bottom drawer where she'd stored a super-size flashlight. She located the switch on the long handle and then there was light, a large round beam of light. Still not enough to make all the willies go away, but enough to ease the thudding of her heart.

Immediately, she headed downstairs to light candles and was reminded of the first time the power went out after her parents moved. Nothing had ever seemed as frightening as the house she knew like the back of her hand for her entire life.

There had been an electric storm that night and thunder had rumbled eerily overhead. An occasional flash of lightning at the windows provided just enough illumination to make her think she'd seen something lurking in the shadows. She'd felt her way down the stairs then shuffled across the living room holding her arms out in front of her, afraid her fingers were going to encounter another human—or maybe something inhuman. She'd remembered tossing her purse on the couch earlier that evening and knew her car keys were tucked inside the front pocket. She'd grabbed it on a run, opened the front door, dashed through the pouring rain, jumped in her car, locked the doors, and stayed there until the break of dawn. Never mind that her neighbors were just a stones throw away. She'd been scared out of her wits. A chicken. Feeling weak and helpless went against her Jersey girl nature, but like it or not, alone in the dark, she was as chicken as chicken could be.

Tanya wasn't about to panic and run out to her car this time, but neither did she feel brave enough to go back upstairs and attempt falling asleep in her bed. Tonight it was going to have to be the couch, and its close proximity to the front door suited her just fine.

Guided by the flashlight beam, she walked to the kitchen to look for the utility lighter she normally used for candles and the outdoor grill. She loved candles and often lit them for atmosphere and fragrance during quiet evenings at home, rare though they were. Consequently, there were enough scattered about in holders of all shapes and sizes so that by the time she had them all burning, they threw a sufficient amount of light for her to see without having to waste the battery power in the flashlight.

When she returned the lighter to the drawer, she looked out the window over the sink. Nothing to see. All black, just as she expected. The power was out on the entire block, possibly the entire town. Walking to the other side of the kitchen, she touched her nose to the glass sliding doors and watched the wind whipping the backyard cherry tree. The rain was still coming down in torrents and bouncing like a million beads off the decking. There was barely a mile of land separating the bay from the ocean in most towns along the barrier island. There was bound to be major flooding.

A battery operated radio. That's what she needed to add to her power outage survival list and made a mental note to pick one up, along with extra batteries. At least then she would know what's going on out there.

Staring out into the storm, for lack of anything else to do, she was thinking of Lisa and John and hoping they made it home safely when she thought she heard knocking coming from the front of the house. Her head turned toward the sound but with her pulse pounding loud in her ears, she wasn't sure if she heard it a second time or not. Tanya padded lightly across the kitchen tiles. She peered into the candlelit living room and paused to listen. She heard it again. Someone was knocking on the front door.

Her throat constricted. Stretching across the counter, she grabbed the flashlight. She often thought it would make a good weapon, but that didn't mean she ever wanted a reason to find out. Again, treading softly, she entered the living room and started towards the front picture window on tiptoe. Suddenly the knock came again, this time harder and accompanied by a voice.

"Tanya, it's Mick. Open up, I'm getting drenched out here."

Shock had her tumbling off her toes and ramming her foot against the leg of a chair. She hissed, twisted around and straightened herself out on the spin. Holding on to the back of the chair, she checked her heel to see if it was bleeding then rubbed it against her shin to ease the pain.

"Tanya!"

Again, the hard knock and again her feet stumbled backward. With her hand splayed across her chest, she stared at the door as if Big Foot was pounding. Mick had never come to her house before. Never ever, in all the years they'd known each other! Not that he'd ever been welcomed.

Okay, focus Tanya, focus. You can do this. She closed her eyes, seeking strength and guidance from any source that might be tuning in—God, Papa Reese, Lisa, anybody? Mustering all that remained of her stamina by this hour of the night, she drew a deep breath, squared her shoulders and crossed the room in long, brisk strides. Elevating her jaw, she unlocked the deadbolt and threw the door wide. "This better be good," she said to him.

Mick lowered a big black umbrella and left it outside next to the door. He'd been standing under the portico but it hadn't offered much protection from the driving rain, especially when it blew sideways. He'd flipped up his jacket collar to keep the back of his neck dry. Hunching his shoulders, he entered the house, running a hand down the side of his face where a splash caught him on the way in. It was as if the wind stole some of the breath from his voice as he looked into her eyes and said huskily, "Trust me it is. Your mother just called me."

Mick imagined he must have had the same look on his face when the bartender rang his office at The Cove to tell him Carol Morgan was on the phone for him. He'd replied back "*You mean Tanya Morgan*" and Pete's response had been "*Well, if you say so, but she told me her name was Carol.*" The initial shock had paralyzed him. He'd probably stared at the blinking light for a full minute before pressing the button.

"Let it go, love. Your hardwoods are getting wet," Mick said now, peeling each of her fingers off the handle in order to close the door.

"Oh God, my father?" Tanya covered her mouth with her hands and braced herself for the bad news.

"No, no," Mick assured her. "Nothing like that. Your mother is just worried about you. She saw on the weather channel that we are having a nor'easter and she's been trying to reach you to make sure you're okay. She said she tried you here at home, at the pub, your cell, one of your neighbors, I guess, even your friend Lisa. She couldn't get through to anyone. There's a repair truck at the corner already so your landline will probably be fixed soon."

"Oh." Tanya blinked the mist from her eyes and dropping her hands to her heart for a moment, she sighed with relief.

Mick pulled his phone out of his jacket pocket. He held it out for her to take. "Call her. I told her I'd come right over. She'll be expecting to hear from you."

Tanya looked down at his phone while her mind continued to whirl in confusion. Her mother actually called Mick? He had to be telling the truth. It was too easy to verify. Her gaze blinked up the front of his jacket. "Wait a minute, wait a minute. This doesn't make any sense. Why on earth would she call you?"

"My thoughts exactly. If you don't know, I certainly don't. I'm sure she had to be pretty desperate which means she must be pretty worried." Again, he offered the phone. "Will you just call her, please?"

His patience began to falter and affect his voice. For chrissakes, did she forget she was standing there braless in a tight white undershirt? He could see her nipples without even trying, even by candlelight. And whatever the hell she had on for bottoms, he wasn't complaining. He believed they were underwear, though they looked more like black skin-tight short shorts. Mick wasn't sure how much willpower he had left but from the way his body was reacting, he had a feeling he was running on empty.

Reading his thoughts, Tanya folded her arms instead of taking the offered phone. Her hips shifted. "It's not like you haven't seen them before. Besides, I'm sure you have daily access to somebody's."

The comment dripped with sarcasm and had Mick raising a brow. "I'm sure you have no intention of answering this question, but would you mind telling me what the hell that's supposed to mean?"

It was a silly thing to have said, and she regretted it the moment it came out of her mouth. "Nothing," she muttered and with downcast eyes brushed the subject away with a wave of her hand. Anxious to get past it, she shook back her hair and looked up at him again. "I'm not sure of my parents' phone number. It's programmed into my house phone, which is obviously dead at the moment, and in my cell, which is upstairs in my bag. Thank you very much for coming over here to give me the message. I'll be sure to call her right away." Her half step forward was a signal for him to leave, excusing him from any further obligation.

"Oh no," Mick returned adamantly. "I'm not leaving until I know you were able to reach your mother and you've told her that I was here to check on you. I have no idea what your parents ever had against me, but I'd rather not add anymore fuel to that fire."

Tanya considered that a valid reason, although it had been eight years now and her parents had been in Florida for more than two of them. She would have thought *Mick Leighton* to be the farthest name from her mother's mind after all this time. And yet, not only did his name cross her mind, she'd actually called him for a favor?

Mick was now standing in almost the exact same spot her father stood the night he'd lambasted Mick's reputation and forbade her to see him. After that, she, her mother, her father, they'd all gone about their business pretending the incident never happened. Mick's name was never mentioned again. Of course, little did they know she immediately began meeting him behind their backs, and little did she know, Mick would end up proving her father right.

She could have saved herself a whole lot of heartache if she'd only had the sense to heed her father's warning that night. With that thought embedded in her tone and attitude, Tanya tossed up her hands. "Fine, if you insist. I'll be right back."

She'd only taken a few steps toward the staircase when she remembered she hadn't lit any candles upstairs, and the flashlight she needed was back on the coffee table behind her, opposite from where she was heading. Without breaking stride, Tanya switched direction, veering left to walk around the back end of the couch. She stepped on to the area rug, picked up the flashlight and came full circle, walking by Mick again.

Though she didn't glance at him once, his eyes followed her every step of the way. "Last I heard, the Park still had power," he said to her as she passed by him. "Will you just get what you need while you're up there and come home with me?"

"No."

"You want to stay here all night in the dark? All by yourself?" He called after her.

"Yes."

"You do not. You hate being alone in the dark." He watched her hesitate then continue up the stairs without comment.

Mick sighed heavily after she disappeared from sight. Stubborn female. What the hell was her problem? Tired from a long lousy day and weary from this senseless rift between them, two fingers came to rest on the bridge of his nose.

While his eyes were closed, he just had to treat himself to an instant replay of her walk around the room. More times than he could remember over the years, he'd stopped what he was doing to watch that walk—those straight sexy shoulders, and the healthy stride of her long shapely legs. At times on the boardwalk, counting on his sunglasses to conceal the subject of his gaze, he'd get a fix on that curvy backside then feel the need to look to the cool blue Atlantic for relief.

Halfway across the room just now, she'd lifted a hand to her hair. Also familiar, unless the braid was in, the habit she had of diving one hand into her waves and tousling the shiny mass from one sexy look to another. He swore the girl was born to make him weep.

Mick rested both hands on his hips. Sliding his gaze up the staircase again, his head shook at the irony of it all. He nearly laughed at the circumstances he found himself in. He highly doubted Carol Morgan intended for him to come over here and find her precious daughter prancing around in her underwear. At this hour of the night, her mother must have realized Tanya wouldn't be dressed for visitors, but since they do make something called a bathrobe, she probably assumed her daughter would make sure she was properly covered by one before answering the door. If that's the way Carol Morgan had it figured, she obviously didn't know her brazen offspring very well.

Since Tanya didn't come right back down, Mick assumed she was making the call from upstairs. Having no idea how long she would be, he unzipped his jacket and took a look around.

Make yourself at home, Mick, he muttered under his breath. *Why thank you, Tanya, don't mind if I do.* He'd been standing on a small entry rug and made sure the bottom of his shoes were dry and clean before stepping onto the glossy hardwoods. The framed photographs lined up between the burning candles on the fireplace mantel drew his curiosity to the left end of the room. Moving at a slow stroll, he made his way there, absorbing every detail along the way.

That day on the boardwalk when he'd finally decided he'd waited long enough and asked her to go out with him, the plan had been for him to pick her up here at her house. He imagined that part of the evening to be fairly routine. He would park his car out at the curb and walk up to the front door. Tanya would invite him in to say hi to her parents. From rubbing elbows on the boardwalk with them over the years, the ice was comfortably broken enough to make the getting acquainted process painless, or so he'd thought. He would shake hands with her father then they would all sit around and make small talk before leaving. Dating etiquette.

Tanya was only seventeen. He expected her parents to ask what their plans were for the evening. Though they hadn't really decided, he'd done his homework and checked out the movies playing in Toms River just to have a prepared answer.

Tanya had told him at some point over the years that she lived in Lavallette on an ocean block, but he hadn't known exactly where until he called out to her that day. "*Hey, what's your address?*" She'd turned around but continued walking backward while the sunlight and sea breeze played with her long unbound hair. "*25 New York Ave.,*" she'd hollered back, flashing him a smile that sparkled straight up into her deep blue eyes and left him without a prayer.

Anticipation ran through his veins like a drug while he showered and dressed for their date. The phone rang just as he was about to leave. He could tell she'd been crying. Don't come, she'd said. My parents won't allow me to go out with you. It was the hardest hit to his pride he'd ever taken, and the first of many nights he poured himself one too many letting it get to him.

Probably built in the mid 1900's, 25 New York Ave. sat on a lot approximately 75 by 100 and had around 2000 square feet of living space. Small by today's standards but those were rough calculations based on what he could see. Most likely about half of that space was original and the other half new construction added on over the last decade or two—a couple of upstairs bedrooms, a second full and possibly a third half bath, along with new windows, new siding, new roof, the hardwoods. No doubt the kitchen had been remodeled.

Unlike Seaside Heights with its honky tonk boardwalk, corner bars and dance clubs, Lavallette was a quiet town, mostly residential. The homes here had curb appeal as they say, and many of their owners lived in them year-round. Seaside Park was becoming similar. Because 25 New York Ave. stood about sixth in line from the Atlantic ocean, its pristine, sugar sand beaches and protected dunes, in any market, the house and small patch of land it sat upon would probably catch a cool million plus.

The room he stood in was broad and spacious, serving as a living room front and center, a dining area tucked in the rear left corner with a wide window view of the backyard, and a mini office conveniently located between. An executive style computer desk sat inside a nook against the opposite wall and was outfitted with a Mac, a printer, a landline phone, and a skinny gooseneck lamp. Yellow sticky notes were tacked here and there and a stack of papers was piled neatly beneath a large crystal weight to the left side of the wireless keyboard and mouse. A framed color sketch of Paradise Pub hung above the desk.

The furnishings were showroom quality and magazine worthy. He would have expected nothing less from her. In the middle of the room a nearly white sofa scattered with deep red and dark chocolate pillows along with twin leather chairs the color of espresso overlooked a large square coffee table. In the center of the table sat a bronze wrought iron base supporting a shallow glass bowl as big around as a hubcap. A fat candle with about five wicks burned in the hollow giving off an aroma of coffee or cinnamon, something homey like that. He couldn't pinpoint the fragrance. He only knew it was subtle and he liked it. Also on the table was a New Jersey Life magazine, a hard cover book flipped over so that the author's picture was face up and a spiky green plant surrounded by shiny black stones in a clay dish, and there was still plenty of room on the table to spare. The two large area rugs beneath both tables were thick and rich in predominantly dark colors. The fireplace he stood in front of was white with black glass doors.

The first photo on the mantel was of Jim and Carol Morgan. His lips curled, but not in the shape of a smile. Based on the palm trees and swimming pool in the background, he assumed the picture was taken at their new residence in Florida. *Some house*, he thought. As often as he'd seen him over the years, he'd never said two words to Jim Morgan, or vice versa. Never found him very approachable either. Her mother had been kind and friendly enough whenever their paths crossed. In any case, they'd always seemed like decent people. Obviously the feeling hadn't been mutual. Looking at their faces, all the hurt and resentment came barreling back to the surface. Their approval might have made all the difference.

The next photo took him back to a happier time and nearly made him laugh out loud. She had to be all of eleven or twelve, seventh grade maybe. She was dressed in her softball uniform. Her red cap was dangling from her hand, and her braid was falling down in front of her left shoulder. She was squinting against the sun wearing a quirky, up to no good, smile. Her head was tilted slightly as if she was running out of patience with the photographer.

He'd never told her about the day he got his driver's license—that he'd been out riding around getting a feel for the old Buick his grandfather decided would be good for him to cut his teeth on. He'd driven 35 all the way up to Point Pleasant and on the way back through Lavallette noticed a game in progress at the ball field. He'd parked and stood at the end of the bleachers thinking he'd just watch an inning or two. On a hard hit grounder, Tanya rounded first and slid like a pro into second. The ump, who'd been all of about 16, called her out. Jumping up, she went nose to nose with him arguing the call until the coach had to come out and remove her from the game. He'd gotten back in his car and laughed all the way home.

She always looked good in black, even if it was a long shapeless gown. She looked both happy and proud of the degree clasped in her arm as she stood between her equally beaming parents. Even the day looked bright and cheerful with red tulips bordering the campus grounds behind them and sunshine glittering down through leafy branches overhead. He'd considered sending her flowers, or at least a congratulatory card, something to let her know he was proud of her too. In the end, he'd come to his senses and done nothing—because, as he painfully continued to remind himself—she wouldn't welcome his sentiments. She'd moved on and was out of his life for good.

The photos displayed in the double white frame painted with tiny rosebuds stopped his heart before making it reboot to a rhythm he'd never felt before. Tanya was holding a newborn in her arms. A sleeping baby wrapped in soft pink lay against her chest. One of Tanya's hands cradled the infant's bottom. The other supported the back of the small head. Tanya's eyes were closed as she pressed her cheek in a loving way against the baby's delicate crown.

In the second photo, the baby was a few months older and held Tanya's braid in a chubby little fist. In wide-eyed fascination she stared at the treasure in her hand while the camera caught Tanya laughing in the process of trying to reclaim her hair.

"That's Jennifer, my Godchild."

Every nerve in his body leaped. She stood directly behind his right shoulder. He'd been so deep in thought, he hadn't even heard her come down. When she spoke, with her voice soft and sweetened by the love she obviously felt for this Jennifer, he'd been thinking they might have had a baby by now if things had worked out. He'd been imagining what it would have been like, impregnating her, watching their child grow inside of her, building a family and spending their lives together. When Mick turned to face her, every one of those thoughts glowed hotly in his eyes, open windows providing a clear view to the depth of his soul.

Tanya's fingers curled tightly around the things she held in her hands; a pair of flip-flops, her car keys, a small duffel. Her purse hung from her shoulder. Upstairs she'd dumped its contents out on her bed in search of her cell phone then realized she must have left it on her desk after Lisa called to thank her for dinner. Since the pub had generated power, she decided she was going to drive back and spend the night in her office. She would call her mother when she got there. Then, maybe, if she was still wide-awake, she would try tackling those invoices again. At least her sleepless night would be productive.

She concentrated on those good intentions until her nails nearly punctured her palms. But who was she kidding? The only man it seemed she was ever going to love in this lifetime was standing in her candlelit living room in the middle of a stormy night looking at her now as if he wanted to virtually step inside her body and become one with her—as if nothing less would satisfy him. Sometimes, in her weakest moments and wildest dreams, she wondered in the end if anything less would satisfy her.

He didn't move a muscle, yet somehow he was already gathering her in. Tanya didn't move a muscle yet could feel the surrender begin with the hard shell of resolve she'd clung to for the past eight years crumbling into pieces. One last effort was made before the dust settled, and she went looking for that shield of bitterness and bitchiness she'd been using to guard against him—but it was gone. Nowhere to be found. Her pride was another matter and fully aware it demanded she be strong, her head shook, but it shook only once. "No," she tried to say, but the word made no sound.

"I'm dying a slow death without you," Mick confessed and sounded achingly vulnerable as he begged her to take pity on him.

A wavering ghost of a smile revealed the admission hadn't come easy for him while the weight of it pulled on Tanya's heartstrings. Fresh out of pretense and ammunition, she could only react with open and honest feelings. The release of all her pent-up emotions poured into her eyes, lighting the blue as brightly as the flame glimmering on the mantel behind him. Her belongings fell from her hands. Her purse slid down her arm. Yes, she nodded now in agreement. Oh God, yes. Like a slow death, the yearning for him had been killing her too.

Their last night together that summer had been cut short at the most inopportune time. When the phone rang in Mick's bedroom with news of his grandfather, the pause button had been hit, leaving the need and the hunger idling for eight years. Fighting their feelings for each other for so long had been an exhausting effort. They might as well have been trying to change the ebb and flow of the tide.

Their lips sank into each other on a sigh of relief. The desire they'd both buried beneath secrets, heartache and stubborn pride went soaring, unleashing a passion that had yet to be tapped between them. Moaning sounds rushed to the surface and strained against the barrier of their sealed mouths. The kiss was all feeling and raw emotion, almost too much to bear. Tenderness, technique and the subtle nuances used to arouse were neither sought nor applied. Those elements of their kiss were unnecessary. More would never be enough. The tighter they clung, the deeper they ached.

It was a race to the finish that neither seemed able to control. Their hands swept each other from shoulder to hip looking for an opening that would bring them closer to what they craved. Their jackets were restrictive and cumbersome. Tanya was the first to lose patience. Her frenzied search found his to be half open. Cursing its very existence, she slid the zipper to the bottom, pushed it off his shoulders and down his arms. A whimper of frustration escaped when the sleeves wouldn't budge beyond his wrists.

"I've got it," he murmured, drawing back for a moment. Putting his hands behind him, he released himself from the stubborn cuffs and let his jacket drop to the floor. In the time it took him to accomplish the task, Tanya had pulled her windbreaker over her head and stripped off her top along with it.

Mick's knees nearly buckled. He thought she was braless until he noticed the skin-tone straps. In the candle's glow her cleavage glistened and the smooth full mounds of her breasts looked as luscious and irresistible as a prize-winning dessert. She'd put pants on, cropped, cargo style pants that snapped about two inches below the sparkle in her belly button and ended below her knees. She'd left her hair loose and wild.

Afraid his mouth was hanging open, Mick clicked his back teeth together. A rough hand slid over his face for a reality check. An hour ago, he'd been closing up The Cove in no particular hurry. With nothing but longing for Tanya waiting for him at home, he usually took his time about it. Now, by some surprising twist of fate after all these years, here they were in the middle of the night, face to face. She, half clothed, looking like some modern day goddess, and he—terrified. He feared it was just another fantasy and if he reached for her, there would be nothing but a memory where she stood. His heart knocked against his rib cage. That familiar anticipation raced through his veins flowing towards one destination.

If this was a dream, Tanya never wanted to wake up. She closed the space between them, eager to feel the solid press of his body against her own. On contact, she savored and trembled. A gasp lodged in her throat when his hand cupped her breast. Her mind emptied of everything but the wonder of being back in his arms.

He'd been suffering for so long without her, Mick had to fight the urge to drag her to the floor. If there'd been carpet instead of wood beneath their feet, he might have done just that. The strain of behaving himself tightened his muscles and sharpened his cheekbones. He would have sold his soul rather than change the course they were on, but before he took the next step, he had to be sure. Grasping her jaw, he drew her head back in order to see her face. When he saw her eyes reflecting what he knew was in his own, he unhooked her bra.

With that action, the frenzy seemed to ease. Tension waned and pure pleasure intensified. The change took them higher. Straps were lowered and shirt buttons undone while the passion behind their kisses grew deeper and stronger and drove them to the point of no return.

"Where?" he ground out, hiking her off her feet and guiding her legs around his hips.

"Couch," she answered, flinging her bra into the air as they passed the leather chairs.

Mick pressed one knee into the seat cushion and began removing the pillows to make room for them to lie down. When they were all gone, he lowered her the rest of the way with his own weight bearing down over half of her body. His lips reined kisses from her face to her neck to her breasts where they stayed to devour.

Tanya felt him opening her pants and the press of his knuckles as he lowered her zipper. His fingers slid under two layers of cotton. The intimacy of his hand touching where it had never touched before nearly drove her up and over. She held on to the groan as long as possible, until it began to slip out with her uneven breath.

The sound was music to his ears. It drew his eyes to her face to watch her reaction as his hand slid lower.

Her hips lifted eagerly. "Please," she begged softly, feeling her way down his chest and stomach to the snap of his jeans.

Mick swore and sucked in to avoid her touch before it was too late. He held her wrist captive to keep her hand out of trouble then found a safe place for it at the back of his neck. He had second thoughts about that when her other hand joined in, ran caressingly through his hair and pressed him down hard onto her lips. The kiss she gave him said she was all in, mind, body and soul.

He'd waited a lifetime or so it seemed, and the need for her spiraled through him like a dangerous whipcord spinning out of control. Ripping his mouth from hers, he rose up, fisted her pants and began sliding them over her hips when suddenly the power came on.

They froze, except for their lungs, which continued to heave from exertion. Disbelief turned their features to stone as their eyes met. She'd left one light on downstairs and it was the one on the couch table now shining bright as the morning sun upon her bare breasts and stunned expression. If that wasn't bad enough, laughter and clapping from the SNL audience spilled down the stairway segueing into a commercial with an obnoxious boost to the volume. Even the returning hum of the refrigerator and air conditioning system seemed loud and intrusive, which at any other time might have gone unnoticed.

Mick reached up and turned off the lamp. "It's okay," he whispered against her lips but when the phone began to ring his body sagged in defeat. A growl licked moist heat against her neck. "Please tell me you called your mother."

Tanya plowed all ten fingers into her hair and wasn't sure what she was going to do next, scream, cry or go crazy. "Noooo," she wailed and kicked her heels against the couch. "I couldn't. I left my phone at the pub. Oh my God, why isn't it going to the answering machine?"

Covering her ears, she closed her eyes. Her head rocked from side to side. She couldn't believe this was happening to them again. Drawing him to her, she crushed her lips against his in the hopes of recapturing that mindless passion. Weakly her fists pummeled his back.

Mick was certainly giving it his best. Six rings, seven rings. He was losing her, suffering the same torment and very much afraid if he couldn't make love to her right now, at this very minute, she was going to see a grown man cry. "Shhh, please, Tanya. Relax. It's okay. We'll just wait it out. Don't think about it," he pleaded, trying to calm her with gentle strokes and tender kisses. But she'd become tense and rigid, a stick of dynamite ready to explode. Her breathing was labored. She was losing the battle. Ten rings, eleven rings…

"Let me up, damn it."

Swallowing a litany of curses, Mick pushed himself into a sitting position and gave her room to roll off.

Tanya reached for the throw she kept draped across the back of the sofa. Rising unsteadily, she wrapped it around her shoulders. Her pants were adjusted on her way to the desk. She wanted to rip the phone off the base, heave it through the window then chase after it and beat it with a stick.

Instead she looked down at the name *Morgan* displayed on the screen, did what she could to compose herself and pressed the button. "Hi Mom." Her voice came out flat and scratchy. Injecting any levity into her greeting was out of the question.

"Oh, thank heaven, Tanya. I've been so worried. Is everything all right?"

Weak, wobbly, she tilted forward and let the desk take her weight.

"Tanya, are you there?"

"Yes." She cleared her throat to smooth out her tone, pulled out the chair and stooped like an old woman collapsed into it. She crossed her thighs, hoping to relieve some of the throbbing. "Yes, Mom, I'm here. It's raining and it's windy but I haven't been swept out to sea yet."

"I know, I know honey. I worry too much and I'm sorry but the weather channel is showing pictures of LBI and saying—"

Tanya sighed. "Mom, they would have evacuated if it was going to be that bad. I'm fine, really. I don't even hear it raining anymore. I would have called you back, but I left my cell at the pub and the house phone has been out for awhile."

"Oh? Then Mick came by—and—told you—I was trying to—reach you?"

The discomfort in her mother's voice was obvious. The hesitant climb said she hated to ask but couldn't resist. God, how on earth was she supposed to handle this conversation, especially with the subject of their discussion within earshot? The less said the better, she supposed.

"Um, yes actually, he did." Okay Mom, your move.

When her mother didn't make one, Tanya stumbled over a few more words about the weather and looked back at the couch. He was sitting on the edge of it with his legs widespread and his forearms braced on his thighs. His fingers were threaded loosely together between his knees. He appeared to be staring at them, very solemnly. He was shirtless and shoeless and looked magnificent sitting there. The throbbing intensified.

"Is he there now?"

"Hmm? What? Oh, umm, yes. Well, no. I mean he was just leaving. We both were. I was going to go back to the pub and then we saw the lights come on in the house so I...I came back in and um, heard the phone ringing."

"Oh, I see. Well, I know it's late darling and I won't keep you. I just knew I wouldn't sleep a wink until I knew you were safe. Oh, I nearly forgot. I also wanted to tell you quickly that Nan broke her ankle today."

"Oh, my goodness. What happened?"

"She fell out of the golf cart."

"She fell out of the golf cart?"

"Yes, your father and I nearly died when we saw her tip over?"

"It tipped over? With Nan in it?"

"No, no. The golf cart didn't tip over. Nan put one foot down on the ground and she tipped over...lost her balance."

"Oh, bad enough though. Is she in a cast?"

"A walking cast. You know, one of those things. She's on pain medication. She's a trooper. She'll be fine."

"Well, give her my love. I guess she'll be off the greens for a while. She won't be very happy about that."

"No, that's all she keeps talking about. She needs to give it time to heal properly, of course, and we've told her if she's not going to behave herself, we're going to drag her up north with us when we come rather than leave her here alone. You know she's not fond of traveling very far by car."

"Mmm, any idea when you'll be coming?" Tanya asked, and out of the corner of her eye noticed Mick stand up. Half listening to her mother, she watched him walk over to the switch on the wall, turn on the overhead light for the landing and go upstairs. Imagining him stepping foot into her bedroom made her lose concentration. Maybe he was just looking for the bathroom. If he went into hers, she hoped she hadn't left anything embarrassing lying around. The lights had gone out while she was in there preparing for bed. Before panic took complete control, she saw him coming back down and realized he had just gone up to turn the TV off. Good Lord he was gorgeous. She wondered if Melanie was waiting up for him somewhere. No doubt he'd turned off his phone in case she called looking for him. The thought made her ill.

"Not exactly. August, I believe. We'll be stopping in Maryland on the way up to visit Aunt Jackie and the family for a few days. I have to call her and see what their plans are for the summer. Don't worry though darling, we'll give you fair warning."

"Oh, umm," Tanya put two fingers of pressure against her brow and squeezed her short-term memory to rewind what she'd missed. "I don't care about that, Mom. I was just curious."

"I know, just teasing. Well, I'll let you go. You sound so tired, and no wonder it's after midnight. I really think you've taken on far too much up there, Tanya. Your father wants to talk to you about hiring someone to manage the music stand until it sells. You have your hands full with the pub, and he doesn't like you having to go up on the boardwalk and close on the nights Sonny can't do it."

"Mmm, I wouldn't say no to that but having Dana and Stephan back is making a big difference. Everything is fine, going well. Tell him not to worry."

"All right, I'll tell him. Sweet dreams, honey. I love you."

"I love you too, Mom. Bye."

His hands were kneading her tense shoulders. She felt the impression of a kiss on the top of her head. Tanya cringed away from him and stood up.

Mick gripped the back of the empty chair and stared at the Apple logo on the computer monitor wondering if he'd imagined the way she shrugged him off. He didn't think so, and his head hung for a moment with a collapse of hope. Here we go again, he thought, so weary he wondered if he was up for the fight. Turning, he rested his hands on his hips and watched her walk around the room.

Tanya gathered up their clothing by the fireplace, draped her own over the chair where her bra landed then handed him his shirt and jacket. "Goodbye, Mick." She began picking up pillows and arranging them across the couch. Something glistening on the floor caught her eye and she realized it was the fragments of a crystal bird that had been knocked from the couch table, probably by one of the pillows. She walked across the hardwoods and stared down at it, amazed at the disorder they'd created in their haste to… to mate. The word seemed apropos. They'd behaved like animals.

Mick dropped his clothes on the coffee table and walked over to her. "Be careful with your bare feet," he told her caringly. "Why don't you get me a broom and a dustpan or something, and I'll clean this up." He could tell she was beating herself up over what happened between them. Why, was the sixty-four thousand dollar question. Even without the grand finale it was the best fifteen minutes of his life—and if she didn't claim the same, she'd be lying through her teeth.

"I'll get it later. I'd appreciate it if you'd just leave."

"I'm not going anywhere," he stated plainly.

Tanya blinked her gaze up from the broken bird. "What do you mean you're not going anywhere?"

"Exactly what I said. I don't know what the hell has been going on with you but tonight just proved—"

"Tonight proved nothing, Mick. Absolutely nothing." Tanya went to gather her hair to one side and nearly lost the blanket. It parted down the middle and began to slip off her shoulders. She yanked it back and marched over to the clothes she'd left on the chair.

Mick couldn't believe what he was hearing and sliding his hands in his pockets, his back bowed as if physically struck by the load of bull in her denial. The corners of his eyes creased with amusement as he chuckled deeply, venting some of the anger before he spoke. "Oh, I beg to differ sweetheart."

Coming up behind her, he twirled her around. He had his shirt and jacket in his hand and shook them in her face. "What it proves, Miss Morgan, is that nothing's changed, not in the last eight years. You couldn't get these off me fast enough!"

Tanya gave his clothing a cursory glance as she leaned over to extinguish the candles on the coffee table. "Is that what happened? I really didn't notice."

If he wasn't so teeth gritting mad, his jaw would have dropped. "You want proof?" Adrenalin pumping, Mick shrugged into his shirt, shoving his arms into the long sleeves with joint snapping movements. He held the right shirt tail out, pulling it taut for her to see the loose threads dangling where buttons used to be.

"Look at this," he gestured to them as he counted, "two, three, four. I'm listening baby. How do you want to explain?"

Tanya was actually stunned to see how many buttons she'd torn off. She'd forgotten how intoxicating it was to be in his arms and lose all control, all awareness of anything outside of them. She might not have much experience to go on but to her the chemistry between them was even more powerful than she remembered, which was terribly sad really because she knew in her heart of hearts she would never connect the same way with any other man. It was a pity he'd destroyed what they had, what she truly believed was meant to be.

His loss, she told herself. With a roll of her eyes, she tossed back her hair and sighed. One shoulder shrugged as she ambled around him. "So, what do you want me to do? Sew them back on? Buy you a new shirt?" Tanya wasn't sure where it had gone earlier but at the moment she was chock-full of bad attitude and using it to get herself out of the predicament she'd created.

At the end of his rope, Mick went after her and grasped her by the shoulders. He could barely speak. "Why, Tanya? I'm not leaving here until you tell me what kind of game you're playing and why." When she looked up at him, her soft lips were parted and a mere breath away.

Aching to be welcomed back into her arms, he lowered his head to kiss her.

Tanya turned her cheek.

Determined, Mick drew her hair aside and began kissing the slope of her neck in a way that used to make her body melt into his.

"Stop!"

"You know this is what you want," he insisted lowly. Moving the blanket aside, his lips grazed along the smooth bridge to her shoulder.

"Mick, I mean it. You're wrong, I do not want this."

His hands roamed boldly from her breasts to her bottom in an attempt to rekindle the mood she was in before the lights came on and the phone rang.

She squirmed to get free. "Don't!"

Gathering a fistful of her hair, he drew her head back to make her look at him. "Tell me why and I'll let you go. Tell me why your hands were all over me a minute ago when for the past eight years you've acted like you hated my guts."

Tanya closed her eyes against his anger. It was fueling her own and she had more than enough brewing. The answer he wanted and she wanted to be rid of was coming. She could feel the tremors beginning to shake it loose. "Just—let—me— go!"

"Why don't I show you how much you mean that." One good yank stripped her of the blanket. Tanya tried pushing away from him but he manacled her wrists. Their struggles caused her to fall against him.

"Ahhh!" Mick looked down at the red mark on his chest where she'd bit him. "Mother of, jeez! Holy! What the hell!" He wiped a finger over the spot to see if she'd drawn blood. Damn that hurt.

"What the hell is the matter with you?" The pitch of his voice was high, as if it squeaked back out of the breath he'd sucked in. When he looked up from his chest to see where she had gone, something came flying towards him. Tanya had slipped on a long sleeve white t-shirt and her arm was in full swing by the time he realized what was happening. His head whipped to the side, and he immediately raised his hand to cradle his jaw. "What the f—?"

"You want to know what's wrong with me?"

The voice alone chilled his blood. When Mick opened his eyes to look at her, he thought he could feel his skin turn green from the anguish in her expression.

"I saw you," she said to him, and the quiver of her mouth and the dagger shooting loathing in her brilliant blue gaze gave him every reason to believe he was going to be very sorry he ever asked. "I saw you," she said again, her voice shaking as if an internal quake had finally erupted the buried secrets inside of her. Her eyes raked him coldly, turning as dark and stormy as the clouds on their way out to sea.

Keeping that night to herself had never been deliberate. There were many times over the years she'd considered telling him, wanted to tell him, but the words would never come…until now. And they were coming with feelings fresh and raw, as if time had done nothing to assuage the pain. They were coming steeped in all the heartache and loneliness of the past eight years, all the shattered dreams and tear-drenched pillows. The closest place to sit was the coffee table and bending her knees she folded against it, trembling from the initial release.

By the slow visible bob of Mick's Adams apple, it was clear his swallow hadn't gone down easy. "Tanya, I don't understand. You saw me where? When?" He didn't have a clue what she was about to say and his mind spun quickly through a conscience clear as glass, at least where Tanya was concerned. He couldn't imagine what he could have done to have caused her this much pain but whatever she was about to say had obviously cost him the last eight years and by the looks of her, quite possibly the rest of their lives. A chill raced down his spine. Fear dried up his mouth. "Tanya, please, tell me."

Her throat already felt raw, her voice hoarse. It was a strain to continue but it was too late to turn back now. She raised her head in order to watch his reaction. After all she'd been through, she wasn't going to deny herself.

"I saw you that night at your party."

He frowned heavily. Whatever he expected her to say, it hadn't been that. "Party? What party?" He hadn't had a party in years.

"The one you had Mardi Gras weekend, after your grandfather died."

Mick stared back at her and she could practically see the wheels of time reversing behind that blank, steady gaze. "I'm sorry, you'll have to give me a minute. That was a long time ago. The year you started college. You left before he died." Mick remembered it as the time he'd hit rock bottom. His grandfather passed away, and Tanya had left for a new life. The two people he cared for most were gone.

"I came back, Mick. Did you know that? I came back the weekend after the funeral to see you." Tanya always wondered if his tattooed friend ever told him she'd been there that night. Obviously he hadn't, which explained why he never suspected she'd caught him in the act.

Mick continued to look down upon her, still with that dumbfounded, unwavering stare. "You came back from Boston?" Damn, why couldn't he remember? "No." He was sure of it. "I didn't see you again until November when you came home for Thanksgiving. I saw you go into the drugstore. I followed you, remember? That's when you told me you were seeing someone else."

There was a lengthy pause while Tanya prepared herself. Her hands felt like ice and she pulled her sleeves down over her knuckles to warm them. She inhaled to the top of her lungs, exhaled to the bottom. Ready as she would ever be, her gaze returned to his. "You didn't see me at the party Mick, but I saw you. I saw you in your bedroom, in your bed, having sex with…with some blond."

His intent gaze locked where it had been focused, directly on her face. That was the extent of his reaction until what she'd disclosed suddenly seemed to register. His lashes drifted down. Turning, he walked to the nearest chair as if the effort it took to stand was gone. He sat and bracing his elbows on his thighs, cradled his head in his hands. "Are you sure it was me?"

Tanya stared beyond him into the darkness of the dining room while the images took shape in her mind. The slender white arms crossing his broad shoulders. The scoop of his tanned spine and the edge of the sheet thankfully clinging to his hips and covering their bodies from the waist down. Two profiles were branded into her mind's eye. The downward tilt of his own and beneath it, the arch of a pale throat, the thrust of a feminine chin, a spill of blond hair against his pillow.

Tanya raised her cuff to swipe at a tear trickling along her jaw line. "I'm sure of three things. It was you, you were on top of her, and I will regret stepping through that door until the day I die."

His head dropped low over his lap. A sound came from his heart's center where the words cut through it like a knife.

Tanya was oblivious to his agony, imprisoned in her own as she began to recount and relive the events leading up to that night. Then she would tell him about the aftermath. How her inability to cope took control of her life. It was time he knew, and she was ready. Ready to let it out, let it go. Then, possibly, hopefully, the torture would come to an end.

"It was awful the way that summer ended, for your grandfather to say the least. But for you and I, we never had a chance to say goodbye or make final plans for you to come up and visit me the way we talked about. You said your father had a place on Lake George. You said for my birthday, you would pick me up at school and take me there for a weekend. I thought about that all the way to Boston. Sometimes, I think having that weekend to look forward to was the only thing that got me across the bridge that day.

"When we spoke on the phone and you told me your grandfather died, I could hear in your voice how distraught you were. I started classes that week but it was a waste of time. I couldn't stop thinking about you, thinking how you must need me. I wanted so much to surprise you. That's why I didn't call to let you know I was coming. The sun was just rising when I left that Saturday morning. I got here about noon. My parents were furious with me for returning home so soon, but I tried to convince them I didn't want to miss Mardi Gras weekend.

"We had relatives visiting, which I didn't know about until I arrived. My father was so mad at me, he made me stay home and babysit my cousins while the adults went out for the evening. After everyone came home and fell asleep, I snuck out of the house and drove to yours. I couldn't believe how many people were there, that you were having a party. I went inside and looked for you but couldn't find you anywhere. Your friend came up to me, the one with the tattooed arm. Garrett, I guess his name is. He told me you had left and that he didn't know where you had gone or when you'd be back. I told him I was just going to call your cell and he said you hadn't taken it with you. He said he had just seen it lying on the kitchen counter. I think he knew I was growing suspicious at that point, but it was obvious he had no intention of telling me the truth.

"I'd driven seven hours, waited all day. I was so upset. I left by the front door and started for my car when I remembered your boat was docked behind the house. I thought you might be there so I turned around and walked into the side yard. That's when I saw the deck and the stairs leading to your bedroom. I could see the sliding door was open. I thought maybe you'd gone to your room to get away from everyone, or maybe you were sleeping. I climbed the stairs, opened the screen and stepped inside your room. You were there, but you weren't alone, or asleep."

He was kneeling in front of her. She'd been staring off into space and hadn't even been aware of his nearness or his touch until she stopped speaking. Her legs were crossed. Mick's arms rested along her thighs, his hands grasping her hips. His forehead pressed against her knee.

"I'm sorry. I'm so sorry. I swear to God it meant nothing, Tanya. I can explain. I—"

"Explain?" Tanya severed his paltry apology with cutting sarcasm. The suggestion that having sex with that girl, woman, whatever the hell she was, meant nothing to him was not only insulting, it was laughable. "Oh please, no explanation necessary. She was hot and willing and your girlfriend was three hundred miles away. Or, so you thought." Tanya stood up, nearly knocking him on his backside. "Then I realized *I* was the one who had it all wrong. I wasn't your girlfriend or anyone special." Chilled, she hugged her arms and walked over to the couch table. She hated the tears that kept coming and couldn't swipe them away fast enough. "I was just the next chick in line, right Mick? And once I left town, out of sight, out of mind?"

"No! Never!" He came after her.

"Don't!" Tanya spun around and held out her hand to keep him at a distance. She desperately needed comforting and if he touched her—

"Tanya, you have no idea."

"I thought I did Mick," she threw back, retreating as he advanced. "That summer was so incredible, I thought I knew exactly where we were headed, what we meant to each other." Her head shook. Teardrops oozed from the corners of her eyes as they squeezed closed. It galled her every time the facts smacked her full in the face.

"God, I was so naïve, so stupid. All those years, I thought we shared this special bond. More even…something…I don't know. I thought you'd just been waiting for me to grow up. I thought I meant so much more to you than I obviously did."

"Tanya, you do. You always have." His voice and eyes implored her to believe him. "I went a little crazy after you left. I was afraid I was going to lose you, that you were going to meet someone at college. Then my grandfather died. That night, people just started showing up at the house. Several of them knew my grandfather, and we ended up in the kitchen pouring shots, toasting him and telling stories. I'd hardly eaten anything that day and after a couple of hours, the liquor hit me hard. The next thing I knew, I was being helped up the stairs."

"I don't want to listen to this!" Tanya raised her hands to cover her ears, but Mick gripped her wrists and forced them back down.

"Please, just hear me out," he pleaded. "I swear I don't even know who she was. All I remember is the next morning. I remember walking into the bathroom and seeing the note she'd left on the mirror. It was written in lipstick or something. She'd signed it, Tara. Beneath it was written, not Tanya."

He'd blocked that night from his mind years ago. It started coming back to him though when she began to describe that Mardi Gras weekend. He didn't remember much about the party, or the girl that climbed into bed with him. The next morning was the only thing he recalled with disgusting clarity—the message on the mirror, the used condom in the wastebasket and feeling like a pile of trash washed up in the gutter.

Tanya's reaction was far from understanding, more the opposite. Fury bled through her low, dry laugh as she wrenched her wrists from his grasp. "Don't you dare imply you were pretending she was me and called her by my name. If you think for one second that's suppose to make me feel better, you are sadly mistaken, and for you to even suggest such a thing, disgusts me even more."

Mick gripped the back of his neck and looked upwards in search of divine guidance. He was at a loss to explain and desperate to do so. "I didn't tell you that to make you feel better. It's just—the truth."

"Right," Tanya jeered, nodding, about to divulge a few truths of her own. Finding herself at the end of the couch, she sat back against the rolled arm and closed her eyes, briefly. After a moment she began. "You know, it's funny but I can actually relate to what you're saying." Finding it too unnerving to meet the heavy weight of his stare, she settled her gaze on the fine blue stripes of his shirt.

"After that night, I went numb. I couldn't bring myself to care about anything, not my classes, my grades, friends. I had no interest in anything. I pretty much crawled into a shell and just wanted to die. I hardly ate, rarely left the dorm. My roommate let me wallow in self-pity for a while, and then on my 18th birthday, she finally talked me into going to a frat party. There was this guy there, Jason. He kind of reminded me of you. We all started playing this drinking game and long story short, I got drunk and slept with him. I didn't know anything about him, where he came from, last name, nothing. Never saw him before and never saw him again, but that night I went into one of the bedrooms and gave him my virginity. Since I wasn't saving it for you any longer, it didn't really matter anymore. Nothing seemed to matter anymore. I just wanted to be rid of it. I guess you could say that was the second worst night of my life."

Tanya heard the sound he made and had a distorted view of him moving about, but she was too blinded by tears to see exactly how he reacted. Not that she cared. It was a shameful, painful story and she only wanted to finish it and put it out of her mind forever.

"That day over Thanksgiving weekend when you followed me into the drug store, I'd gone in there to buy a pregnancy test. I was a few weeks late. When you came up to me, I took one look at you and wanted to hit you like I did a few minutes ago." Her voice cracked as a fresh pool of tears filled her eyes. "I wanted to scream at you that my life was falling apart and it was all your fault.

"I bought the test but I couldn't bring myself to take it. I was terrified it would be positive. Can you imagine me saying to my parents, I'm pregnant, but I'm not really sure who the father is, let me ask around at the frat house and see if I can find out. It was about another two weeks before I knew I'd just panicked, and it was only a false alarm. I guess my cycle was just affected by my emotions.

"By then though my GPA was so low, I was asked not to return the following semester. Just before the Christmas break, my parents received the letter. They came right up to Boston, unannounced. I knew they were concerned about my weight loss when I was home in November, but it wasn't as noticeable as it was weeks later. They took one look at me and thought I was on drugs. I told them I wasn't, but they didn't believe me until my test results came back. Obviously, I couldn't tell them the truth. I just told them I wasn't happy there, that I was depressed and homesick."

A wry smile appeared as she continued. "Can you believe it? Me? Tanya Reese Morgan, straight A student, senior class vice-president, recipient of three scholarships and the most likely to succeed award, kicked out of Boston University the first semester? How's that for a tail-spin? I could barely even stand how pathetic I'd become, but I couldn't seem to pull myself out of it.

"We spent Christmas that year in Florida with my grandparents. While we were there, my grandfather was diagnosed with cancer and after a few heart-to-heart talks with him, I guess I grew up a little and finally began putting things into perspective. I went back to school, formally apologized to the Dean and appealed to the Board. I guaranteed them no less than a 3.5 GPA every semester if they would grant me a second chance."

After a moment of silent reflection, Tanya breathed a deep and surprisingly restorative breath. She raised her chin and found Mick leaning against the wall across from her. There was no sign of life in his expression, or his eyes, which appeared to be glued to the floor. Looking her fill of the beautiful picture he made standing there in his soft Levis and open shirt, she felt tremendously deprived of what could have been, but finally prepared to accept a future without him.

Despite everything, her gaze softened as it settled on his face. Maybe having purged all that poison inside of her would enable her to forgive him someday. "I ended up graduating with honors, but I've never been able to overcome the way I feel when I look back on that night. I wouldn't know how to trust you again, Mick. Seeing you like that, it broke my heart. I was crushed. Believe me, I have tried, but I just can't get past it, and I know by now that I never will."

Her tongue emerged to lick the salty collection of tears from the corner of her lips while the flat of one hand wiped both cheeks dry for what she promised herself was the very last time. She sniffed and pressed her shirt cuff up under her damp, itchy nose. Big girls don't cry, according to Fergie. Well, it was high time she became one.

"Goodbye, Mick." Tanya looked down and found she'd been clutching his jacket against her with no recollection of how it came to be there. As she stood and handed it to him, her body suddenly felt cold and empty. For all her newfound bravado, she was terribly afraid it would remain that way forever.

CHAPTER 5

"Has anybody seen Mick for crying out loud?" Garrett strolled down the boardwalk in the shade of the red awning questioning the two teenage boys working the stand, and Charlie, the old timer Mick kept on the payroll to do odd jobs and run errands. Each of them gave a negative response in one manner or another.

One of the boys stopped him with a question of his own. "Are you going to hire somebody to replace Kevin? He was scheduled to be on tomorrow. I know I can't fill in for him. I'm having oral surgery. I'm having my wisdom teeth—"

"Yeah, yeah, yeah, don't worry about it," Garrett muttered, his thoughts elsewhere. This was the third day Mick hadn't put in an appearance on the boardwalk. It wasn't like him…unless. Cursing under his breath, he proceeded down to the seafood bar and rounded the corner. "Seen Mick?" he called out. Four heads shook.

Garrett took out his cell as he continued down the ramp to the street. Since he already left two messages, he pressed end when Mick's voicemail came on. The Cove was only two blocks down and three blocks over. It was lunchtime. Hopefully he was there. Hesitating on the corner, he checked his watch. Even though he was pressed for time and the temperature was pushing ninety, he decided to hoof it. By the time he walked up one block to where his car was parked and fought his way through traffic, driving over would probably take longer.

He swung open one half of the wide double doors, appreciating the blast of cool air and relief from the noonday sun. The anteroom with its gray plank walls adorned with seafaring artifacts and scenic artwork by local artists was empty at this hour of a weekday, but there were a few customers sitting at the bar, as well as in the main dining area, from what he could see of it.

He greeted the familiar hostess on duty with a tilt of his mustache. As his Doc Martens angled left across the embossed carpet, his right arm reached out in the opposite direction, acknowledging the bartender who'd looked over his way. Pete was busy pouring from two bottles at the same time, making some kind of fancy concoction. Reaching Mick's office, he rattled the doorknob but it was locked. Turning around, he backtracked a few steps and wrapped a knuckle on the door marked *Manager.*

Jack opened it within seconds with his usual gusto. When he saw who it was, his blond brows jumped and his cheekbones lit with a color that matched the pinstripe in his crisp oxford shirt. He laughed in surprise and a bit of discomfort. "Hey man, what's happenin?"

Garrett braced himself for the high five but was thankfully spared. Just because he played in a rock band, had a sleeve tattoo and sported a few earrings, Jack took it for granted that he spoke in slang, like a hippy high on weed or something. He supposed he was only trying to fit in or be friendly.

"Seen the boss man lately?" Garrett asked him, and listening to himself, he sighed, chuckling inwardly. Apparently he did speak like he looked after all. Tired, he was just tired. Maggie was in her third trimester and having trouble sleeping, but he refused to let her sleep in the spare room, afraid she'd need him in the night and he wouldn't hear her.

"No man, not since Saturday night," Jack answered, releasing minty puffs of air as he spoke, though this time there was no laughter filtering through. Trying to look cool, Garrett imagined, unless it was just nerves, Jack shifted his weight from one designer loafer to the other. He crossed his arms then uncrossed them, all in the same motion. From there, his hands slid neatly into the pockets of his professionally pressed Dockers. "I open and close Sunday through Tuesday, but he usually pops in and out of here all day. I've left two messages on his cell and was just starting to get concerned myself. I double-checked his schedule but there was nothing entered for these past few days."

"I haven't seen him since the storm. How about you?" Garret asked him, with growing concern.

Jack pulled one hand from his pocket to splay across his heart. "No, now that you mention it. Damn. That didn't dawn on me. I hope—"

"I'll let you know." Garrett cut him short since their conversation suddenly took a turn he didn't like.

"Right. Call me," Jack said in parting, straddling the threshold as he watched him walk down the short corridor and back out into the vestibule.

Garrett departed with a roll of his eyes and a shake of his head, hoping Jack wasn't back there checking him out. Mick was of the opinion his openly gay manager talked to him like that because he got all flustered when he came around—because he had a crush on him. Considering the odd couple the two of them would make, Mick thought that was hilarious. Got a real kick out of it. Thinking about that, Garrett hoped he found him alive just in case he decided to pound him for it some day.

There were a couple of newspapers scattered across the porch, rolled up in rubber bands. Even the Sunday paper was there. Today was Tuesday. Not a good sign. The company van was in the driveway.

"See if his Jag's in the garage, Maggie," he called out to his wife. She was standing on the front lawn with worry clouding her otherwise clear as sea glass green eyes. Her hands joined in a prayer against her lips after Garrett tried the front door and found it locked.

Maggie walked around the back of the van and down the newly installed pavers. Lifting herself up on her toes as best she could, she shaded her eyes and looked in one of the garage door windows. "It's in there," she called back, biting her bottom lip as anxiety mounted over their friend's well-being.

Garrett knocked hard on the front door. He didn't hear Mick coming and knocked one more time. He turned his head to look over the porch rail at his wife. Maggie stared back, sharing his silent concern. Jogging down the steps, he joined her in the drive.

"Oh Garrett, I'm scared," she said, in her pretty Irish brogue, taking the hand he held out to her and squeezing it tight. Together they continued down the pathway of pavers that continued from the drive around the side of the house.

"He's fine," her husband insisted, his deep voice resonating a confidence he was far from feeling. "You know Mick, he gets in these moods sometimes."

"At least the boat is there," she said when its aft came into view.

"Stay here while I try the back door." As Garrett's left boot hit the second of four steps, he saw him. He was across the deck, semi-reclining on a thick cushioned lounge chair. He was facing the back of the house instead of the picturesque bay. Beside him was a tall glass filled with a clear liquid, a couple of ice cubes and a lemon wedge. He was wearing a pair of sun bleached khaki shorts and dark glasses. It didn't appear as if he'd shaved in a few days—or that he could crack a smile if his life depended on it.

Garrett walked over to him, picked up the glass and sniffed.

"It's only water."

"Well, how about that Maggie, he's conscious and he can even put together a complete sentence."

"You're a riot and a half Garrett. Now why don't you get out of the way so I can say hello to your wife and child." Leaving his elbow on the arm of the chair, Mick raised his hand to welcome the approaching redhead. "How are you doing, Irish? Junior still trying to kick his way out of there?"

Maggie gave Mick's hand a comforting squeeze then placed it on the sudden bulge in the left side of her belly. "We just came from the doctor's office. Looks like we're still a go for the 4th of July." They all watched as the baby kicked, and kicked again, as if to say, *hey you guys, I'm in here!*

"Holy—" Awed by the feeling against his palm, Mick looked up and found his two friends sharing a Hallmark moment, smiling at each other, happy as a couple of turtle doves. He removed his hand and drank some water, hoping to squelch the pang of envy. Returning the glass to the small table beside him, he said, "That's still a couple of weeks away. You think he'll stay put that long?"

"Well, he—or she, better," Maggie replied, giving Mick a pointed look as she emphasized the feminine pronoun. Since they learned she was pregnant, both Garrett and Mick referred to the baby as *he*. She and Garrett decided against learning the baby's gender ahead of time, and now she worried if it wasn't a boy, Garrett would be disappointed.

"Actually, I'm afraid if I go into labor any earlier, he's going to make me squeeze my legs together," she joked, giving her passionately patriotic husband a cheeky grin. The Ames family boasted a long line of war veterans, and Maggie knew it would mean a great deal to him to have their child born on the 4th of July. Samuel or Samantha, he wanted the name to be.

Maggie transferred her grin to Mick and watched a small dent appear in his cheek, as if that was the best he could do. She'd never seen him quite like this. She thought she'd felt a tremor in his hand when she raised it to feel the baby and wondered if he'd been eating properly. Hoping he would open up to Garrett if she left them alone, she placed her palm on her brow. "Whew, I think I better get out of this heat for awhile. Mind if I go in and catch Ellen, Mick? I heard she's having some male strippers on today."

"Go on in and put your feet up. No drooling on the furniture though," he teased.

"I'll try to control myself," she returned, giving her husband a wink.

Without Maggie's spirited brogue driving the conversation, the two men on the deck fell silent. The last sound to be heard was the metallic click of the kitchen storm door as compression eased it closed behind her. Garrett took a seat in a navy and white striped cushioned chair, one of the ensemble pieces matching Mick's lounger. It was positioned on an angle a few feet away, facing the bay. He hiked a boot up onto his knee and enjoyed the view while he wondered if Mick was going to spill this time or clam up as usual.

"There's beer in there if you want one," Mick finally said. He didn't stand on ceremony with Garrett and Maggie. His house was their house and vice versa.

"Thanks, but I'll pass," Garrett declined. When Mick didn't have more to say, he picked the ball back up. "I fired Kevin yesterday. Found him leaving with his pockets full of quarters." Garrett had a chuckle remembering. "Caught him red-handed. He was so weighted down he could barely waddle. They always think they can get away with it," he mused aloud, shaking his head.

Mick wasn't surprised. He had a bad feeling about the kid. *Shifty*, his grandfather would have called him. "Go ahead and replace him. I think Justin said he has a friend that's looking." Normally, he handled new hires for the boardwalk but if Garrett wanted it, he could take over that responsibility. At the moment Mick was having trouble caring one way or another about anything. "Got any cigarettes on you?"

"No. I only smoke outside the clubs now and then with Maggie being pregnant. Trying to cut back."

Mick looked over at him nodding, his sunglasses concealing his bloodshot eyes. His mind couldn't rest, wouldn't let him sleep. "Good, that's good."

Garrett threw him a scowl. "I thought you quit."

"I did. Few years ago." Mick let the back of his neck relax against the cushion. Raising his arms, he threaded his fingers together and rested them on top of his head. His gaze traveled up the stairs to the sliding doors of his bedroom, his old bedroom. "Why didn't you tell me Tanya Morgan was here that night?"

Well, what do you know, Garrett thought to himself. He finally said her name out loud. Wonder of wonders. Contemplating the question, nothing rang a familiar bell. "What night would that be?"

"What night?" Mick snapped back, cocking his head with unmistakable meaning. "How many times have you spoken to Tanya Morgan in my house?"

Mick's sudden attitude along with the caustic tone had Garrett's dark gaze narrowing. "What's going on?"

Mick shrugged. "It's a simple question. Why didn't you tell me Tanya was here that night? Mardi Gras weekend, right after Pop died," he supplied.

Garrett's knee jerk reaction was to be pissed at anyone who spoke to him that way. But this was Mick and obviously the question had everything to do with the reason he'd been hold up here at the house shunning the world for the past three days. For that reason, along with a whole list of others, he kept his cool and tried to remember.

After a moment, his memory began to cooperate. "That was the night everybody started piling in here, thinking you were having a party. I swear there had to be fifty or sixty people here at one point." He thought some more. "Yeah, I remember now. I remember seeing her walking around the house. She tends to stand out in a crowd."

"And?"

"I'm trying to think where you were. I went up to her and she said she was looking for you. She asked me where you were." Garrett paused as a wave of recollection washed over him. He snapped his fingers. "You went upstairs with that blond that was hanging all over you in the kitchen. A bunch of you were doing shots then all of a sudden I see her helping you up the stairs. Not long after that, I found Tanya walking around the house so I figured I better—"

"Why the hell didn't you ever tell me she was here?" Mick sprang upright, throwing a leg over each side of the chair. The question that had been burning a hole inside him for three days seemed to spew from his gut in a fireball of frustration.

"What are you talking about? I did tell you!" Garrett insisted, dropping his boot to the deck.

"When, for chrissakes? If you told me then why didn't I know anything about it until she told me herself the other night?"

"How the hell should I know? If you don't remember, it was probably because you were still drunk off your ass when I told you the next day. What's the big deal anyway? I sent her packing. I followed her out of the house and watched her walk down the street to her car. I knew you two had been sneaking around that summer. I could never figure that one out," he scoffed.

"We were sneaking around because her parents wouldn't allow anything else. How did you know about that anyway?"

"I have eyes for Pete's sake. I saw her in your car a few times and besides that, you've had the hots for her as far back as I can remember. Did you think nobody noticed?"

"Wait, wait." Mick held up a hand. "We're getting sidetracked." Feeling shaky, he reached for his water and sat back.

Garrett leaned forward, drew in his boots and stared down at the space in between. Gradually it came to him. He looked up. The sun was beginning its evening descent, making him squint against the horizon while he formed his thoughts.

"I spent the night here. I had more than a few beers and didn't want to drive home so I crashed on the couch in the den. In the morning, I made coffee and heard you walking around upstairs. I waited for you to come down and when you didn't, I went up to tell you I was leaving. You had gone back to bed. When I walked into your room and passed the bathroom doorway, something caught my eye. I remember it freaked me out at first because from a distance, it looked like there was blood on the mirror. I went in and saw it was a message. Tanya's name was written at the end of it. I believe it said *not Tanya* to be exact. When I came out of the bathroom and walked over to the bed, I asked you if you'd seen it. You said yes, and I said to you, speaking of Tanya, she was here last night.

"I can't remember how you responded, or even if you responded, but I know you were awake. I wouldn't have been carrying on a conversation with myself." Garrett's eyes followed a pair of seagulls sweeping the water's surface. After a moment passed without getting any further argument from Mick, he pulled in his gaze just in time to see him backhand the tumbler and send it sailing across the deck.

Garrett didn't realize the glass was plastic until he heard a thud instead of shattering glass. The lemon wedge and what was left of the ice skidded across the boards and slipped over the edge into the bushes. He'd known Mick more than twenty years and not since he'd taken out Rusty's death on the little pine tree, had he seen him unleash his feelings to that extent. Garrett always believed that to be part of his problem. He kept everything that mattered to him all bottled up inside.

Mick planted his feet on the deck floor again, straddling the chair. As if he'd just spent the last of his energy, he hunched over and removed his glasses. They hung from one finger while he massaged his tired eyes. Sliding the glasses back on his nose, he raised his head to the same view he'd been staring at all afternoon, the stairs leading to the upper deck.

"I don't remember. I just don't remember. Or maybe I did at the time and figured I dreamt it. She didn't leave Garrett, not when you thought she did. She turned around, came back to the house, went up on the deck and walked into my bedroom at the worst possible time."

Garrett made a sound through his lips like a descending missile. He had a feeling the story was going to go something like that. That had to top the list of relationship killers. Even though he thought better of it, he still couldn't resist asking. "Mick, if you and Tanya were involved at the time, whatever possessed you to—?"

"Do you think I haven't asked myself that question a million times?" And without knowing the answer—why he would have jeopardized his future with Tanya for a lousy one night stand—the question just kept wrapping around him, tying him up in a coil of twisted knots he couldn't escape from. It was evident in his voice, his actions, the veins ready to burst through his skin. "God, I wasn't even remotely attracted to that girl. In fact I seem to remember her being loud and annoying. I know I didn't make the first move. I wouldn't have. Not that it makes any difference."

Mick tore a hand through his hair wishing he hadn't let his cousin walk off with his grandfather's boxing bag. He would have pinned his own picture on it and beat the everlovin shit out of himself. "For eight years I've been trying to figure out what happened. Why she ended it, just like that." His fingers snapped. "She was away at school at the time. The possibility that she came home that weekend or somehow found out about that night never even crossed my mind."

"Mick, even if she hadn't walked in on you buddy, you still would have had to tell her."

"I know, I know, and I still might have lost her in the end, but it wouldn't have been nearly as bad as her actually seeing us with her own eyes. She said she can't get that night out of her head. She hates me for it and how can I blame her?"

"Why the hell did she wait so long to tell you?"

Mick shrugged, a slight movement barely achieved against the weight of despair rounding his shoulders. "I don't know. Pride, I guess."

She had her share of it, for sure, but he certainly couldn't fault her for that. He'd spent the last three miserable days unraveling the last eight miserable years, thinking how blind and stupid he had to have been not to see there was something more behind her behavior. The puzzle pieces all fit neatly together now, from her brush off the day he called her at school, to the way she'd looked through him at the retirement party, to her mad dash from the luncheonette a few weeks ago. She'd been carrying a grudge the size of Alaska and with damn good reason.

Back in grade school, he never went out of his way to cultivate friendships. He and Garrett clicked the first time they hung out together and they had developed a genuine affection for each other over the years. He couldn't imagine life without him. On occasion, he'd pal'd around with some neighborhood kids, especially when his parents were both at home and couldn't find a decent word to say to each other. He'd always enjoyed his grandfather's company and was pretty content with his own—but when Carol Morgan began bringing her curly haired daughter up on the boardwalk, there was something about her that drew him like a magnet. He knew it sounded weird and to this day couldn't define what he felt all those years ago, but whatever it was settled deep into his soul and over time became as much a part of him as his heartbeat.

Words like fate and soul mate had become cliché, half the time tossed around by two people who tripped over each other in a bar and got engaged three months later. They didn't have a clue. The other night she'd mentioned them sharing a bond. Same thing, he supposed but it was also as she said, something more…something unexplainable.

He'd lived thirty-two years, traveled more than half the globe and couldn't begin to count the number and variety of women he'd met—from feisty frauleins to sultry senoritas. Not to mention the thousands of bikini clad girls that paraded up and down the boardwalk every summer. Whether he'd slept with them or not made no difference. None touched him beyond the skin. There'd never been one who could make him yearn the way Tanya Morgan could with one look from those midnight blue eyes. That's just the way it was, that's the way it had always been and God help him, that's the way it would always be.

Which is exactly why he'd lost the will to get up each morning and face the day. For the past eight years, he at least had hope. Now he had nothing. When he left her house the other night, there was closure in the way she said goodbye to him, as if she'd made peace with her decision, locked the door and threw away the key. His punishment, a lifetime sentence without her. The thought made him want to curl up and die.

"Eat this."

Mick looked over his shoulder to find Garrett placing a sandwich on the table.

"Maggie made it for you."

"I thought she was watching the strippers."

"Yeah, well she tore herself away just for you. She thinks you're losing weight."

Mick reached over and raised the top slice of bread to assess the meat. "I didn't even know I had ham in there. This stuff must be ancient."

"It smells fine, so eat it. You look like hell."

Mick ran a hand over his incoming beard. His jaw still felt tender. Man, for a girl she had some swing. "I know, I know. I've just been doing some thinking that's all." Mick left the sandwich on the table, not trusting the ham. He'd get something later at The Cove.

"I saw her last night," Garrett blurted out, still standing over him.

"Is that so." Mick really didn't want to hear about it, figuring he had enough torturing his brain for the time being.

"Yep, I saw her all right," Garrett exaggerated the sigh, massaging his chest as if the memory was almost too sweet to bear. Resting his hands on the hips of his low riding jeans, he began to set the stage for more serious chop busting with the hopes of bringing this self-pity party to an end.

"Maggie had a craving for fajitas so we went to Paradise. We were sitting out on the patio when I happened to look out towards the street and see a pair of long sexy legs climbing out of a shiny new Beamer. It was Tanya. I watched her walk up the sidewalk and come into the pub. I'm telling you that black dress she had on—holy Toledo!" Garrett grunted and groaned, conveying raunchy thoughts through facial expressions. "She had on these long sparkly earrings and her hair was pulled back all sophisticated, like they were going someplace fancy. A few minutes later she walked back out and got into the car again. I don't know who the guy was but the license plate read MD."

"Thanks a lot, my friend. You know you're a real big help. Next time why don't you save your breath and just pull the trigger."

Garrett's grin spread until it turned into a low laugh. "So what are you going to do now, sit here and feel sorry for yourself over something you think you can't change? Or are you going to get up off your ass and try changing something you still might be able to change?"

Mick looked up, springing a half a smile and a dimple. "You want to run that by me again? You confused me with all those changes in there."

Yeah, he was coming around. Garrett began to feel better about leaving him. "Don't give up so fast is all I'm saying."

"So fast? It's been eight friggin years and she's just getting around to telling me *why* she hates me."

"My point exactly. You hurt her in the worst way a man can hurt a woman, but you'd think she would have let it go by now, found somebody else and made a new life for herself. But she hasn't, Mick. If you ask me that's a pretty clear indication that she's still as crazy about you as you are about her."

The next day Mick returned to his somewhat normal routine—boardwalk in the morning, lunch and dinner at The Cove and the hours in between, running Leighton Holdings LLC. Professionally at least his life was on track, thanks to his grandfather. This month marked the eighth anniversary of the company's start-up. Michael Shane Leighton Sr. had lived barely three months into their joint venture. They shook hands over their John Hancock's in the lawyer's office and suddenly, he was gone.

The idea of forming the company had been a twinkle in his grandfather's smiling eyes from the moment Mick came home from the Marines. He'd said he'd been working for him since he was knee-high to a grasshopper and thought they made a pretty good team. Unless he had other plans for earning a living, there were local opportunities beyond the souvenir shop he'd been exploring, and he would need a full-time partner to handle the added responsibilities. They'd both tried urging his father on board, but Mike Jr. had turned to the serenity of Lake George, New York after his divorce and he was in the process of realizing a lifelong dream of building his own log cabin. He had no interest in returning to the coastal town where he'd met, married and lost the love of his life.

Prior to and during his stint in the service, Mick managed to accumulate approximately half of the college credits required for a Bachelor's degree in business. He considered himself a jack-of-all-trades but knew it was time to master one of them if he wanted to get anywhere in life and provide for the family he expected to have one day. Though he wasn't particularly eager to continue his education after the Marines, he would have done so out of necessity if his grandfather hadn't offered him the partnership. A partnership, he soon discovered, that came with a caveat. His grandfather demanded his word that he would return part-time and earn his degree. It had taken him awhile but that promise had been fulfilled.

That was also the summer he secretly began dating Tanya, and confiding in his grandfather had not been the exception. He didn't want him to think he had a special girl at the top of his *to do* list every day instead of the objectives outlined in their business plan. Mick had every intention of doing whatever it took to keep Leighton Holdings moving in the right direction. He didn't want him worrying that his attention was being compromised when there was work to be done, even though it had been damn near impossible staying grounded that summer with thoughts of Tanya's nighttime kisses luring him into daytime fantasies. He'd always regretted not telling his grandfather about Tanya, but it's very possible he'd known all along. As Garrett pointed out, people noticed. Apparently he'd been wearing his heart on his sleeve all these years without even realizing it.

His grandfather didn't exactly have an eye for the ladies, so to speak, but they sure had an eye for him. Mick had vague memories of his paternal grandmother. She'd died tragically when he was five years old from a respiratory infection, but there were enough pictures around his grandfather's house for Mick to see what she meant to him. It wasn't until several years after her death that he would occasionally see him with a female friend. None of them lasted very long though. He'd never said as much, but Mick had a feeling he never found another woman to compare to his grandmother. It seemed the Leighton men were doomed when it came to holding on to the women they loved.

Losing his grandfather that September had knocked the wind out of him, as well as the confidence to make a success of the company on his own. His break-up with Tanya a short time later left him without a reason to even bother. He'd floundered for months, prowling the house, drink in one hand, smoke in the other, nourishing his body only when his hands started shaking. Everyone was gone. His parents had moved away, his father north, his mother west. Tanya was up in Boston with her new man, or so he thought, and on one brilliantly clear Saturday mid-autumn, he and his father had chartered a boat, aimed for the open waters of the Atlantic and scattered his beloved grandfather into the wind. After that, it was the longest, loneliest winter of his life.

Not until the sun began clinging to his bay-view windows every evening and taking its sweet time sinking into the horizon did something begin to stir deep inside of him. Summer. Like the Grinch that couldn't stop Christmas from coming, another summer was fast approaching whether he liked it or not. It was at that point, he knew that unless he stopped feeling sorry for himself and got his rear in gear, Leighton Holdings LLC was not going to be ready for it. He'd already left too many loose ends dangling.

The Seaside Park boardwalk began a few blocks from his house. Aside from an occasional resting pavilion, nothing but boards bordered dunes for a good long mile until the commercial stretch began near the Heights. He'd walked it one day, knowing he needed the brisk March wind to clear out the cobwebs and whip some sense back into him. He'd taken the padlock off the souvenir shop and sat inside for hours, thinking, reminiscing, looking for inspiration. Not long after, the exterior walls came down and nearly forty feet of red awning went up bearing his surname in bold white script. That summer, Leighton's Seafood Bar and Amusements opened for business.

Mick believed his grandfather would have approved. He'd hung an 8x10 of him beneath the menu board, to the right of the standing beverage cooler and the left of the fresh lemonade mixer. It was one of those priceless photos he was thankful to have found. The picture was taken during a deep sea fishing excursion a few summers before his stroke. About a dozen locals had gone out on a party boat from a marina in Point Pleasant as they did from time to time. His grandfather caught a 38-pound striped bass that day. In the picture he stood on deck, holding it up proudly, his Mets cap tipped back topping the windswept feathers of his silvery blond hair. Surrounded by the deep blues of the ocean and a cloudless sky, he looked tan and fit and healthy enough to have lived another twenty years.

His grandfather's friend, Sophie, liked to stop by the counter occasionally and gaze at the photo. "*I swear that smile could melt the sun right out of the sky*," she would often say, leaving Mick to wonder if there had ever been more between them than friendship.

This morning Mick woke up with his grandfather on his mind, hence the reason for all the nostalgia before he dragged himself out of bed at seven a.m.. He showered then took his coffee, eggs and newspaper out on the deck. He steered clear of thoughts of Tanya as best he could and tried to stay focused on the day ahead. By eight a.m., he was rolling up his proverbial sleeves and getting back to work.

Garrett let him know stock was running low on Yankee caps and t-shirts at the sports stand. Anything bearing logos of the local pro teams moved like hotcakes and since storage space behind the stand was limited, he stored additional inventory in his garage and hauled them up to the boardwalk as needed.

Garrett was there to help him unload. It was becoming another scorcher as the day progressed, unusual for this early in the summer. After working up a sweat, Mick walked into the back entrance of the seafood bar to get a couple of drinks out of the cooler. He passed a bottle of water over the counter to Garrett as he came up the ramp.

Leighton's Seafood Bar was located on prime corner boardwalk property and consisted of twelve weatherproof booths, two restrooms, an enclosed food prep and refrigeration area, and the walk-up service counter. The menu on the wall offered several seafood options, two sides and a variety of beverages; Shrimp cocktail, grilled or southern fried, steamers, scallops, mini crab cakes, calamari, coleslaw and the best french fries on the Seaside boardwalk, according to popular opinion.

A Portuguese family of seven ran the place in shift rotations with the efficiency and precision of a well-oiled machine, and he paid them considerably well to do so. Nevertheless, it was the *Leighton* logo printed on the awning hanging over the counter. *Your name, your responsibility,* his grandfather drilled into him growing up. Therefore, he took nothing for granted and made frequent inspections based on his own personal criteria of the way he expected the place to look and the food to taste.

George was chief cook in charge and his wife, Lilia, a workhorse. Mick swore you could eat off the floors even in the bathrooms where customers tracked sand in all day long. He dreaded the day they might come to him with the news they were opening their own place. Finishing the inspection without a single complaint, he gave the couple a thumbs up and headed back to the sports stand to help Garrett unpack the cartons.

It was uncanny how he knew she was going to be there even before he looked over his shoulder. She didn't spend much time on the boardwalk anymore with only one stand to oversee and the new pub to manage, but somehow he knew she was going to be there when he turned his head.

His first thought was that she'd worn that *eat your heart out* dress for his benefit just in case they ran into each other—and there was always a good chance of that at this hour of the day, which she knew full well. The dress was hot pink with nothing but a halter strap holding it up. The neckline dipped just low enough to tease. He couldn't see any cleavage from this distance but any guy tall enough and close enough was probably getting an eyeful. He rarely saw her in a dress at this hour of the day, and she knew damn well she'd stand out in that color, like a flamingo in a forest, and he'd have no trouble seeing her and how good she looked.

He faced forward again and continued walking a few more feet until seafood and lemonade turned into a veritable locker room of sports paraphernalia. In fact, over time, regular customers had dubbed the stand *Leighton's Locker Room.* In appreciation, this year he'd ordered a couple of hundred red t-shirts screened with the nickname to be handed out as comps over the course of the summer.

At the moment, there were a fair number of patrons standing at the betting counter watching the wheel of fortune spin—a typical family of four, a young teenage couple with one hand in each other's back pocket, and a skinny boy in swim trunks who kept pressing the button with comical vigor as if it made all the difference where the arrow stopped. Mick saw the kid's arms shoot up into the air when it landed on the word *Dad* and felt a momentary lift to his own mood.

Watching the boy select a Giants jersey for his prize and run down the boardwalk waving the shirt in the air, Mick removed the cap from his Snapple and took a swig. The kid hadn't been able to control the wheel with the button, but he supposed there was something to be said for all that positive exuberance. He could sure as hell use some of that.

Recapping the bottle, he turned his head in the other direction, unable to stop himself. She was still there, still holding a conversation with an older woman who looked vaguely familiar. He recognized her from someplace down on the next block, the Sawmill maybe or Berkeley's. Uncertain, and not particularly caring anyway, his gaze switched back to Tanya. He was surprised she didn't have her hair tied up or braided on a hot day like this but no, she was wearing it the way he liked it best, loose down her back. When she moved her head, he noticed she had on the silver hoop earrings she usually favored. Her bare shoulders and limbs were becoming lightly tanned and looked smooth as silk. Felt like silk too. That fifteen minutes in her arms the other night had been pure heaven. They'd been sixty seconds away from making love. Thirty maybe. It was a miracle he hadn't cried like a baby.

Knowing he was standing in the line of boardwalk traffic basically ogling a woman who made it all too clear she wanted nothing more to do with him, he began to feel like a stalker. He soaked up one last look and was just about to go about his business when he saw a man walk up to her. The way Tanya reacted, it was obviously someone she knew. Mick thought maybe it was a friend of her fathers until he saw a kiss land on her lips instead of her cheek.

What the hell? Judging him by his hair color and boring business attire, he appeared old enough to *be* her father. When they started walking in his direction, Mick realized the gray was premature. His age could have been anywhere from thirty to forty. He watched the guy draw Tanya's hand out of her pocket and hold it in his own.

Mick thought he was going to lose his breakfast. This had to be the MD, and Tanya or no Tanya, he didn't like the snooty look of him. He was wearing a white short sleeve shirt and gray dress slacks. His skin had about as much color as a Rolaid. He looked like a pansy. Okay, a distinguished pansy. He'd give him that much.

Mick watched them turn and take the exit ramp. Who the hell was she kidding? The two of them looked like fire and ice—a mismatched pair if he ever saw one. If she ever sunk her nails into that milquetoast, he'd probably run for the disinfectant.

So much for his theory she'd worn the dress for him. Mick scraped his knuckles along his jaw. He still hadn't shaved. He'd looked in the mirror this morning and came up with the desperate notion she might find the rough shadow appealing. Thinking about the MD's smooth lily-white complexion, he figured that made him 0 for 2. Hell, he just could not win for losing.

Feeling an urgent need to work off some steam, Mick began unpacking cartons, taking inventory and re-organizing the storage area and front display—more or less getting in everyone's way. He grew increasingly irascible, wore a fixed scowl and snarled and snapped at the least provocation. Garrett told him he was being a general pain in the ass, and he was sorry he talked him into coming back. Mick had to agree with him and doing everyone a favor, he took off for his office at The Cove.

Chapter 6

She wanted so much to feel something for him. He seemed like such a good man, a fine dedicated doctor, and handsome enough when the lights were low. He shouldn't wear white shirts though, she decided, unless he teamed it with a sports jacket. The navy blazer he'd worn the other night had given his shoulders a boost and threw some color in his rather ice pale eyes. He had very clean looking hands. Certainly not a bad thing, but his fingers were unusually slender for a man, the nails rather shiny and pink.

He wasn't happy to be sitting on the patio, but she thought he would have preferred that to the rather raucous event going on inside. It was a party of nine lively women celebrating a 65th birthday. They'd brought presents and balloons and were having a grand time laughing themselves silly. Tanya hoped she looked as good as most of them when she reached that age and had as much zest for life. She sighed lethargically then smiled to herself when she heard the cheer from inside and more bouts of laughter. At least somebody was having fun.

Not far from their own table, there were two honeybees minding their business in The Cove's courtyard. Charles was keeping a close eye on them, just in case they attacked, she supposed. He said they reminded him of a young boy who once raced into the emergency room with a wasp in his ear. That was the second story he reported in graphic detail. Previous to that interesting saga, he'd recounted his mother's unfortunate mishap with the razor-sharp lid from a canned ham. It nearly sliced her finger in two.

Getting a sleepy spell, Tanya rested her chin on her hand and played with her salad. She gazed at him while he spoke. He enjoyed talking about his work—medical stuff, bones, blood, infections, things that swelled, oozed then burst open. There was nothing wrong with that, she supposed, coming to his defense as if it were someone other than herself who suggested he was a bit odd and self-absorbed.

And so what if he had called Paradise *cute*. So what if he continued to point out that he was finding the heat oppressive and wished they had gone someplace else, even though Tanya thought it wasn't so bad sitting under the wide umbrella in the shade of the crape myrtle. It was, after all, summer. And, so what if he'd complained more than once that his garden salad was missing radishes. He loved radishes.

Who on earth *loved* radishes? People liked radishes, of course, but love? When they first arrived, Dana accidentally dropped his menu when she went to hand it to him. It had been entirely his fault. If he'd been paying attention instead of inspecting his silverware, he wouldn't have caused the mishap in the first place. Together Dana and the doctor bent over to pick up the menu and ended up bumping heads, which he openly sighed about. On top of that, he didn't even say sorry or no problem when Dana expressed her sincere apologies. Time and again, Tanya's eyes had been drawn to that circular red patch above his right eye that bloomed after the collision. She had a sudden urge to tell dear ol' Chucky he could find a radish on his forehead.

Good Lord, what in the world was she doing with this man? "Will you excuse me? I just need to use the ladies room." Without waiting for his response, she rose from the table, walked through the french doors and headed straight to her office.

When Dana saw Tanya enter, she was just passing by the birthday table. One of the ladies happened to catch her eye and call her over to weigh in on a, *wink wink*, important topic they were debating—which Grey's Anatomy co-star was better looking, McSteamy or McDreamy? Dana called out her opinion and in the wake of a chorus of boos and cheers, she hurried to catch up to her boss. Following her into the office, Dana closed the door and turned to watch her collapse into her chair.

"I can't go back out there. That's all there is to it. I can't do it. He is the biggest jerk."

"And not your type at all. I've been trying to figure out why you would go out with him in the first place," Dana proclaimed, knowing she was out of line but unable to stop herself from reacting with such fervor. Especially after the arrogant way the, *yes*, jerk treated her after they'd bumped heads.

"I know, I know," Tanya slumped forward moaning. Planting her elbows on the desk, she covered her face with her hands. She shook her head at the question. She'd been desperate that's why, desperate for someone to take her mind off Mick—in particular the heart wrenching, amazingly wonderful, frustrating, upsetting events of last Saturday night. But, she wasn't about to pour her heart out to an employee at the moment, if ever. Even though Dana was unfailingly loyal and trustworthy, and Tanya was becoming increasingly aware that her assistant manager was attempting to bond with her on a more personal level, especially after that incident with Mick and the twins, Tanya was very protective of her private life. It was hard for her to share any more than a portion of the truth.

Tanya raised her head and made it brief. "I met him at a charity function a few months ago. We exchanged business cards. When he called, I thought, why not? He seemed nice enough. We've only been out twice but both times we were in mixed company, and I didn't realize—he seemed okay." Her fingers combed through her unbound hair, all the way to the base of her neck. Leaving them there, her head hung wearily between her forearms. Oh God, why do I even bother, she stopped herself from adding.

Dana had been on her way to the office to deliver the mail when she found herself a participant in the fun loving ladies' *Mchotty* debate. Consequently, she had a large manila envelope to hide her smile behind in case her boss wasn't ready to appreciate the humor. "You should have seen your face while you were sitting there. You looked bored to tears. I know I saw your head bob. I can't believe he didn't notice you were falling asleep."

"No, he was clueless, or too busy finding fault with everything." Ordering herself to get a grip, Tanya came up on a gulp of air, arched her spine then pressed it against the back of the chair. Playing with her hair always helped her release tension. Gathering it all to one side, she began to braid with a speed and dexterity of one who'd performed the task so often it had become second nature. Her gaze lowered while she considered her options.

"What time is it?" she muttered, more to herself as she paused one hand to check her watch. "He has an appointment at 2:45." It was 2:15. The braiding continued. "Thank God. I should be able to get rid of him soon."

Dana followed her boss's fingers with a bit of awe. "Do you want me to go out there and tell him you've received an important call or something?" she offered, willing to help in some way. She noticed Tanya hadn't been herself for the past few days. She seemed distracted, quiet, sad somehow.

Tanya was tempted by the suggestion and lifting her lashes, revealed over-bright eyes shimmering like moonlight on water. She *had* nearly fallen asleep at the table and even though she could feel the strain of exhaustion burning behind her eyelids, the rest of her felt restless and over stimulated. She'd hardly slept since Saturday night and when awake, never stopped moving, working, doing. She would have loved to take the easy way out, but Charles had annoyed her sufficiently so that combined with her stress level, she was almost looking forward to giving him the old heave-ho.

"No thanks, Dana. I believe I can handle it," she stated, and on that affirmation stood up as if ejected from her seat.

Dana hopped back hastily as Tanya whirled around the desk. "Are you okay?" she asked, frowning after her boss. Less than a half hour ago she was practically nodding off, and now she looked recharged as if she'd downed a gallon of Red Bull.

Striding towards the door, Tanya looked back over her shoulder. "I'm fine. Why?"

"Well, for one thing you forgot your shoes."

"Oh!" Tanya stopped short and looked down at her bare feet. Spinning around, she tossed up her hands and hurried back to her desk to slip into her sandals.

"You're sure you're okay?" Dana repeated, unconvinced as she watched her head to the door again.

"Uh huh," Tanya assured on a high note. "Positive."

Actually nothing could have been further from the truth. Tanya returned to their table only to find it empty save for the remains of her salad and now watered down green tea. According to their waitress, her guest had received a page. Charles had nearly reached the exit when Tanya caught up with him.

"I'll call you," he said, glancing back at her.

"I'd rather you didn't," she replied, with a smile to lessen the sting.

He nodded and neither one looked back. Who knows, she thought to herself, maybe that page had been his way of dumping her. Either way, the deed was done. Hallelujah and Amen. The only problem was it left her with rushing adrenalin and energy to burn, especially after she'd gone back to the table and discovered he hadn't even left Zoë a tip. Cheap bastard. She'd told him lunch was her treat but the least he could have done was leave a few dollars for the waitress.

Back in her office, Tanya paced, contemplating various ways to decompress. She had personal errands to run— banking, a few groceries to pick up, a Coach bag to return. She'd bought the purse to cheer herself up then decided the style didn't really suit her. But zigzagging all over town and across the bridge to the mall wasn't exactly the outlet she had in mind and would likely lead to more, not less anxiety. She needed something physically exhausting to help her sleep tonight. A run along the beach might have done the trick but it was really too hot for that kind of exertion today.

Suddenly, a thought struck her. On the back seat of her Jeep was a tote bag containing a bathing suit and beach towel. It had been there since Memorial weekend, intended for use at Lisa's picnic/pool party. With Dana and Stephan scheduled through closing, Tanya thought she could easily slip away for a swim.

Well, maybe not easily. There always seemed to be something requiring her attention, and she was detained on her way to the car to get the bag, on the way back to her office after getting the bag, and after changing into her suit, on her way out again. Consequently, it wasn't until four p.m. when she finally managed to slip out the back kitchen door.

Crossing the boardwalk and seeing the ticket booth vacant, Tanya realized the beach attendants had turned in. Her timing turned out to be fortunate then. She held a season badge in Lavallette, but it had been so long since she'd been on the Seaside beach, she completely forgot she would have had to pay the daily rate if she'd arrived before four. Except for the towel, she'd come empty handed. No purse, no money, no cell phone, nada. There was no one to watch any personal belongings while she was in the water, therefore it seemed pointless to bring them along. Brian was on shift at the music stand, but he had enough to keep an eye on without worrying about the safety of her purse as well.

Tanya bypassed the booth then stood to one side rather than try and dodge the small army trudging up the ramp. It appeared to be one beach-worn extended family looking like a bunch of pack mules with all they carried. Children of all sizes were bringing up the rear and pointing to Casino Pier in the distance where the Skyscraper had come to a stop, dangling its, no doubt, screaming passengers upside down. The children were chattering excitedly about the rides they planned to go on that evening.

Wishing life could be that simple again, Tanya continued down the ramp and removed her sandals. The feel of the soft white sand between her toes reminded her again of how much she loved the beach and how seldom she was able to take advantage of being so close to it each day. She supposed that would probably hold true for any business owner in a resort community, particularly in the Northeast where peak season lasted all of three months. Work, work, work and then poof, summer was over.

Seaside Heights public beaches were generally packed on a hot day like today. Tanya was relieved to see the crowd had already thinned. Typically, by late afternoon vacationers headed back to their rentals or motel rooms to get ready for dinner and an evening of boardwalk activities.

It wasn't really that far from the ramp but by the time Tanya reached the lifeguard stand, sweat was pooling between her breasts and running down the back of her neck. The foamy waves beckoned and feeling the affects of the high humidity just from the short walk from the pub, she could barely endure the wait. There was just one thing she had to do first, and she hoped Ty Harding wasn't in a talkative mood.

Tanya slipped out of her halter dress, dropped it on top of her towel then walked around to the front of the lifeguard stand. Shading her eyes from the late day sun, she looked up. "Hey Ty, mind if I leave a few things under your chair while I take a swim?"

The lifeguard leaned forward, delighted to see her, even though he'd taken himself out of the running. By late afternoon, he was more than a little anxious for the day to end. His butt was sore from the hard wooden bench. Even though he'd raised the umbrella for the majority of the day, he still felt like a slow roasted side of beef. Other than a few squealing kids running in and out of the shallows, there wasn't anyone in the water to keep an eye on at the moment. Tanya Morgan's surprising appearance broke the monotony and then some. "Hey, honey bunch, what brings you down here? Playing hooky?"

"I guess you could say that," she chuckled wryly, knowing the guilt would be waiting when the fun was over. Apparently he'd come to know her well.

"Hello," Tanya tilted her head, acknowledging Ty's cohort, since he appeared to be leering her way. She didn't know him. He looked young, a rookie most likely.

"Well, well, well, hel-lo to you too," the other lifeguard replied deeply and by his rather obnoxious response and posturing, Tanya wasn't surprised by his next maneuver. Making an event out of adjusting his shades, he angled forward with a flexing of his deeply tanned, bulging bicep and a cocksure grin that cried, *Come to Papa.*

Tanya hoped he exerted as much energy saving lives. No doubt he was mistaking her for one of the beach bunnies that often made pests of themselves by hanging around the lifeguard stations. It didn't help either that Ty had called her *honey bunch*, but that was just his way.

Ty performed a casual introduction.

"Nice to meet you," Tanya said halfheartedly, this time barely meeting his gaze, which she sensed was buried in her cleavage anyway. There was nothing left of the smile she started with. "What's the water temperature?" she asked, looking to Ty for the answer.

"Sixty-six very chilly degrees, but on a day like this, who's complaining?"

"Hopefully not me," she returned, beginning to shuffle backwards, anxious to make her departure. "Be back in a few."

"Have mercy," the rookie groaned, looking his fill as she turned away. "Where the hell did she come from and how fast can you hook me up?"

Ty leaned back, resuming a lax position. He watched Tanya run into the surf and dive into an unbroken wave with the fluid grace of a mermaid. "Put your eyes back in your head doofus, you'd have to take a number."

New Jersey ocean waters rarely warmed up until mid season. Since summer had barely begun, the temperature didn't surprise Tanya. Having lived at the shore her entire life, she knew it was better to submerge yourself as quickly as possible rather than prolong the agony by standing in front of the breakers trying to adjust one body part at a time. Still, she had to admit the shock to the system seemed to have less of an impact when she was a child. Kids, she mused, they had it made. Too bad it wasn't possible to fully appreciate all the perks until you were all grown and they were long gone.

Tanya swam out where the waves were high but gentle. She floated on her back and stared up at the hazy, faded blue sky while the buoyant, repetitive motion lifted her up and down like a carousel pony.

Heavenly. Sunlight sparkled on the whitecaps, surrounding her like fairy dust. Water lapped at her ears. Other sounds were distant—the waves breaking after they rolled past her and rushed to shore, the high playful pitch of the children at play in the shallows, a deep droning sound of a powerboat that seemed to be getting louder and louder. And closer?

Dropping her legs, Tanya treaded water and looked out to sea. The boat was moving parallel to the beach heading south. It appeared to be the same boat she saw heading north as she ran into the water a few minutes ago. This time however, it was running much closer to shore, angling inland and heading straight towards her.

For safety reasons, of course, all boats were restricted from coming in too close to public swimming areas. She didn't know the distance they were required to maintain but this one was obviously going to surpass it—and she was directly in its path.

With her heart about to leap into her throat, she was on the verge of swimming for her life when everything seemed to happen at once.

Realization dawned that it was Mick and at the same time a commotion started up on the beach. Tanya could hear people shouting. Both lifeguards stood tall in their chair, waving their arms and blowing their whistles. A beach patrolman came on the loud speaker ordering the boater to vacate the area immediately. Tanya could barely hear him and doubted Mick could hear him at all. Not that it would have mattered.

Mick didn't obey the command but he did stop and position the craft to face seaward. He let the engine idle and rode the waves while he left the controls to come to the side of the boat where he could see her. He called out, motioning with his hand for her to swim to him.

He was nuts! A lunatic! The boat was beginning to buck like a bronco. The waves were going to tip him over or soon wash him up on shore. "Get out of here, Mick!" Tanya screamed, her arms flailing. "Are you crazy?"

He shook his head and motioned for her to come.

Dear God! Tanya looked back over her shoulder and saw Ty and the rookie jump down off the chair with their rescue tubes and run towards the surf. Beach patrol was continuously issuing a stern warning—*Under strict penalty of the law, the driver of the boat was to vacate the area immediately!*

Tanya looked frantically back at Mick again. The boat had moved in even closer, rocking precariously about three car lengths away. The fool. She was going to take great pleasure in killing him for this. That vow was repeated over and over again as she swam towards him, her arms slicing through the water as though a shark nipped at her heels. Swimming against the tide was exhausting and it seemed as if it was going to take forever to reach him. She kept a wary eye on the boat, praying it wouldn't capsize, especially once she got within range.

Tanya reached for Mick's outstretched hand and grabbed the edge for leverage as he hauled her up and over the side. She was panting heavily and would have landed in a heap if he hadn't caught her under the arms to help her stand. Once she was able to get her legs beneath her, she gripped his hand tightly and followed him forward. She hesitated, crying out as she balanced herself surfboard style when the boat surged and seemed to point its nose at the sky. As soon as it leveled, they were able to get into their seats. Once they were down, Mick opened the throttle.

Now that she knew they were safe, Tanya's emotions flew into a frenzy. She glared at Mick repeatedly, but he chose to ignore her and gave all of his attention to piloting the boat. Flying against the sea air chilled her to the bone and had her searching the immediate area for a towel or a shirt, anything to cover herself. There was nothing within reach. Goosebumps began rising on her arms and legs, and she couldn't seem to stop shaking.

Thankfully, it wasn't long before they were rounding Barnegat Inlet and within minutes, Mick was guiding the boat up to the bulkhead behind his house. Tanya was on her feet before he even cut the engine. As soon as she had access to the dock, she was out and marching across the lawn. Her heart was banging against the wall of her chest. Fed up with his abuse no doubt and trying to get free. She didn't think she'd ever been so frightened. Her determined stride took her as far as the shrubbery bordering the deck before she went spinning around to march back again.

Mick was kneeling down on the dock securing one of the lines to a piling. Raising her voice wasn't exactly her style, but she might have let him have it at the top of her lungs if she hadn't spotted a neighbor a few backyards away grilling his dinner. Tanya turned her back to the man before speaking to the one crouched at her feet. "You are insane," was the first thing that shivered out of her mouth with controlled fury. "What made you do something so stupid? You could have killed us both!"

Tanya stopped there, noticing another neighbor on the opposite side looking over at them, though the woman quickly averted her gaze, trying to appear all about her plants as she watered her potted begonias. She and Mick made spectacles of themselves this afternoon, providing entertainment for at least half the Seaside beach. She preferred not to continue the show for his entire neighborhood. Shoving her wet, windblown hair out of her eyes, Tanya walked back up into the yard, propelled by a surge of adrenaline.

Unfolding himself, Mick calmly followed in her turbulent wake. "We weren't in any danger. I've been handling boats since I was fourteen. I knew how close I could get."

Tanya spun around again but continued moving backward up the sidewalk path. "Oh, well that's okay then. Excuse me, I must have forgotten I was talking to the all mighty, all powerful, Mick Leighton, who can control a two ton motor boat on the beach at high tide and leap tall buildings in a single bound. Take me home." Livid, she turned and continued to the front of the house.

Mick followed at a much slower pace. He wasn't about to take her home, and she wasn't going to be too happy about it either.

Fate. It was the only explanation for what took place out there on the ocean. Either that or somebody up there decided to take pity on him. Unless it was a holiday, he rarely took his boat out at this time of day, especially a weekday. And, he couldn't say for certain, but he believed it had been years since Tanya went for a swim at the Seaside Heights beach, probably not since high school.

Mick didn't know what made him look over at the very moment she ran into the water. But he did. From that distance, she was little more than a stick figure with long flying hair. Something, some spark of recognition, made him reach for the binoculars he kept close by. Just before she dove under, he saw that it was Tanya. The rest had been an act of pure desperation, along with a little positive exuberance of his own, he supposed. He could have ended up looking like a damn fool but positive attitudes were said to reap positive rewards. He knew it was going to take a hell of a lot more than that to win her back, but this was at least a start.

When Mick turned the corner of the house, he found her leaning against his Jaguar combing her fingers through her hair. If that wasn't the most fantastic sight he'd ever seen, he didn't know what was. It had been a long time since he'd seen her in a bathing suit. Not since the night they'd gone for a moonlight swim and she'd taken off her shorts and top to reveal a string bikini that nearly put him into cardiac arrest. They'd skipped the swim in favor of cocooning themselves inside a blanket, and he was sure if it hadn't been for the sudden sound of voices, he wouldn't have been able to resist her fervent pleas to make love to her that night.

Mick tore his eyes away. This time it wasn't going to be about sex. "Why don't you come into the house and get a towel," he said to her as he walked around the hood of his car.

"Why don't you just bring one out to me," she threw over her shoulder, determined to stand her ground. Besides, she didn't trust him behind closed doors—herself either for that matter.

Mick paused on the porch steps to look back at her. "I'm not coming back out Tanya, so please, will you come inside? I'd like to talk to you."

Despite his faultlessly cordial tone, Tanya was about to spout something back when she noticed the woman next door was now in her front yard bearing her watering can. *Doesn't anybody work around here?* Tanya muttered to herself and faced forward again with a huff and crossed arms. Casting a furtive glance up and down the street, there didn't seem to be any other nosey neighbors in sight, thank goodness.

Tanya debated her safest course of action while giving her hair a few shakes and scrunches. A bundle of nerves, she continued to fidget. Both hands rubbed vigorously over her face trying to remove the residue left by the wind and saltwater. She crossed her arms again, then her ankles, looking around, still debating. Her fingers drummed. What just happened for heaven's sake? One minute she was enjoying a refreshing swim and now here she was standing in Mick's ninety-degree driveway, shoeless and half naked. Otherwise, she definitely would have started walking home, even if it was five miles.

Tanya scooted down to the Jaguar's front fender, closer to the garage door where the face of the house cast shade onto the pavers. Two minutes later the soles of her feet were still baking. Closing her eyes on a curse and a prayer, she blessed herself, rounded the car, walked up the porch steps and entered the house.

"I'd really like to know why," Tanya began, only to cease wasting her breath when she realized Mick was nowhere in sight. She was familiar with the layout of the rooms having circled the staircase several times that fateful night long ago, but nothing else looked as she remembered. He'd told her he'd bought the house to renovate. Obviously, he'd done so. She didn't want to like it on principal but it was quite beautiful really in a casual, masculine way and much more spacious than she remembered. A wall had to have been removed, she could only imagine. She didn't want to picture him here after she left and would have preferred to just cover her eyes before she took in too much to forget, but it was already too late. Curiosity got the best of her the minute she walked in the door.

There were a few things that stood out and brought all the neutral tones to life. The two very comfy looking, overstuffed cream and pumpkin couch pillows and the stunning sunrise and sunset landscapes on the long wall to her right were the first to capture her eye. Beneath the latter was a long dark cabinet with two wooden drawers in the center and four rattan drawers on each side. The center accent rug and two bronze-based lamps similar in style were gorgeous and of obvious quality. She'd forgotten about the massive stone corner fireplace and imagined how cozy and romantic it must be on nights when—Tanya gritted her teeth and brought an immediate halt to that line of thinking.

Good Lord, where was the man? She could hear him moving about somewhere on the other end of the house. Finally, he came through a doorway carrying a fluffy green bath towel. "I want to go home, Mick," she said insistently. "Please, just get your keys. I want to go home right now." Tanya was careful not to venture too far into the house and stood front and center between two long windows, just a stone's throw from the tiled foyer and front door, or to her way of thinking, the quickest escape route.

She wanted there to be no misunderstanding that he had placed her in a precarious position out there on the water by forcing her to choose between complying with his request, or bearing responsibility for the consequences if she didn't, which she feared could have been dire. Therefore, he was not to, in any way shape or form, misinterpret the situation as her willingness to spend another evening rehashing what happened to their relationship eight years ago. And just as soon as she felt like telling him all that, she would!

Mick put his keys in his pocket after he unlocked the front door. Normally he would have tossed them in the ashtray on the side table but this time he thought better of it. He wouldn't put it past her to swipe them and run off with his car. There was no way he wouldn't catch her but he wasn't about to take any chances. If he had to tie her down, by God, she was going to stay here and listen to what he had to say!

For now he simply walked up to her and handed her the towel.

"Thank you," she said with dripping sarcasm and continued on in the same vein. "Now may we go, please?"

Walking further into the living room, he stopped and turned to face her. "Not until we talk," he stated evenly. "Will you please come and sit down?" he asked her, motioning to the couch.

"There is nothing more to talk about. I believe I made that clear the other night," she replied coolly.

Mick jiggled the keys in his pocket. "You made a lot of things clear the other night, Tanya. Incredibly clear. As I recall, you did most of the talking. Would it hurt for you to stay awhile and listen to what I have to say?"

Tanya dropped her gaze rather than keep looking at how good he looked—all summer sexy in his surf shorts with his sunglasses hanging down around his neck. The white undershirt he had on was a ribbed tank style that gloved his lean torso and left his sun-kissed shoulders bare, and her hands aching to touch them.

She kept them busy, very, very busy. Gathering all of her hair to one side, she blotted the long strands. She'd been running on adrenaline since Saturday night, filling every second with any task she could find. At home, she'd even accomplished the three things she disliked to do most; lawn-mowed, flowerbeds-weeded and windows–washed. Most of them at least, plus the patio door. As a reward for all her hard work, she went on a shopping spree and bought herself the Coach bag and a knockout dress for her dinner date with Charles. Don't stop. Don't think. Don't look at the couch. Don't remember the look in his eyes when you told him goodbye. And don't, under any circumstances, walk by the fireplace again and step on one of his damn little shirt buttons.

Tanya assured herself time would do the trick. The secret was out leaving nothing to cling to. She hoped it would make a difference, and she could finally begin putting the whole nightmare behind her. So far, not so much, but it had only been a few days after all.

Suddenly, Tanya realized she was stalling, actually considering the invitation. Thankfully, she snapped back to her senses. "There's nothing you can say to change my mind, Mick, and you'd just be wasting your time. It just so happens I have a date tonight, so I really don't have anymore time to waste."

Mick had been meandering about the living room, waiting with forced patience and baited breath for her answer. Hearing what she'd come up with, he threw her a look and snickered a laugh. "Not with that bozo I saw you with this morning, I hope."

Tanya stopped drying her hair in order to square her shoulders. She opened her mouth for the comeback before realizing she didn't have one. Still she managed to save face with, "Not that it's any of your business but no, not with him." Her date was with Lisa. Tanya had been avoiding her calls and decided to ride over there tonight and make amends, but she wasn't about to tell him that.

Mick's jaw clenched. Damned if it wasn't his business. "So, who is it this time then?"

"Nobody you know."

That made him chuckle with deep disdain. His brows lifted as he scratched one thoughtfully. "I imagine so. You've already been through all my friends, a couple of the cops in town, the lifeguards—"

Tanya gaped at him before erupting with a hollow laugh. "Oh my God, you have to be kidding me. Not only are you greatly exaggerating, I cannot believe you have the utter gall to even go there. I doubt there's a woman left in Ocean County you haven't been out with—and slept with. Don't you dare give me that double standard routine."

"Well, I sure as hell wasn't about to turn into a monk after you dumped me."

"After!" Tanya exclaimed, whipping the towel from her neck. "I wasn't even gone three weeks! I suppose I should feel lucky you waited until I crossed the bridge. If you even did." Her throat vibrated with a husky growl. "I should have listened to my father. He knew what you were like. He knew the price I would pay if I got involved with you. He knew—"

"Your father knew shit!" Mick rebounded vehemently, believing this was all Jim Morgan's fault to begin with.

Tanya gasped, incredulous. "Apparently not! He knew you'd end up hurting me! He knew you'd end up breaking my heart! Now I know exactly what he was talking about. Now I know why he was trying to protect me!"

Overwhelmed with frustration, Mick reached the end of his rope. His sunglasses came off and went sailing across the room to land on the couch. An ottoman got in his way and was upended with a shoving kick. After he'd vented physically, he strolled towards her for a verbal release.

"Well, there's one thing I know for sure sweetheart! I know I should have balled your brains out when I had the chance!"

Mick saw her recoil and stood rooted to the floor watching the color drain from her face. He watched her beautiful eyes well with tears, her throat clench and her lips begin to quiver, except for the spot she'd drawn between her teeth.

"So that's what this is all about," Tanya rasped, though barely able. "I should have known."

She was in motion long before he managed to extract his feet from the quagmire reserved for stupid assholes. He caught her at the door as her fingers were curling around the handle.

Mick leaned one shoulder against the door and trapped her in by stretching his other arm out behind her and flattening his hand against the wall. "I'm sorry." Turning his head, he drew a steadying breath, giving himself a minute before he said something else he might regret. He looked back at her, unable to see much more than her hair.

"I didn't mean to say it that way. I shouldn't have, but you know what that summer was like and how close we came. Do you think what happened right here in this foyer hasn't haunted me every day for the last eight years? I was in the fight of my life that summer trying to keep my hands off you. I was just trying to be the kind of guy your father would approve of, and—"

Sighing, he gathered some of her hair and moved it behind her shoulder in order to see her face. "Will you please look at me?" When she didn't but rather squeezed her eyes shut and pressed her brow against the door, he went on. "I can't talk to you like this. I've ended up starting in the middle. Will you just come and sit down? Please, Tanya."

He waited a moment but when she refused to budge, Mick bowed his head nearer to her own. He could feel her trembling and heard her sniff. She was chilled, her shoulders hunched. She'd wrapped her arms tightly around herself in her efforts to ward him off. He wanted to hold her, warm her, but he was sure she'd resist. Her body language couldn't have been clearer.

Knowing this might be his best and possibly his only opportunity, he struggled with the words and ordered himself to swallow his pride and just say what needed to be said. "I'll admit it, wanting you is making my life a living hell, but that's not even the half of it. What you told me the other night changes everything. All this time, I thought you didn't have feelings for me anymore. I wish I'd known what happened, I would have explained long ago. I know. I know. What I did was unforgivable, and I know I don't deserve a second chance. But I'm asking anyway." He swallowed. "Okay, I'm begging, I—"

Hearing how desperate he sounded, Mick paused there to ease up on the pressure and soften his tone. "Please, Tanya, let's at least try. I know I can fix this. I know I can earn back your trust. Please, just tell me what I need to do and I'll do it."

What he needed to do couldn't be done, and what he'd done was bring all the pain back to the surface again. Still too hurt and angry to even look at him, she raised her head barely an inch and with just the slightest turn asked him scornfully. "Can you go back in time and make it so that night never happened?"

Mick closed his eyes with true remorse. "I'd give anything if that were possible. I promise you, I will go to my grave hating myself for what I did. I can barely stomach my own company anymore, knowing what you went through and how much I hurt you."

He gave her time, sensing he might be getting through. Gently, slowly, he slid his hand beneath her hair. Resting it on the back of her neck, around the curve of her shoulder, his thumb rubbed up and down her nape soothingly. "Will you at least stay awhile so we can talk about everything without all this tension for once?"

He wasn't encouraged by the fresh onslaught of tears until he heard her say with weary resignation, "I can't do this anymore. I'm so tired. I give. I give. I can't fight this anymore. I can't do it."

Beneath his hand, Mick could feel changes taking place little by little. The weakening. The release. The resolve. The surrender. With that same hand he urged her around and into his arms. She came willingly and burrowed against the warmth of his t-shirt. Her arms circled his waist.

Mick's other arm hovered over her, uncertain but ready. He swore he had no heartbeat. He knew he'd pushed her to the breaking point and everything inside him was on standby, waiting. He wouldn't believe it until he heard the words.

"I'm done," she cried on. "I'm done. I can't live like this anymore. Yes, yes, yes. I want to be with you. I want to try. I have to."

He couldn't have gathered her closer without injury. Kisses rained across the top of her head and down her brow to her cheek. He tilted her chin. Framing her face with his hands, his lips pressed into her own with such tender passion and gratefulness, fresh tears squeezed from the corners of her eyes.

Tanya clung to his wrists while the pads of his thumbs swept her cheekbones dry. Their lips, sharing the taste of salt from her tears, tried to hold fast but there was too much emotion bubbling inside. Green eyes met blue, communicating a message they both seemed too shaken to voice. Suddenly, Tanya's gaze turned quizzical. Breaking free, it roamed his face, returning with a twinkle of amusement. "Are you growing a beard?"

Mick grimaced and put a hand to his jaw. "No. Sorry, I know it must scratch. I've just been a little out of it lately."

"Me too," she admitted softly. "I'm sure I must look like a witch," she said and raised both hands to sweep her hair from her face.

His lips touched her forehead. "You are beautiful. Always, so damn beautiful."

Tanya's heart swelled as he hugged her close again. He'd never said anything like that to her before.

"Will you stay for awhile?" Mick would have said forever but knew it was too soon.

She nodded. "For awhile. I would really love a shower. I don't suppose you have any conditioner? And something else I can wear?"

Ten minutes later, Tanya stood under a hot shower biting down on a smile that might have stretched from ear to ear if she allowed it the freedom to do so. She'd done it. She'd agreed to give Mick another chance. She wasn't sure if she was ready to forgive, but she'd accepted his regrets and promises and trusted he spoke from the heart. It was enough, for now.

For a few seconds, she paused the bar of soap over her heart. The way it was palpitating reminded her of another summer day—the day following high school graduation. Seventeen. Ready for life. Ready for love. Ready for the only man she ever wanted to be with. Flying up the stairs to her room, rummaging through her closet for the perfect outfit to wear on their first date, she remembered feeling the same giddy, irrepressible excitement.

Now, once again, filled to the brim with anticipation, Tanya couldn't even allow herself to think too far ahead to what the rest of this night might bring. Wondering why she was wasting so much time in the shower when all she really wanted to do was be with him, she rushed to finish.

Mick had hung two items from the silver hooks on the back of the bathroom door, both compliments of his mother, though she wasn't aware. The first was a yellow bathrobe, a gift from her that he never used. The second was a three-section toiletry bag with the initials JWL embossed into the tan leather. She'd left the bag behind during one of her visits, and *lucky for you,* Mick had said, tossing a grin over his shoulder that had Tanya's toes curling into the plush throw rug in front of the sink, she hadn't remembered it since.

While he'd been busy making sure she had everything she needed and showing her how the shower worked, she'd asked him a few questions about his mother. He told her that after the divorce, Joanna Winifred Leighton had moved back to southern California where she was born and raised. At least twice a year, she flew back to New Jersey to visit him and other family and friends. He added that, like herself, he closed up The Cove and spent an extended holiday season first with his mother in San Diego then on Lake George with his father.

Tanya dried off the bottles of the hair products she'd used and returned them to the appropriate pouch. She ran a finger across the clear plastic as she perused the other items inside. She thought about the woman they belonged to and wondered what she looked like, if they would like each other. Tanya unzipped another one of the pouches thinking if the contents of this bag were anything to go by, they were probably going to get along just fine.

The framed mirror was as wide as the vanity, making it easy for her to critique her appearance. She turned this way and that, fluffed her drying hair and smoothed her brows. She unwrapped the bath towel she'd been wearing and slipped into the yellow robe. Catching a glimpse of her body during the exchange, her lashes dipped languidly, acknowledging the power he was able to wield without even being in the same room. Already she could feel the heat rising beneath her flesh, the swelling ache in her breasts and a heaviness filling her thighs. It was as if her senses were all joining forces, singing hallelujah, and stirring him up a feast. They'd waited so long for this night.

Fortunately, the robe wasn't overly large and only required a few adjustments here and there to suit her frame. She opened the lapels to expose her neckline, rolled back the cuffs then smoothed the fabric over her hips. Hoping to rid herself of a little anxiety, she took a deep breath and released it in a rush. She palmed her cheeks. They felt feverish and looked it. Hand-fanning them, she wondered if she should suggest he turn off his cell and unplug the house phone. She would absolutely die if they were interrupted again while they were making love. Later she would mention it to him. Not now but later. They were going to talk first. Good, good, Talking was good.

Phone, phone, thinking of the phone, she suddenly remembered Paradise. No doubt Dana and Stephan would be wondering where she was since her Jeep was still parked in her usual spot. Hopefully, they didn't think she'd drowned. Actually, she wouldn't be a bit surprised if the news had already reached Paradise that her archenemy, Mick Leighton, had fished her out of the sea. If so, there would be plenty of long looks and whispers tomorrow. Refusing to carry that thought any further and allow anything to spoil this night, Tanya took another deep breath and reached for the doorknob.

He was waiting for her directly across the hall. He'd showered as well and shaved off the beard. Either way, he was unbearably handsome. His tawny blond hair was still damp and swept back. He'd changed into linen trousers and a lightweight t-shirt. He looked casually sexy, especially the way he was standing with one knee bent and his hands buried deep in his pockets.

Tanya lifted her gaze. The back of his head and shoulders were braced against the wall. Under the cover of dark lashes he was looking her over with the same intensity.

"Come here," he said huskily, shooting a flaming arrow into the pit of her stomach and with a roll of his hips he pushed off from the wall. Taking one hand out his pocket, he held it out to her.

Her mouth watered as she padded over to him. He did nothing more than curl an arm around her neck and draw her against his chest. She felt a shudder course through him.

"I was afraid you were in there trying to climb out the window or something."

Tanya chuckled and tilted her head to look up at him. "The thought never entered my mind."

"Good, we're making progress then," he said, smiling back with both dimples in play. Keeping his arm around her shoulders, he guided her towards the staircase. "So I can turn my back on you down here and not worry that you're going to run off with my robe or anything?"

"Well, I'm not so sure about that. It's really comfy and very soft inside. I just might steal it from you. But I'm not going anywhere. I promise."

Mick thanked her for that reassurance with a one-arm squeeze and a kiss on her brow. "Can I fix you something to eat? I don't keep much on hand but I can have something brought over from the Cove, or we can order a pizza or something?"

Tanya shook her head. "I'm not hungry yet. Are you?"

"I'm good right now. How about a drink? Wine, iced tea, soda?"

"I'd love a glass of white wine. Chardonnay preferably, or—"

"Got it," he answered and letting go of her at the couch, he continued on into the kitchen.

"Oh, I need to make a few calls," she remembered. "Can I use your phone?"

"I'll bring it to you," he answered and returned with it a moment later.

"Thank you." Bracing one knee on the couch cushion, she reached across the end table to take it from him. Immediately, she began pressing in the number with both thumbs.

"You're welcome," she heard him answer as he headed back to the kitchen.

Grinning, she shook her head and curled up in the corner of the couch. It was almost funny how polite they were being to each other when just a short time ago she'd been ready to rip his head off. This was definitely going to take some getting used to.

If the reason she didn't return from her swim reached Paradise, Stephan didn't let on. Nor did he ask when she didn't reveal her whereabouts. He told her the pub was very busy. They were currently filled to capacity with about a twenty-minute wait but everything was running smoothly. Tanya left a number where she could be reached, assuming Mick still had the same number, but then suddenly remembered the caller ID. If Stephan bothered to look, *Leighton* would have come up on the phone. Not that it mattered. Everyone would know soon enough anyway.

Tanya made one more phone call to make sure Sonny had relieved Brian at the music stand and would be there to close then placed the phone on the table beside her. She wondered what time it was, glanced around the room but didn't see a clock anywhere. Probably about 6:30 she imagined, judging by the lengthening shadows outside. Through Mick's front window she could see the reflection of the lowering sun, bright as a ball of fire in the second story windows of the house across the street. Tanya was glad the room she sat in faced east. It was already growing dim and cozy. Not that she was eager for night to fall. They had some talking to do. Important talking. But then what?

Mick returned carrying her glass of wine and a can of coke for himself. With her legs drawn up beside her, Tanya was in the process of covering her bare feet with the robe when he handed her the glass.

"Are you cold? Do you want me to turn the air down?"

"No," she answered and thanked him as she accepted the stemware. "Actually it feels good in here."

Tanya took a sip of the wine and while her palate savored the delicate burst of flavors, she watched Mick drag a side chair closer to the couch until it was positioned directly across from her. He sat down on the edge of it, as if he had some purpose in mind but didn't intend to stay long. Less than two feet separated them.

He looked tired, she thought, noticing deeper creases than usual in the corners of his eyes. She probably did too. They'd been to hell and back as far as she was concerned. It was a long trip.

Tanya took another sip, watching his index finger trace around and around the edge of the can he held between his widespread knees. He was watching it too. Gathering his thoughts, she imagined. She waited, rather than begin prattling about the exceptional wine or how much she liked what he'd done with the house. When at last he raised his head, her expression welcomed him back from wherever it was he had gone.

"I love you, Tanya," he said deeply. "More than I know how to handle apparently." Placing the unopened can on the floor beside his chair, he wiped his palms down his thighs then laced his fingers together. "And that's long overdue," he admitted. "Way long overdue. I should have told you that summer. Maybe it would have changed everything." He rubbed the back of his neck, sighing inwardly. "I knew it then. I knew it even before then but you were just a kid with college ahead of you and a lot of living to do. That scared the hell out of me." He scratched his brow. "I didn't know what to do about it. I didn't know how to let you go and still make sure you'd come back to me. Your parents didn't approve of me. I wasn't expecting that. Our age difference seemed to keep working against us."

Tanya's eyes began to pool as she watched and listened. Eventually the tears blurred her vision, making her lose sight of those adorable nervous gestures he was making. Oh God, she had no idea he was going to come out with that now. If and when he told her, she'd thought it would be during the prelude to passion, or in the heat of it. But not like this. The way he'd said it was so unbearably sweet and forthright, she wanted to ask him to say it again, in exactly the same way.

Setting her glass on the end table, she dropped to her knees. "I love you too, Mick. I love you too. I always have."

Driven by all they nearly lost and a future that now promised everything they always wanted, everything they always believed was meant to be, they kissed and kissed and kissed, until the need for oxygen interfered. Still they clung to each other, holding on for dear life.

Finally with a short groan and a parting kiss, Mick raised his head from the silky curve of her neck where he could have easily lingered if she wasn't on her knees and he wasn't fully aroused. Whatever it took, he was going to do it right this time. "C'mon. Up," he said, bringing her to her feet and placing her back on the couch. "Uh oh. Tissues?" he asked, seeing her wiping her cheeks dry.

"Yes," she sighed with more than a hint of irritation, wishing she could stop leaking like a faucet. "I don't usually cry."

"I know, I know. You never whine and you never cry," she heard him call back teasingly as he walked towards the kitchen.

Returning, he handed her a small box of pop-up tissues and sat beside her on the couch, spacing the distance so she could swing her legs up and across his lap. Tanya adjusted her position to face him and slid one of the pumpkin pillows behind her back for support.

"I'll never forget the first time I saw you cry," he said, flashing deep dimples while he helped her adjust the robe over her legs. When he started sliding one hand up and down her shin, Tanya sent up silent thanks that she shaved in the shower that morning.

"When was that?" she asked him curiously and reached over her shoulder for her wine. She couldn't ever remember crying in front of him before Saturday night.

"Oh, I guess you must have been almost two. Let's see, your birthday is in September and it was probably early summer that year, so a little less than two. I guess I would have been about eight by then. The fireworks were about to start on the boardwalk and I came out of the shop to watch them. Your mother was sitting on one of the benches along the rail holding you in her arms. You were looking over her shoulder, facing me. As soon as you heard the first boom you jumped and started howling. Your mother was trying to calm you down, but you kept looking up at the sky and then back at me. I guess I went to pat you on the head or something, but you grabbed hold of my hand and wouldn't let go until they were over."

Tanya stared at him in awe. "That's amazing. I can't believe I did that. I can't believe you remember it."

"I remember everything that ever happened between us. Every summer. Everything. That was the first time I touched you."

He made it sound as if it had been a momentous occasion. Tanya pressed her lips together and tried blinking the tears away but it was no use. She reached for the tissue box she'd set on the floor.

"I bet you don't remember the time you covered me with custard either."

"No." She chuckled deeply, shaking her head. Like him, she had a picture book of memories in her mind and was pretty sure she remembered everything that happened between them as well, but covering him with custard certainly wasn't one of them.

"It was a couple of years later," he went on to say. "You were running all over the boardwalk giving your mother a hard time. I offered to treat you to a frozen custard and sit with you for a while to give her a break. You proceeded to force-feed me the entire cone. You absolutely refused to eat any of it. By the time you were finished, I looked like I had shaving cream all over my face. The rest of it dripped all over our clothes. I don't think your mother thought I was much help."

Tanya laughed heartily just imagining. She could totally picture herself doing that. Recollecting something, a small frown waved across her brow. "You hate frozen custard."

"I know," he replied, with a curl of his lip that had her sputtering another laugh.

Tanya joined her hands together and held them beneath a trembling smile. His sentimental memories of their past touched her more than words could say. Never in a million years would she have suspected they were so dear to him. He'd never mentioned any of these things that summer. She blotted her eyes again, feeling like a bottomless well of emotion. Lowering her gaze, she played with the terrycloth belt, folding it this way and that. "I can only remember as far back as the necklace. I still have the heart," she told him softly.

His hand stilled on her knee and by the way he tilted his head and studied her beneath the veil of his lashes, she could tell she had touched him as well.

"Now you've surprised me. I can't believe you've kept it all these years. I remember that day clear as a bell. I remember you picked out one of the grab bags then looked up at me with these incredible eyes. You handed it to me to open and when I pulled out the necklace, I swear they lit up like there were stars shining through. I fastened it around your neck and I think I said something like—"

"Good choice." They spoke in unison and shared a reminiscent smile. Mick took hold of her hand and kissed her knuckles. His other hand returned to rubbing her leg. "You were adorable at that age." Feeling the need for a stretch, he winged his arms and flexed his shoulders. Fighting a yawn, he gave her a sidelong look. "Then you grew up, got sassy and became a royal pain in my—"

"Hey!" Tanya saw that one coming a mile away. Sweeping her legs off his lap, she kneeled on the cushion and lunged.

The laugh he'd held in expelled in one gust as he stalled the impetus of her weight by catching her forearms. "You knew I couldn't resist," he ribbed her, dodging her swing and a miss.

"You just can't handle the fact that you were never able to beat me at skee ball." She tried breaking free but Mick held her arms fast. "Let go. I'm not going to hurt you."

Her smile had the look of a Cheshire cat. "Yes you are," he returned with a half grin, half grimace, anticipating her shifting knee landing in his crotch and rendering him useless for the night. God forbid. He wondered why he was surprised by her strength after she nearly cold-cocked him a few days ago. They continued to arm wrestle, neither taking their eyes off their opponent. Mick got lucky and throwing her off balance, toppled her against him.

Tanya breathed in the scent of his aftershave and wondered if that was fair play since it went straight to her head and made her almost dizzy with desire. Suddenly feeling weak as a kitten with cuddling in mind, she curved her hip onto the cushion and lay across his lap, supporting herself with her elbow on the other side of his thigh. Reclaiming her other hand, she smoothed the front of his shirt then walked up his chest with two fingers. "Is that really how you think of me?" she was curious to know, all kidding aside.

Mick cradled her head in his hands, caressing her features with eyes that had warmed to deep velvet. Little by little, his expression relaxed to a clean slate, all playfulness put to rest.

Mesmerized, Tanya gazed back, something soulful in that look kicking the beat of her heart into a drum roll of anticipation. Having yearned so long for things to be this way between them, the moment seemed somehow surreal, a dream coming true before her eyes.

"The truth is, what I feel for you, Miss Morgan," he began in a thoughtful tone, watching the pad of his thumb smooth her hair back from her temple, "goes much deeper than what I imagine might be normal between a man and a woman. How I think of you goes hand in hand. This thing between us has been building for a long time and in the process you've somehow become a part of me. The best part of me."

He fell silent, in a contemplative way, and slid one hand under the robe's collar. Tunneling deeper beneath the fabric, he palmed her shoulder with the intent to part the lapels and expose the curve of one breast. He gazed at the luster of her skin in the twilight then lifting his eyes to hers, his head shook slightly in frustration. "I could spend half the night trying to put my feelings into words and I would still fail to do them justice. The short version is, you are everything to me and I don't know how much longer I could have survived without you. It's as simple as that," he confessed, covering her hand with his own where it had come to rest over his heart.

Tanya was so moved by his candor and eloquence, the breath required to activate her vocals became lodged in her throat, rendering her speechless. She could not have said it better if she had been the one to speak first and express the depth of her feelings for him. She wanted him to know that he had indeed found the words, but she was so overwhelmed, stunned really to hear him open his heart in such a way, like he'd never before, like she'd never expected. The sting in her eyes soon manufactured a tear. It spilled over her bottom lashes, crested her cheekbone and seeped into the corner of her lips. She couldn't help it, didn't care. "Oh Mick," was all she seemed able to say.

"I love you," they breathed against each other's lips. Knowing they'd said all that was important for now and their long agonizing wait to consummate what seemed born in their hearts had finally come to an end, flames of passion licked like wildfire. With tongues engaged and hungry hands on the move, Mick began to adjust his position, thinking neither of them were wearing underwear, it would take him to the count of three. It was because of that, he set her aside and removed himself from temptation. He'd be damned if their first time was going to be a quickie on the couch.

Tanya flopped back into place, facing the back of the sofa as she had been, but without Mick to lean on. Twisting her torso, she looked to see where he had gone. Not far. He'd only taken a few steps and was turning around. Rolling off the cushion, she stood up. "I think..." she began.

"No, no. Please Tanya. I beg of you. No more thinking." Mick bowed his head, knowing he'd reached the end of the line, the absolute outer limits of his sanity, especially after that thigh-high view she'd just given him swinging off the couch. "Just say yes or no. If it's yes, we go upstairs right now. If it's no—"

"It's y—" Tanya let out a yelp instead of a yes as she was swept off her feet and cradled in his arms. "Mick, let me walk!" she insisted, clinging to his neck. "Really Mick, I'm too heavy for you to carry up the stairs!"

"You're not heavy. I can leap tall buildings in a single bound, remember?"

Tanya chuckled. Mindful of the handrail, she drew herself in closer against him. "Hmm, what other super powers do you have Mr. Leighton?"

Surprisingly, he didn't seem to find the question all that amusing. Interpreting the heated look he gave her, no longer did she. If Saturday night was any indication, their sexual need for each other seemed to have built upon itself, gathering momentum, gaining strength, reaching a level beyond the ordinary. Blood rushing, hearts pounding, they stared each other down, both of them wondering if they'd be satisfied by sunrise.

He placed her in the middle of the bed upon cool sheets and tumbled covers, untied the sash, and whipped the terrycloth apart. He made no apology for his bold devouring gaze and neither did she when the shirt came off and he began to unzip. Looking into her eyes, he pulled her into a sitting position, pressed a hard kiss on her lips and swept the sleeves from her arms.

"I swear I've wanted you like this forever," he vowed with a warning light in his eyes. "If you're looking for slow and easy you'd better take your best shot, because I swear to God I feel like I could—"

Tanya didn't wait to hear what fate he had in store for her. Freed from the robe, she reached up to grasp his shoulders. "Just do it," she whispered, bringing him down with her.

If the phone rang this time, they wouldn't have heard it. If sirens blared, if hail plummeted, if winds howled and a freak ferocious storm hammered the Jersey shoreline, picked up the house and tossed it into a raging sea, it would have failed to distract two lovers so absorbed in the wonder and glory of their long awaited union, the world might have come to an end while they soared in ecstasy to the top.

Spent, they slept, limbs entwined, deeply and peacefully for hours. The digital clock on the nightstand read 2:24 a.m. when Tanya felt his lips roving. His tongue swirled around the ring in her naval. Her hand slid up his back and into his hair. "Mick?"

"Hmm?" Kissing his way up her body by way of the valley between her breasts, he made his way to her lips. He could see her face through the darkness thanks to moon glow and a street lamp, especially her sleepy eyes. "Hello," he said softly, looking into them.

"Hello," she whispered back, wondering if she ever thought it possible to feel so wonderful.

He kissed her lightly. "Do you know where you are?" he asked her, sensing she wasn't fully awake and might be a bit disoriented.

"Mmmhmm," she purred, turning towards him. "Where I've always belonged."

She had a way, with just a look or a few choice words such as those, of either knocking him flat or filling him up. Either usually required a recovery period. He took this one wrapped in her arms, grateful beyond measure for the second chance she'd given him. Thinking he might have been a little rough on her earlier and she might be a little tender, he was about to pull the sheet over them, go back to sleep and not wear out his welcome when she rubbed that luscious body against him again and curled one leg around his.

He'd been ready, willing and able since he woke up ten minutes ago and by now she had to know it. Drawing back, he looked to see if she was fully awake. With her lashes lying seductively low, she returned his warm glittering gaze. Instantly spellbound, and for a space of time drawn into a world reduced to nothing but sensation and emotion, he entered her by slow degrees. He found her incredibly snug but moist enough to take all of him in again. Still he ached for more of her and stroked his thumb across her lips to part them. His tongue slipped inside. Joined mouth to mouth, heart to heart, body to body, they rode the crest of the sweetest wave, climbing higher and higher until a plateau was reached that brought tears to the eyes and cries from the soul.

They surfaced again at 8:02 a.m. when the sun broke through a cloud-covered sky to shine through an unadorned window. Mick was the first to wake. Squinting against the invasion of bright light, he muttered a curse. He shaded his eyes with one hand, holding up the other to block the worst of it until another cloud came along.

Woven shades were drawn on two of the windows in the room, but he remembered now that he'd pulled on the third the day before and the hardware on one side had come down along with it. Since he hadn't been in the mood to play handyman, he'd left it that way. Fortunately, the window offered only a bird's eye view into the bedroom. A good thing since they were both bare ass naked.

Tanya was lying close beside him stretched out on her stomach—not that she could have ventured much farther in the double bed. Since she was facing the other way, Mick had no idea if she was awake or still asleep until she stirred slightly, and he heard her give a long muffled groan. Probable translation…*I feel like I've been run over by a Mack truck by the name of Mick Leighton.* Grinning at the thought, he rolled onto his side and propped himself up on an elbow. "Good morning to you too," he said and pinched her bottom.

"Owe." Tanya opened her eyes only to shut them against the glare.

"That didn't hurt, did it?"

"Yes." Blindly she felt for the pillow she thought was nearby and dragged it over her head.

"I'm sorry. I'll kiss it and make it better." Cupping the underside of her bottom, he leaned down and pressed his lips against the blush mark. "God, you have the most beautiful ass I've ever seen," he remarked unthinkingly and while his hand caressed, he went back for seconds. It was easily a vision he could have happily stared at 24/7 for the rest of his days.

He was lucky, she thought, that her spirits were too high to risk spoiling by asking him just how many he was comparing hers to. Besides, other than feeling a bit uncomfortable lying in front of him stark naked, in broad daylight no less, especially with him nibbling on her derriere as though she were breakfast in bed, which did feel sinfully delicious to be perfectly honest, she had the feeling something wasn't quite right.

Tanya pulled the pillow off her head. Her half-opened, curious gaze went bouncing around the linen colored walls of what was obviously a bare bones spare bedroom. Gathering her hair to one side, she rose up on her forearms and turned her head in the other direction. There were no sliding glass doors leading to the deck, no king-size bed or connecting bath. Winding up her visual tour of the room with the man lying beside her, she studied the face just inches from her own. "This isn't your bedroom," she concluded aloud.

"It has been since Saturday night."

Her gaze lowered a bit while she processed that information and came another step closer to forgiving him. Appreciating his thoughtfulness, she leaned over to say it with a kiss.

He was hoping the subject would never come up again, but he supposed that was too much to ask. Relief washed over him when she came towards him and touched her lips to his. Meant to ease his mind, it seemed. It did that and then some, turning him on in a way that had nothing to do with the physical. He didn't deserve her and vowed to change that. Following her back to her space, he rolled her over and buried his face in her hair. Over time he supposed these moments would pass when it rocked him to the core that she was finally back in his arms.

They held each other in silence, putting all else behind them, or at least aside while they let realization sink in and savored their first morning together. Tanya began to feel her stomach rumbling and sliding her hand down to his buttocks, she gave it a squeeze. "Are you ever going to feed me or do I have to start nibbling on *your* behind?"

He came up on a growl, stamping a kiss on each breast before he rose to sit on the edge of the bed. "God, don't start talking dirty to me now or I'll never let you out of here."

The choice between another shower or a quick bath was easy, especially when she happened to see a sample bottle of Jasmine Vanilla foam bath on the top shelf of the linen closet. She decided not to worry about how it got there. It was hers now. Her body was achy from sleeping in a strange bed and she was tender in places she'd never been tender before. A hot bubble bath was just what the doctor ordered.

When the tub was full and foamy, Tanya lowered herself with a deep sigh of satisfaction. Oh yes, there was nothing like a hot bubble bath. Well, up until last night there'd been nothing like a hot bubble bath. Twenty-six and she was just discovering that. Boy, she certainly had a lot to learn.

She reclined and relaxed thinking of the empty wrappers she'd seen on the nightstand once she'd finally found the strength to get out of bed. There were also a few unopened as well. *Probably buys them at Costco,* she muttered to herself. It must have been a case of the hand being quicker than the eye because she had no recollection of him ever pausing to put one on. Birth control was something she hadn't even considered. Thank God he'd taken the precaution though. He could have assumed she was good to go since she hadn't paused the action to question him.

Not that she wouldn't love to have his baby someday. The very idea seemed to tug on her ovaries and drag her deeper into the water. Down girl, she commanded. If her insides got any mushier— her grin felt so silly, she tried to adjust it with her fingers. Mick said he would be back in a few minutes. She didn't want him to think he'd been that good. Just at that moment, there was a tap on the door.

"Are you decent?" he asked her before entering.

"As decent as you can get in a bathtub."

"Do you want your coffee?"

"Yes, please." Tanya watched him enter carrying an attractive cobalt blue mug, though she was much more interested in the fine appearance of her handsome server. Mm mm mmm, yummy dude indeed. He'd showered and put on a pair of jeans. Soft, well-worn in all the right places, unsnapped jeans. He was shirtless and barefoot. Just the way she liked him. She wondered if he'd put on any underwear this time.

"Thank you," she said, accepting the mug.

Mick came down on his haunches and watched her take a sip. "How is it?"

"Perfect." She'd asked for extra light and extra sweet. It was just as she ordered.

"I'll fix you breakfast when you're done with your bath." He didn't know what she'd used but she'd tied up most of her hair. A few strands had come loose and were curling about.

"Okay."

"The only thing I have is eggs and toast, unless you'd rather have a bowl of bran flakes." Considering the night they'd had, her eyes were crystal clear. Her lashes looked incredibly long. They were damp and a little spiky, probably from the humidity in the room.

"Eggs and toast will be fine."

"How many do you want and how would you like them cooked?" She had some pair of lips. Years back, he used to have to be careful not to stare at them. They drove him to distraction, making him think of things he shouldn't, even when she was too young to know, and he was old enough to know better.

"One egg, scrambled, and one slice of bread lightly toasted please."

"I don't have any wheat bread." She had a flawless complexion. She hadn't changed much at all in eight years, only matured, beautifully. Either the heat from the bathwater put all that color in her cheeks, or it's possible she was blushing.

"That's okay. Do you have white?"

"Yeah. I have white." The shape of her face was oval from the front and a little angular in profile. There was a high curve to her cheekbones and a perfect slant to her jaw. Even her nose was somehow sexy, kind of long and straight with a rounded down tip and small flaring nostrils.

"White will be fine then."

"How tall are you?"

"About 5' 6". Why?"

"If you'd been a little taller, you could have been a model. You have a helluva face squirt." Dipping his index finger in the water, he ran it down her nose.

She grinned at the nickname he used to call her and rubbed the tickle off her nose with the back of her hand. She had a *helluva* face? "You do have a way with words, Mr. Leighton."

"I get my point across, don't I?"

"Loud and clear." She was thinking about the things he said to her last night while they were making love. One thing in particular came to mind and she found herself tugged a little deeper.

"How soon will you be ready?"

"What?" Tanya set the mug on the tub's edge before it slipped from her grasp. "Oh, umm, ten minutes?"

"Whatever you say." He stood and walked to the door.

Tanya rolled her eyes at his back. Here her breasts were bobbing through the bubbles like buoys on the bay and he had spent the entire five minutes dissecting her face, not even glancing at them.

Before he opened the door, he looked back and caught her admiring his backside. Tanya quickly raised her gaze, her smile the picture of innocence. She saw his eyes slide into the water and a dimple appear before he closed the door.

Lord help me, she prayed as her chin broke the surface.

On schedule, Tanya headed downstairs wearing her bathing suit and one of Mick's t-shirts advertising *Leighton's Seafood Bar, Lincoln Avenue and the Boardwalk, Seaside Heights, NJ*. She heard his voice and followed the sound into the kitchen. He was standing at the screen door, looking outside, talking on the house phone.

He'd put on a slate gray t-shirt. The kind that gave his biceps just enough flexing room, his ribs just enough breathing room and ended just about where his jeans began. She wanted to walk up behind him, wrap her arms around that lean waist, nuzzle his back and have her fingers check to see if he still had that snap undone.

But she didn't. Instead she found herself battling an unexpected attack of nerves and hoped he continued his conversation until she found a way to shake them. This, after she'd just spent about ten hours naked in bed with the man? Go figure.

Walking over to Mr. Coffee, she refilled her mug halfway. She looked around for the sugar bowl and found it on the granite counter next to the stove. A frying pan full of fluffy scrambled eggs sat warming on the front burner. Two cobalt blue dinner plates were laying in wait and two slices of white bread stood up in the toaster.

She opened the refrigerator, took out the milk and poured some into her coffee wondering if she was going to be able to eat anything after all. She was suddenly feeling a little out of her element and was rather relieved at the moment his attention was focused elsewhere.

Once outside the intimacy of the bedroom and bath, what did new lovers say to each other the morning after? How about those Mets? How did two people who'd just packed a decade of pent up desire into one night carry on a conversation as if their world hadn't spun off into another galaxy?

At least that's how she felt, as if he'd led her into a new and glorious land. Last evening they'd shared their deepest feelings. Through the night they'd shared their bodies. The things he'd said and done to her she couldn't stop thinking about.

Leaning back against the countertop, Tanya sipped her coffee. It sounded like he might be talking to someone at The Cove. She heard him say, "*hang on.*"

Gripping the phone by the mouthpiece, Mick looked over at her. "What's on your schedule today?"

The question caught her off guard and coupled with the way his eyes skimmed her body in his t-shirt, she couldn't for the life of her remember what day it was, never mind what was on her schedule. She was absolutely lost without her cell, her car, her clothes, her—

"Tanya?"

"Oh, umm. Well, I have to work, you know, at the pub. And, um, I have to, umm. Oh, I have an appointment at three," popped into her head just as he put the phone back to his ear.

His gaze lingered before he told the person on the other end he would be there in a few hours. He hung up and set the phone in the charger at the end of the counter.

Her swallow got stuck.

"You could have started without me," he told her, pressing down the lever on the toaster.

Tanya cleared her throat. "That's okay."

"Do you want butter or jelly for your toast?"

"Just butter."

Mick handed her one of the plates. "Take as much as you want and I'll eat the rest."

She did as he suggested and sat down at the kitchen table with her coffee.

Mick looked down at the small amount of eggs she'd taken. There was hardly more than a mouthful on her plate. She'd been avoiding eye contact and seemed to be at a loss for words. Her mood certainly took a nosedive since he'd delivered her coffee.

He took half of the remaining eggs for himself and turned off the stove. Setting a slice of buttered toast on each of their plates, he pulled out a chair and joined her at the table. "Okay, what's wrong?"

"Nothing's wrong, not really." She shrugged, taking a small bite of her eggs.

"Something is obviously bothering you." Even he didn't like the way that sounded. Mick covered her hand where it rested on the table. His fingers curled around hers.

"I don't know." Her head shook. Dumbfounded by the butterflies in her belly, she half-laughed. "I'm beginning to think I'm more comfortable being intimate with you than I am making conversation."

Munching on a wedge of toast, Tanya glanced at him during the ensuing silence and found him staring back at her, apparently mulling over the statement she made. There seemed to be a splash of color around his neck that hadn't been there before.

There she went again, blindsiding him. So she could say that to him as easily as pass the salt, but carrying on a simple conversation was suddenly out of her comfort zone? He shook his head in wonder of the female mind, especially this particular female—which he had to admit was a big part of his attraction to her. And why wouldn't it be when her mind had her blurting things out that turned him on as easy as a light bulb.

"I don't know whether to be concerned about that or elated," he finally remarked. Swallowing a forkful of egg, he leaned back in the chair. "You didn't seem to have any problem talking to me last night."

"Well, no. No, I didn't. But that was before the—you know, the night we had. And, it was—you know, pretty intense. At least for me it was. So now it's a little different. It's just a little different," she finished quietly, looking down at her plate.

"How so?"

Clearly he wasn't getting the picture and wishing she had never begun to let on what she was attempting to let on, she shrugged. "It's nothing, really. Never mind. Let's just eat."

"Obviously, it is something, so why don't you just come right out and tell me?"

Tanya set down her fork, suppressing a sigh. "Okay, you know, this is just not typical behavior for me. That's all. I know it sounds silly, but I'm pretty much new to this."

"New to what? Eating breakfast?" He was being deliberately obtuse. It was beginning to dawn on him what she was implying, but since it didn't make a damn bit of sense, it was stalling his thought process. "So, you're saying you've never done the whole overnight thing when you—" Mick hesitated there, not really sure how much he wanted to know. If she'd slept with any of his friends or anyone else in town, they'd kept the lid on it. Part of him was curious. The other part wasn't a masochist.

Agitated, Tanya began to peel the crust off her toast. "Right. I've never done this before, so I guess that's why I'm feeling a little uncomfortable."

"You've never done what exactly? Spend the night?"

"Well, yes, but I mean there was never a reason to."

"Stay all night you mean?"

"Right, since I've never slept with anyone, no reason to spend the night." Her tone only implied the, *duhhh.* She abhorred that kind of attitude but obviously something more was required to drive her point home.

"You said you slept with that guy at college."

"Yes, there was that particular disaster, but there was just him and now you."

"That's impossible."

Whiplash might have occurred if she'd turned her head any faster. "Excuse me? Oh, trust me. It is possible. Maybe it's not normal in your book, or much fun, but it is possible." Deciding it would be best to end the conversation there, Tanya pushed back her chair, rose from the table and exited the kitchen.

Mick was hot on her heels across the living room. It seemed he was forever chasing her and thought today was going to be different. He reached for her as she rounded the newel post but she managed to evade him.

"Where are you going?" He called after her. "I didn't mean that the way it sounded." He sighed, angry at himself for not thinking before he spoke—again.

"I'm going to make the bed and then you can take me home," she called over her shoulder. "Can you please show me where the clean sheets are?"

"Tanya." Mick had followed her up the stairs and into the bedroom. "Hey." He took her arm gently as she began to gather up the top sheet. "Look at me."

Still bristling from his insensitive remark, she couldn't resist doing so with an indignant toss of her head.

He held her steady, wrapping his fingers around her neck and tucking his thumbs beneath her chin to make her look up at him. "You should have told me last night. I would have done things differently. I definitely would have taken it slower. I just assumed all these years that you were—"

"Were what? Doing what you've been doing?" she grated. "You know, I don't even know why I told you. I should have let you go on thinking…but I wasn't sure. I thought maybe it showed, and I just wanted you to know why."

Mick began to move his hands, his voice deepening, softening, convincing in its sincerity. "The only thing that was apparent to me last night is how much I love you." He kissed her, dragging his palms across her shoulders. "And how much you love me." His hands continued down the sides of her breasts and tucked under her arms. "And how perfect we fit together." He kissed her again. Gathering the t-shirt in his fists, he pulled it taught across her chest. "Like I always knew we would." Another kiss before he angled back to look down at his shirt. "Now that is something I have been waiting to see for a long time."

Tanya followed the direction of his gaze and saw the name *Leighton's* stretched across her breasts. Raising her head, she shook it in amused dismay. "What am I going to do with you," she sighed, wrapping her arms around his neck.

He released his grip on the t-shirt. "I'll tell you what you can do *for* me." He reached around her to the nightstand. "Here, hold out your hand. I need both of mine."

Tanya looked down at the small package he'd placed in the middle of her palm. At the same time she gasped feeling the fuller parts of her body give way as he stripped her bathing suit down to her ankles. With pleasure, she stepped out of it and kicked it aside.

His mouth opened hers while his hands went a little crazy at the feel of her bare bottom through his cotton t-shirt.

With a soft, needy cry she arched into him. He was hard as steel behind the denim and almost bruising against her softness. It only made her want to press closer.

"Mother of God, you feel good," he swore, his voice scraping a depth of desire he'd thought he'd already reached by now. He assumed last night would have taken the edge off this all consuming need he had for her that never seemed to wane and give him a moment's peace. Now knowing making love to her lived up to all his fantasies, he was afraid he was in deeper trouble. Tumbling her onto the bed, he drew her wrists up beside her head.

One palm fell open revealing the package she'd been holding. Her eyes, heavy-lidded with desire, were on his face as he took it from her. Leighton's was now bunched above her breasts. It was true. She did belong to him. She'd come away from that summer they spent together with a bleeding heart and a profound certainty that whether or not fate decreed they would live their lives together, she would always be his. Her body was unresponsive to any other man. Without him, she would never have known such pleasure and abandon.

"Make love to me" she whispered urgently, as she had whispered to him that summer.

The plea, along with that breathless catch in her voice that said she was lost in the magic between them, took him back in time. Looking into her eyes, he became twenty-three again, she seventeen. His beautiful temptress, soft and sensuous, passionate and eager. More than any man could ever hope for. Where, he had to wonder, had he ever found the strength to resist her.

Now and forever his, he swore as they came together and came together and came together, racing to make up for the past.

Chapter 7

"Our meats are top quality, Ms. Morgan. You can't buy better, I assure you. In fact it's our motto. As you can see from my presentation, our beef is prime, grade A, aged Colorado beef. Guaranteed. We buy our poultry from Perdue. In my opinion, it's the best money can buy. Let's see..." Through the lower half of his lenses, the senior salesman perused the tropical design on the cover of the laminated tri-fold menu. *Paradise Pub*, he pondered with a thin slice of cynicism. Well, Seaside Heights might be a vacation hotspot for some people but it was certainly no palm tree island paradise. Damned if the ambience she'd created out there didn't make it feel that way though.

His bushy brows rose as he opened to the first section of the menu and scanned it from the bottom up, looking over the various specialty salads and apps. Making mental notes, he studied each page and took a glance at the back panel to see if she advertised catering. He'd already familiarized himself with the menu online but wanted to make sure what he'd seen there was up to date.

"Other than the ribs, it doesn't appear you're in need of any pork, lamb or veal. From what I see here, you offer beef and chicken, as well as the catch of the day and some seafood, of course, and I'm afraid I can't help you with those." He smiled, raising his gaze to the potential client behind the desk.

There was no change in her demeanor. She was still using her knuckles as a chin-rest and staring vacantly at his laptop screen through eyes the color of a Corvette he once owned. He sighed. The woman seemed to have the attention span of his thirteen-year-old grandson and with her rosy cheeks and long braid, didn't look to be a whole heck of a lot older.

Unless one looked lower of course. Flustered, the salesman arrested his thoughts, as well as his disobedient gaze. Against his will, it kept being drawn to that palm tree and grinning turtle screened above her left—well, he hadn't expected her to be quite so—why, a man would have to be blind not to—closing the menu, he harrumphed. She was the one who initiated the meeting, dissatisfied with her current wholesaler. The least she could do is pay attention.

"Ms. Morgan? The salesman waved his hand in front of those rather incredible eyes. "Ms. Morgan?"

Tanya saw five beefy fingers wagging, interfering with the bright, colorful graphics displayed on the laptop screen. She blinked. "Hmm? Oh. Oh, my goodness. I'm so sorry Mr.—"

"Pierson," he reminded her. "Please, David will be fine."

She returned his tepid smile with one rather whimsical, though she wasn't aware. Through it emerged a voice soft and dreamy. "Fine, fine, David." Tanya's brows began to pucker. She really was trying to concentrate but it was just so warm in the office. Her fingers plucked at the neckline of her polo shirt. She looked down at the folder he'd given her. The wide pockets contained a slot for his business card, a formal letter from Edward R. Moorhead, the company's CEO, and were otherwise filled with sales sheets and pamphlets. At some point she apparently withdrew some of them, but she still hadn't a clue where they'd left off. "Forgive me. I am so sorry. Where exactly were we?"

David Pierson loosened his tie and finding the visitor's armchair a bit dainty for his hefty girth, repositioned himself in search of some comfort. Obviously, this was going to take longer than he expected. Easy on the eyes or not, her trips into *Never Never Land* were beginning to irk him considerably.

Seaside had been his territory for twenty-two years, and he'd been knocking on the door of Jim Morgan's Bar and Grill longer than he cared to remember. Since the daughter took charge and gave it a trendy make-over, he'd spoken to her twice on the phone. First impressions led him to believe he was dealing with a chip off the old block, a pretty tough cookie. It surprised and pleased him more than a little when she actually called him back to schedule an appointment. Now he had to wonder if this cookie was only half-baked. Her head seemed to be up in *La La Land* somewhere, certainly not on the pitch he'd prepared to win her over. David decided to review his presentation again, uncertain if anything he'd said to her had sunk in.

"As I mentioned previously, Ms. Morgan, we have a long list of satisfied customers in the area. In fact, The Cove is one of our larger accounts. I'm sure if you ask Mickey Leighton next door, Moorhead would come highly recommended in his book."

Mickey? Tanya's palm nearly slapped her desk as she went in search of a place to hide her grin. Her monitor sat to the right and she turned towards it feigning the need to reference information for their meeting. She'd never heard anyone call him *Mickey* before. Michael maybe, but never Mickey. She immediately thought of that bouncy song from the 80's she loved so much and the tune began to play inside her head. High on love, her senses succumbed to the lyrics. Mm, oh yeah, *so fine.* That song definitely could have been written for her Mick. Tanya thought she had it under control, but her grin got away from her again when she faced forward.

"Something amuses you?"

The deep, disapproving timber of his voice reminded Tanya of her father and there was nothing more formidable than her father in a foul mood. Even a simulation was enough to make her snap to attention. Noticing, what was it? David? Yes, noticing David's brows drawing down his frown, she straightened her shoulders. Her lashes fluttered, sweeping the stars out of her eyes. God, she really needed to stop reliving last night. Tanya shuffled through some of the literature in the folder.

"Well, yes, as I was about to say, David, I've seen Moorhead trucks frequently in the area, and I am aware that The Cove is one of your accounts. I assure you, Moorhead's reputation has preceded you or you wouldn't be here. I've heard nothing but rave reviews.

"Callenzio has been our distributor for years and as I understand it, they are having some unfortunate difficulties since ownership changed hands. They've been dependable in the past, and I've given them ample opportunities to fill my orders promptly and accurately. To put it politely, they've failed, which is the reason I called you. I can't afford another inconvenience. Therefore, I am very serious about making a change. Why don't I give you a printout of my standing order with Callenzio, and we can go from there. I'd like to make my decision by Monday."

David Pierson gave an agreeable nod. Now we're getting somewhere.

A short time later, the meeting came to a close with the usual exchange of pleasantries. They shook hands across the desk with David thanking her for the opportunity to compete for her business and promising her the requested information within twenty-four hours. She thanked him for coming, handed him her business card and walked him to the office door. She wished him a good day.

Relieved to be alone with her thoughts, Tanya returned to her desk wearing a rueful smile. Her head shook. The man must have thought she was one ditzy broad, at least initially. Serves her right. She should have rescheduled. What did she expect fresh out of Mick's bed, that she was going to be able to keep her wits about her? She could barely think of anything but him since he'd kissed her goodbye about three hours ago with a husky "*I'll see you later*" murmured somewhere between her earlobe and collarbone.

She absolutely could not wait for later but until then there was much to be done, and she was just going to have to be diligent about it if she wanted to spend at least part of the evening with him. Stephan and Dana were leaving for Virginia tomorrow to attend a wedding. They'd be gone through Sunday, which meant she would be on her own at the pub and wouldn't get to see much of him over the weekend. Still, there would be the nights.

Before allowing that thought to turn her all ditzy again, she got busy. For starters, her desk was an intolerable mess between the pile of mail Dana delivered earlier and all the Moorhead literature scattered about. Tanya began to organize the latter when she happened to notice the doorknob turning very slowly. Little by little the door came ajar. Amidst a rustling fumbling sound, Dana backed into her office.

"Somebody got flowers," she sang out, pivoting to face her boss. Cradled in her arms was a long white florists box.

Something giddy and euphoric bounced from Tanya's toes to her larynx and would have escaped on a squeal if four fingers hadn't pressed against her lips to contain it. That, she somehow managed to control but there was nothing she could do about the emotion pouring into her eyes. In her mind she was twirling like a starry-eyed teenager when Dana placed the box into her waiting arms. She could see yellow roses through the cellophane window and anxiously removed the white envelope attached. Her hands shook opening the card.

I can't stop thinking about last night.
These reminded me of how beautiful
you looked in my robe. I love you . . . Mick.

"Oh." Utterly and positively ditzy, her eyes closed as she pressed the card against her heart. "Me too," she whispered. "Me too."

When Tanya opened her eyes, she nearly laughed at the dreamy expression on Dana's face. She imagined it to be a mirror image of her own. "Oh, what's that?" Tanya asked, noticing she had something else in her hand.

Dana looked down at the brown paper bag, grateful for the diversion. It gave her a way to hide her disappointment that Tanya didn't share with her who the flowers were from, although she had a pretty good idea based on the story that spread through the pub like wildfire yesterday. She placed the bag on Tanya's desk. "Your lifeguard friend dropped this off earlier today. Stephan was holding it behind the bar for you."

"Oh, that was nice of Ty," Tanya remarked, opening the bag. Inside were her sandals, towel and pink dress, the items she'd abandoned on the beach yesterday. She cringed and not for the first time thinking of all the trouble she and Mick had caused the beach patrol. Not exactly one of her stellar moments. She hoped Mick wasn't going to be fined, though despite everything, the outcome had been well worth it.

"I'll go and see how the kitchen is doing," Dana said. "Victor had some car trouble on the way in and got here late. Mark only arrived a short time ago as well," she added, referring to one of the sous chefs. "Apparently there was a fender bender on the bridge and the traffic was backed up for miles. Oh, and the twins called in sick."

"Oh wow, of all days," Tanya grimaced, looking down at her watch. "And it's already close to four. I noticed the twins were coming down with colds," she murmured absently. "Looks like it's going to be one of those nights. I'll be out shortly."

"Okay," Dana answered and turned to leave.

Tanya lifted the lid off the long white box and breathed in the sweet summer fragrance. The perfect buds were just beginning to open. "Dana?" Tanya called to her.

"Yes?" she paused, doing a half turn, resting her hand on the doorjamb.

"They're from Mick."

Unlike Tanya, Dana made no attempt to contain her squeal. "I knew it! I knew it!" She jiggled excitedly. "Does this mean…?"

"We'll see," Tanya shrugged, and though her response went as far as the unfinished question, her beaming smile spoke volumes.

Dana couldn't have been happier for her, even if she was bound for Italy now. To be honest, she was torn between the two honeymoon destinations anyway. "Okay if I tell Steph?" she asked, poking her head back in before closing the door.

"Of course," Tanya answered. "Although I'm sure it's common knowledge out there by now."

"There weren't too many around when the flowers arrived but pretty much everyone knows what happened up on the beach yesterday and that your car was still out there when we closed."

"Great," Tanya sighed, not particularly thrilled to know her employees probably, and accurately, believed she slept with Mick last night. Deep down she was just too happy to care overmuch.

"Don't worry," Dana threw back before leaving. "Actually, some of us are wondering what took you guys so long."

With that parting comment dredging up the past and weighing down her smile, Tanya closed the lid to the long white box. *If you only knew,* she thought, with a renewed pang of regret for all the precious time they'd lost. Certainly not her fault.

Refusing to go there, she picked up a stack of envelopes and began sorting only to find herself gazing into near space reflecting on that, *we'll see,* response she'd given Dana. Had that been her subconscious telling her in the deep recesses of her mind and heart she had little faith this was going to last? It had been less than twenty-four hours and although she had every reason to believe they were back on solid ground, was she afraid to look too far into the future? Despite all of the beautiful things he'd said to her, the incredible night they'd shared and now the roses, had he hurt her so deeply she might *never* recover enough to trust him again?

Unable to bear the thought, Tanya banished it from her mind and finished sorting the mail.

The Thursday night barbequed baby back ribs special drew quite a crowd, and tonight every employee in Paradise Pub was doing their best to impress—including the proprietor.

No biggy, Tanya thought, rather enjoying the rush, both literally and physically. Over the years she'd done everything from flip burgers, peel potatoes, mop floors, wait tables and tend bar. Running a restaurant was hard work. You had no business being in this business if multitasking didn't come naturally.

Cooking wasn't exactly her forte, but she liked to think she had a keen business sense, a flair for advertising and a certain knack for managing people and bringing out the best in them. And, if she did say so herself, the mass of bodies standing out on the sidewalk waiting to get in confirmed she must be doing something right.

It was a beautiful, balmy evening. Thanks to a Canadian low that swept through overnight and chased away the humidity, the wait for an outdoor table was currently fifty minutes. Customers were lingering over their cappuccinos, a decadent dessert or a second glass of wine. They were enjoying themselves and to Tanya, there was no higher praise. To rush them from their pleasure was forbidden. *Welcome to Paradise! May you relax, linger and enjoy!* It was the first option on the menu.

At seven p.m., she turned on the patio lights and changed the satellite station to a softer blend. It was also a signal to all waiters to begin lighting the candles on their tables as they introduced themselves to their party and announced the specials. Lighting the candles for parties with dinner already in progress was left to the waiter's discretion. Most people welcomed the added ambience when dusk began to fall but it was never safe to assume. Ask first, she always advised.

She had an efficient, hard-working team this summer. Tanya imagined a bird's eye view of the pub would showcase the entire staff moving as if in a choreographed dance, herself among them. Grabbing a handful of napkin wrapped silverware, placemats, a new bottle of ketchup, a couple of straws and a small dish of lemon wedges, Tanya returned to the patio and began distribution as she threaded her way through the tables. Dana was coming from the other direction with a tray full of filled water glasses which she began serving to new arrivals. Tanya set the placemats and utensils down on the vacant four-top for Dana to arrange and started helping Zoë bus the six-top next to it.

"I wonder what happened to Colin tonight," Tanya said to her when he suddenly appeared at her side. He was in the process of tying his apron and catching his breath.

"Sorry I'm so late, Miss Morgan. My mother had an accident driving home from work, and I had no other way to get here until my dad got home."

Tanya stopped what she was doing to give him her undivided attention. "Oh no, Colin, was she hurt?"

"She's okay. Her car is pretty messed up though."

"Was it the accident on the bridge? Mark was just telling us about it."

"Yeah. It wasn't my Mom's fault though. She stopped for the drawbridge light and the girl behind her was texting or something and rear-ended her. The bumper and part of the trunk is smashed in."

"Well, thank God she wasn't injured. That's the main thing. You know it wasn't necessary for you to come in tonight. Just call me whenever there's a problem, okay?" The poor kid looked a little shaken but still trying to maintain his *cool* surfer image in front of Zoë, who Tanya sensed he had a thing for, although she had to have four years on him.

"It's okay. I get my license in a few days, and I already bought a car so—"

He was all *cocky* surfer dude with that comment, jerking his head to the side to toss his silky, maple syrup bangs out of his long lashed, brown sugar eyes. He certainly was a cutie. Another *yummy dude* in the making. Tanya let him have his moment before sliding the pile of dirty dishes under his nose. "Good, that will give your mom a break, and be careful you don't make the same mistake. No cell while you're driving," she ordered in a mother hen tone.

"*Yes, ma'm*," Tanya heard him answer as he lifted the heavy tub and headed for the kitchen. She raised her head to watch him go. "Did he just call me, ma'm?" she asked Zoë.

"Yeah, but don't feel bad. He calls all older women that. I keep telling him it's okay to call you Tanya, but he says his parents are real sticklers for manners."

"Amen to that," Tanya murmured as Zoë disappeared to wait on the four-top and Dana appeared with all the necessary items to prep the six. They began to work in harmony when Tanya happened to look up and see Mick standing just inside the open french doors watching her.

It was actually pretty amazing, she thought, that a heart could flutter that fast without flying off somewhere. And seconds later, when Melanie stopped to talk to him on her way back to the hostess station, it was equally amazing a diffibulator wasn't needed to restart the beat. At the opposite end of the patio, Tanya stepped inside and headed for the kitchen. She had the swinging door in sight when she felt his hand clamp the back of her neck and steer her in another direction.

"Hey squirt, can I see you in your office for a minute. There's a good girl." Finding the hallway empty, two of his fingers threw her into a tortuous squirm. They were very ticklish spots he was pressing and knew it. The moment he had her on the other side of the door, his body flattened hers against it. A bold, sexually stimulating kiss was used to transform her squealing anguish into long passionate groans. Mick wanted to grab her hand, drag her out the nearest exit and take her to his house again—anywhere they could be alone and do what they did last night and this morning, over and over and over again.

"I missed you."

"I missed you, too," she echoed breathlessly and went to say something else but apparently there was more mind-blowing kissing to be done.

Before he was too far gone to pull back, Mick unpinned her from the door and walked deeper into the office. When he turned around, he'd already counted on the question in her eyes.

He shook his head, thinking of Melanie, like so many others he'd dated out of desperation, hoping to make her jealous. Or yes, even hoping something would come of it and put him out of his misery.

"I went out with her once knowing she worked here and you'd hear about it. Since that was my only interest in her, I'm sure I came off like a real jerk. We went out on my boat with another couple. I never touched her or kissed her. I barely even talked to her. In fact, I'm surprised she even spoke to me just now."

One hundred percent truth or embellished to sound good, Tanya was satisfied with the answer, and it showed in her expression as she pushed off from the door. She felt foolish now reacting the way she had, turning her back on them as they talked in the doorway and fleeing as fast as she could. Obviously, she was sensitive when it came to Mick and other women, particularly ones he dated. She was definitely going to have to work on that. Walking up to him, her arms circled his waist and gave it a hug. "Thank you for the flowers, Mick. They're beautiful. I love yellow roses."

"You're welcome. I'm glad you like them." He looked over his shoulder at her desk. He'd wondered all afternoon if he should have sent red or something more exotic. It struck him when he walked into the florist that he had no idea what she preferred. He thought he remembered her liking daisies at one time. Probably all girls liked daisies, he'd thought to himself, but Tanya wasn't a girl anymore. He'd been at a complete loss until he noticed the yellow roses in the cooler. "Where are they?"

"I put them in the refrigerator. I'd rather take them home and arrange them. I have the perfect vase for them."

"Do you now?" Mick murmured, hearing only the word *home* in that statement and liking the sound of it. Sitting on the corner of her desk, he drew her between his legs. She felt so good, smelled so good—all feminine and sexy mixed in with a hint of barbeque. It just made him want to gobble her up.

Only too willing to oblige, Tanya tipped her head with a lazy purr, giving him easy access to her neck while she posed the suggestion she'd been thinking about all evening. "I have an idea what we can do tonight."

Mick's chest rumbled while his lips stayed busy. "Oh, trust me sweetheart, I am way ahead of you on that one."

"As long as it involves nourishment. I'm about to collapse from hunger."

Mick worked his way to the other side of her neck. "You've been in a restaurant all day. You couldn't scrounge up a chicken leg or something?"

Tanya chuckled. "Mm mm." Her head shook a little while his reared back.

"Seriously? You've had nothing since breakfast, which you hardly touched?"

"I did grab a slice of cucumber from the kitchen earlier and I always have a bottle of Vitamin water nearby but that's it. I've just been so busy, there wasn't any time."

"Okay, first priority. You need a good hot meal. Name it. Where would you like to go?"

Tanya leaned into him feeling the roller coaster she'd been riding for the last few days starting to run out of steam. Her head rested comfortably on his shoulder. "I'm pretty sure I could do justice to a small feast from your seafood bar."

His chest rumbled again.

"I don't feel like going up to the boardwalk though. Would you mind picking up a little bit of everything and meeting me at my house in about half an hour? No clams, unless you want them. Just shrimp cocktail, calamari and um—"

"Scallops?"

"Oh yes, definitely scallops. Don't forget the french fries. Oh, and a crab cake."

Mick thought that sounded perfect. "I think I can handle that. Should I bring my pajamas?"

"You wear pajamas?"

She asked him in a way that Mick found so comical he started laughing. It was possible he'd just blown his image for good.

When a knock came at the door, he slid his hand out from under her shirt. Tanya backed out of the spread of his thighs and turned. It was Dana. "Sorry to interrupt, Tanya, but a Mr. and Mrs. Gallagher are out here having dinner. They'd like to say hello. They said they are old friends of your parents. I told them I would let you know."

"Okay, thanks Dana. I'll be right there."

Returning to Mick's embrace, she sighed audibly. "Better make that an hour, and you can stay over as long as you promise *not* to bring your pajamas."

Fortunately the Gallagher's were also pressed for time and forty-five minutes later, Tanya was lip-syncing to the song playing on her stereo as she arranged the yellow roses in a china vase her mother had left behind. She didn't know Michael Buble's, *Everything*, by heart but played the CD often enough to know most of the words. It was one of her favorites and as with every romantic song, she thought of Mick and yearned. This time though, knowing that yearning would soon be fulfilled by the man she loved and was loved by, her bare feet barely touched the tiles as she bustled about the kitchen preparing for his arrival.

Her pulse leaped each time she heard a car coming up the road or a door slam shut but so far it hadn't been him—which was probably a good thing. She'd spent so much time upstairs in her bedroom debating what to wear and straightening up, she hadn't even set the table yet. Finishing the bouquet, she carried it into the dining room. The tall vase was ivory with an elegant curve. Lenox most likely. She hadn't checked the markings on the base, but she knew her mother worked for the company fresh out of high school and had several pieces she was able to purchase at cost. Most of them she'd taken to Florida. Just as Tanya expected, the arrangement looked stunning against the table's dark glossy surface.

Returning to the kitchen, she discarded the debris from the flowers and began filling a large tray with things they would need for dinner. Hoping she'd thought of everything, she carried it out on the deck. She was happy to see the mixed annuals she'd planted in large patio pots a few weeks prior were looking full and healthy. No doubt from all the rain.

She set down the tray and checked her watch. She supposed it was a little late to be eating outside, but it was such a perfect summer night, she decided she could always put the deck light on if the candles she brought out weren't bright enough to see by.

Before heading back in, Tanya looked bayside once again. As it often did this time of year, the sun had departed in glorious splendor. From her vantage point, she could see neither ocean nor bay, only the skies above them. To the west, a vibrant shade of pink swirled across the rooftops and to the east, mountain size cumulus clouds hung over the ocean reflecting the sunset with an ethereal glow. It was a breathtaking sight. One of the most beautiful sunsets she'd ever seen, and she wished Mick was there to share it with her.

She imagined the view from his upper deck must be pretty spectacular this time of night. Soon she would talk to him about moving back into the master bedroom. It was twice the size of the spare room, and there was a connecting bath. Not using it wasn't going to change the past. They'd be much better off making new memories there instead of shunning the room as if something evil lurked behind the closed door.

Tanya re-entered the house with the feeling she had just risen to a new level of maturity and found him walking through the kitchen doorway. Even after these brief separations, it was almost startling to see each other again. Being together again seemed too good to be true.

"Hi," she smiled.

"Hi," he smiled back and after his eyes skimmed her body from head to toe, he wasted no time setting down their dinner and the six-pack he carried in his other hand.

Incredible. If she was asked to describe in a word what it felt like to be swept up in Mick Leighton's arms and kissed like there was no tomorrow, Tanya would have to say incredibly sensual. No that was two words. Okay, so it was a stupid thought and truth be told, she no longer cared about food or the sunset or anything other than dragging him up to her bedroom as quickly as possible.

"I guess we better eat before everything gets cold."

"Hmm?" Her lashes fluttered open. Toes touched down. He'd made her lips feel hot, swollen, as well as other parts of her, and she was more focused on that than his deeply uttered words.

"I said we better—" One caressing hand paused, moved, then paused again. "Do you have anything on under this?" he scowled, feeling for underwear evidence beneath the pretty print sundress draping the shape of her body.

"Yes, I have panties on," she insisted.

Mick looked down at her skeptically. "Where?" He hiked up the calf length skirt against her sputtering protests. One hand felt boldly around her bottom until he came across a triangle so tiny it could have doubled as a slingshot. Groaning, he closed his eyes. She looked so beautiful with her long hair flowing and her satiny breasts cuddled up in the bodice, all soft and welcoming, he was having enough trouble fighting the urge to take her right where she stood. "You're killing me, Tanya. You know that don't you? How do you expect me to think about dinner knowing you're basically naked under this?"

"Well, I didn't know you were going to go in search of my underwear the minute you walked in the door." Repossessing her skirt, she turned to pick up the bag of food.

"Get used to it," he said as a matter of fact, taking one beer out of the carton and putting the rest in the refrigerator. "Especially if you're going to wear stuff like that."

Secretly pleased but for some silly reason conveying otherwise, she exchanged a long look with his twinkling eyes. "May I have one of those too before you put them away? Everything else is out on the deck."

"Since when do you drink beer?"

"College." Tanya was so engrossed in satisfying her appetite; salting, dipping, finger licking, chewing, moaning, then tipping the bottle back and washing it all down, a one word answer was all she had time for.

Sitting at the square glass table in the chair to her right, Mick kept stealing glances at her, enjoying watching her chow down more than he was enjoying his own plate. "Everything okay?"

"Mmmm, fantastic," she practically slurred, popping a butter bathed baby scallop into her mouth.

"You're just so hungry anything would taste good right now."

"Oh no, I'm totally serious. You know I never stopped at your seafood bar for obvious reasons but I've heard great things about it. This is really, really good. Speaking of beer, I seem to need another already. How about you?" she asked, wiping her hands on a napkin as she made to push back her chair.

Mick touched her arm. "No, stay. I'll get them. I don't want you to break your momentum."

"Funny," she jeered, but after the day she'd put in, Tanya was perfectly happy to have someone wait on her for a change. "So? What's your secret?" she asked him when he returned and set an open cold one in front of each of their placemats.

"Secret?" Mick frowned. Given their history and all it entailed, the word made him a little uneasy. He didn't have any secrets—at least, not anymore.

"About your seafood, and your famous fries, as long as we're on the subject," she coaxed sweetly but then changed her mind and shook her head. "I'm sorry. I know that's privileged information. You really don't have to tell me if you don't want to."

"There's not much to tell," he shrugged. "Seafood has to be fresh and cooked exactly right. It's as simple as that. I've taken some crash courses, and I'm just lucky enough to have found people who are on the ball and care about doing things correctly and according to my instructions."

"Well, that is fortunate but what about this cocktail sauce and whatever this dip is for the calamari. It's addictive. And these crab cakes—oh my God, they are the best I've ever tasted. They have so much flavor and a little heat. So good."

Flattered she was giving something he'd worked very hard at and meant a great deal to him such high praise, Mick pushed his finished plate aside and folded his arms on the table. "The sauces are all made fresh as needed. They're just a combination of ingredients I played around with until I found the exact taste I was looking for. Some ideas I picked up during my travels in the Marines. Some I picked up from the food network."

"Wow, no kidding?" The man was just full of surprises.

"No kidding."

"Do you like to cook as well?" Tanya had a feeling he did after tasting his light and fluffy scrambled eggs this morning. He'd added fresh herbs. He appeared to be very efficient in the kitchen.

"I do, when I have the time."

"That's actually a relief because I'm not much into it and hard as I try, not very good at it."

Mick chuckled at the way she apologetically wrinkled her nose. He touched it affectionately with his index finger. "That's okay. Believe me it won't be your cooking I'll look forward to every day." He was going to say it would be her *company* and he would have meant that too, in many ways, but the flush had already started at her delectable cleavage and was working its way up. He was too much of a tease not to sit back and enjoy. With the candlelight enhancing every aspect of her beauty, he was just able to discern the glow overtaking her skin. The breeze played along, fluttering her dark waves and making the flame dance over her features.

When he came close to drowning in the vision, he withdrew his gaze, ironically in need of a good size breath. He was in love with her, deeply. No newsflash there. But for eight years he'd believed it to be unrequited and lived with a band of barbed wire squeezing his heart. Now that he knew the truth and she'd granted him a second chance, there'd been moments over the past two days like this one when not only had the heartache subsided but the swell of emotion replacing it intensified to a degree he wasn't quite sure what to do with unless he had her in his arms.

Mick cleared his throat along with his head in order to continue the enjoyable evening they were having. He was glad she seemed more relaxed tonight and appeared to be overcoming her discomfort with him *outside* the bedroom. Although the idea of her being more comfortable with him *inside* the bedroom stayed with him throughout the day, messing with his head until he thought he was going to have to kidnap her for a little afternoon delight.

One dimple, the right one and the more deep-set of both, appeared at the thought. "I do find it a little strange you're in the restaurant business and don't like to cook," he said, resuming their conversation the way it had paused, on a humorous note.

Tanya swallowed the last fry and grimaced in response. "I know, right? Actually it's the business side of it I'm good at. At least I think I am, and that I enjoy, most of the time. Even the hectic pace of a night like tonight I enjoy. I have no idea why that appeals to me but it does. Probably because it means we're paying the bills." Stating the obvious put a slant on her smile.

"The cooking I leave to the experts," she went on to say. "Sometimes I think if my parents didn't already have Morgan's, I probably would have ended up working nine to whatever in some stuffy office building somewhere. I would have hated that."

Remembering something it was important to her to mention, she slid her hand towards him on the table in a gesture of sincerity. "I am sorry about taking Victor away from you, Mick. The conversation I had with Connie just sort of snowballed and before I knew it—well, it wasn't intentional—or maybe it was. I don' know. My mind was in a very bad place at that time, and I guess I did want to try and hurt you with whatever means available."

Touched by the apology when he didn't deserve it, Mick's hand covered her own and gave it a squeeze. "Don't worry about it. Vic's happier, less stressed. I've talked to him, and it seems to have worked out for the best for all of us. Besides, I can hardly blame you. Come here." Wrapping his hand around the back of her neck, he urged her to meet him halfway.

The kiss was the perfect ending to a perfect meal, sweet and satisfying and knowing they could be seen from a few neighbor's windows, tame. However, when lips eased open and tongues embraced, and it became mutually clear control was slipping away, they parted.

"Um, thank you for dinner, Mick," Tanya said, a little lightheaded and more than ready to retire so to speak as she rose to clear the table.

"No problem," he replied, feeling the same after that kiss.

Carrying out the garbage can from the kitchen, he caught her yawning. "Tired?" His hand swept her waist as he walked behind her to reach for the bag she'd set on the deck floor.

"Mmm," she nodded, loading up the tray. "Oh, I just remembered it's garbage day tomorrow. Would you mind adding that bag to the can in the garage and taking it out to the curb?"

"So that's why you invited me over tonight, to take out your garbage."

"Actually, to feed me and take out the garbage," she bantered back, reaching for a stray napkin.

"Is that all?"

There was that voice again. He knew how to pitch it low and slide it right into home base. Her hand knocked over an empty beer bottle.

His arm curved around her from behind. "You sure get flustered easy squirt."

"Yeah, I know," she agreed, losing vocal power because of the way he was *damn the neighbors* kissing the side of her neck. "You do it on purpose though."

"Yeah, I know. Serves you right." This time unerringly locating her panties through the dress, he gave them a snap before walking away.

Tanya was still chuckling over that maneuver as she stood at the kitchen sink watching the tap water run through her fingers. She decided to do the few dishes they'd used by hand rather than bother with the dishwasher. She might not have a grand passion for cooking but to her Mother's delight, she'd always loved the feel of hot soapy water. Helping with the dishes was one chore she never tried to shirk.

Turning off the faucet, Tanya submerged her hands into the basin with a mental *ahhh* and reflected on how perfect the evening had gone. It left her with an overall sense of euphoria. Her tummy felt pleasantly full, her head buzzed lightly from two and a half beers and her body seemed to hum in anticipation of making love with the man she was absolutely crazy in love with. Her eyes closed. It was gloriously liberating after suppressing her feelings for him for so long.

It was also a miracle she'd gotten through dinner without jumping his bones because he was certainly looking quite appetizing himself tonight, she thought with a tipsy smile. She probably would have if she hadn't been so hungry and the food hadn't tasted so good. She loved that shirt he had on. He really was a great dresser. He made it seem effortless. Some people had that knack. Not so difficult, she supposed, when the clothes were surf shop quality and the physique was, well, hot to say the least.

Placing the last item on the drain board, Tanya filled her lungs with the blissful aura in the air surrounding her and was about to exhale a sigh of pure and utter contentment when he spoke and startled her.

Coming up behind her, Mick chuckled an apology and steadied her shoulders. They'd jumped about half a foot. "Come on, let me finish up here. You're half asleep."

"No, I'm fine, I—" she began to argue but he was already taking her hands and drying them with the dishtowel. "Everything in from the deck?" He looked over at the screen and saw that the outside light was still on.

"Yes, but—"

"I'll take care of it. Garbage is out. The front is locked up. Go. I just want to make a quick call to The Cove and I'll be right up." Planting a kiss on her forehead, he pointed her in the right direction and gave her bottom a push.

She'd folded the spread to the bottom of the bed and moved the sham-covered pillows to the chaise in the corner. The far window was open, catching a light, refreshing breeze. He could feel it all the way across the room where he stood with a thumping heart looking down at her. His call lasted longer than expected so he wasn't at all surprised to find her fast asleep. He would have felt a whole lot better about it if she'd pulled up the covers.

She'd replaced the thong that had his imagination revving all through dinner with bikini style panties. Both the panties and the skimpy top were a deep silky blue trimmed with lace of the same color. He didn't know if the ensemble was meant to be nightwear, underwear or just designed for the sole purpose of dropping a man to his knees, but the latter seemed to be where he was headed. He had a sudden flash of déjà vu and since he sure as hell had never been in her room before with her stretched out on the bed like Victoria's Secret version of sleeping beauty, he knew it had to be spun from a fantasy.

Considering a cold shower, Mick pulled the top sheet and blanket over her. He removed his shirt and shoes, took a few things out of the duffel he'd carried up and decided if he didn't look at her again and kept his mind on something really unappealing, he just might be able to forego the shower. He used the bathroom then walked around to the other side of the bed, turning off the wall switch on the way. Unsure of her routine, he hadn't left any lights on in the house but the bathroom night-light spilled into her bedroom well enough to see by. He supposed she'd be all right with that. Stripping down to the buff, he climbed into bed, careful not to wake her.

Arms flailing, Tanya bolted upright.

"Whoa, whoa, it's me." He reached out, catching her shoulder before she could scramble out of bed.

Tanya glanced halfway back. "Oh." Sagging with relief, she lay back down and with eyes closed, stayed quiet for a minute sorting her thoughts. "I was dreaming. I was running towards the edge of a cliff, but it was okay because I knew I could fly." If there was a hidden meaning there, she really didn't want to wonder, or worry about it. Turning her head against the pillow, she looked at him and smiled. "I was trying to stay awake for you. I can't believe I keep jumping like that but I guess

I'm not used to having company, and I'm definitely not used to sleeping with anyone."

Mick had propped himself up on his hip leaning on one folded arm. He felt the drowsy smile she gave him slide like a tongue down his midsection. He took her hand and held it where it rested between them on the sheet. "Well, I can't say I'm sorry about that but since we're going to be living together, it might be nice if you start remembering I'm around."

Tanya tilted her head back and through the semi-darkness tried reading the look in his eyes. Did he mean living together like tonight? Late dinners and sleepovers? Or actually moving possessions into one house or the other? "I'm sorry, what?"

"You heard me," he murmured huskily. "Get over here." With a grunt of exertion, he scooped her up and settled her on top of him. His fingers moved a dangling wave out of her eye before wiggling her loosely woven braid that had fallen onto his chest. He traced the curve of her cheek with its banded tail. Stall tactics while he prepared something to convince her. "With our crazy schedules, we're going to have a heck of a time figuring out every day when and where we'll have time to see each other. If we live together, we'll at least have the mornings and what's left of the night when we get home."

He'd hoped for a little enthusiasm, but she remained unresponsive with those seductive blue eyes giving nothing away. Bracing himself for disappointment, Mick broke the silence with, "Well? Any objections?"

He'd taken her by surprise fresh from a dream—unless she was still in it. *Control yourself, Tanya*, he hadn't popped the big question, only the second rate one. But, was it just too soon for either? Returning his patiently waiting gaze, she remembered another time he'd posed that question. "*Any objections?*" Then it had been about sex. Living together was a much bigger commitment, and quite possibly, one she wouldn't recover from if he had a change of heart somewhere down the road. Was she prepared to take that risk so early in their relationship? Silly question.

"It's a big step, Mick. At least, to me it is. I have no reservations but you have to be absolutely sure."

"Are you kidding me?" he half laughed. "In my whole life, loving you is probably the *only* thing I've ever been sure of."

Rejoicing in that answer, Tanya's arms hugged his ribs as she turned her head and rested her cheek against his heart.

Mick's hand smoothed up and down her spine. Was he rushing her? Damn straight. He actually hadn't planned on talking about it tonight, but the more he was with her, the more he kept falling, and the more he kept falling, the harder the impact if he lost her again. Until her faith in him was fully restored, he knew she had him on probation. "*I want to try*," she'd said when she agreed to give him a second chance, and he wasn't about to take those words lightly. Amazing as the past few days had been, one wrong move and there was no doubt in his mind, she'd be done with him. This time for good.

No way in hell was he going to let that happen, but time is what he needed to make sure it didn't. Time to earn back her trust. Before he even had the chance, what if something happened to make her rethink her decision? Would she pull the rug out from under him like she did in the drugstore eight years ago? A ten second kiss off without explanation? Building a wall between them again he couldn't penetrate with a jackhammer? If they were living together, he'd have more control over all of the above, more opportunities to make up for the past and prove to her just what she meant to him. Then he would concentrate on the next step.

Mick rubbed her back, a swift motion this time to encourage some dialogue on the subject. He wanted to hear more than just, *no reservations*. His head angled slightly to better see her face. "Am I wrong or do we both already know this is forever?"

Tanya wasn't quick enough to catch the tear before he saw it.

He rolled her onto her back and gazed into her sparkling eyes. "Are those happy tears, or how do I tell him I'm not ready tears?"

"Happy tears," she replied, smiling tremulously. She blotted the fresh ones with her knuckles before they ran down her temples.

His own eyes took on a squint while he scanned her unreadable features and questioned the sincerity of that answer. "Sure?"

"Sure," she stated, nodding and sniffed.

"Well, can you try and control your excitement? It's kind of getting on my nerves."

Tanya's smile relaxed, widening at his droll sense of humor. Then as if finally allowing herself, she threw back her head and laughed. Folding her arms behind his neck, she gathered him close and rocked joyfully from side to side. Her fingers ran through his hair, combing and clutching the short strands.

Lying against her soft supple body, he breathed in the fragrance on her skin while the summer breeze danced across his back. "I love you so much," he whispered into her ear and felt that swell of emotion again, rising, filling him. Treasuring the words she echoed in return, he tightened his embrace.

A few moments later, Mick raised his head as if revived by her answer. He dotted her face with kisses. The last one landed at the left corner of her lips. "Did I tell you how beautiful you look tonight?"

Her head shook while her hands began to roam.

"Did I tell you how sexy you look tonight?" he moved to the right corner of her lips.

She chuckled softly. "Thank you. Mission accomplished." Her hands grew bolder.

His lashes dipped warningly. "You laugh, but keep dressing like this," his hand snaked under her top and raised it above one breast, "and you're going to be spending a whole lot of time on your back."

"Mmm," came from all e-zones stirred by his promise. Her nails gently grazed. "Well, I definitely have no objections to that."

There were kisses for the pub, kisses for the deck, kisses for the kitchen, and then there was this. A passion he turned on behind closed bedroom doors she could barely fathom the reality of yet, novice that she was.

Her breath quickened at the stroke of his fingers. Her breasts ached for more when his mouth moved beyond them. She gasped as he lowered his head, clutched her pillow as his lips descended, moaned feverishly as his tongue explored and worried the next day that her wanton cries had been heard on the moon, never mind by her neighbors.

Much later, clinging together in the aftermath, Mick pressed his brow against her own. No words were necessary.

Chapter 8

In order to keep tabs on both houses, they decided to spend Saturday through Tuesday at his and Wednesday through Friday at hers. Spare keys were exchanged and extra drawer space created. Mick managed to adjust to the arrangement with a minimal amount of fuss. For Tanya, moving five miles away for four days every week presented some wardrobe dilemmas which she eventually decided wasn't worth the worry. Whatever she forgot to pack was only a ten minute drive away.

Since neither kept a particularly well-stocked fridge or pantry and both found appetites growing healthier due to a major increase in physical activity, a trip was made to the local A&P. They went late one week night to avoid the summer renters who typically flooded the food stores on weekends. Finding themselves hungry, and as a result so many things to their liking, they ended up with a full cart and enough food to feed a small army.

Mick's weekly cleaning lady continued to do his laundry, however her schedule was adjusted to service Mick's house every other week and Tanya's on the alternate, still on his dime. Tanya felt positively pampered having a cleaning lady but insisted on doing her laundry herself. Other decisions were left up in the air, assuming they would figure things out as they went along.

Learning each other's routines, habits, likes, dislikes as well as little idiosyncrasies was a gradual process they thoroughly enjoyed every minute of. Like all new lovers in love, each found the other to be a fascinating study.

Tanya discovered that Mick was a bit of a fanatic about three things; his breakfast, his Jaguar and recycling. Breakfast was the same every morning—two eggs, generally over easy with lots of salt and pepper, dark toast, buttered, and freshly brewed black coffee with a teaspoon of sugar. He prepared it himself and did his own dishes, more often than not while she showered or went for a run. Since his morning routine included reading the Asbury Park Press while he ate, she began having it delivered to her front door.

His silver Jaguar sparkled inside and out and heaven forbid she forget to clap the sand off her feet or dare enter it's hallowed domain with her Vitamin Water in hand or she would pay when they got home—usually in a way that left her exhausted from the chase and limp from laughter.

With regard to recycling, Tanya liked to think she did her part, particularly at the restaurant where it was almost mind boggling to imagine there'd been a time, and not so long ago, when not only food establishments but nearly everyone in general did not recycle. However, Mick seemed to take it to a conscientious level above and beyond her own. One evening, nibbling on her grin while he gently scolded her, she saluted him, promising to be more mindful in the future about where she accidentally tossed the cardboard toilet paper roll. For that, she received a dishtowel swat on the behind as she walked away.

Her best discovery— his genuine goodness and heart of gold.

Mick discovered Tanya rarely sat still unless she was reading, on the computer or beneath him. Depending on what she was reading, she occasionally wore a pair of very cool designer glasses that for some crazy reason made him instantly hard. And if it wasn't her glasses, it was usually her mode of dress, or rather lack of dress that landed her on her back, just as he'd forewarned.

Her one weakness, she openly admitted, was clothes. Somewhat embarrassed the day he peered inside her huge walk in closet and muttered, "*Holy shit!*" she sought understanding in the comfort of his arms quickly pointing out that although she did buy high end, she waited for post-season sales. Usually.

Nearly every day, and mostly from the pub, she talked to her mother on the phone and hadn't once mentioned his name. He knew because he'd asked her and she said, no. She was also very disciplined about emailing status reports to her father. Strictly business, she told him which meant the change in her personal status was never included.

His best discovery— the day he found the grab bag heart tucked inside her blouse, hanging from a long silver chain. Moved as he was, he had every intention of replacing it with the real thing at his first opportunity.

With eight years to catch up on, they enjoyed long conversations. Sometimes late in the evening snuggled together on Mick's deck watching the sun go down. Sometimes in bed in the quiet of the night after making love. Tanya wanted to hear about his parents, his business, his experiences as a Marine, which she'd been too immature to think to ask him about that summer. They talked about the possibility of him being recalled should the need arise. Something she couldn't bear thinking about.

Together they discovered three very important things; they were magnificently compatible living together, each enjoyed traveling, had visited some of the most beautiful places on earth, but neither had any desire to live anywhere but the Jersey Shore. And lastly, not so surprising, they couldn't keep their hands off each other.

Each morning they discussed their plans for the day. Schedules permitting, they met for lunch, or if either had a late night in store, they met for an early dinner. Though no formal announcement was made, the first sighting of them holding hands was all it took to start spreading the news around town. Mick took a lot of ribbing from Garrett, with no big surprise there, and Tanya took her share from Lisa, that is after the screech and her hearing returned to normal. She grew accustomed to Stephan's overactive grin and Dana's romantic sighs. Melanie took great pains to avoid her.

The nights were too short, their workdays too long. As a result, the mood often struck when and where it wasn't exactly appropriate, namely their respective offices. Clinging to that last shred of propriety before he turned her into mindless putty, Tanya dug deep to find the willpower to call time. She knew what she looked like after Mick got done with her and shuddered to imagine another story about them, this time x-rated, circulating Seaside like front-page news. Grudgingly, Mick bowed to her better judgment and a pact was formed that they maintain a safe distance between them at work.

Lack of communication was often responsible for destroying a relationship, she'd often heard. Tanya sincerely doubted they would ever have any problems on that score. In fact, Mick was beginning to read her mind, gauge her moods and know her body better than she knew it herself. What he didn't know, he asked about, out of the blue, in a casual fashion, even in non-intimate settings—which usually left her stuttering and him showing off a dimple. Being intimate was one thing, talking about it was another. Tanya was sure that in time, led by his example and so forth, she would rise to her own comfort level in that area. But until then, he was leaps and bounds ahead of her and taking full advantage. As far as secrets were concerned, she was beginning to think she no longer had any.

Well, except for this one, she amended, feeling distinctly out of place in the waiting room of her gynecologist's office. There were four other women besides her listening to light FM and reading baby magazines. All were in various stages of pregnancy. All but her that is. Beneath her gauzy white cardigan was an apricot color cami. The fitted style was unsuitable for anyone without a perfectly lean torso and board flat stomach. Tanya crossed her arms and rested them there in the hollow beneath her breasts wondering what it must be like to watch your belly expand as a new life grew inside of you. A few weeks ago motherhood was the farthest thing from her mind. Now the thought of having Mick's baby someday made her feel all warm and fuzzy inside, not to mention aroused.

The waiting room décor was a cut above most and catered to the comfort of its patients from the plush almond color carpet underfoot to the thickly padded armchairs to the pretty white and fern green table lamps projecting a soft glow through their linen drum shades. A flowering Bonsai sat on the far corner table and on the one next to her, rows of popular magazines on good health and parenthood fanned around a clear glass vase of pink tulips. Tanya doubted they were real but even from two feet away, wasn't one hundred percent sure. A fifteen-minute patient education video played repeatedly up on the wall mounted TV.

Brochures on the topics covered were available in a wall rack below, as indicated in the video.

Growing restless despite the amenities, Tanya shifted her position and happened to lock eyes with the attractive redhead sitting across the room and two seats down. The woman commiserated by way of a smile. Tanya reciprocated then turned her attention to the selection of magazines. It wasn't the first time she felt the weight of the woman's stare, and she began to wonder about her frequent regard. There was something familiar about her but Tanya couldn't place her. She imagined the feeling might be mutual.

Switching her focus to the video once again, Tanya practiced what she was going to say to Doctor Levin of Levin, Yang and Upland. *I'd like a prescription for birth control pills please.* In early March, when she arrived home from Florida, she'd seen Upland for her yearly exam. Stating the purpose for this visit would only take two seconds. She shouldn't even have to undress. Why was she so nervous? Levin wasn't going to counter with, *I'll need a note from your mommy.* Her chart would clearly indicate she was old enough to be sexually active. Tanya nearly laughed at that ridiculous thought. Twenty-six and she was just getting started. In this day and age, she was probably a bit of a phenom.

Tanya leafed through Working Mother without any real interest at this point then returned it to the table. She checked her watch again. 3:16. Her appointment had been for 2:30. Why did doctors always assume their time was more valuable than their patients?

When the door opened again to the inner sanctum, she wasn't even going to look over. So far it had only been patients departing. But alas, this time a nurse actually stood there framed in a beacon of heavenly florescent hallway lighting. The vision in mostly white looked down verifying the name on the chart in her hand. Five women held their breath, their eyes filled with hope. And the examination room goes to—

"Tanya Morgan?"

Across the room and two seats down, Maggie Ames followed the stunning brunette with her Irish green eyes until the door closed behind her.

Tanya filled her prescription then returned to Paradise. She heard her phone ringing from the hallway and dashed into her office to catch it before it transferred to the automated menu. It was Mick calling to let her know he would be home about eight. He mentioned having left her a message on her cell, which reminded her that she hadn't turned the ring back on since the doctor's office.

While they spoke, she retrieved it from the side pocket of her purse and told him she was hoping to be home a little earlier than that to get ready. It was Friday night and they were going out socially for the first time. Garrett's band was playing at a club in town. His wife would be there as well. Tanya was gradually coming to know Garrett but would be meeting Maggie for the first time. They were special friends of Mick's. She hoped the night went well. Before they hung up, Tanya was tempted to tell Mick where she had been that afternoon, but she decided to surprise him with the news at home.

He was late. Tanya was debating between crystal chandeliers and hand hammered silver and black onyx hoops when she heard his car pull in. A few minutes later the front door opened and closed. His footsteps sounded on the stairs. It was as if everything inside of her sent up a cheer. Silly, but true. Deciding on the hoops, she returned the other pair to her top bureau drawer. When he entered, she looked to the doorway with a welcome home smile.

The long, somber face was unexpected. Off and on all week, they'd been talking about Garrett's band playing tonight. He'd reminded her twice to be sure to give Dana and Stephan a heads up that she would need them to close. Tanya thought he would be in more of a TGIF frame of mind when he got home, although for a restaurant owner that acronym took on a whole different meaning. "Bad day?" she asked, pressing the clasp on her watch as she rounded the foot of the bed.

Mick managed a fraction of a smile. "Not anymore."

Even his voice sounded drained, Tanya thought, yet she sensed something more, especially when he wrapped an arm around her shoulders and drew her hard against him. The way he pressed his face into her hair and breathed, it was almost as if he was drinking her in, restoring himself, or maybe his faith. Stepping back, his eyes raked her. "God you look hot."

"Thank you," she replied, but it was a thoughtless response as her priorities shifted from worrying whether she was going to be too warm in jeans to worrying whether he might be coming down with something. Whatever it was, his behavior was completely out of character. Not that he wasn't entitled to an off day. "Sure you feel up to going?" she asked him. "You don't look…"

"No, no. I'm fine. Garrett's looking forward to us coming and I'd like you to meet Maggie. I'm just going to grab a quick shower."

"Okay." Tanya touched her lips to his. "I'll get out of your way then."

The shower seemed to have worked wonders and washed away whatever blues had followed him home. Looking like his old gorgeous self again, he took a possessive hold of her hand and led the way through the club's crowded tables. Clearly he was well known in this circle, Tanya noted, hearing his name shouted out more than once. Tanya saw that he was responding in typical *guy* fashion—a casual lift of the hand for those at a distance and either a clutch or a slap and a fist bump or whatever it was he was doing for those they practically scraped against passing by. With one acquaintance, he simply exchanged a good old-fashioned handshake. Tanya smiled to herself, finding men's communication methods a mystery. How did each one instinctively know which gesture the other was going to use?

Destination apparently the far side of the room, it wasn't until he finally stopped and leaned down to greet Garrett's wife with a kiss on the cheek that Tanya actually saw that Maggie Ames and the redhead pregnant woman from the doctor's office were one in the same. Oh dear, Tanya thought, when Mick straightened and began the introduction. By her expression, Tanya could tell the woman was about to mention the coincidence of seeing each other that afternoon.

"I thought that was y—" Maggie began until she suddenly noticed widening eyes and a shivering head. Reading the signals, she hesitated.

Tanya extended her hand and filled in the pause with, "It's great to finally meet you."

They both tossed Mick a glance to see how well he had been paying attention to the exchange. Fortunately, he was preoccupied rounding the table and sliding out two chairs, preparing to settle in.

"Thank you," Tanya mouthed with a grateful look, following Mick around to the other side, where they, like Maggie could face the band. Tanya hated to begin their friendship under any false pretenses, but it was either that or have Mick start grilling her right then and there as to why she had been to see the gynecologist that afternoon and didn't tell him. And she knew he would do exactly that. Avoiding the subject until they got home was just better for everyone.

Mick held out the chair next to Garrett's wife for Tanya and the conversation was off and running. They talked about Maggie's hometown in Ireland. Tanya believed she had passed through it during her graduation trip abroad. One of her college roommates was also from Ireland, she explained to Maggie, and they'd stayed a few nights with her relatives in the town of Killarney, which Maggie was also familiar with. From there the conversation switched to the baby, her due date and how she was feeling. Tanya wondered how long she was going to survive the discomfort of the hard wooden chair, but Maggie had come prepared and pointed out the two cushions she'd brought from home, one for her back and one for her bottom.

Conversation flowed effortlessly between the three of them, with one interruption from the waitress to take their drink order, and the second interruption when seven band members appeared to the roar of the crowd.

Wow. Tanya looked around. You would have thought Bruce Springsteen and the E Street Band stepped onstage. Mick told her during the drive over that *Back Alley* was a popular group who'd been touring the Jersey coast every summer for about nine years. After all that time, they had gained quite a following, and since their very first gig was at the Beachcomber, they were especially popular in Seaside Heights.

Tanya couldn't remember for sure but thought she might have seen them play at one time. She and Lisa had turned twenty-one during the month of September so it wasn't until the following summer they frequented many of the Seaside Heights clubs. But that had been the extent of their so-called clubbing days. The year after that, Lisa married John, shortly after she graduated from Stockton. Tanya had also graduated that year, and after her trip to Europe, she began spending all of her time at Morgan's, working and learning the restaurant business.

Looking forward to seeing what she'd been missing, Tanya sat back, enjoyed her beer and focused primarily on Garrett. He wore the *rocker* look well, she thought, especially the way his hair fell around his face as he tuned his guitar. Before they began, one band member wearing a bandana over the crown of his long, straight platinum hair, stepped up to the center microphone and shouted at the top of his raspy voice, *"What's up Seaside!"*

Once again, the crowd roared and whistled. Garrett struck the first cord to their first song of the night, *We're An American Band,* and again they cheered. For the next hour, the incredibly talented Back Alley played classic rock, covering artists such as Bob Seger, the Rolling Stones, Bon Jovi and Def Leppard. In the second set they mixed in some AC/DC, Aerosmith and U2. Justice was done to all and then some. More than half the room was up dancing. Although she couldn't quite picture it, Tanya wondered if Mick liked to dance, or if he even could.

Garrett played lead guitar and sang back-up on a few songs with that beautiful baritone of his. During each break, he came over and sat with them. Like Mick he was a man of few words, preferring to sit back and observe rather than lead the conversation. Except with Maggie. By the end of the second break, Tanya was well on her way to getting to know him. There he sat, looking for all the world like the quintessential bad ass, and she was quickly discovering that underneath those lean, mean tattooed muscles, that tight white t-shirt and black leather vest was nothing but a big softy, completely besotted with his pregnant wife. He held Maggie's hand for the full twenty minutes, asking her if she was getting uncomfortable, was she tired, did she feel okay, did she want to go home? Even while he talked to Mick, he kept a close watch on his wife.

When Garrett left to begin the third set, Tanya asked Maggie if she knew the location of the ladies room. Feeling the need as well, she offered to go with her.

"Thanks for covering for me when we first arrived. I just haven't told Mick yet that I..."

"Oh my God, are you pregnant Tanya?" The question nearly burst from Maggie's lips once they were out of earshot. It was the first thing she had thought of that afternoon seeing her in her OBGYN's office, even though she knew there had hardly been enough time to even suspect.

"Oh, no, no, no," Tanya assured her, spilling a laugh. "That's not the reason I didn't want him to know. Mick and I have only been together a short time and—" Tanya wasn't even sure where to go with that. "Well, I just didn't have a chance to tell him today that I had this appointment. I will though. Mick and I have been through a lot I guess you could say, and he tends to get a little upset with me now when I keep anything from him."

Maggie chuckled while holding onto Tanya's arm as they squeezed through a tight spot near the restrooms. "Please, say no more. Trust me, I've seen the man doing his best to hold it together over you. I'm sure I'm not telling you anything you don't already know, but if there's even a shred of doubt, Tanya, do away with it. Mick is completely and utterly devoted to you." The last sentence was thrown over her shoulder as they entered the ladies room.

Fortunately there was no line, just a few girls crowded around the mirrors over the twin sinks reapplying their lipstick and checking themselves out. Conversation lapsed between the two women while they went their separate ways.

"Sorry." Maggie grimaced, seeing Tanya waiting patiently by the door. "Takes me some time to put everything back in place."

Tanya grinned. "That's okay. How are you holding up out there?" she asked, raising her voice enough to be heard over the running water as Maggie washed her hands. "You know, as soon as you've had enough, just let us know. We'll leave whenever you're ready."

"Oh, I appreciate that. I'm hanging in though. Just another set I think and then I'll probably be needing my feet up." Maggie turned off the faucet and pulled a paper towel from the dispenser. "After the baby's born, who knows when I'll get out again to see the band play so if it's all the same to you, I should probably make the most of tonight."

As Tanya opened the door to exit the ladies room, Maggie dropped the towel into the trash receptacle and continued. "You know let me just say this, Tanya, I'm so happy you and Mick are finally together. Garrett too, of course. Actually that happens to be a huge understatement. The two of them are quite a pair you know. Like brothers almost. Garrett says Mick is a changed man and I can see that for myself."

"Thank you, Maggie." Tanya was touched by her candor. It seemed they were off to a good start at becoming friends, and she could listen to that musical brogue all night.

Due to the wall-to-wall tables, along with a few people standing and mingling nearby, Tanya didn't realize someone was sitting in her chair until she was almost on top of it—and lo and behold if it wasn't goldilocks, practically sitting on Mick's lap. The girl had pulled her chair in close, twisted her body to face him and was posed provocatively on one forearm. At first Tanya thought she was coming onto him until she saw how fast she was talking, as if what she had to say was very important.

Thanks to Maggie's hand slipping into her own and giving it a squeeze, Tanya recovered enough to simply take Garrett's chair until she knew what was going on.

It was another minute or so before the girl finished speaking then without even nudging her chair back for clearance, she rose slowly, sinuously within the confines of that small intimate space, making sure Mick received the full affect of her so called charms as she stood.

Mick still hadn't raised his eyes to her, or Maggie, or to the pair of boobs now looming over his nose. Rather, they appeared to be boring a hole through his empty glass while his fingers continued to spin it within the same circle. Tanya wasn't sure if his cheekbones were flushed from discomfort or suppressed fury. Possibly a combination of both. A pulse was thumping behind his jawbone.

Tanya was doing her best not to let on that jealousy was clawing its way up her windpipe and nearly choking off her oxygen. She was also trying not to let her imagination run rampant when it suddenly went up in flames at the sight of ten feminine fingers with turquoise blue nails curling over Mick's shoulders. Using them for balance, the girl squeezed between the back of his chair and the person sitting behind him. She arched her spine for no other reason than to make her breasts brush his head. Even though Mick lunged forward to avoid them, Tanya's stomach churned, as if she'd swallowed something vile. Unfazed, the blond even took the liberty of dragging her hand caressingly across his back before walking away.

Not once did the spoiler of their previously enjoyable evening acknowledge Maggie or herself, though there was no doubt in Tanya's mind that the girl's rude, disgusting performance made all the more offensive by her unflattering skintight mini dress, was strictly for her benefit.

The mood at their table no longer matched the upbeat music being played by the band. Mick still hadn't looked at her. She couldn't look at Maggie. So much for their first night out on the town. Tanya pictured something like this happening on every occasion. Somehow she knew this wasn't the infamous blond she found in his bed, but it didn't matter, the urge she had to get up and walk out of his life for good said it all.

An Eric Clapton ballad began with an intro from Garrett's guitar. A song she'd always loved. She didn't want to go with Mick when he wrapped his hand around her wrist, but to do otherwise would have created an embarrassing scene in front of Maggie. The strength of his hold practically lifted her out of the chair anyway. He headed for the dance floor, leading her to the darkest area near the wall.

"I'll explain everything when we get home," he told her. "Whatever you do, don't jump to conclusions."

It helped. A little. But Tanya wished he had asked her to dance when she was feeling more receptive to his hard embrace.

The three of them continued to abide their own awkward silence at the table until the band broke again, then by mumbled, mutual agreement the decision was made to call it a night. Garrett escorted Maggie outside to say goodbye. Tanya made her way out alone. She could have waited with Mick while he waited for the waitress to settle their tab, but she was nearly suffocating on the blond's presence as she continued to draw attention to herself by slithering past their table over and over again on one pretense or another.

Though the strained silence made it seem longer, it was only a short ride to the Ames' pretty cape in Ortley. Tanya wished Maggie goodnight and watched Mick walk her to the door and see her safely inside. For the remainder of the drive to Lavallette, she stared straight ahead, unable to see before or beyond what happened at the club.

Mick locked the front door then turned to watch her cross the living room. She'd slipped off her shoes, as she always did upon entering. They dangled from her fingers as her bare feet padded across the hardwoods. He was surprised she didn't try to club him with the narrow heels the minute they got into the house. He would have preferred some kind of physical or emotional release to her stone-cold silence and weary gait. He followed her, just as weary, on top of being scared shitless to tell her the truth.

He entered the bedroom just in time to see her walking into the bathroom, this time with clothing dangling from her hand. She shut the door. He heard the lock click. She'd started dressing and undressing in front of him almost from the start, never in the bathroom. Mick cursed, took off his shirt and shoes and emptied his pockets of his wallet and some loose change. Waiting for her to come out, he practically wore a path in the carpet.

When she finally opened the door, he saw that she was dressed in something she might have worn to hang out in her college dorm. The boxers were red and gray checkered. The BU t-shirt was thin from wear and roomy, not the figure hugging kind she usually wore. In fact, he hadn't seen her wear anything so modest to bed since they'd been together. Her message came through loud and clear—*Hands off buster, don't even think about it.*

Starting to smile against his will, Mick cupped his jaw in his hand and gave his night shadow a rub. She actually looked so damned adorable, he swore if the situation wasn't about to get worse, he would have carried the smile through to a good laugh. Maybe he'd given her reason to believe otherwise, but it was absolutely beyond him how she could think he'd be interested in anyone else.

He watched her remove the surplus pillows from the bed, place them on the chaise and return to fold back the comforter. "Do you want to talk about it?"

"Not really, no." Tanya started to gather the summer weight blanket and top sheet but paused. Her tense frame slackened. "All right, yes," she sighed. "I suppose we might as well get it over with."

Mick leaned back against the bureau and slid his hands in his pockets. He found himself crossing his fingers for luck. "She's a waitress at The Cove, and the reason I was late getting home tonight."

All support systems crumbling, Tanya dropped down on the edge of the bed. Bracing herself for the rest, she studied the new polish on her nails as if it mattered. "Go on."

"I'm having a problem with her. She's been coming in late, leaving early. She has trouble getting along with a few of the other waitresses. There's no question she's the instigator. I put her on probation tonight."

"Why didn't you just fire her?" Tanya looked up at him, perplexed. "It sounds like you have enough grounds. Have you been documenting everything?"

"I realize that, Tanya, and yes, everything has been entered into her file. My intention was to let her go tonight but she gave me this sob story about being in a financial bind right now. She asked me to give her another chance, and although I'm now regretting it, I agreed. What you saw was just a follow-up to the talk I had with her before I left The Cove tonight."

"Really?" Tanya's tone couldn't have been more sarcastic. He actually had the nerve to call that woman's appalling behavior, *just a follow-up talk*? She chuckled sardonically. "Wow, I would like to have been a fly on the wall during the private meeting if that's how she handles herself in public."

Mick looked at her squarely in the eye. "It was strictly professional, Tanya, I swear. That act she pulled tonight had a fair amount of booze behind it. It was for your benefit, just to cause trouble between us. She's never done anything like that at The Cove."

Tanya suspected as much but felt only marginally better hearing Mick confirm it. "How did she know you were going to be there tonight?"

"I have no idea. I certainly didn't tell her, but she knows Garrett plays in Back Alley and that he and I are friends. She may have assumed she'd find me there. I don't know. It could have been just a coincidence."

What the hell did it matter at this point, Mick thought with a shake of his head. She managed to ruin their evening and then some, which was precisely her intent. Mick rubbed his eyes, beat, both physically and mentally. Tanya probably was too and here they were, after midnight, giving credibility to something, someone, who had no real significance in their lives. Except that she made it appear that way.

Tanya gazed up at him thoughtfully, wishing he had kept his shirt on for this conversation. His bare chest only served to remind her how handsome and virile he was. "Do all of your waitresses touch you like that, Mick?"

"No," he answered abruptly, adamantly, then after a silent prayer, a long exhale prepared him to face the inevitable.

The young woman was more than just a difficult employee. That much was becoming evident, Tanya realized, as she watched Mick's demeanor change little by little. Something, perhaps guilt, seemed to be causing his gaze to shift, his head to hang, his hand to start working on whatever was troubling the base of his neck.

Oh please. "You've slept with her, haven't you?" Tanya didn't need verbal verification. It was written all over him. She felt profoundly ill at the thought of them together.

She had one final conversation with Mick about what he had done to her eight years ago and she'd begun to accept it for what it was. Or at least what Mick told her it was. A terrible mistake caused by excessive inebriation. A mistake that would have cost him everything, is how he'd put it, if she hadn't found it in her heart to forgive him.

This was different, regardless of whether they were together or not at the time. As far as she was concerned, it spoke to his integrity, his morals. She couldn't even bear to look at him and turned her head aside in both disappointment and disgust. Disillusioned as well, she closed her eyes and struggled not to feel as if she might also be in the midst of making a terrible mistake. "You didn't think of the risks involved, sleeping with an employee?"

Though far from funny, again Mick couldn't help chuckling to himself. It was ironic, he thought, that these last eight years were now set to come back and bite him. The eight years that never would have happened if he hadn't screwed up in the first place and never should have happened the way they did if she hadn't kept that night a secret. She was all he ever wanted and no matter how hard he tried now, his behavior over these last eight years was going to make it an uphill climb to convince her. He supposed he couldn't blame her for all her doubts, especially after tonight, which was precisely the reason he wanted them living together. He was on the verge of losing her again. He could see it in her eyes, and by God she was going to have to call in the National

Guard to remove him. Transfixed by his thoughts and feelings, his gaze clung to her profile, wishing she could just somehow see into his heart.

"I'm never going to risk losing you by lying to you, Tanya, and there's nothing I can do now about the past. She worked for me one summer several years ago then quit to go back to school. A year or so after she left, I ran into her in Klee's. We dated a few weeks then I ended it. It was the same with every relationship I ever had—if you could even call them relationships," he shrugged. "They just weren't you so there was no point in continuing. This spring she came back to The Cove looking for evening work. I was in California at the time. My mother had surgery, and I flew out to be with her. Since she was a model employee the first time, Jack saw no reason not to rehire her. I had no idea until I returned. Initially things were fine then she began to take advantage, expecting preferential treatment because we dated. At least, that's how I saw it. I gave her a warning, and she seemed to get her act together, until she heard about you. Since then, she's developed a real attitude."

"Did she offer to sleep with you again in order to keep her job?" Tanya wasn't sure why she even bothered to ask that question since tonight's little performance had been a blatant invitation.

"In a manner of speaking," Mick replied quietly, sticking to his full honesty policy.

Tanya harrumphed. Having a front row seat to her brazenness, she could just imagine what manner. "What did you tell her?" Reaching over to her nightstand, she pumped moisturizer into her palm. Rising, she rubbed the lotion into her hands and smoothed the excess into her arms as she walked towards the door.

Mick cut her off at the end of the bed by stepping in front of her. "I know you're upset and I don't blame you. I'm sorry she was there. I'm sorry she made an ass of herself doing what she did and spoiled the night for us, but what do you think I told her Tanya?"

When her only response was to drop her gaze, Mick went on to answer the question himself. After the last two weeks that she would even have to ask? "I told her no, Tanya. What the hell do you think?" By the lift of her lashes, he saw firsthand the hurt she was suffering, and it was clear tonight hadn't done him any favors in his quest to regain her trust.

"Well, I think maybe you should reconsider. Leave some of your many options open, you know? Just in case things don't work out between us."

As she made to move past him, Mick grasped her arm. "Tell me you don't mean that."

"I wish I could." The retort rolled off her tongue without even having to think about it. Seeing the look on his face, she softened slightly, took a much needed breath and rubbed at the pressure pounding between her brows. "Just…just leave me alone for awhile, okay?"

He gave her an hour in which time he laid on her bed and studied the container of pills he found in the pharmacy bag in her purse. Mick headed downstairs with them in his hand. She was sitting cross-legged at the end of the couch. Her elbow was bent on the arm. Her hand supported her head. A curtain of waves hid her face from his view as he walked past her and sat down on one of the leather chairs.

"What the hell is this?" he asked, tossing the dispenser on the coffee table.

In a meditative mode that nearly put her to sleep, Tanya opened her eyes a slit and began to lift her head. When she saw it was the birth control pills, she resumed her position. She had forgotten all about them. "I'm sure you know, so why are you asking? Is there some reason you were going through my bag by the way?"

"Your cell phone rang. Considering the time, I thought it might be important. It was a wrong number. Have you been taking these all along?"

"No. I just got them today." He was obviously angry. Tanya couldn't imagine why.

"How?"

"How what?"

"How did you get them?"

Tanya sighed and sat up straight. Obviously her meditation time was over. "I went to the doctor and got a prescription."

"Why?" Mick shrugged.

"Because I asked for it." Tanya copied the shrug.

"Why," the pause was deliberate for emphasis, "did you ask for it?"

Tanya closed her eyes so he wouldn't see the shimmer of tears. "I don't want to talk about this now, Mick."

"Well, I've got news for you." Rising he swiped up the pills and came around the coffee table. "We are going to talk about it. You know I always use a condom. Are you still so unsure of us, so afraid of me getting you pregnant, that you've decided to take these for added insurance?"

Shocked he would think that, she looked up at him. "That isn't the reason I wanted them."

"What other reason could there be?"

"I...I can't talk about this now. This is very bad timing." Bristling that he was insisting they discuss a topic that was meant for an entirely different set of circumstances, in fact circumstances quite the opposite, Tanya untangled her legs and made to get up.

"Stay," he demanded, pressing his hand upon her shoulder. "Were you even going to tell me about them?"

"Yes, of course I was. It was supposed to be a surprise."

"A surprise," he stated flatly, obviously stumped by her line of thinking. "As in a good surprise?"

"No, a bad surprise," Tanya jeered. "Let me up."

"No. Watch your feet." Mick stepped over them to sit beside her. "Tell me."

"Mick." It was a plea for him to leave her alone. Leave the subject alone. At least for now. How could she tell him now? The mood was all wrong.

"Did you get them because you don't like me using condoms? You don't like the way they feel? It's distracting when I have to stop?"

Tanya rolled her eyes, her face warming. Flustered to the point it was either vent or strangle, she vented, even though her hands itched to do the latter. "It's not that exactly. I just thought...I was thinking..."

"What, what? Just tell me."

"I was thinking it would make things easier for you." Under pressure, the words came out in a heated rush, certainly not as she planned or pictured herself telling him. "And, and..."

"And?"

"And." Tanya closed her eyes and took a moment to find her center, along with the emotions that led her to the decision to start taking the pill. "I just don't want there to be anything between us when we..."

"Come here." Mick wrapped his arm around her and pulled her hard against him. His face dove into her wealth of hair. "You should have told me. Don't ever keep something like that from me."

Tanya ran her hand through the smattering of hair on his chest. Closing her eyes, she breathed in the musky essence of her man blended with the soap and cologne he favored. A strong possessiveness filled her making her tighten her embrace. Those scents belonged to her now and her alone, and she resented that woman for having once had the pleasure and trying to lure him back. Her expression, had she allowed him to see it, mirrored her thoughts. "I would have thought you'd feel the same."

"I do," he answered gruffly. "Look at me." He cupped her chin and raised it. "I don't want you taking birth control pills. Did you read the crazy side effects to those things? We'll look into some other options. Okay?"

Tanya nodded, fighting back the tears that were sitting on the brink.

He hugged her close, his other hand rubbed up and down her arm lying across his chest. It slid up inside her t-shirt sleeve and palmed her shoulder. "Okay, now that we have that settled, what are you doing next Saturday?"

She shrugged, watching her newly manicured nails scrape gently across his skin. "The usual. Why?"

"Let's get married."

Tanya pressed against him and bolted upright. Throwing her hair back with a swift hand, she scanned his features trying to gauge his sincerity. As marriage proposals go, it wasn't exactly cut from a girl's dream. The setting was hardly romantic and there was no sign of a ring. Three hard clues he'd pulled the idea out of his *get out of the dog house free* emergency kit. Yet despite all of that and the reason she was barely speaking to him, the tender tone of his voice and the fierce way he gathered her close had given her goose bumps, making up for all the rest—that is, if she were inclined to go easy on him. It just so happened, she wasn't. Her eyes narrowed. "You're just saying that because I'm mad at you."

"I'm saying it for a dozen reasons. The first one being I love you, I've always loved you and I'll never stop loving you. But yes, far down the list is the fact that you scare the hell out of me when I know I've hurt you and there's nothing I can do about it."

Mick framed her face with both hands. "Tanya, I had no idea what was going on inside your head all these years. I thought you just lost interest in me and moved on. When I wanted sex, I chose women I knew were a certain type and made sure they understood that was all I wanted. Without you, I might as well have been dead inside. I would have married you when you were seventeen but that wouldn't have been right for you. I'd have given anything to be with only you. That's all I ever wanted."

Savoring every syllable, hanging onto his every word, Tanya returned his gaze with all the boundless love in her melting heart. Her head, not so gullible. Okay, so maybe she would believe everything up to but definitely not including, "*I would have given anything to be with only you.*" Somehow that one seemed a little hard to swallow, particularly given his penchant for slutty blonds.

Thinking of which, acting on impulse, inspired by her competitive nature and certainly not to be outdone by an ex, Tanya came up on one knee and threw the other across his lap. A single rotation of her hips found him a warm, snug fitting home. "Promise?" she asked him, affecting a sultry whisper through moistened, pouty lips.

What the—? Mick looked up at her with a raised brow and a randy smile full of winking dimples. "Promise," he vowed thickly, thinking now *this* was a surprise. She'd never taken the initiative, not like this anyway. Probably because he usually had her flattened somewhere before she even had a chance to—*uhhh God.*

Pleasure overtaking him like an avalanche, his head rolled back, lolling against the couch. Watching her slowly grind against him, his green eyes turned languorous. Lost in the moment and loving it, he clutched her undulating hips. His thighs hardened, filled with a keen throbbing. When she pulled off her shirt, he nearly lost what little control was letting her still run the show.

Tanya guided his hands to her breasts and joined in with her own as he fondled and watched. His skin felt hot to the touch when she slid gentle fingertips down his forearms, lowered them to his waist and unfastened his pants. Slowly, she began working the zipper down. He became an inferno of lust and need while her mouth treated him to deep, wet, wanton, tongue sucking kisses. The kind she thought might go nicely with a lap dance.

Her hands ran through his hair. Rising up on her knees, she let her breasts fill his hungry gaze. "Mick," she murmured softly, suggestively, bowing to his ear with her warm, moist breath. "Will you do something for me?"

He was sure a dead man would have found a way to say yes. "Anything baby, anything." Cupping the firm mounds to draw them near, he suddenly felt her retreating. She'd lowered one foot to the floor. Overdosed on foreplay, he looked up at her through a hot, hazy gaze, eagerly anticipating what kind of finale she had in mind.

Bending over, Tanya rubbed noses with him. "Tell that little bitch to keep her hands to herself." Snagging her t-shirt off the cushion, she tossed it over her shoulder and sauntered away in her short, sassy boxers. The *coup de grace,* well it went without saying.

"Ahhhhhh— damn it—son of a—you—oh baby, you are going to pay! You are going to pay big!"

Tanya heard him wail like a wounded wolf to the moon. Then began the disjointed phrases filled with emphatic curses muttered in disbelief. More importantly, she heard the sound of his feet hitting the floor.

Had he jumped over the back of the couch? Tanya looked over her shoulder, saw that he had, shrieked and ran up the stairs. Turning on the landing, she glanced down to see him taking the first set two at a time. She shrieked again and ran faster. Racing down the hallway, she dashed into her room feeling his breath on her back. On a burst of laughter, she felt herself scooped off her feet and sail through the air.

True to his word, Mick made her pay. And in the end, believe.

Chapter 9

Everyone wished for good weather for the 4th of July but no one wished harder than shore lovers—those residing, those vacationing and those on their way for the day. When the morning dawned clear and bright, homage was paid appropriately and all seemed right with the world, at least for the next three days. They were lucky enough to have the holiday fall on a Friday with the forecast for the weekend promising more blue skies. The latest traffic update reported heavy congestion Parkway South, North Jerseyan's lifeline to all shore points. Mathis bridge flashed with silver lights as the sun bounced off a steady stream of windshields and car bumpers. The barrier island prepared for the invasion.

Typical of holidays and summer weekends, the bay was also a beehive of activity. Crabbers anchored their smaller boats in the shallows, frequently checking their traps for Jersey blue crabs, large enough to call keepers. Wave runners swirled out in deeper waters, sending up a wall of sparkling spray on their figure eight turns. Larger powerboats, similar to Mick's, as well as luxury yachts, headed out to sea around Barnegat Inlet or were content to navigate the calm bay waves while their passengers enjoyed the vibrant beauty of the waterway and its scenic shoreline.

Pretty sailboats as well eased gracefully across the channel, catching the light morning breeze. They were especially peaceful to watch, Tanya thought, as she and Mick took time for a leisurely breakfast on the lower deck. Knowing they were in for a long busy day, they poured a second cup of coffee and moved from the table to share one lounge chair. Young lovers in love, they snuggled close, her body curled into his. It was their first holiday together and whether their hearts expanded from the spirit of Independence Day, the visual effects of a perfect summer morning, being with the one you love or the harmony of all three, after everything they'd been through, it was a treasured time neither took for granted.

It was also Maggie's due date. They called her before leaving the house but there was no change in her condition. There was, however, a change in Garrett's. He woke up with a miserable cold. Mick had to argue with him to stay home from the boardwalk and keep Maggie company in case she went into labor. Barring the birth of a new little Ames, they all planned to meet at Mick's house early evening for a barbeque and fireworks.

For Tanya, time flew by with a steady flow of customers. The dinner crowd was just starting to arrive when Stephan and Dana relieved her. She scheduled them from 4 p.m. to closing but gave them Saturday off as well as Sunday morning, allowing them time to enjoy at least a fair portion of the holiday.

On her way out of Paradise, Tanya ran into the kitchen trying to stay out of everyone's way while she threw together a salad of mixed greens. Mick assured her he had everything under control but since he wasn't high on anything with leaves, she doubted he would think of it. Passing the market, she stopped to buy a dozen ears of corn she happened to notice advertised in the window. She thought it was a little early for Jersey corn, thanks to that old adage, *Knee high by the 4th of July,* embedded in her brain, but the clerk assured her it was indeed homegrown. As an afterthought, she grabbed a six-pack of Stewart's root beer from the cooler in case she and Maggie felt like a soft drink. Mick would probably drink beer, Garrett would be loaded up with medication. If Maggie had to go to the hospital, one of them had to be the designated driver.

Tanya pulled up in front of Mick's house and parked her Jeep Cherokee behind the Ames' Ford SUV. Collecting her purse and packages, she walked around to the back rather than try to open the front door unassisted. No doubt they were out on the deck.

Maggie was the first person she saw stretched out under an umbrella. The soon to be mom had been on her mind much of the day. Tanya couldn't imagine what it must be like to know you're about to see your child for the first time. Would the baby be okay? Ten fingers, ten toes? Would the delivery be smooth or would complications develop? God, it must be frightening. Lisa had delivered Jennifer five days late. The wait had her bouncing off the walls. Hopefully, Maggie wouldn't be kept in suspense that long.

"Well? How are you doing?" Tanya asked her, walking over to her chair and eyeing her wan features.

Maggie removed her dark glasses and looked up. Her jewel green eyes spoke volumes. "I do feel like a beached whale as they say. Other than that, everything is quite normal. There are no signs yet. I'm sure it's not going to be today."

"How's Garrett taking it?" Tanya knew he was hoping for a 4th of July baby. A descendent of many war heroes, he was very patriotic.

"He made me wear this."

Tanya peered over her armload to see her swimming in a simulated American flag t-shirt. Her lips pressed together. "It looks…comfortable."

Maggie rolled her eyes. "I packed another shirt in my bag just in case I do go to the hospital from here. Although with Garrett's cold, it would probably be best if I don't deliver today."

On that note both men came out of the house. Garrett was wiping his pink tipped nose with a cloth hanky. "Hey, Tanya."

He sounded like a cartoon character. "Wow, you have a doozy."

Garrett shook his head in disgust and dropped into the chair beside his wife. "I haven't had a cold like this since I was a kid. We shouldn't even be here but Mick started bawling when I told him we might not come. I hope you guys don't catch it."

Tanya's brows rippled in sympathy. "No worries," she assured him. The frown deepened with an overlay of amusement as her attention swerved to the man emptying her arms.

"He hallucinates. You'll get used to it."

She smiled. "Okay." Ribbing seemed to be common practice between these two, she was discovering. "Hi."

"Hi yourself." They both leaned in for a kiss. "What is all this stuff? I told you I had everything."

Tanya followed him into the house. "I just bought some corn and soda, and I wasn't sure you would remember a salad since you never eat one."

Setting everything on the kitchen table, he turned and opened the refrigerator door to point out the tri-color salad she frequently ordered at The Cove, which he had his kitchen oversize for company. Closing the door, he took her in his arms for a better greeting than he'd given her outside.

Mick always kissed her hello as if they'd been apart for days instead of hours. When the kiss ended, she slipped away but doubled back for a quick apology peck. "I'm sorry. I should have known you wouldn't forget. Why don't I just husk the corn really quick then I'll run up and change. Do you have a large pot?"

"It's okay, slow down. There's no rush. They're not even hungry yet."

"I don't think I can slow down. This is the pace I've been going at all day. I gave too many people off on the early shift. We were a little short."

"Well, you're off duty now, so just relax. Go on up and change." Mick ripped the brown bag apart to use as a mat for the debris and started on the corn.

Tanya hesitated, standing beside him. She rested her hands on the back of the chair. There was something else she wanted to ask him but it slipped her mind. "Oh, did you light the grill?"

"Yup, the ribs are already on."

"Did you bring a few crab cakes from the boardwalk?"

"Yes."

"How about the shrimp?"

"Ready to serve."

"You know, I don't know if pregnant women are suppose to eat shrimp. I think I remember hearing something."

"It has to do with the mercury. Don't worry, I have plenty of food for just four people...and now corn and enough salad to feed this side of town." He grinned adorably, husking away.

Point taken, Tanya pursed her lips. "I guess I should have brought dessert instead."

"Mixed berry pie and vanilla ice cream. I told you *not* to worry about anything."

"Haagen-Dazs?"

"Of course." He knew it was her favorite.

"You're all right you know that?" she murmured earnestly, beginning to regard him through new eyes. It was taking her awhile to see the man he'd become—beyond their past and beyond his—but she was getting there by way of his sweet, thoughtful ways. He really was a pretty wonderful guy, she mused, swaying towards him for one more kiss. "Careful, you may spoil me."

"I fully intend to spoil you," he returned against her waiting lips, then deepened the kiss since she was sticking around.

"Mmm, I am so fine with that." Tanya managed to mumble, mouth to mouth.

Mick's chuckle disengaged the kiss. "Thought so. Now get your fine self upstairs and change."

Having a clear view through the living room, he watched her cross it in a brisk stride. Her steps quickened even more when she neared the staircase. More often than not, she moved at an accelerated pace. Not that she didn't manage her time properly. In his opinion, she just tried to accomplish too much in one day. Unless they woke up in an amorous mood, she generally rose at seven cranked with energy the minute her feet hit the floor. Weather permitting, she'd be off for a run while the coffee dripped and the washer spun. She rarely took a full day off from Paradise, and at least five days a week she put in ten to twelve hours and had trouble unwinding when she got home. He'd found two ways to break her stride; tackle her and make love to her slow and easy, his personal favorite, or sit on her and give her a back rub, which usually led to the former anyway.

His mention of marriage that night might have slipped off his tongue impromptu, but it had been sitting there since she walked out of the bathroom in his yellow robe. And God knows it had been in his mind long before that. He'd regretted it instantly. Not the offer, just his poor timing. He'd botched a moment that was meant to be special, memorable…blurted it out because they'd had their first fight and he wanted to prove to her how much he loved her.

She'd seen right through it though, which didn't surprise him. Some proposal, she must have thought. Well, he was in total agreement. It fell far short of the plans he'd been contemplating. She deserved all the romantic bells and whistles he supposed most women dreamed of, and he hadn't given her that. She had to be disappointed.

Since he couldn't retract the question, and she'd given him a mind-blowing lap dance instead of an answer, he broached the subject again the next day. She said yes, and they were going shopping for a ring the following week. As far as he was concerned, they were engaged. If he had his way, they'd be getting married tomorrow. The only thing stopping them was her parents. Tanya knew they would be deeply hurt to learn she opted for a quickie wedding without their blessing or attendance.

Never mind missing the wedding, Mick thought it would be nice if she started by telling them they were seeing each other. But whenever he brought it up, she'd brush him off. It was on her list, she'd say, then change the subject. A bad sign. A very bad sign. Obviously, she had grave doubts about their reaction. No doubt, her father's. He couldn't believe her mother would be so opposed, especially after she'd reached out to him personally to check on Tanya's welfare during the storm. That night had been the turning point for them, and he would be forever grateful to Carol Morgan for that phone call. It was almost as if she— No, that idea had crossed his mind before and always circled back to the same conclusion. He was grasping at straws there, reading way too much into it. She'd been in a panic about her daughter's safety. It was unlikely her intent was to play Cupid at the same time. And why would she if she knew her husband wouldn't approve?

But what the frig did the man have against him anyway for chrissakes, especially after all this time? Whatever Tanya's reasons were for not telling them, it was making him antsy. Hell, it was doing more than that. They managed to have worked through everything else and come out of it for the better, but this thing with her parents, whatever the hell it was, he was very much afraid it could turn out to be a problem he might not be able to solve.

Thinking about Tanya's father never did him any good, especially today when he swore off alcohol in case of a hospital run.

Dumping the cornhusks in the garbage with more muscle than necessary, Mick turned around and saw the root beer sitting on the counter. He uncapped one with his fingers and took a long swig. It was a sorry substitute for his favorite brew but just going through the motions made him feel better and helped shake Jim Morgan off his back, at least for the time being. Screw the bastard, he thought and taking the rest of the six-pack with him to put on ice, he went out to join his friends.

~

Maggie picked at her food, complaining of indigestion. Garrett tried but found he could only do one or the other, breathe or eat. He grumbled that he couldn't taste anything anyway. Mick and Tanya were the only ones doing justice to the meal. Their guests looked on with envy, badgering them about their appetites or bantering with each other over who was suffering more. Tanya discovered Mick and Garrett were like a comedy team when they got rolling. Both masters of deadpan, their dry, poker-face humor had the two women in stitches until they feared of wetting their pants.

Over the mixed berry pie, the sky dazzled while the mood turned mellow. The fireworks were going to have a hard time topping the sunset, Tanya thought, as everyone rose and began clearing the table. Both she and Mick urged the other couple to move to the upper deck and relax while Mick dealt with the grill and she took care of the leftovers, but it wasn't until everything was carried in that they finally caved in.

Tanya began filling up containers, planning to send most of the food home with Maggie and Garrett since neither of them was in any condition to be doing much cooking over the next few days. Light of heart and foot, she glided around the kitchen feeling the urge to whistle while she worked. Lacking any skill in that area, she decided to turn on Mick's under the cabinet entertainment system. There was no CD in the drive so she went with the radio and began scanning the stations. As always, South Jersey's 101.5 came through loud and clear. Monday through Friday they broadcasted talk radio and as per their slogan, *On weekends the music comes out to play*! Big Joe Henry, their #1 DJ, was a familiar face in the area, hosting beach events and fun competitions for charities throughout the summer. Tanya had met him a few times. Mick probably had, too. Tanya didn't know if she was in the mood for oldies, which is all the station played, but when she heard the beginning of Don Henley's, *The Boys of Summer,* she left the setting there. She'd always loved that song. Smiling to herself, she wondered if they would play *Mickey.*

The next song wasn't that, but it had a down and dirty party beat that soon took control of her hips.

Standing at the sink, filling up the corn pot with hot sudsy water, Tanya slipped into her own little gyrating world. Suddenly, she felt Mick's hands on her waist and the pressure of his lower body moving in time with her own. Her hair was tied up in a semblance of a ponytail. Her navy tank top scooped low in the back. His mouth was making love bites on the sensitive curve of her neck. Going weak, her head rolled back against his shoulder. His lips moved up and around her throat. His hands traveled, one north, one south.

Tanya gasped and shook him off. "Mick!" They had company who could walk in at any moment!

"They're half asleep up there. Don't stop, dance with me." Swinging her around to face him, he held her close, lowered his hands to her derriere and continued the same bump and grind. Moving in perfect time with the provocative beat, he dipped his knees, ducking his face beneath her jaw, then between her breasts.

The heat of his breath moistened her cleavage. His tongue scorched it, spreading shockwaves to tingle her nipples. Her breath caught and held, leaving her with no voice to object when his fingers slid up inside the back of her white knit shorts. She closed her eyes in surrender and let Mick and the music turn her on. She should have known he had rhythm. Unfortunately, the song ended at a very inopportune moment, breaking the sensual spell.

Mick released her with two smacks, one on her bottom with the palm of his hand, and the other on her forehead with his lips.

Swaying like a drunken sailor, Tanya blinked back into focus and sought the closest chair. She felt a yank on her ponytail.

"Look alive squirt or you're going to miss the fireworks."

"Paybacks are tough," Mick uttered lowly when she finally came up the stairs, and he saw that the fireworks had already started—in her eyes.

Wearing an expression that revealed the restraint it was taking to resist tipping him out of the chair, Tanya watched him spread his legs and pat the cushion in between. His grin reminded her of the crafty wolf in a children's storybook. "I was under the impression you made me pay the other night," she replied in an undertone, and sat down.

"Oh right, I did, didn't I? I must be one up on you then. Guess you'll have to give me another lap dance to even the score."

She'd kicked off her flip-flops and was half reclined when she realized what he said. Stiffening, she sighed, then threw their guests a sidelong look before serving him an admonishing glare. "Are you going to behave yourself?" she whispered.

Mick bent forward to scoop her up and draw her against him. "Now what fun would that be?" he breathed into her ear. Sliding his hands across her belly, one slipped beneath her top.

Tanya caught it before it could wander. It was quite dark but Garrett and Maggie were just a few feet away, stretched out in the same tandem position. Tanya noticed their eyes were closed when she came up from the kitchen, although she could hear them now conversing quietly about something.

"Where are you going?" Garrett asked Maggie, aware of her attempts to work her way off the chair. "We just got comfortable." He supported her back as she squirmed this way and that to the edge.

"Sorry, but I've a dire need to use the bathroom. A little more of a push please, Gar."

Tanya overheard her say the word bathroom. "Go in this way, Maggie. Use the one in our bedroom." She got up to open the sliders and put the deck light on for her. "Watch your step," she said, indicating the sill wasn't exactly even with the deck. "Hold on a minute." Tanya walked across the carpet to the nightstand and turned on the lamp.

Maggie thanked her, and Tanya went back outside and climbed back on the chair with Mick.

A few minutes later the celebration began with the faint whistle of what sounded like a soaring rocket. Simultaneously, they heard Maggie's voice at the door. "Hey guys, my water just broke."

The three on the deck jumped up, bumped into each other and tripped over themselves and the chairs, as if the explosion in the sky had scared the wits out of them.

"Oh, for the love of God, don't kill yourselves or I'll be delivering this baby myself." Maggie laughed, thinking their antics bore a striking resemblance to the Three Stooges.

There was an initial flurry of activity and a lightning round of questions from Larry, Curly and Moe which Maggie answered with far more composure than they were asked. Once they were all up to speed, they went downstairs to the living room. It was there, just as Maggie rounded the couch to sit down that she buckled with her first hard labor pain. She immediately phoned the doctor's answering service. Within ten minutes, Dr. Yang called back and based on her symptoms, she was advised to get to the hospital, pronto.

Per Garrett's request, Mick drove their SUV and as Murphy's Law would have it, they encountered one delay after another—first the drawbridge, then nearly every red light on their way to Community Medical.

Under normal circumstances, Mick was an excellent driver, a little heavy-footed on the highways but always alert and in control. For the most part, he remained unflustered by idiot drivers.

These were not normal circumstances, and the idiots seemed to be out in droves. Tanya could tell his nerves were getting the best of him, particularly when the driver in front of them was going more than ten *under* the speed limit in the fast lane and decided to move over just as Mick decided to do the same. Shortly after, when an ancient VW van pulled out in front of them, stalled and coasted off the road, he didn't exactly mince the words he muttered to describe the driver.

Ears burning, Tanya reached over and gave his shoulder a squeeze. Maggie's contractions were coming faster and intensifying in strength making them all begin to wonder if calling the rescue squad, located just a few blocks from Mick's house, wouldn't have been the wiser course of action.

Doing his best to remain calm in the back seat, Garrett took the opportunity to call his mother who lived in a retirement complex in the nearby town of Brick. Since he was an only child, this would be her first grandchild and he knew she'd been counting the days. Even without the aid of the speaker, Mrs. Ames vocals filled the car when he gave her the news that Maggie was in labor and they were on their way to the hospital. Her excitement and enthusiasm turned out to be the elixir all four needed to settle their nerves a bit.

Since it was the middle of the night in Ireland, Maggie told Garrett to hold off phoning her parents for a few hours. To keep the conversation rolling and help hasten the last few miles, Tanya asked them if they had decided on a name for the baby. If it was a boy, Maggie wanted to name him Garrett Jr. If the baby was born before midnight, Garrett wanted to name him Samuel and call him Sam, in honor of Uncle Sam. If it was a girl, Maggie wanted to name her Emma Grace. Garrett wanted to name her Samantha and call her Sam, in honor of Uncle Sam. Mick and Tanya listened from the front seat, quietly chuckling.

There was a collective sigh of relief when the SUV pulled up in front of the hospital's emergency entrance. The two couples parted with well wishes. Garrett encouraged his friends to return home but they insisted on staying and after locating the appropriate parking area, they made their way to the Labor and Delivery waiting room. Garrett told them he would meet them there after Maggie received a progress report. At that point, they would decide whether to stay or go.

"I doubt they'll allow him in the room with her," Tanya said to Mick. He had taken a seat in the comfortably appointed lounge and picked up a newspaper from the table. She remained standing, gazing at the wall mounted TV where they were showing the Macy's fireworks display over the Hudson River. Thinking about the couple down the hall, her head shook as she finally sat down beside Mick. "I could be wrong," she continued, "but even if he washes up and covers up, he has a classic head cold and he's doing a lot of sneezing. Even some coughing. I just can't imagine Dr. Yang—"

Sure enough, as she was voicing her concern to Mick, Garrett came striding through the door.

"They won't let me stay! I'm no good to her in there anyway. I can't do the breathing exercises with her. I can barely breathe myself. I'll infect everybody!" Garrett dropped disconsolately into one of the chairs across from them. His shoulders lunged forward. Between them, his head hung low. "She's scared. She won't admit it but I can tell. She wanted her mother to come but she's afraid to fly so Maggie didn't ask her. Her sisters all have families over there and couldn't spare the time. I knew I was going to be the only one she could count on and look at me." Leaning back, he pulled a hanky out of his jean's pocket, turned his head and produced a monster sneeze. Beside himself, a string of curses hit the four walls and seemed to reverberate around the room. "Why the hell did I have to get this mofo stinking cold today!" Rising in a fit of angst, Garrett snatched up the magazine that was lying on the seat beside him and gave it a hurl down the row.

"I can do it."

Mick's gaze had been clinging heavily to his friend, and Garrett was so wrenched with worry over Maggie going through it without him that both men suddenly looked at Tanya as if she had sprouted wings and a halo.

"You know Lamaze?" Garrett's expression held sincere doubt, his eyes a ray of hope.

Tanya nodded. "I was Lisa's coach when she had Jennifer," she half addressed Mick. "Lisa's a good friend of mine," she explained to Garrett. "Her husband passed out when their cat gave birth, so she didn't think he'd be able to handle it. I went with her to all the classes. I was her coach, her support partner, whatever you want to call it," she shrugged.

Garrett had to think about it for all of two seconds. "I'll show you where she is."

"Wait." Tanya stopped him. "First you have to ask her if it's okay. We're only getting to know each other. She may not feel comfortable with me in there."

Garrett agreed and told them he'd be right back. He was gone less than five and rounding the corner in a hurry, he spotted Tanya hovering by the waiting room door. "You're on kid. C'mon," he gestured to her. "The nurse will show you where to scrub."

Tanya found Maggie in the midst of a difficult contraction when she entered the room. "I'm here, I'm here," she assured her, rushing up to the side of the bed. Wasting no time, she clutched the hand that reached out for her and got her on track. No sooner did they get into a steady breathing pattern when Dr. Yang came in to perform an internal. Maggie's normally pale complexion began to blend with her bright hair as her pretty features contorted during the painful exam. She gripped Tanya's fingers so tight, Tanya looked aside and did some grimacing and panting for her own relief.

Finished, and none too soon to suit Maggie, the doctor disposed of her gloves then adjusted her patient's gown and blanket. She walked around to the head of the bed to speak with her. Her arm was given a comforting pat as she proclaimed her cervix almost fully dilated and the baby perfectly positioned. A speedy delivery was anticipated with no complications.

As she stepped from the room, Maggie and Tanya both looked up at the clock. It was 10:55 p.m. Their eyes connected, their thoughts in sync. If Garrett couldn't be in the room to witness the birth of his child, the least Maggie wanted to do was give him his 4th of July baby.

Tanya smiled. Eyes dancing, she adopted her new friend's brogue, albeit exaggerated. "Well lassie, it looks like you have some work to do. So what da ya say we cut the blarney and get down to business."

Maggie exhaled a quivering chuckle and giving her a teary eyed nod, the two women joined forces and braced themselves for what was to come. Locked eye to eye, hand to hand, together they brought 8 lb. 8 oz. Samuel Garrett Ames into the world at 11:57 pm on the 4th of July. Hearing his first cry, they collapsed against each other and wept like babies themselves.

Tearing off her cap, Tanya raced down the hall, beating Dr. Yang. "It's a boy! It's a boy!"

Garrett whooped for joy. Catching her on the run, he swung her in a circle. "How's Maggie?" he wanted to know immediately.

"Exhausted but wonderful. They both are. Go see for yourself. She was able to hold him for a few minutes but now the nurse is going to bathe him and let you see him through the window. He's perfect." It was enough after midnight for him to be wondering which side of twelve his son was born on, not that his birth date would be at the top of his list of concerns, but since he didn't ask, Tanya didn't tell. She would save that special news for Maggie.

Before he could get away, Mick offered Garrett his congratulations with a hearty handshake and a back-slapping embrace. Tanya was touched and a little surprised by the mist she saw in both their eyes.

For her, the adrenalin drained in a rush. Putting a hand to her hair, she realized how disheveled she must look. She untied the gown at her neck and waist. This experience with Maggie, as it had been with Lisa, was exhilarating, life affirming. After Lisa's late night delivery, however, she remembered saying goodbye to the happy family and driving home alone. It had been a Saturday, December 14th, around 2:00 a.m. Normally she would have been in Florida by then, but she had delayed her plans that year to be with Lisa. As the miles passed, she became engulfed in self-pity, masochistically allowing all the lonely hearts Christmas songs playing on the radio to drag her into a well of melancholy so deep, she was almost afraid to drive onto the bridge. By the time she crossed over, the sadness had manifested into a longing so profound she nearly gave up the fight then and there and followed the road that bordered the bay and led into the Park.

She hadn't done that, of course. Instead, she somehow found the willpower to steer left, towards Lavallette. At home, she'd climbed into bed fully clothed while great sobs wracked her physically and emotionally spent body. Remembering that as Mick stood before her now with open arms, she pressed both hands against her trembling smile.

He caught her in a crushing embrace, his heart so filled with love and pride, he thought it might burst wide open. Her hairline was soaked with sweat. Dried tears marked her flushed cheeks. A shapeless green gown covered her from neck to foot. When she'd flown through that door, he didn't think he had ever seen her more beautiful.

Chapter 10

"These invitations are adorable," Lisa remarked, studying the grinning turtle on the cover. The lovable looking reptile was occasionally included with the Paradise Pub logo. He was mainly used for promotional apparel and advertising material. Sitting on a little oasis of land, he lounged against the trunk of a palm tree. His knobby knees were casually crossed. There was a Margarita glass propped in his hand. For this purpose, the graphic designer added a party hat on his cute bullet shaped head.

"Come celebrate a birthday in Paradise," Lisa read aloud. "Oh, that name just keeps on giving, doesn't it?" Making herself comfortable in the guest chair in Tanya's office, she raised the flap of the invite. "Paradise Pub invites you to attend a birthday celebration in honor of Jim Morgan, Sunday, August 12th, 6 p.m., R.S.V.P., dit dit da da. How old is he going to be Tan?"

"Fifty-nine."

"Get out. I swear he doesn't look a day over forty-nine, or something like that. Of course I haven't seen him since…did I see him last year?" Lisa's chin angled up as she thought back. "Maybe it was the year before. Anyway, based on the last time I saw him, he was aging well. Very well. I find your dad kinda hunky, actually."

Aghast, Tanya threw her a look that went from surprised to sour. "You are just not allowed to tell me that."

"Sorry. I've always thought so."

Tanya looked down into the ridiculously long-lashed aquamarine eyes of the one-year-old baby girl sitting contentedly on her lap. Her own eyes swirled, suggesting her mama had gone loco.

Jennifer thought her Godmother was making very funny faces and trying to copy them, they both got into a silly spell.

"What are you two up to over there?"

"Nothing," Tanya answered in a prim tone, wiping her features free of anything but innocence. Again, Jennifer tried to copy her Godmother's expression and they both giggled again. "Oh my gosh Lisa, she is so funny. She may look more like John, but she definitely has your personality."

"I know, that's what everyone says. I hope her hair stays that color but it probably won't. So go ahead, you were talking about your parents," she reminded her, not that she was desperate for adult conversation or anything.

"Mmm, well Florida does seem to agree with them. I think they're both happy they made a permanent move. They got tired of the winters up here, you know? You like my earrings, don't you sweetie?"

Jennifer stared at the swaying blue stones that sparkled like her Godmother's eyes.

"Careful, she'll rip them right off your ears," her mother sang the warning like a sweet lullaby.

"Don't worry, I'm ready for her," Tanya sang back in the same melody. "Yes I am," she cooed, rubbing noses with the tot. She had a light hold of Jennifer's wrists, prepared to thwart any sudden yanks.

"So, when are they coming?"

"The third. A week from Friday." Tanya sighed inwardly, feeling guilty for dreading their arrival. Opening the lap drawer of her desk, she felt around for the plastic spoons she kept on hand. Pulling two of them out, she waved them in front of Jennifer and managed to draw her attention away from her earrings.

"I guess that's going to throw a damper on your little love nest," her friend teased.

"You can say that again." This time Tanya's sigh was audible, and long and worthy of her dilemma. "I'm really worried to be perfectly honest. I have this horrible feeling my father is going to have the same reaction to Mick that he had eight years ago." She'd given Lisa a watered down version of the story one night, omitting certain details that were just too personal to share. "How's your ESP? Any predictions?"

"Mm mm," her head shook. "I'm not getting anything. I'd need some kind of personal connection. Is that the reason you're planning this little birthday bash? Doing a little sucking up?"

Tanya chuckled dryly. "I don't know. Probably. I admit it was my idea, after I spoke with my mother and found out he's already grumbling about nearing sixty. We doubt he'll be in the mood for a party next year so we thought, why not have one this year. Fifty-nine sounds like a much better birthday to celebrate. And by throwing him a party, he gets to see all his old friends at one time while he's here."

Jennifer pretended to feed her with the spoon and Tanya pretended to like it. "Hopefully, we'll all be on speaking terms by then," she added drolly. "The more I think about it, the more I wish Mick and I had eloped as he suggested. I could have moved the rest of my things into his house and let my parents have their house to themselves. It would have all been settled then, whether they liked it or not. Now we'll have to live apart for almost a month."

"They're staying that long?" By her tone and expression, Lisa was even more sympathetic to her plight.

"Close to it, and I know my father will have a coronary if I even try to spend one night at Mick's place."

"Tell them, Tanya. Now, before they get here. If it were me, I'd rather do it over the phone instead of in person. It will eliminate the face-to-face shock factor. Plus, it will give them time to adjust."

"I've tried Lisa, but the words just won't come out. I think I'm afraid they're going to come running up here and ruin everything."

"Well, they're coming anyway, and soon, so you're just delaying the inevitable. Besides, you might be getting all worked up for nothing."

"I know, I know. I guess I'm not so much worried about my mom. I actually think she's always had a soft spot for Mick, which I know sounds strange when she went along with my father that night. But my father . . . you know I love him dearly but let's face it, the man is overbearing and intimidating and for some stupid reason that makes me want to please him all the more. Sometimes I wonder if that isn't why I'm driven to work so hard, just so he'll always think highly of me. When we interact professionally, there's rarely a problem. Personal issues were and still are a whole different story. *It's my way or the highway.* That's his favorite expression.

"I don't know," resting her head against the back of the chair, Tanya gazed up at the shaft of light projecting through the high window. "Now that I'm with Mick, it will seem strange having them home this time. I feel like a different person, kind of all grown up I guess. I know my father is going to get bossy, and I'm just not going to stand for it. I'm too old for this. Last winter he kept trying to fix me up with a few of the men he'd become acquainted with at the golf course. I eventually gave in and dated one of them. Dan Wakefield. We went out a few times. Nothing clicked, of course. My father couldn't understand why. He's good looking, financially secure and a pillar of the community, to quote his exact words. Mix all of that in with the fact that the man is a golf enthusiast and even played in a few charity tournaments with some pros and my Dad's ready to book the church. "*What more could you possibly want?*" he asked me."

"Well, there was your perfect opportunity. You should have told him Mick Leighton."

Tanya grinned derisively. "Easy for you to say." Hearing two taps on her partially open door, she glanced up to see the subject of their discussion. She turned a little warm, wondering if he had heard them. "Hi, c'mon in. Is it one o'clock already?"

Lisa glanced over her shoulder to see who she was talking to. Turning back she crossed her eyes and mouthed WOW!

Dressed in a black shirt and dark trousers, Mick was looking incredibly sexy today. He had a meeting with someone somewhere and left the house a little earlier than usual this morning. Yup, WOW pretty much covered it, Tanya thought, pressing her lips together to keep from laughing at her friend's antics.

"You remember Lisa, don't you Mick? And this is Jennifer." Tanya stood up and settled the baby on her hip so he could see her sweet, angelic face.

Coming to stand at the corner of the desk, Mick offered Lisa a friendly greeting and caught the bundle of pink that flew at him with outstretched arms.

Jenny's headlong dive startled Mick and Tanya, but not her mother. Lisa rose, tossing her hands. "I told you, Tan, she's crazy about men. It really worries me. Come here you little flirt. Daddy's waiting." She took Jenny from Mick wondering if she should begin her mother-daughter talks now at this age then with any luck all the warnings will be drilled into her head by the time she began dating. Wasn't it only yesterday she was teaching her the barnyard animals?

Perhaps the two subjects should be combined, Lisa began to think, noticing the way Mick's eyes zoomed in on the front of Tanya's shirt. The top two buttons were open when they arrived. Jenny's busy little fingers must have undone the third while they were talking. When Tanya stood up, the material parted, offering a sneak-peek at her boobs and the pale lace demi bra struggling to contain them. Lisa began gathering their belongings, preparing to leave. "Oh, the invitations," she remembered.

"Don't worry about them," Tanya replied. "I'll put them in the mail along with the others. Remember to keep the date open though." Ironically, she'd been addressing the Malone's envelope when Lisa unexpectedly appeared. Spooky.

Still, her friend held out her hand. "Don't be silly. Why waste two stamps? I'll be seeing my parents tonight anyway." With her back to Mick, she started to signal Tanya about her shirt, then on second thought decided to let Mick have his fun before big daddy arrived to cool him down. Whew, sandwiched between the two, she could almost feel the heat wave shimmering between them, like some kind of force field.

It reminded her of that day on the boardwalk when she and Tanya were all of sixteen, and they ran into Mick just home from the service. There had been something in the air then too. Something so palpable, if Jim Morgan happened to have his eagle eye on them, no wonder he blew a gasket at the thought of them dating.

Feeling a little flushed herself, Lisa gave her own top a quick adjustment before hooking her bag over her shoulder. Maybe she would dig out some sexy lingerie after Jenny went to bed tonight, see if she could get John to look at her like that again. Since parenthood...well, the before and after was like night and day.

"Okay, I know it's here. I already addressed it, but what did I do...?" Tanya was still shuffling, trying to locate Lisa's parents' invitation. "Oh, here it is." She handed them both over. "Tell them I said hello." She walked mama and baby to the doorway. "Bye sweetheart." Jenny had perfected her bye-bye wave and proudly flapped her hand. "I'll call you," she told Lisa. Tanya closed the door, turned around and collided with Mick.

Looking down her blouse, he reached behind her and turned the lock. He took her in his arms. "Have you been walking around like that all morning?"

She followed the direction of his gaze and gasped. "No, I don't think—oh, Jenny must have done that," she realized and went to fix it.

Mick intercepted her hands and guided them around his waist. He reached inside her shirt and bra to palm one breast. He was very gentle. "Still tender?"

She gave a nod.

"They feel different when your period's due. Heavier but more delicate."

Another nod.

"Your skin feels even smoother. Did you get it yet?"

She was losing concentration. "What? Get what?"

"Your period."

"Oh," her color bloomed. "No, not for a few days probably. Why do you keep asking me that?"

"Just curious." He made slow delicious love to her mouth.

When he stopped, she was reeling.

"Ready for lunch?" he asked deeply.

"No. I'm not ready for lunch. I can't even see straight when you do that. You know we have an agreement about the office."

"Sorry." His grin was anything but. Removing his hand, he buttoned her blouse all the way to the top. "There, now you're ready to go public."

She looked down. "Now I'm ready for a convent you mean." She released the top two buttons again. "Wasn't I suppose to meet you at The Cove for lunch today?" Tanya suddenly remembered and looked up to find his features turning a tad grim.

Mick merely shrugged. "I thought we would walk up to the boardwalk, get some seafood instead." He strolled over to her desk and picked up one of the invitations. Having seen them already, and frankly looking forward to the event as much as he might passing another kidney stone someday, he tossed it back down. “Is that all right with you?” He glanced at her as she came around behind him.

“I guess. Although, I kind of had my heart set on that new strawberry walnut salad.”

“I can always bring it home for dinner tonight.”

“I’m not sure I’ll make it home for dinner. Stephan and Dana are here until closing, but I’ll probably work late and catch up on some paperwork. These invitations are taking longer than I expected, especially trying to track down everyone’s address. I wish I’d been able to send an e-vite but without email addresses that wasn’t possible. Anyway, I’d like to finish them today. We could stay here but my mouth is kind of watering for that salad,” she smiled at him with sweet persuasion. “Let’s just go over to The Cove, okay?” Tanya locked up her desk and pocketed her keys as she talked.

Studying the carpet on his way, Mick followed her to the door. “Wait up,” he said before she could open it. When Tanya turned, he braced a hand above her head. “I don’t think you’d enjoy having lunch there today.”

“Why?” She frowned.

Mick tucked in his chin and stared at his shoes. Things had been going so well, he hated to start all of this up again. “Nicole is working today. She’s filling in for someone.”

“Nicole?” Tanya couldn’t imagine who he was talking about. She didn’t know anyone by the name of— *Oh, her.* The employee he’d given another chance who thanked him by making an ass of herself at the club a few weeks ago. The waitress he’d…been with. She hadn’t wanted to know her name anymore than Tara’s, the girl she found in his bed.

Mick raised his head, looked at her and shrugged. “We can still go there. I just wasn’t sure how you would feel.”

“It was fairly dark in there. I didn’t get a very good look at her face. You have other bleach blonds working at The Cove so I may not have recognized her. Is she very pretty?” Foolish question, Tanya thought. He wouldn’t have dated her otherwise.

His gaze roamed her features. “Compared to you, there is no comparison.”

"Looks aren't everything. There must have been something special about her since you slept with her a few times. By the way, I'd be interested to learn your definition of few." Tanya gave him a demeaning once over and pushed away from the door. She didn't have the vaguest idea why she was goading him and tormenting herself in the process.

Mick ground his back teeth together. "In this particular case, six or seven." Hell, if she wanted to know, he'd tell her.

"Six or seven?" Tanya threw back airily, winded by his answer and trying not to show it. "Well, I'd consider that many, not few. She must have been pretty good."

"She was there and I got off. That's all I cared about. Any more questions?"

Her throat closed and her eyes stung but damned if she'd let him see. "I've lost my appetite. If you don't mind, I'd like to get back to work."

Before she could round the desk to her chair, Mick spun her back. "Would you like a list of every woman I've had sex with and how many times we did it, Tanya? Would that make you happy?"

"No, Mick. Do you know what would make me happy? Being in your position. I wish I'd gone to bed with every guy that tried to get me there just for the satisfaction of throwing it in your face. Now that... would make me happy."

His eyes blazed. "If you'd done that, I wouldn't be standing here."

Which meant what? That if she'd slept around, *he* wouldn't want *her*? Tanya nearly choked on her laugh. "My God, Mick, how is that any different? I'll tell you what, why don't you make up that list. Maybe that will help me make up my mind about you once and for all."

That one hit home and regretting having handed her the ammunition on a silver platter, he raked a hand through his hair. He took a breath and a few paces. Turning back, he implored her to see reason. "C'mon, Tanya, we've already been over all of this. Please, can we just put it behind us for good?"

"I would love to put it behind us Mick but it seems every time I begin to, it gets shoved down my throat again."

"I'm not shoving it down your throat. I was trying to be sensitive to your feelings just now."

"If you wanted to be sensitive to my feelings, you would have let her go. According to everything you told me, you certainly had good cause. You may be sympathetic to her problems, but don't expect me to be. How do you think I feel knowing you see her almost every day? When you look at her, can you honestly tell me you don't have flashbacks of what it was like being with her?"

"I don't! I'm always too busy thinking about you!"

"That's a little hard to believe. You told me she offered to sleep with you again. You told me she expects you to give her preferential treatment. And I'm sure there's a hell of a lot you haven't told me—like why she fights with the other waitresses? Could it be because they are all vying for your attention? I'm sure she's spread the word that you two have slept together. How do you think that went over with the rest of the staff? Sounds like she keeps you on your toes over there, Mick. I can't imagine when you have time to think about me. She was all over you that night knowing I was right there watching. I think you enjoyed it."

He turned around and walked out.

Tanya grabbed the first solid object she could lay her hand on and flung it at the door. The rush of satisfaction was hardly worthwhile, lasting mere seconds before it turned to regret. She slumped forward, flattening her hands on the desk, wishing she could have that last ten minutes to do over. She raised her head. Through a sheen of riled emotions, she stared at the mark the stapler made in the new paint. Her features crumpled. "Idiot!"

She wasn't upset with Mick or the gash in the stupid door. She was angry with herself for behaving like a jealous shrew. He was right. They had been over this, again and again. Enough! Was she still so insecure, so suspicious that she was going to blow up and bring up the past every time she felt threatened by another woman? And why should she feel threatened? There wasn't a single doubt in her mind that he loved her and only her. Since they'd been together, he'd shown her in a hundred different ways. If she didn't start believing in him, believing in that love, she'd wind up driving him away, possibly back into Nicole's waiting arms. The thought had her rushing for the door.

Tanya walked hurriedly through the pub. Stephan was taking inventory behind the bar. Dana was writing the dinner specials on the chalkboard. "I'll be back shortly," she told them dividing a glance between the two.

Both assistant managers turned to face each other after the door closed behind their boss. One common thought passed between them—*uh oh, trouble in Paradise.*

"Hi Jack. Did Mick come back here? Is he in his office?" Hoping for a yes to both questions, there was only a slight hitch in her stride as she crossed paths with him in the vestibule.

"He just went in," he told her, pausing to take in the full effect of her ensemble. In relaxed white linen with accessories of deep ocean blue, she was a vision of summer loveliness, as always. "Great outfit," he called to her, considering himself an authority.

Tanya didn't quite catch the compliment but threw back a smile nonetheless. Jack was always very friendly and pleasant and she enjoyed their occasional conversations but today her mind was elsewhere, set on one thing and one thing only—erasing her argument with Mick before anything remained to fester. A little anxious, she smoothed her palms over her hips and tapped on his door. She heard his call to enter. Tanya noticed a flicker of surprise in his eyes when he saw her. After all the horrible things she said to him, she was probably the last person he expected.

She closed the door behind her. In her haste to catch him before he disappeared somewhere, she hadn't exactly come prepared. From a woman's perspective at least, it was a delicate matter to discuss, and she found herself searching for the right words to explain her behavior, other than jealous shrew that is. Her hands slipped into her pockets as she paced back and forth in front of his desk. Sneaking glances at him, she struggled how to begin.

As he waited, he watched her and remained unnervingly silent. From his behavior, Tanya gleaned he had no intention of making this easy for her. She strolled some more, avoiding eye contact, which was much less disconcerting. Evidently, she wasn't keeping him from anything. His desk was quite clear and neat as a pin. His black leather chair had been pushed to an angle, tilted back to accommodate the supine curve of his spine. His ankle was hiked up to rest upon his knee. With his forearm flat on the desk, his thumb and index finger turned a pencil end over end. He once told her she took his breath away. When he stared at her, as he was doing now, with that veiled, brooding intensity, she knew exactly what he meant.

Deciding on some plain speaking, straight from the heart, Tanya stopped her aimless wandering to stand directly before him. "I'm sorry, Mick. I didn't mean to pick a fight with you or imply that I don't trust you. It was just a spontaneous, thoughtless reaction, compounded by a little PMS, I suppose." She stared down at her fingernails as they flicked the edges of some papers stacked near the edge of his desk. "When I think of the way you make love to me, I…I can't bear to imagine…it's hard for me…I don't like to think…well, normally I don't think about it unless I'm reminded, like before when you mentioned…"

In an effort to get her point across, the feelings she tried to convey came out jerky and jumbled, bumping together without really reaching fruition. Not to be forestalled, however, once she got started, she carried on, even as he gave the pencil a toss, shoved back his chair and walked around the desk. Taking her by the hand, he led her out of his office. She didn't know where they were going, just that his grip was tight, his jaw determined and every muscle in his body seemed engaged.

The hallway, with offices on one side and restrooms on the other, was brief. When it opened into the waiting area, he let go of her hand and moved his own to the small of her back. Tanya was forced to lengthen her stride to keep up with him as they made their way to the exit. Someone called his name just as they stepped outside. "*Later,*" she heard him throw back before the door eased shut behind them.

Taking her hand again, he proceeded to the parking lot. There were two ways to access the lot on foot; by walking out to the street and up the sidewalk, or by taking the wide tree-lined path with its pretty weathered benches and potted coleus and sweet potato vines nestled in beds of river stone. Mick chose the latter, the shorter of the two routes that wound around the side of The Cove. Tanya saw the rear end of his Jaguar come into view. She heard the locks release. He opened her door, guiding her inside with a firm hand on her spine then on her shoulder as she folded into the passenger seat.

The ride to his house was a blur of familiar scenery, made in record time. Tanya flinched when he pulled into the driveway and cleared the garage door by a whisper as it was opening. It closed behind them, shutting out the world.

He released their seatbelts, reached for her and she was taken on another ride—a rocket ride of sensations. Shirt unbuttoned, bra unhooked, *bada bing bada boom*. How he accomplished so much so fast she didn't know or care because his hands were molding her flesh as if he owned it and could do with it as he pleased. His tongue was bold, his lips masterful, causing spears of white lightning to shoot where he'd cupped his palm. He let her come up for air and while she dragged in a lungful, he plunged a hand into her hair to expose the deep, delicate curve of her neck. As if an addiction drove him, his mouth descended and drew blood to the surface. At the same time, the pad of his thumb scraped an aching nipple. Her reaction was a spike of arousal that had her crying out.

"Get out."

She heard the soft slam of his door and stared dazedly at the tinted glass and superior leather as if it might answer back. Her own door opened abruptly, and she swerved her head, heart pounding. She swallowed. He was angry. To an extent she'd never seen before. For a moment just now, it was as if he'd turned into some wild beast on steroids. By the look on his face, she was about to be ravished. Dear God in heaven, she couldn't move her legs fast enough. "I'm coming, I…"

"Not yet baby but be prepared." Taking hold of her arm, he helped her out, bent his knees and settled her over his shoulder. Upstairs in their room, he lowered her feet to the floor. Again his hands were quick and adept, making white linen slide from her limbs like water. He reached around her to the spread and threw back three layers as one to the end of the bed. Sweeping her up, he laid her down on ivory sheets with a satin sheen.

As he disrobed, his eyes feasted on her wonton disarray. Her dark glossy waves fanned across the pillow. Her lips were enflamed from his rough kisses in the car making them look like they were begging for more. Her bra was in a state of dishabille, the lacy cups lying beside her lush breasts as if some madman tore the link apart in his desperation to fondle them. The mate to her bra was a sweet triangle created for a woman to tease her man. He swore God gave her those damn eyes for him to drown in.

Lowering himself on top of her, he held her head steady between his hands and stared into those eyes until he was certain she could see what he needed her to see. "My heart, my hands, my body, have always belonged to you, Tanya. I don't know why that is, but I stopped fighting it a long time ago. Loving you makes all the difference in everything we do together, whether it's how we make love, share a meal, take a walk, or just sit and talk. Knowing you love me in return is the only thing that makes my life worth living and without you beside me or to come home to…well, then life to me is just a series of meaningless days looking for ways to get you off my mind until it's all over. That's where I was before you came back to me. Do you believe me?"

Tanya tried to nod while he kissed the last of her doubts away.

"Good, now pay attention. I'm giving you a quiz later."

One hour and forty-two minutes later satiated and half dozing for the second time, they lay facing each other with limbs still entwined. His hands were buried beneath her hair. Hers rested against his warm chest. He heard her sniff and slid a hand out to brush his thumb across her cheek. It came away wet.

"Don't cry." Mick gathered her against him and kissed the crown of her head.

"I'm not."

His lips curved. The phone rang, disrupting a tender moment, making him curse under his breath and swear once again that he was going to cancel his landline. He reached backward to grab the receiver from the nightstand. He recognized the number. "Yeah."

"Where the hell are you? You said three o'clock."

Mick looked back at the clock radio. It was well after. "Sorry about that. Something came up." He rolled onto his back bringing Tanya with him. When he felt her head depress his bicep, he knew without looking she was peering up at him. Tucking in his chin, a crinkle of amusement accompanied his return gaze. The phrase he used had been a slip of the tongue but from the look on her face, he doubted she would believe him. Mick gave her a squeeze and tuned back into Garrett.

"All right, I guess we'll take care of it tomorrow then. What are you doing tonight? Maggie wants to know if you and Tanya want to come over and see Sam."

"Hold on." Mick rested the receiver against his shoulder. "Garrett wants to know…"

Tanya sprung upright. Leaning over him, she added her hand to cover the phone. "Mick," her hushed tone reprimanded him. "I heard what he said but now he's going to know I'm here with you and figure out what we've been doing."

"So."

She closed her eyes, sighing. Men. Where were their marbles sometimes? Lying back against his arm, her eyes opened and slid down the well-equipped one beside her. Well, there was her answer she supposed. The thought had her stifling a laugh. It was decidedly unfair and untrue of her Mick, and wasn't even that funny, but she was in her happy place and life was just so good at the moment. "Tell him yes," she said, "and ask him what time."

Sensing she was amused by something, and at his expense, Mick's gaze swerved towards her again and narrowed. "What time?" he asked Garrett.

"Whenever, but if you want to see him awake, be there by eight."

"Right, see you later." Mick hung up and relayed the information to Tanya.

Coming up on one elbow, she took a look at the clock. "I can't believe it's going on four. I better take a shower." Rather than work her way all the way over to the other side of the king-size mattress, she rolled over him and nearly got away.

"Wait." Mick caught her at the waist and was completely unprepared for the impact when she looked back to see what he wanted.

He didn't know what he wanted, aside from her back in his bed. They had their late nights and their early mornings but lazing away an entire afternoon was a luxury for them he wouldn't mind indulging in more often. He would have just come out and told her that if he'd been able to suppress all the emotion welling up inside of him.

He searched her face and wasn't sure but something about the way she tilted her head maybe or the glow of her complexion. Something about the way she looked at him took him back into the past. Having known her through all the stages of her life, it just became another one of those poignant moments to see his squirt wearing the sultry look of a woman who'd been thoroughly debauched at midday and clearly enjoyed every minute of it. Knowing he was responsible did amazing things for his ego. All the loving they'd done had painted her face with vibrant colors. Her eyes never looked so blue, or her mouth so pink and lush. Over the past weeks, he'd watched her innate but still somewhat guileless sensuality begin to blossom into something he had trouble tearing his eyes from. He started to become aroused again, not believing it was possible. Rising up on his forearm, he grasped the back of her head.

"God, I love you." He had to kiss those lips one more time before she left the bed.

Tanya cupped his jaw, feeling the slight scrape of his beard coming in again. "I love you, too." When he started to deepen the kiss, she withdrew with a husky chuckle. "Oh no, I know what you're up to." She twisted away from his hand when it shot out to grab her.

Mick climbed out of bed and followed her into the bathroom. "We'll take a shower together. It'll speed things up."

"No, Mick. It takes longer to shower with you than without you."

"I promise. I'll just wash your back…or something."

"That's what you always say."

"This time I mean it. Honest."

Opening the door to the linen closet, she nearly banged him in the head. She took out a towel and closed it.

He dashed around her.

"Go a-way."

"I'll just turn the water on for you." He did so and stepping quickly over the rim of the tub pulled her in after him.

It was nearly five by the time he drove her back to Paradise. On the return trip she began to question her sanity. "This is crazy. I should not even walk in there looking like this."

"Looking like what? You look perfect."

"I have on different clothes. My braid is damp and I've been gone for more than three hours. Everyone is going to know how I spent the afternoon. I really didn't want to get my hair wet. I should just cut it all off. It would be so much easier."

Reflex had her grabbing the dash, even though the seatbelt tightened with a jolt and kept her from flying forward. Mick was already slowing down on the approach to a stop sign when he slammed on the brakes a few yards short, for no apparent reason. Tanya glanced into the rearview mirror on her side. Thank heaven nobody was behind them or they probably would have been hit.

With a slow meaningful turn of her head, she glared at Mick as if he had indeed *lost* his marbles. He was looking back at her with an almost horrified expression Tanya would think about later and find hilarious.

"You'd better be playing me," he warned.

"Mick, I've had a braid since I was like ten, probably even younger. Aren't you getting sick of it?"

"No. I love your hair. It's beautiful. You wear it all different ways. Promise me you are not going to cut it."

Since he looked about to cry, she promised.

"I tried not to get it wet but you're a slippery devil," he said, coasting to the corner.

"I was trying to get away from you."

"Not for long." He pulled out.

"That's beside the point."

"Well, I don't remember hearing all these complaints at the time. I guess you'll have to tell me what it means when you start moaning and groaning and scraping my skin off. I assumed that meant..."

Tanya held up a hand. "Please, spare me your graphic details or you'll probably be turning the car around."

He chuckled and upon her request, took her down the alley behind Paradise, which would enable her to go in through the kitchen door. "The presents for Sam are at your house. I'll meet you there when, seven? Seven-thirty?"

"Seven should be fine," she responded, and deciding to go blissfully down with the ship in the event of an upcoming gossip fest, she leaned towards him with the memory of their lovemaking still warm in her eyes. Her hand curled around the strong column of his neck. "Thank you for a beautiful afternoon, Mick."

"You're welcome." His eyes were soft and loving in return, a peace and contentment filling him like never before. It was felt in the kiss they were sharing, for both of them. The depth of their love surprising even them sometimes.

Even so, Mick had to hear her say the words. "Hey," before she could climb out of the car, he tucked two fingers beneath her chin. They guided her face around until he was satisfied with the view. The pad of his thumb caressed her bottom lip. "We okay, or are you still making up your mind about me?"

She smiled. "Oh, I think you've finally managed to convince me."

In parting, his index finger tapped the tip of her nose.

Tanya walked around the hood of the Jag and looking into the windshield, she blew him a kiss.

Tanya Morgan blew him a kiss. After spending the last few hours crawling up one side of her naked body and down the other, why such a simple gesture of affection rendered him brainless, he didn't know, but it was a full minute before he remembered where he was going and how the hell to shift into reverse.

Chapter 11

"Here, let me hold him while you open the gifts." Sam was fresh from his feeding and his bath, Maggie told her when they arrived, and Tanya's fingers itched to cuddle him. He looked so precious in his soft Pooh Bear sleeper.

Maggie handed him over. "Take this in case he spits up on you," she said, draping a cloth diaper over Tanya's shoulder.

Cradling the infant in her arms, Tanya walked over to the couch and sat down. Maternal instincts had her bowing her head and filling her senses with the sweet scent of new baby. Her gaze gobbled him up as she brushed his silky patch of dark hair with her index finger. She spiked it up like a rock star then smoothed it back down. Mindful of her nails, she ran a knuckle down his velvety cheek. Sam's glassy eyes stared up at her as if trying to bring her into focus. Since the trauma of birth, his features had filled out a bit and had begun to resemble a miniature of his father.

"I can't get over how much he looks like you, Garrett," Tanya remarked. "Doesn't he Mick?"

Suddenly, Sam's tiny, bow shaped mouth puckered in search of something to suckle. With nothing forthcoming, he appeared to fantasize. Wearing a whimsical smile, his gossamer eyelids fluttered. A dreamy expression crossed his peaches and cream complexion. Watching him, they all chuckled.

Mick was seated on the other couch cushion beside Tanya. He agreed with her observation, adding his own point of view. "Actually he does look like you, Garrett, especially after you've had one too many."

Maggie clapped her hands together, laughing. "That's exactly what I told him last night."

They all smiled into the new daddy's face and received a sober if not sullen look in return.

"He didn't appreciate it when I said it either," Maggie murmured aside and knelt down on the carpet. Feeling the weight of her husband's gaze she gave him a loving smile and opened the envelope attached to the gift box. It was from Tanya. She ran a hand over the wrapping adorned with little toy soldiers. "This paper is adorable, Tanya. I'm going to cut a square to put in Sam's scrapbook. Wherever did you find it?"

"Oh, they had it at Babies R Us," Tanya answered.

How cool and collected she sounded now, Mick thought. Reflecting on that evening in the store, it was an entirely different woman oohing and ahhing over every cute and cuddly thing. He didn't know much about babies and was frankly amazed by the warehouse full of supplies they seemed to require. He knew one day it would be his turn to learn about it all, but at the time he was just happy to be tagging along watching Tanya's reaction to everything.

His arm rested along the cushion behind her, only inches from the back of her neck. Mick gave it an affectionate brush with his finger in fond remembrance of that night, especially after they got home. The topic of babies had continued up in her bedroom with regard to their own future. Two, they decided but not for a few years. Still, there was something different about her body that night, an incredible softness and a heightened sensitivity to his touch. The way she gave herself to him, it was as if the subject served as an aphrodisiac. She couldn't get enough of him. He'd counted four orgasms. God, what a night.

Tanya turned her head in response to his caress, beaming him a smile that pierced his heart sure as Cupid's arrow. The longer they were together, the more he was coming to realize that sharing moments like this was almost as good as…

"For crying out loud, didn't you two get enough of each other this afternoon?"

Garrett's sudden outburst drew three different reactions. Mick unabashedly grinned. Tanya mashed her lips together and served an *I told you so* look to the blabbermouth sitting next to her. His wife dropped her shoulders and sighed.

In the process of lifting the lid from the box, Maggie paused. "Garrett be nice. You'll have to excuse my grumpy husband," she addressed the couple on the couch. "He told me about this afternoon and the only reason he's pouting about it is because he's still out to pasture so to speak. The doctor hasn't released me yet to have relations and he's just sulking because he's jealous and feeling deprived."

Mick hiked up his ankle and rested it on his opposite knee. His foot jiggled like a puppy that wags his tail uncontrollably when he can barely contain his happiness. He eyed his friend with a mixture of genuine sympathy and suppressed gloating. "Sorry man, I wasn't aware."

Garrett gave him a long dour face. "Right, you look real sorry."

"Oh, look at all this. How adorable!"

Grateful for the diversion, Tanya turned her attention to Maggie who had proceeded with opening the gifts. She watched her hold up and examine each and every article of clothing she'd arranged in the deep rectangular box. Tanya had so much trouble making up her mind, she'd bought a little bit of everything from daywear to sleepwear to special outing outfits. Some were decorated with baby animals, others sported choo choo trains and athletic themes. She'd purchased sizes from newborn to twelve months thinking if he was going to take after his father, he'd probably be growing like a weed.

Maggie rose up on her knees and scooted over to the couch for a hug. "Thank you, Tanya! You really shouldn't have gotten so much."

"You're welcome. Baby clothes are so adorable, I could have bought out the entire store," she returned truthfully.

"Thanks kid," Garrett rose and walking by her, he passed a gentle hand over his son's head. "Sam's going to be the best dressed baby in town."

"Oh Mick, you already gave us the rocking chair!" Maggie shook her head at the generous check enclosed in the second card. She handed it up to Garrett as he walked around her. "Will you do something with this man, please."

Garrett looked down at the check amount. "Mick, c'mon."

"The rocking chair was really from my mother. She just happened to add my name to the card." That wasn't exactly the truth but hopefully it made them feel better. Thanks mostly to his grandfather, he had it and was sure they could use it. Besides, it wasn't that much.

Maggie rose and walked over to him. "You are much too kind," she said, leaning down with a thank you kiss. "Now, I hope you guys haven't eaten. Garrett's mum has been bringing casseroles over nearly every day and we have lasagna warming in the oven."

"Oh, that sounds wonderful Maggie. Here Mick, you hold Sam while I help." Tanya stood and turned to lower the baby into his arms. She grinned as he tightened his frame and pressed into the corner of the couch as if she was about to hand him a cobra, although he probably would have been less apprehensive. "Loosen up," she told him. "Relax your elbow against the bolster. Just remember to always support his head. That's the most important thing. He feels light as a feather compared to Jennifer, doesn't he?"

"If you say so," he muttered.

Although Mick was clearly out of his comfort zone, Tanya thought he looked absolutely adorable the way he was holding Sam so gingerly in the crook of his muscled arm. Her heart took wings at the sight as she trailed after Maggie into the kitchen.

Garrett went to follow the girls.

"Hey, where are you going? I've never held a baby in my life and you're going to leave me alone with him?" Mick kept his tone moderately low when he called out to his friend. He didn't want to scare the poor kid who was looking up at him so trustingly.

Garrett turned back around. "Do you want a beer or not?"

"Well, I can't very well drink a beer with your son in my arms. Get one for yourself and get back in here. I'll have one with dinner."

"Poor Mick, I think he's afraid Sam is going to shatter if he even breathes too deep," Tanya said to Maggie after Garrett got his beer and went back into the living room. The table was preset for four but taking a quick inventory, Tanya saw a few things she could add. She pulled out four napkins from the holder, folded them in half and placed one under each fork. Seeing the salt and pepper shakers near the stove, she moved them to the table.

"I had no idea he'd never held a baby. I'll let him get in a little practice before I put Sam to bed," Maggie said as she opened the refrigerator door. She took out a large glass bowl full of iceberg lettuce with thin slices of tomato and green bell pepper arranged on top. "Garrett was like that too at first, although it was a couple of days before he could even go near him. I don't think he'll ever forgive himself for getting that cold."

Drizzling a homemade dressing over the salad, she gave it a toss and set it on the table. Turning around she took Tanya's hand. "I just wanted to thank you again for helping me through the delivery. I felt so utterly alone when Dr. Yang made Garrett leave and so relieved when they told me you were coming in to take his place. I don't know how I would have gotten through it without you and not knowing what to expect, I really didn't understand how necessary it was going to be to have that support. Your presence changed the entire experience for me Tanya, and I can't begin to thank you."

"Oh, I'm sure you would have been just fine." She gave her a hug. "Actually, you wouldn't have had much choice." The two women chuckled. Tanya rubbed Maggie's back affectionately becoming even more aware of her new slenderness beneath the roomy pink shirt she imagined she wore for nursing ease. "You know, no one would even know you had a baby just a few weeks ago. How did you manage to get your figure back so quickly?"

"Ah, the luck of the Irish I suppose," she answered with a wink and slipping on quilted mitts, she opened the oven door to remove the lasagna. She placed it on the hot pad in the middle of the table. "My sisters were the same after giving birth. The weight just seemed to fall off them as well. I was hoping to be as fortunate. Although, if Garrett's mum doesn't stop delivering these wonderful casseroles, I'll probably be piling the pounds back on in no time.

"Help yourself to a drink, Tanya. There's water, Pepsi and beer in the fridge and Garrett has a nice bottle of wine breathing over there on the counter if you like red. I'm going to put Sam in the bassinette and tell the men dinner is ready."

"You're awfully quiet." Reaching across the console, Mick took her hand. "Something wrong?"

Tanya withdrew her gaze from the traffic light. Giving him a half glance, she briefly answered, "No." It was a lie, but there was no point in raising the subject tonight. Her parents' visit would be lurking in the back of their minds throughout the coming week. She'd rather not spoil what time they had left by discussing it.

The mood swing had snuck upon her as she stood at the sink rinsing off the pretty dinner plates and putting them in the dishwasher. Sam had started to fuss for his next feeding and Maggie had excused herself to tend to him. Tanya assured her she would see to the dishes. Mick and Garrett helped clear then sat back down at the table nursing their beers.

Tanya didn't know what miscreant wandered in to spoil the end of such a pleasant evening. She could only imagine it had slithered into the Ames' happy home while a good time was being had by all. Standing in the cozy low-lighted kitchen as night closed in and darkness fell, listening to Mick's voice engaged in quiet conversation behind her, which was enough to make her bones melt anyway, a yearning seeped into her soul to fast forward and have what Garrett and Maggie had together. Marriage. A family. A binding pledge of eternal love, till death do us part, what God hath joined together let no man put asunder. Now, today, right this minute, or at least within the next nine days. Otherwise, there was always a chance, that slim but definitely possible chance, something or someone *could* come along and tear them asunder.

She would have only herself to blame. Mick had asked her to elope, so to speak, and she supposed the offer was still on the table by way of a quick trip to Vegas or the use of a local cleric. She doubted very much if Father Dimitri from her church would perform a ceremony on such short notice. Even if he would, she couldn't do that to her mother. She just couldn't. Shopping for a ring the previous week hadn't gained them any ground either. There were a few she admired and one she secretly fell in love with. Luckily she hadn't made it obvious *before* looking at the price tag. Mick knew of another jeweler he wanted to take her to as well, but they just hadn't gotten around to it yet.

It was only during semi-idle moments like dish washing when her mind became free to wander and wonder. Then, trepidation always seemed to be waiting in the wings ready to storm her newfound happiness and fill her head with all sorts of worry.

It would be fine. Everything would be fine, she kept telling herself. Instead of getting married, she and Mick would just have to put things on hold for a few weeks, that's all. Indeed, soon she would be sharing the house with her parents again instead of Mick, not to mention sleeping solo in her bed. Temporary or not, a weekend without his warm body to snuggle against she could handle, maybe. But nearly four weeks was just too much to ask.

If her father had a change of heart over the last eight years, and she prayed that he had, Tanya planned on inviting Mick to spend every available evening with them at the house. When it was time for him to leave, she could just picture the two of them kissing good-bye at the front door while Mommy and Daddy looked on.

There was small comfort in reminding herself that just might be the best-case scenario. The worst, of course, would be another scene like the one that occurred eight years ago. The night she informed her parents she was going out on a date with Mick. The prospect of facing that same situation again left her with a numbing fear that history was about to repeat itself.

"Do you want to go up to the boardwalk with me for a few minutes?" Mick asked her before the light changed. "We have a couple of new guys working the stand on their own tonight. Garrett was going to drive over and see how they're doing but I told him I would check in on them. If you're too tired, I can run you home and come back."

"No, no that's fine. I don't mind. You might have trouble finding a parking place any closer than The Cove though." Tanya glanced at the dashboard clock. "The fireworks will be starting soon."

"That's right, it's Wednesday," he responded absently. "No wonder there's so much traffic." In spite of the congestion he was able to hop on 35S and drive from Ortley to the Heights in less than ten minutes. Avoiding Ocean Terrace, Mick navigated the side streets and made his way over to The Cove. "Here's one. It's still a couple of blocks away though. Do you mind walking?"

"No. I could actually use a walk after that meal. I ate way too much."

"Mrs. Ames was always a great cook. I probably ate more meals at Garrett's house than my own growing up," he told her as he cut the wheels and backed into the parking place.

Tanya took the hand he extended when he joined her on the sidewalk. They were in a residential neighborhood where more than likely most of the houses were rentals. It was quite dark at this hour, except for an occasional streetlamp, a random porch light or landscape illumination. Rock music drew their attention to a plain white cottage set back from the curb. Young adults were milling about, both inside and out. They seemed to be in high spirits ready to party the night away. Tanya didn't miss those days, not that she was ever much of a party go'er. She wasn't sure she could say the same for her ol' pal, ol' buddy.

The traditional Seaside Heights Wednesday night fireworks drew thousands of spectators, especially on a clear July night such as this. The boardwalk was so jammed with people, it was hard for them to even walk side by side. Tanya stopped in at the music stand and finding everything satisfactory she strolled towards the red awning. She caught Mick's attention and indicated a point just beyond the seafood bar where she would be waiting.

Standing out of the pedestrian pathway, she watched the fireworks begin. Shot from the beach, a ringside seat would have been at the midway point of the boardwalk about three blocks north from where she was standing. That's where most people congregated. Tanya had seen so many Wednesday night fireworks in her lifetime, spectacular as they were, they'd lost much of their *wow factor.* The crowd always seemed to enjoy them though and that was always gratifying. Plus, the take on Wednesday nights at the music stand was sometimes triple that of any other summer weeknight. For that reason alone, she mentally cheered them on.

"Feel like walking a little farther?"

Tanya gripped the forearms that suddenly circled her waist. Turning her head, she glanced up. "Okay, where did you have in mind?"

"The beach. Let's get away from all the noise and go down to the Park."

Tanya agreed and within minutes they left the masses and bright lights behind. Continuing beyond the metered parking lot, they took the next beach access between the dunes. They both kicked off their sandals and leaving them alongside the walkway stepped onto the cool, smooth sand.

The weight of her braid wasn't helping the pressure building along her brow, undoubtedly brought on by all her restless thoughts. With a word to Mick, she took back her hand and unraveled it as they walked. Running her nails through her scalp and loosening all the strands felt wonderful.

She sighed, feeling so much better. There was the softest beach breeze romancing her gauzy blouse and now her unbound hair. "Mmm, what a beautiful night," she moaned, appreciating its calming effect as she took in the nearly full moon and it's glistening reflection across the tranquil sea. Another spectacular sight she was accustomed to, though this one she'd never tire of. Someone had given her a relaxation CD of the surf at low tide, but there was nothing like a live concert under a moonlit sky.

"I wish we had a blanket."

"Too bad we don't have a blanket."

They spoke in unison, looked at each other and smiled. His arm curved over her shoulders. Hers wrapped his waist.

"Do you still have that bikini?" He drew her close and murmured against her ear.

"Probably. I think so."

"We'll have to re-enact that night sometime. Only with a different ending this time."

Tanya slid her other arm around the front of his waist and locked her hands together. She burrowed against his chest. "I wanted you to make love to me so badly that night."

"I wanted that to. Believe me, you have no idea how much. If it wasn't for those voices, it would have happened."

In response, her arms tightened. She pressed her face into his shirt, breathing him in, storing up his love as if she could stockpile it for a rainy day when she'd need to make due without.

Mick kissed the top of her head. Stopping short of the water's edge, he turned her in his arms. "Okay, what's up? I felt your mood crash tonight."

Tanya looked out over the ocean and tried shedding the weight of it all with a long exhale. It didn't work. She'd been avoiding the subject over the last few weeks. Talking about it would only upset him. "Nothing."

He lifted her chin. "Is it Sam? You seem pretty taken with him. Do you want to have a baby sooner?"

"No, not exactly. I really just want it to be you and me for awhile, but—"

"But?"

Until admitting her fears about her parents' acceptance of Mick to Lisa today, she'd done pretty well these past few weeks pretending they didn't exist. Now that she'd opened up that Pandora's box, it seemed to be all she could think about. Eventually the strain of keeping it to herself was going to show anyway, like now, so she might as well come clean. "Oh, I just wish the next few weeks were behind us, that's all."

He gave a short grunt. "I don't know why you haven't told them Tanya, but you're freaking me out here. You were seventeen then. I was twenty-three. As much as it pissed me off that they forbid you to go out with me, I guess I can understand now that I look back on it. But you're twenty-six now. What are you afraid of? Why would they care? I wouldn't think they'd want you to end up an old maid."

Her jaw dropped. "Excuse me?" Insulted, she gave him a playful shove.

Knocked off balance, Mick stumbled sideways at the precise moment two separate and rather energetic waves raced past the shoreline and overlapped. Salt water covered the hem of his jeans while their clash created a spurt that shot all the way up to the front of his shirt.

Watching the scene unfold, Tanya's jaw dropped even further. They weren't even that close to the water. How had that happened? Her hands covered her mouth, mainly to hide her amusement. Seeing the look on his face, she started backwards.

"Now you've done it. Come here you little devil."

"I'm sorry!" She couldn't help laughing. "It wasn't my fault. There was a rogue wave."

"A rogue wave." Despite his attempts to appear threatening, he started to smile.

"I said, come here. Just come here. Just for a minute." He followed in her retreating footsteps.

"No, why?"

He made a face. "C'mon Tanya, I could drop you on the count of *one* if I wanted to."

"Wow, there's a newsflash."

His brows rose. "Never looks to me like you suffer much. Are you complaining?"

"No."

"Then why are you backing away from me?"

"Because I don't wish to be dropped in the sand or—"

"Watch out!" Mick looked down at her feet.

"What!" Falling for his bluff, she went up on her toes imagining sand crabs and slimy creatures. She looked behind her.

"Suckerrrr."

Swept off her feet, she yelped as Mick started for the water with her in his arms. "Oh Mick, please don't." She laughed anxiously, breathlessly. "Please, please don't." Clinging to his neck, she looked down at the ground. He was in over his ankles with an incoming wave not far away. "Mick, no! I hate wet clothes. Mick, please."

"Tell me about it. Mine are soaked thanks to you." He let his arms go slack to scare her.

She cried out, laughing harder, and tried to climb back up his body. "Please, please, I'll do anything."

He fell still on that comment and looked down at her face. "Now there's an interesting offer. You'll do…anything?" He backed up avoiding the next wave for the sake of his own jeans.

"Well, um," Tanya hesitated catching the glint in his eyes. She could just imagine what he had in mind.

He started forward again.

"Okay, okay, I will. I will. I'll do anything," she chuckled deeply. "I promise." She held onto him tight, swinging her calves as if the rapid motion could make him go in reverse.

Mick carried her up to dry sand and set her on her feet.

"Okay." Tanya gushed with relief and adjusted her clothes. She brushed off her capris checking her outfit for damage. Eyes bent to the task, she queried dryly, "Well, what is it you want? As if I don't already know."

Mick finished rolling up his pant legs so they wouldn't collect sand on their walk back. Coming up, he clamped the back of her neck.

Tanya's spine arched. Looking up at his dimpled smile, her throat squeaked.

"Sometimes I wonder what goes on in that mind of yours squirt. You might want to clean it up a bit before your mother gets here."

His fingers pressed on a ticklish spot, making her laugh and squirm. Bowing down low then under his arm she was able to twist up and away from him. "That's your fault. You've corrupted me."

"Is that right? Well, for your information, what I want has nothing to do with what you're thinking." Slinging an arm around her, they started to walk back.

Tanya reached up and took the hand hanging over her shoulder. "It doesn't huh, that's a first."

His look threatened again until she leaned in and gave him a quick kiss. "So what is it? What's my punishment," she asked teasingly. He was silent and thoughtful for a length of time, building Tanya's curiosity.

"I want you to say yes to going with me on Friday to Atlantic City. We'll spend the night and come back by Saturday afternoon. We'll only be gone twenty four hours." He threw that in off the bat, knowing her first refusal would have to do with time away from Paradise.

Tanya's initial reaction was surprise and a glowing smile. After a second to think about it, she asked. "Why Atlantic City? To gamble?"

"No, not necessarily, unless you want to. It's just someplace nearby that has good food and entertainment. Do you realize that you and I have never even been out to dinner? We either eat at The Cove or the pub, which really doesn't count, or we throw something together at home. We haven't done anything special for fun or relaxation."

They'd just spent three hours in bed this afternoon. That, along with an evening spent with the Ames' set her back nearly an entire day at the office. She believed Stephan and Dana were scheduled to close Friday night but needed to verify. If they were off, they might have already made plans.

If Dana and Stephan weren't on the schedule or available to work, it would have been impossible for her to go, which is why he checked with them days ago and swore them to secrecy. "I can practically hear your brain buzzing with a bunch of excuses, but you can't say no. You already promised. A deal's a deal."

"Oh Mick, it's a wonderful idea and I would love to, but I just don't feel right going away. What if there's an emergency? You have Jack and Garrett to back you up if something goes wrong."

"And you have Stephan and Dana," he pointed out emphatically, intent on winning this argument. "You praise them all the time and say how competent and loyal they are. Atlantic City is less than an hour away, Tanya. You're nearly thirty minutes away when you go to the mall. We'll be back within twenty-four hours. C'mon, you work your butt off. You deserve some R&R before your parents get here."

"Okay, you've talked me into it." She smiled up at him.

Well, that went better than he expected. Just plain happy about it, Mick put her in a headlock and gave her a noogy. "That's my girl."

Friday morning dawned bright and breezy. Perfect weather for a romantic getaway, Tanya thought, as she opened her suitcase and decided what to bring. Let's see, a dress for dinner, an outfit for tomorrow, lingerie, jewelry, toothbrush, toiletries and her make-up bag. Thirty minutes later, thinking of the million things she wanted to take care of at the pub before they left, she finished dressing.

A multi-color sash was fed through the belt loops of her black cropped pants. After tying it at the hip, she shrugged into a white denim jacket to cover the black cami that otherwise would have been a bit inappropriate for daywear. The heart necklace went over her head before she gathered her hair to lift it out from under the jacket collar and chain. She'd left her hair loose the way she thought Mick would prefer and spent a ridiculous amount of time this morning giving it a smoother, sleeker style for a change.

He was downstairs eating his eggs, reading the paper, waiting to take her to Paradise. Mm mm mm, when didn't the man take her to Paradise. Her lips curved on that thought as she packed a few special occasion items he'd never seen before, selected with his particular taste in mind. Her body stirred anticipating the evening ahead. She was tempted to close her eyes and wallow in it for a few minutes but knew it would leave her brain all befuddled and there was no time for that until they were on their way.

As it turned out, they were actually lucky to be going at all. The previous afternoon Mick called her at the pub to tell her he'd been on the phone all morning trying to find a room but all the hotels seemed to be booked. Even though it turned out that Dana and Stephan were already scheduled to close, she'd still been struggling with her decision to go—until she learned they might not be. Her spirits had plummeted and remained there until he called back a few hours later to tell her he'd finally managed to get them a standard double at the Borgata.

Taking one last glance around her bedroom, Tanya began to zip the overnighter when she remembered she hadn't packed her heels. "*Be still my heart*," she murmured, patting her chest as she walked across the room. Had she forgotten them, she supposed she could have purchased a pair at the hotel, though at boutique prices, she would not have been happy about the unnecessary extravagance. While she was in her closet, she also grabbed a thin shawl. The dress she packed was sleeveless and it might be chilly in the restaurant.

By one o'clock they were heading south on the Parkway. Relaxed now, thanks to a productive morning, not to mention deliriously happy, Tanya slumped low in the bucket seat and gazed up at the blue sky and billowy clouds through her side window. She always enjoyed traveling this long black ribbon of highway curving through the pinelands. Midday traffic was surprisingly light for a summer Friday, and although the Jag was cruising the fast lane and they stood to make good time, she wished she had the power to flip a switch and make everything move in slow motion. This was one of those moments she would liked to have languished in, when the colors of the landscape looked sharper and clearer than ever before, when the song playing on the radio spoke about real love and could have been written especially for them, and when the hand folded over her own made her feel weak and strong at the same time. But time and scenery sped by and soon they were veering off on the Atlantic City Expressway, heading towards the towering hotels lined up across the horizon.

In the spacious Borgata lobby, Tanya stayed in the background while Mick went up to the front desk. They'd agreed to turn off their ring tones and leave their cell phones on vibrate while they were away. Since hers had been in her bag on the backseat during the drive, she took the opportunity to see if anyone called. They'd only been gone an hour but she knew she was going to have to check periodically for peace of mind.

They'd arrived a little earlier than the designated check-in time. Seeing Mick in the process of a transaction, Tanya assumed there was no problem getting into their room. Filling up with butterflies, she watched him walk back to her, all adorably preoccupied with returning his wallet to his back pocket and sliding the card keys into the one on his shirt. Although an unwed couple sharing a hotel room was no longer taboo, she was suddenly feeling rather risqué about it—probably because it was their first time. She had a sudden urge to throw open her jacket, cock her hip and deliver a pick-up line but he was too fast for her.

"Unless you want some action in the elevator, you might try saving that look for the room," he uttered lowly. "This way," he told her and led her to the bank of them on the other side of the lobby.

How did he always manage to stay one step ahead of her, Tanya wondered, as they rode the elevator up and up and up. Every other passenger got off floors ago and they were still climbing. Good thing she didn't have any phobias about heights or elevators. Finally. There was one short aisle and one long one, then a brief alcove to get to their room number.

Mick slid the key into the lock and opened the door. Stepping inside, he held it wide for Tanya to enter. He was able to gauge her first reaction then followed in her footsteps until she stopped altogether.

Full-blown surprise parted her lips and held her features in suspended animation. Her first impression was that the immense view of the blue sky and white cotton clouds made her feel as if she was floating above the earth. Tanya continued her dream walk until a panoramic view of the bay rose up to meet her through the wall of floor to ceiling windows. The room had to be three or four times the size she'd expected and she hadn't even seen a bed yet, which meant this was just the salon.

The décor was very chic, ultra contemporary, pleasing to the eye as well as the senses with both comfort and style. Other than artwork, a modern sculpture and the cream damask draperies, bisque and ebony were the predominant colors of the furnishings. On the wall to her right was a multi-media entertainment center and a pair of open double doors leading into the bedroom. No standard double this. Obviously they were in a penthouse suite, or something.

There had to be two dozen of the most perfect ruby red roses arranged in a stunning art deco vase on a cocktail table in front of the sofa. Beside the flowers, a bottle of Dom Perignon chilled in a silver bucket. Accompanying the champagne was a crudité platter, an assortment of cheese, crackers, red and green grapes, decadent looking truffles and chocolate dipped strawberries—all of her favorite things.

"Oh my God, Mick." Other than that outpouring of emotion, she was at a complete loss for words and blinked the moisture from her eyes to turn and look at him. "I can't believe this room. I can't believe you did this." Knowing it was trembling, she pressed a hand against her mouth. The tears spilled when he took her in his arms.

"I'd do anything for you. Don't you know that by now?"

The knock on the door had him stifling a curse. "Hold that thought," he whispered against her hair. Walking back into the foyer, he let the bellman in with their bags. After the man politely and efficiently performed his duties and wished them a good day, Mick tipped him generously and closed the door. He found Tanya standing in the bedroom, running her hand across the lustrous bedding.

She heard him come in and looked over her shoulder. "We could get lost in this bed," she said, still a bit dazed by it all. She felt as if she were walking on air and wouldn't be coming down anytime soon.

"Well, if I had three wishes, that would be one of them," he said in response.

Knowing him, it was a bona fide statement. It earned him a bona fide smile. Tanya aimed straight for his arms laughing with pure joy.

Mick caught her in a hard embrace and held himself to one potent kiss before lowering her feet to the floor. "C'mon, let's get out of this room before I decide to take you up on that idea."

Tanya followed him out and passing the dressing room saw that their luggage had been placed on racks. Their garment bags were hung inside the wide mirrored closet. A built in wall unit provided ample nooks and drawer space for their folded clothes and accessories. Tanya poked her head in the bathroom and gazed around at all the marble and glass, the huge oval Jacuzzi tub. A fresh exotic arrangement sat just outside the rim. Tanya grabbed a tissue from the dispenser on her way out and dabbed her eyes.

The impact of the view and the sheer magnitude of the salon struck her again as she walked into it. Slipping out of her shoes, she tucked a leg beneath her and sat down on the sofa as though she'd been sucker punched. "You are very good at surprises, Mr. Leighton," she said to him as he walked around the other side of the table to sit down beside her. "So you were just able to snatch up a standard double, huh?"

"Just trying to build the suspense. I had to play that one out over the phone. I couldn't have kept a straight face if I told you in person." He squeezed her knee. Reaching for a square of cheddar, he popped it into his mouth and handed her an envelope he'd picked up from the table.

Tanya lifted the flap and pulled out a spa schedule with one of the services circled in red.

"You have a Svedish massage at ten a.m. If there's anything else you want to schedule, feel free to pamper yourself. Nails, toes, mani maxi mini. Whatever it's called. I've already requested a late check-out so take as much time as you want. We'll just order room service at some point."

Tanya chuckled and collapsed against his shoulder letting it all sink in. Raising her head, all she could do was stare at him. "How—? When did you arrange all of this? Have you been here before? In this suite?" Her eyes narrowed. "You've never brought anyone else here, have you?"

Leaning forward, he picked out a strawberry and plugged her mouth with it. "I'll answer the stupid question first. No, I have never brought anyone else here. I spoke to the concierge on the phone, told them what I wanted and asked them if they could accommodate. Wednesday morning I drove down here, checked out this suite and a few others and made final arrangements."

Tanya nibbled on her strawberry, gazing into his eyes. "I never knew you could be so romantic."

"You never knew a lot of things." He wasn't sure he could ever make her understand, but he'd die trying. Lifting her arm, he kissed the inside of her wrist, the palm of her hand. "Let me open the champagne."

Tanya slipped out of her jacket and swept her hair back, making herself comfortable. She accepted the glass from him and watched his eyes slide over her appreciatively. Their glasses tipped towards each other with a light ping. I love you's were spoken. Mick finished his glass first and set it on the table. He took Tanya's from her hand and set it beside his own.

The kissing began soft and light with fragrant palates. Mick slid his hand up her spine beneath her top to release the clasp of her bra.

Tanya took it from there. Reaching under her cami, she pulled it out. It wasn't one she wore often and now she remembered why. She sighed with relief, stood up and switched her position to lie across his lap.

Mick eyed the black strapless she'd tossed on the table. "If I'd known you were wearing something like that, I would have taken this off instead," he indicated her cami. "Although this ain't so bad either," he added, feeling her body through the smooth fabric before lifting the hem.

"Later," she promised, thinking of how deserving he was…thinking how she could give back…give of her love in a way that would transport him to a place beyond the clouds and raise him up to the level of emotion she was experiencing right now. She wanted to do for him as he often did for her, leaving him mindless, helpless to do anything but feel profound pleasure.

"Right now, I just want to say thank you," she whispered, beginning her journey with the sweet seal of her lips against his own. By the time she had his shirt unbuttoned and jeans unsnapped, she could smell the fire beneath his skin, taste the heat on her tongue, feel it in the rough sweep of his palm as it traveled her curves and dove into her hair. She could feel it under her own palm as she gave to him in ways previously withheld. Until now. Until the moment felt right for her and her faith in him was fully restored. Giving generously, she felt him burn and burn and burn, pleading for mercy with the clutch of his hands and the tight, ragged spill of his breath. In the end, leaving him as stunned with his gift as she'd been with hers.

They rode the elevator back down to the casino level, picking up other passengers during their descent. Mick and Tanya became separated, ending up on opposite sides of the car.

He hadn't had very much to say since she'd left him quivering on the sofa, Tanya thought, as she rocked back on her heels to bring him into view. She wished he would lift up those lashes. They'd been at half-mast, hiding his thoughts from her. There was a crease at the corners of his eyes. Usually, that happened when he was amused about something, yet the pull of his jaw and the indentation of one of his cheeks, which had nothing to do with his dimples, appeared to indicate some degree of dissatisfaction. Possibly even anger? If he was angry, Tanya didn't have the faintest idea why. And dis-satisfied? No way, uh uh, not possible.

At least she hoped not. Having zilch experience in that area, she supposed she had some degree of knowledge to gain but based on her instincts and his response, she was pretty sure she'd knocked his socks off—that is, had he been wearing any.

Exiting the elevator, they reunited.

"Hold up," Mick said to her, pulling her aside while the car emptied. Making a quick sweep of the area to make sure they were alone, his gaze returned to her face and examined it fully, as if he had much to consider, as if he was looking for something he'd never seen before. "And just where did you learn how to do that?" He was a little ticked she was that good at it and for the life of him had no idea why.

Tanya had just popped a stick of gum into her mouth. Holding his waiting gaze, she gestured to her jaw, chewed hurriedly, swallowed then swept the gum over between her molars. All that concentration helped hold the poker face while she wracked her brain for a killer response. Such a ridiculous question deserved an equally ridiculous answer.

"Actually, I don't believe lessons are available on the subject, but then it's not exactly rocket science, so..." Leaving it at that, she resumed chewing, blew a small bubble and popped it with a snap.

Mick closed his eyes, turned his head and controlled the choke as he stepped away. He supposed he asked for that and should have known she'd come back with some smart-ass answer. Sighing inwardly, he dragged a hand over his face. It felt warm to the touch. Unbelievable. He didn't think he'd ever blushed in his life. Apparently, he had corrupted her. He turned back around. "Very funny, Tanya. Very, very funny." Still finding that kind of talent a bit suspect based on a history of one guy, one night, he studied her again at length but chose to say nothing. "C'mon, let's go play some blackjack."

Walking into the casino, he threw an arm over her shoulder. He was still deep in thought on the issue when suddenly something extremely important came to mind. "You know, you never really thanked me for fixing that leaky faucet in the kitchen the other night."

"Yes I did. I said thank you," Tanya argued.

"Oh no baby, not like that you didn't."

"So, what are you saying, I owe you now?"

Mick lowered his arm and patted her hip. "I'll work up a list."

He was up two hundred dollars. She was down fifty and not taking it well. Waiting for the next deal, her nails beat a galloping rhythm on the green felt. "If I get one more lousy hand, I'm quitting." She was dealt an eight and a four and snickered. "Twelve. Do you believe this?" Tanya glanced over at Mick's cards. He had a pair of queens, which he decided to split when he saw the dealer ended up with fifteen and a strong probability of going over. Tanya took a hit and was dealt a deuce. Muttering to herself, she flattened her hand above her cards, indicating she would stay. Mick ended up with blackjack on one hand and nineteen on the other and made himself another hundred when the dealer busted. "Well, I don't believe it," Tanya mumbled dryly, "I actually won. Good, we're getting a new dealer. Maybe my luck will change."

Tanya thought differently when seconds later she looked up from her meager pile of chips and saw the stocky middle-aged man had been replaced by a blond bombshell with a Dolly Parton bustline. Upswept wheat blond hair, porcelain skin and a black beauty mark dotted above the corner of red velvet lips gave her the look of a bordello madam from the old west. The new dealer bade a husky good evening to the five players at the table and hadn't those whisky brown eyes lapped up the sight of Mick as though he'd been delivered by the local sweetshop? And didn't they keep coming back for more? Tanya squinted in order to read the nametag on the dealer's abundantly filled vest. *Angel.* Oh please. Thank goodness the woman was old enough to be his mother, well almost anyway.

Sneaking a peek at Mick, who was seated dead center with a full frontal view of the dealer's chest, she found him trying like hell to find any other point of interest.

"Well, I'm ready for dinner. How about you?" Tanya picked up her chips.

"Don't you want to—?"

"Nope, nope, I practically broke even. That's about as lucky as I get when I gamble. Ready?" She flashed him a sunny smile.

Mick shot her an amused look and unhurriedly rose from his stool. Collecting his own chips, he remarked, "I guess I don't have a choice."

"That's right, you don't. C'mon, we'll go find a cashier."

Wisely he made no further comment.

They had dinner reservations for eight and tickets to the ten o'clock show Mick told her while they were riding the elevator back up again.

This time they were alone in the car and Tanya was able to cuddle against him. "You thought of everything, didn't you?"

"I tried."

"That suite must have cost a bundle. I feel terrible we're not going to be spending much time in it."

Outwardly, Mick watched the numbers climb above the door. Inwardly, there was a vision in his mind that just wouldn't quit, and it had nothing to do with a pair of balloon size breasts across a blackjack table. Hours later and he was still feeling the lethargy in his thighs. "Are you kidding me?" he slurred, drawing her close. "It's already been worth every penny." Exiting the car, he caught the elbow before it caught him.

Storm clouds with silver linings had rolled in while they were downstairs in the casino. Mick turned the lamp on by the sofa but otherwise let the changing light in the sky set the stage. He found some mood music on the Bose system provided and poured them each another glass of champagne while they dressed for dinner.

He took the first shower while she opened her suitcase and unpacked. While he dressed in the bedroom, Tanya took over the bathroom. Since she had taken a shower that morning and wasn't about to let her hair near water, she gathered it in a high knot and dashed in and out just to freshen up. At the sink, she flossed, brushed, refreshed her make up and smoothed lotion into her limbs. She donned a red satin push up bra and matching thong, brushed out her hair and considered a few style options. Undecided, she left it loose then went out into the dressing room to finish.

Dangling Swarovski crystals were fastened into her earlobes and although she'd also packed a bracelet and dress watch, the drop earrings seemed to be all that was necessary to compliment the black sheath. Sweeping her hair around to one side was not only expedient but seemed to suit the dress as well—simple and sexy. Anxious to join Mick and get their evening underway, she stepped into her shoes while zipping and managed to hit a snag.

Tanya groaned in frustration but before she made it worse, she walked out into the salon to find Mick. She stopped short when he turned around. It was possible her heel caught on the carpet but she was more inclined to believe she'd tripped over her tongue. Really, could anything make a woman feel more feminine than a sharp dressed man? One hand rested in the pocket of his well-fitting pants while the other held his champagne glass. She'd never seen him like this, dressed to kill yet still managing to own that casual beachcomber grace. Above his starched open collar, his face looked smooth and lean and drop dead handsome. She opened her mouth to tell him about the zipper but hadn't a clue what came out of it. Apparently, she'd gotten her point across though since he was drawing her back into the dressing room where he could see better.

Locating the problem, he worked the fabric loose, pulled up the zipper and fastened the hook and eye. He turned her to face the long mirror and took his time admiring every inch of her from the top of her head to the tips of her painted toenails.

Knowing what this night meant to him, Mick found his hands unsteady as they curved over her shoulders. His breath staggered in. "The first time I saw you in a dress was that night at the retirement dinner, the summer after you graduated from college. I remember it was the color of that champagne, he nodded towards the glass he'd set down. Your hair was loose and you had on earrings that kept catching the setting sun. You looked like you stepped straight out of heaven. I couldn't take my eyes off you. I couldn't believe how beautiful you'd become. How is it that you've managed to improve upon perfection?"

Tanya raised her hand to cover one of his on her shoulder. She smiled, nearly chuckled. Wow, he was certainly waxing poetic tonight. Taking a closer look, she could tell he'd slipped away to that place where his thoughts were deep and provocative, a mood of his she found to be such a turn on. "I'm in love and happier than I ever imagined. They say it does wonders for a girl's complexion."

Surveying the rather sophisticated looking couple in the mirror, Tanya drifted back in time along with him. They'd come a long way since that fateful day in the souvenir shop. The heart was currently tucked inside her bra. Since they'd reunited, she was never without it.

"You clean up pretty nice yourself, you know," she murmured and before the little bit of drool proved what an understatement that was, she caught it with the tip of her tongue. Leaning back against him, she pressed her cheek against his. She could have told him he was possibly one of the hottest guys on the planet, but she was starving and wanted to make sure he'd be able to fit his head through the door on the way out.

He took her hand as they made to leave. "Come sit down for a minute. I want to ask you something before we go."

Tanya glanced at him expectantly and let him guide her out into the salon to a chair by the window. When he reached into his pocket and lowered to one knee, she nearly fainted. She didn't know why. He'd already popped the question but oh dear God, it never dawned on her that's what this night was all about. She didn't know if her heart could take any more surprises. Tanya looked down at the ring he held between his thumb and index finger. It was the one she fell in love with. "Oh my God." Her hands flew to her face. She'd been so careful not to let it show.

"Will you marry me, Tanya Reese Morgan?" He had a hard time holding her hand steady enough to slide the ring on. The way she was gasping and groaning, it sounded as if she could do with some oxygen. "You okay?"

She nodded swiftly, silently, fanning her face with her other hand.

"Shopping for a ring together didn't seem to be working out, so I took matters into my own hands. Is that all right with you?"

"Yes, but this one was so expensive, Mick!"

"Sh sh sh, no buts, no arguments. I told you to stop looking at the price tags. I knew this was going to be the one the minute I saw it on your finger." Mick cupped her jaw, setting it on an angle that would make her look into his eyes. "I only ask one thing Tanya. This ring does not come off your finger until the day we get married. Agreed?"

She understood. He didn't want her to remove it when her parents came which meant she had to tell them beforehand or be prepared to tell them as soon as they arrived. She nodded her promise with eyes sparkling bright as the solitaire between them.

Holding onto her hand, Mick continued to stare down at the ring. The biggest fear he'd ever faced in life was that this day would never come. He stood, bringing her with him and began to release the breath that had been lodged in his chest for days, years maybe.

Locked in an emotion packed moment and a hard embrace, Mick opened his eyes and gazed out the window. The lights were beginning to glitter around the bay and marina. *Not very original Leighton. Nothing like taking her to her own backyard for the big event.* He'd wanted to make their engagement special and under the circumstances, this was the best he could come up with. It wasn't exactly Paris or any of the super romantic venues popular for marriage proposals, but the honeymoon he had in mind would hopefully make up for it. Hew drew back to look at his future bride. "Well squirt, this is it. It's for real now."

"It always was for real," she vowed softly and as their eyes met, they seemed to mirror a love that in some mysterious way seemed to have been born within them, mind, body and soul.

Mick raised her hand to kiss it.

Gazing at the ring and the touching way he held her fingers against his lips, she breathed his name.

He felt her cool palm on the back of his neck, her lips soft against his brow and at once their arms and mouths were clinging, their hearts hammering against each other. Love words were whispered as they both neared the decision to wave their plans in favor of a more pressing matter.

In an all fired hurry to flee the temptation of the nearby bed, Mick started to pull her along behind him. "I brought you here to wine and dine you and show you a good time. If all we're going to do is have sex, we could have stayed home."

Tanya steered him to a side table where she'd left her shawl. "We could always skip the show," she suggested.

In the foyer, Mick stood back and held the door open for her. She saw his dimpled smile descending and paused to catch the kiss aiming for her cheek. His hand pushed her rump out the door. "Yeah, I always knew you and I were going to make a great team."

Mick ordered the rib eye. Tanya ordered the filet with béarnaise sauce and roasted asparagus. Mick started with a Jack and ginger. Tanya started with a Cosmopolitan. The seats were comfy, the lights low and above the fine white linens and the crystal globe where a small candle flickered, they only had eyes for each other. Whether everything was truly as perfect as it seemed or being officially engaged just made it feel that way, they would never know, or care.

Afterwards, sticking with their decision to forego the show, they left the restaurant at a slow stroll, intent on walking off the heavy meal before returning to their suite. Following no particular direction, they came upon a dimly lit lounge with live music and decided to go in for a nightcap. They chose a table in a dark corner, ordered drinks and slid their chairs together. Tanya leaned back against him while they enjoyed the timeless classics played by the four-piece band. One particular ballad soon found them on the dance floor.

It was the third time they'd danced together, though the first two hardly counted. The first time she'd been mad at him and the second, he'd bumped and grinded her into a state of delirium. This time, cheek to cheek, they swayed to the music, barely moving. At times they murmured quietly to each other, teasingly, flirtatiously. At others, they listened to the moving lyrics of the song and tightened their embrace.

Mick was feeling mellow after the second highball but it was nothing compared to the affect her perfume was having on him. It was a new scent wafting up from her cleavage, making him want to find a private place where he could hike up her skirt and see what other forms of torture she had in store for him. She'd probably smoothed lotion over her thighs, up to her bikini line, as she called it, and the curve of her bottom. She had a variety of panty styles in her lingerie drawer and unless she was wearing something new, he'd become adept at feeling her through her clothes and knowing which pair she had on. Pushing her rump out the door earlier, it felt au naturale. He'd immediately known she was wearing a thong. It would be red. He'd seen the color of her bra strap when he was fixing her zipper and more often than not, she wore a matched set.

Because his randy thoughts were making his blood flow a little too fast for the middle of a dance floor, he nuzzled her cheek, tuned back into the music and let the feel of her in his arms keep building the anticipation.

Tanya was acutely aware of the hard press of his cheekbone against her temple, the delicious scent of his jaw and the way his muscled thigh kept slipping between her own. The alignment of their bodies felt seamless, as if they had been custom made to fit together. The limited view she had of him was arousing in itself—one broad shoulder, a strong bronze neckline and the crisp, expertly tailored collars of his pale shirt and dark jacket. She loved the quality of the fabric and the smooth feel of it beneath her fingertips. The shirt was sandy beige, a perfect compliment to his skin tone and tawny hair.

He'd seduced her with all of this—the room, the ring, the romance of it all, so much so her head spun, along with a little help from the Cosmo and the After Eight she'd just downed at the table. Smiling to herself, she turned her lips against his throat, feeling all warm and giving and in love.

For as long as she lived, Tanya would never forget the final song they danced to. Nor would she ever forget how the powerful lyrics moved him to a point that made her wish everyone would disappear but the music would still play on. Closer and closer he held her until the feelings became too great to endure in the presence of others. The rush of love passed from him into her, pouring through her veins into every fiber of her being.

Suddenly the pick-up in tempo called for a bit more than the slow steps they'd been using. Getting into the spirit of the song, Mick waltzed her with an expertise of footwork that brought a smile of pure ecstasy to Tanya's lips. When the crescendo began to build and he lifted her off her feet, she closed her eyes and rode a wave of emotion so strong, she was sure he'd bewitched her.

Any dance after that would have been anticlimactic. Therefore, it was in the natural order of things that he toss a bill on their table and guide her out the door. In their minds there was nothing save this boundless love for one another and an urgent need to express it.

Chapter 12

"Clickety click, clickety click. What are you trying to do, finish that thing before we get to Lavallette? You've been going at it a mile a minute ever since we left Maryland. It's starting to drive me nuts."

Carol Morgan's busy hands paused on purl two then fell heavily into her lap. For the first time in what seemed like hours, her eyes, as true blue and pretty as her bag full of yarn, raised to look out the car window and see where they were. The deep, controlled breath she took was a nerve booster, the kind she often used to help fortify or prepare, especially lately.

They were just coming off the Delaware Memorial Bridge. The *Welcome to New Jersey* sign posted on the grassy knoll in the middle of the turnpike never looked so daunting, only because it meant they were almost there. Any other time, she would have welcomed seeing the welcome home sign. Any other time, the landmark would have begun to stir those old sentimental feelings, get those nostalgic juices flowing and make her think of good memories of days gone by. Any other time, but not this time. Carol closed her eyes, looking within, double-checking, but no, there was nothing stirring but turmoil and trepidation.

Opening her eyes, she bowed her head again watching her slender fingers smooth out the scarf she was making for Tanya. She checked her handiwork for any flaws in the pattern thinking it was a good thing they were wearing them longer these days. Holding up what she'd done so far, there appeared to be more than a yard falling all the way down to the floor mat.

Tanya was so particular, Carol doubted she would ever really wear it. Perhaps it would suit her teenage niece better. That is, if it turned out well enough. Carol shrugged, mentally. The recipient of the scarf hardly mattered. Knitting wasn't a hobby she practiced often but she was afraid she might have bitten off all her fingernails if she hadn't brought along something to occupy both her mind and hands during the long drive up from Florida. So far, it served its purpose.

"Sorry," she said to her husband looking over at him, suddenly remembering why she'd stopped. "I didn't realize it was bothering you. It didn't sound that loud to me. Why don't we play the radio. Here, I'll find something you'll like," she said and reached for the control.

He had no patience with their new Cadillac. They'd picked it up from the dealer two days before they left and he was still getting used to all the new features; the glide-up navigational system, LCD touch screen, backup camera, Bluetooth, satellite radio, etcetera, etcetera, etcetera. Too many bells and whistles this time, he complained. She'd read aloud from the owner's manual for the first hour of their trip and tried to demonstrate in some cases but she could see for the most part her instructions were going in one ear and out the other. All this new technology was beginning to frustrate him and if she were honest, she was feeling the same. They'd mastered various remotes, email, online shopping and the self-check out at the grocery store. They were finally getting used to their iPhones but didn't know or care about most of its capabilities. At their age, it was just a struggle to keep up.

Jim Morgan removed his right hand from the steering wheel to brush his wife's away from the dash. "No, turn it off. I'm not in the mood for music. Next time we'll fly up. My leg has been giving me hell on this trip."

"Did you take Aleve before we left Jackie's?"

"No, I forgot."

Carol looked ahead through the windshield thinking she should have reminded him. His right leg always cramped up after a few hours on the road. Aleve at least took the edge off. Although, since it happened on a regular basis, you'd think he'd start remembering on his own. "I'd be happy to drive the rest of the way." She knew he'd say no. So much was predictable after thirty years of marriage.

"I'll let you know when I've had enough."

Only in an extreme case of fatigue or pain would he ask her to drive. Fine with her. He was a classic back seat driver anyway and wouldn't take the opportunity to rest if they switched places. He'd just try to direct her driving from the passenger seat and constantly criticize the other vehicles on the road. Carol reached over the console to massage his thigh, knowing it relaxed the muscle.

Beginning to feel some relief, he rested his hand upon hers. "I didn't mean to snap."

"I know," she replied, staring at the dashboard clock. They'd be there in a little more than an hour. She was almost out of time. Ever since they'd left Florida more than a week ago, she'd been trying to find the courage to broach the subject that had been plaguing her mind for some time now—their daughter's relationship with Mick Leighton. *Possible* relationship. On the one hand, she wanted to prepare him in case they were seeing each other. On the other hand, why dredge up the past if it wasn't necessary? She'd been doing little else but knitting and procrastinating the entire trip.

It wasn't long after she phoned Mick at The Cove the night of the storm that she began to notice a difference in Tanya. There'd been a significant change in her voice for one thing. It sounded brighter, happier, with a thread of overall contentment weaving through her remarks. Something had obviously changed in her life, for the better.

Carol wondered if that phone call had been instrumental in bringing them back together. Jim would never forgive her if such were the case but if she hadn't done something to help things along, she would never forgive herself. She owed them at least that much.

Mick never married. She made it her business to find that out during her last trip up. Tanya hadn't formed even one relationship with a boy during her entire young adult life. Why they never tried again once Tanya was older was a mystery, but one night last winter Carol walked by Tanya's bedroom door and heard her moaning Mick's name over and over again in her sleep. It nearly broke her heart to think that Jim might have destroyed their daughter's happiness for his own selfish reasons, and that she had stood by and let him.

"Easy, easy." Jim lifted up on his wife's wrist. "You're rubbing so hard, I'm going to have a bruise."

"Oh, sorry," her smile was distracted.

"What's with you anyway? You're acting as if you're on the way to visit the dentist, instead of our daughter."

Here it was, the perfect opening. Carol braced herself. "Well, to tell you the truth, Jim, there is something—"

He reached over to pat her leg. "Looking forward to seeing our baby again, right?"

Carol exhaled audibly. "She's hardly a baby, Jim. She's a full-grown woman. Many of her friends are married with children by now."

He looked at her askance. "It was just a figure of speech, Carol. I know how old she is. In fact, I wish she would find a husband soon before I'm too old to enjoy my grandchildren. I bet you're anxious to start knitting up some baby booties and buntings, or whatever they're called."

"Well, yes, I suppose, but—"

Warming to the subject, he rested his forearm on the console and all but winked. "I'm going to try and talk her into moving down south with us again. I think she's growing to like Florida, and there seems to be a lot of eligible men in our area. In fact, if all goes well, I may even have a little surprise for her."

Carol looked at him sharply. "What? What kind of surprise? Oh Jim, what have you done?"

He gave her a double take and spilled a laugh. "Well, certainly nothing to get all huffy about. I invited Dan Wakefield to spend a few days with us while we're here, that's all. He's in New York on business for an extended period, and he's hoping to find some time to take a ride down. He says he's heard so much about the Jersey Shore and always wanted to see what all the fuss is about."

"Oh Jim, no! How could you? Tanya isn't interested in him. She told you that! I can't believe you would do such a thing."

"Calm down for heaven's sake. They only had time for a couple of dates before he left for China and we were with them that first night for dinner. How could she possibly be sure of her feelings based on a few short hours? I think they're perfect for each other. Tanya certainly made an impression on him, I can tell you that," he added, recalling their last conversation.

"Oh, this is awful, just awful! She's going to be very upset about this." Carol shifted her weight back into the middle of her seat. As if she didn't have enough to worry about, she thought, choosing the view out her side window instead of sharing his of the road. If she couldn't distance herself from him physically, at least she could mentally.

Though it was his wife's displeasure over his matchmaking efforts that rankled, Jim fixed his scowl on the Atlantic City transporter ahead of them. "Damn buses," he muttered. "Can't see a thing when they get in front of you." Turning his blinker on, he switched lanes and resumed their conversation. "Nonsense. That is still my house and I will invite anyone I choose to spend time there. Besides, Dan and I have some negotiating to do on that piece of property on the other side of the golf course."

Flabbergasted, his wife looked back at him. "That property is not for sale! Your mother has been very adamant about that!"

"More nonsense! She wants to keep it just because she thinks those trees look pretty bordering the ninth hole and she's afraid they'll be cut down. You know as well as I do that those acres are useless to her without road access and with Dan's company owning the connecting land, it only makes sense to dump it now before they lose interest. What harm can it do to see what kind of offer they make?"

"Oh, you are just impossible! You think you can bully everyone into doing what you think is best for them with complete disregard for their feelings. Why does it always come down to what you want? I wish just once you would give people credit for knowing what they want and respect their decisions."

"For your information, my mother—*and* my daughter—have a stubborn streak a mile wide. They don't always know what's good for them and need to be steered in the right direction is all. And where is the harm in that?"

Carol made a sound of frustration and grabbed up her knitting needles. It would be futile to remind him that stubborn streak hadn't skipped a generation. He'd only deny it. God save her from egotistical, muleheaded men, she thought, wanting to give him a good hard poke. Now, finding great pleasure in knowing the sound annoyed him, her fingers moved rapidly above her lap. She'd clickety click him all the way home.

The steady hum of a small motor eventually woke him. Mick rose up on an elbow, squinted out the bedroom door and saw the tail end of a canister vacuum going by. He dropped back, rolled onto his side and scooped up Tanya's pillow. He gathered it under his cheekbone, preparing to steel another minute, or two, or maybe twenty, but—

She was vacuuming? With that bit of confusion, he began the morning's thought process. Suddenly he was up on one arm again, whipping his head around. Friday, August 3rd, 8:23 a.m.

The last time he looked at the clock, it had been 3:26 a.m. With Tanya out like a light before the eleven o'clock news, he'd gazed upon her sleeping form with envy, toying with the tail end of her braid lying between them. Not knowing how long they were going to have to go without had made the sex even more incredible. After all that physical exertion, he should have passed out right beside her. That's usually how it went, but this time, no such luck. After a few tosses and turns, he'd turned on the TV and with the volume set low, caught the end of the news then started to scan. He'd watched some of The Deadliest Catch then gave up and got up. He'd prowled around the house and ended up reading a few articles in the paper he'd skipped over that morning. There didn't seem to be a tired bone in his body. His mind had taken care of that with her parents pending arrival keeping him wired.

Now, feeling the effects of the restless night he'd had, he was tempted to linger awhile between the sheets but figured there was no point in delaying the inevitable. She'd given him his marching orders, and he only had a few hours to get his breakfast and wipe his presence from the house before they arrived. Rising, he started the day cursing it, stepped into his jeans, and after a quick stop in the bathroom, headed downstairs to see what the hell she thought she was doing.

Seeing her busily running the vacuum around the living room, Mick nearly missed a step. A scowl zigzagged across his features, revealing mixed feelings about her attire. Peeling his eyes off her body, he searched the windows for peeping Toms. Not that he was complaining, but he didn't think he'd ever known a female so comfortable in her own skin.

Nothing more than a triangle full of faded pink polka dots covered her bottom and a white cotton undershirt that had seen better days skimmed her shoulders and rib cage. She hadn't disassembled the loose braid, only tied it up off her neck while she worked. He was starting to feel the stifling heat and humidity just from walking down the stairs. The way she was exerting herself had bathed her tan limbs with a film of sweat. Running a hand over his chest, Mick let the banister take his weight and thought of the long, lonely nights ahead. Hell.

Good enough, Tanya decided, pressing the off switch. She started for the kitchen, stopping short when she remembered Mick. He better get moving, she thought, and spun around to go wake him. Wiping her brow, she got as far as the bottom step and jumped. "Oh God, you scared me. I didn't know you were up. Coffee's ready." She pivoted on the ball of one foot and retraced her steps.

With much on his mind, Mick stared after her until she disappeared into the kitchen. She was bent over the counter reading something when he walked in. "Is that your cleaning outfit?" he asked, pouring coffee into the mug she had taken out for him. It sloshed over the rim because he couldn't tear his eyes off that luscious behind of hers. He reached across her back to rip off a paper towel.

She was impatient with recipes, always losing her place or feeling the need to double and triple check amounts as if her brain had the memory capacity of a spoon. Halfway down the list of ingredients, she recalled hearing the rough timber of Mick's morning voice, but the words hadn't penetrated. "Hmm?" She turned her head, her gaze bouncing over the rim of her reading glasses.

"I said is that your cleaning outfit?"

Pulling in her chin, she looked down at herself. "Oh, I guess. It's too hot for anything else. The air conditioning kicked off again. Do you believe that? Today of all days." The oven was preheating making it worse.

Straightening, she absently massaged the base of her spine and skimmed over the recipe one more time.

"I'll take a look at it."

"No, don't bother. My father will call the guy when he gets here. He'll take care of it."

The Asbury Park Press was lying on the table. Mick pulled out a chair, set down his mug, and spun the paper around. "Can I ask you why you were vacuuming when Doris was just here Wednesday and did the entire house?"

"I thought I felt some sand under my feet this morning. I probably tracked it in after I ran yesterday." She needed to concentrate on the recipe and couldn't talk at the same time. *Eggs*. Let's see, two she needed. "I hope you left me enough eggs," she muttered, thinking out loud. Turning, she opened the refrigerator and wished she were small enough to step inside.

"There should be a half dozen or so in there. What are you making?" Mick tipped the ladder-backed chair on its hind legs.

"Banana bread and a cinnamon cake."

"Daddy's favorites?"

Eyeing what appeared to be a smirk, she shut the fridge door harder than necessary. "Is that supposed to be funny?"

Mick raised a brow. "I don't know, was it?"

"No."

"Then I guess it wasn't suppose to be."

She gave him a long look that journeyed from his sexily rumpled hair, down his furred chest to the arrow disappearing into his unsnapped jeans. "Don't sit like that. You could crack the tiles."

Eyes darkening, he brought the front legs down with a thump. It was more likely he'd break the chair but she was right. It was a bad habit of his. One that never seemed to bother her before.

She gave him a second glance. "Do you have your things together yet?"

"No. You said they wouldn't be here until noon."

"Noon will be here before you know it. You'd better get a move on."

He swallowed some coffee, returned his mug to the table and looked up from the front page of the paper. "What do you get pre *and post* menstrual syndrome?"

Tanya tucked her hand in her waist. "Oh, is that what this is all about? Are you grumpy because you didn't get enough this week?" Giving him her back, she picked up an egg and gave it a one-handed crack on the edge of the bowl. "I thought last night made up for it but apparently there's no pleasing you. What are you going to do over the next few weeks, find someone else again because…"

Mick torpedoed out of the chair. Gripping her arm, he turned her around. He was so angry his jaw locked. "In the first place, just watching you breathe pleases me. Now you look me in the eye and tell me you believe all the garbage that just came out of your mouth."

Tanya raised her chin a notch. Maybe she did believe it, just a little. But when her eyes met his, she was ashamed of herself for bringing that up again. A lengthy exhale relaxed the tight wire connecting her shoulder blades. She shook her head. Her lashes drifted down. "No. No of course not. I'm so keyed up I don't even know what I'm saying."

Mick went back to the table to get his coffee. "You picked a hell of a day to start a fight Tanya." Though he would have denied it, he was primed for one too.

"I didn't start this. You did, with that remark about me catering to my father. He has a sweet tooth. I always make him something to snack on when he comes home."

Jealousy pricked him, adding fizz to his own mounting temper. "Well bully for you. I have absolutely no idea what you're getting all steamed up about."

"I'm not getting steamed! You are! Now if you don't mind, I'd like to finish what I'm doing here." Tanya turned and cracked another egg.

"Fine." Mick poured his coffee down the drain. "I'll be at The Cove if you want to let me know who wins."

The spatula paused on the edge of the mixing bowl. "Excuse me?"

"You heard me. Let me know who wins, me—or your father."

"It's not a competition, Mick. It's not going to be like that."

"Isn't it? His opinion seems to carry an awful lot of weight with you. What are you going to do if he still disapproves?"

"I didn't listen to him when I was seventeen, did I? Why would I start now when we're engaged?" Emotion building, she mixed the contents in the bowl. Her breasts jiggled behind the thin film of cotton.

Mick watched them. "Just so you don't forget that. You're more mine now than you are his."

"That's an absurd comment."

"Maybe. But that's the way I see it." The frayed hem of her shirt gaped in the front creating a tunnel for his hand to climb up inside. He was only too happy to send it searching and brushed his fingers across her bare breasts. They were as firm as the rest of her, yet felt soft and warm as pillows. The need to have her before he left was about to swallow him whole. "Come here, damn you." He tipped her into his arms.

Tanya pushed away from him. "I can't. I don't have time."

He pulled her back. "Make time. Believe me, this won't take long."

"Mick! No!" Their tug of war ended as quickly as it began.

Disgusted with himself, he backed off and started for the door. He didn't get far before turning around. No way was he going to leave like this. Coming up behind her, he caught the counter's edge on either side of her. "I'm sorry. I'm not exactly myself this morning either." Mick let a few heavy heartbeats go by but she remained silent. He gave her braid a tug. "I'll talk to you later."

Tanya sent her glasses sliding and hooked her finger in the back pocket of his jeans before he could get away. Her arms tucked under his, curling up to holster his shoulders. "I'm sorry too. Don't go yet," she whispered.

Jim and Carol Morgan pulled into the drive at 12:21 pm. Tanya heard a horn beep twice, looked out the kitchen window and sent up one last prayer before going out to greet them.

"There's my girl!"

"Hi Dad. Mom." Leaving her arms open, she turned from one to the other for a hug and a kiss.

Both mother and daughter were dark haired and curvy with Tanya boasting the height advantage in leg length. There, the close similarities ended. While her mother favored her Welsh ancestors with their fuller cheeks, wider brow and a bit more rounded chin, it was the general consensus at a recent family reunion that Tanya had become the near spitting image of her great-great-grandmother Isabella Santiago, based on the few grainy pictures they'd found of her.

Henry Reese Morgan, her paternal great-great-grandfather, eager to see the world at the restless age of eighteen, was said to have stowed away on a ship bound for the West Indies. Discovered during the journey, he was given the boot when the ship docked in Puerto Rico. There he found work as a carpenter's apprentice and began saving to pay for his next voyage when he fell in love with the daughter of a wealthy plantation owner. Though secretly planning to wed, she became pregnant, was disowned and disinherited, and the near penniless couple returned to the Morgan family home in Jacksonville, Florida where Henry began to make a living building furniture. Isabella bore him five more children and they went on to live a long, happy and prosperous life together.

That's all Tanya remembered of the story her grandfather used to tell but someday wanted to visit Puerto Rico and learn more about her Santiago lineage. *There's my girl* was the way Papa Reese always greeted her growing up, not typically her father's way. Funny how those three little words had spun her thoughts in a direction she wasn't expecting. Maybe it was his way of sending her a message of comfort, letting her know not to worry, that everything was going to be okay.

Right, and the moon was made of green cheese. Tanya lifted the heavy weight of her hair and held it there to give her neck some relief from the heat. She rested her suspended elbow on top of the open car door as she continued to watch her mother organize various totes and shopping bags on the back seat. Waiting to lend a hand, her gaze ran over her mother's outfit. Her sporty daffodil yellow shirt looked stunning with her dark hair. Her white capris had a roll up cuff, patterned with the same yellow as her top. Although their age difference made a difference in the styles they preferred, they both loved clothes and accessories and enjoyed shopping together.

Her mother's medium length, sable brown hair swept across her forehead and feathered away from a face that had hardly changed since her Homecoming Queen yearbook picture. Her hairstyle might be outdated, but it suited her. Tanya couldn't picture her wearing it any other way. Upon close inspection, one might find an occasional silver thread running through the dark strands but she didn't seem to worry about them overmuch.

Worry. The word happened to be passing through only to double back when her mother finally straightened and Tanya was able to get a longer, closer look at her face. Maybe she wasn't stressing about the grays but it was clear some issue was clouding up those cornflower blue eyes and pinching fine lines around them. Perhaps she was travel weary or had a headache. Tanya ran her fingers down her mother's arm and gave her hand a squeeze. No matter how much she'd dreaded this day, it was still wonderful to see them. They both looked fit and healthy. Just like typical Floridians.

"You look great, Mom. Did you have a nice visit at Aunt Jackie's?" Tanya felt the gesture return. A smile that appeared to be an effort came and went.

"Yes, it was very nice. They all send their love."

Tanya continued to study her mother after the mechanical reply.

"Notice anything different?" her father called out, looking around the open lid of the trunk.

"Oh my gosh, your new car!" She was so entrenched in her thoughts which seemed bent on veering off in ten different directions, she didn't even notice the shiny new sedan parked in front of her nose. Mick always teased her about having selective vision.

Tanya stepped back for an expanded view. "It's beautiful. I love the color." She joined him to help with their luggage since her mother seemed able to manage the bags from the backseat. "Are you happy with it?"

Carol slid the strap of her white leather purse up her arm and looked over her shoulder. "There's a lot to learn but it rode very nice. We were very comfortable."

Again with the monotone. What was going on in that mind of hers, Tanya wondered, knowing something was up. Either that or her real mother had been abducted by aliens and this look alike zombie had been left to take her place. Not that her mother was ever one to do cartwheels over anything but she appeared so, so…stiff…and not sitting for a long time in the car stiff. More like *bracing herself for an ax to fall* stiff. Contrarily, it was making Tanya squirm. She probably just wasn't feeling well, or her father had upset her about something—more than likely the latter.

"Hey, the yard looks great! Have you been keeping it up all by yourself or did you hire some help?" her father asked jovially, handing her the smallest of their wheeled three piece set.

Well, her mother always said she and her father rarely rode the same biorhythm cycle. Maybe that was all it was. Unlike her mother, her father seemed quite enthused about everything and happy to be home. Tanya dragged her eyes away from the tense profile in front of her, glanced back at the animated one behind her and followed the direction they were both looking.

The red and white potted petunias were flourishing and fluttering in the hot summer breeze. The small patch of grass was green, really green, and neatly trimmed. Large river rocks were now bordering the concrete path instead of those small pebbles they'd always had that annoyingly scattered across the sidewalk and driveway. The pretty decorative stones made a sweeping curve around the lamppost and the far side of the steps to meet the mound of fresh dark mulch beneath the trio of leafy shrubs. Wow, it really did look nice.

"Ummm, yes. Well, you know, it's small enough to take care of and we've had some overnight showers so..." The truth was that left up to her, it wouldn't have looked half as good, especially in August. It had been next to impossible to keep up with everything since they moved and yard work never stood a chance of working its way up her list between Memorial weekend and Labor Day. She remembered seeing Mick's head and shoulders out here a few times from the kitchen window but never realized what a difference he was making. God, love must be making her visually impaired. How did she not notice this yesterday? And how sweet was that man? She'd have to remember to thank him.

"Tanya."

"Hmmm? Oh." Her head shook, realizing she'd slipped away there for a minute. Her father was behind her waiting for her to move on up the driveway. Her mother was already opening the front door, carrying those miscellaneous bags from inside the car.

"So, how was the drive up from Maryland? Did you take the Cape May ferry or come across the Delaware bridge?" Tanya asked him, looking down at her left hand to see how easy it would be for them to notice the ring. She'd turned her diamond around and was making every effort to keep the band out of sight.

Her father grunted. "We thought about taking the ferry but the time we wanted was booked. Next time we fly. My leg can't take this much driving anymore."

"What's wrong with your leg?" Tanya had nearly caught up with her curiously quiet mother.

"Cramps up. It's not easy getting old you know."

"Oh, you're not getting old, Dad. In fact, Lisa was just telling me the other day that you barely look fifty, never mind fifty-nine."

Flattered, he smiled broadly. "I always did like that girl."

They went directly upstairs to the master bedroom. Tanya had asked Doris to give it a thorough cleaning, air the bedding and put on fresh sheets. To welcome her parents home, Tanya purchased a gorgeous gardenia plant at her mother's favorite florist and had placed it on the bureau. She watched her mother walk over to it.

"Oh, how lovely, Tanya." Carol bowed her head to breathe in her favorite fragrance.

Okay, so it really was her mother. Tanya set down the suitcase she carried in then had trouble figuring out what to do with her hands, particularly the left one. She folded it against her hipbone, knuckle side down. Sounding a little breathless, she said, "Well, unless you guys want to unpack first, I have lunch ready. I just made some sandwiches."

"I got a whiff of that cinnamon cake as soon as I walked in the door. I know where I'm heading," her father announced. "I hope you iced it this time."

"I did, I did." She gave him a look as he passed by.

"Good girl. C'mon you two, I'm starving."

"Coming, Mom?" Tanya started to follow him out but the lack of an answer had her pausing in the doorway. When she looked back, she found that the only move her mother made was to turn and face her squarely across the width of the bedroom. Mick had performed a miracle and managed to get the air conditioning working before he left. Knowing it was going to take a while to reduce the stifling temperature in the house, Tanya had gone around and lowered all the shades on the sunny side. Since her mother was standing in a shadow between two of those drawn shades, it was hard for Tanya to read her expression.

She did, however, sense a sudden composure. She seemed to be looking at a woman with an entirely different demeanor than when she first arrived. Her mother appeared at ease now. Her arms were relaxed in front of her. Her fingers were comfortably laced. As she began to walk towards her, a smile was even developing, a rather serene and knowing one.

Coming close, Carol raised a hand to nudge a wave from her daughter's temple. How many times had she performed that simple gesture since Tanya was just an adorable curly-haired toddler? A toddler, she mused. God more than twenty years had passed since then? Impossible. After her birth, it was almost as if she'd blinked and it was time for school and friends, sports and sleepovers. In high school she was as busy as a butterfly, always on the go. Academically, she excelled. Straight A's. Overachiever was the term used in those days. Driven was perhaps what they called it now.

A parent couldn't ask for more. What a perfect child she'd been, never costing them a minute's sleep—until the inevitable happened. The warning signs had always been there, of course, in the model high cheekbones, the gleam of dark long lashed eyes, the full, rosy red lips and lush glossy hair. At fifteen, that promise of beauty began to deliver, along with a figure that made them want to lock her away for a few years.

It wasn't long though before it became evident that there was nothing to fret about because Tanya seemed to have absolutely no interest in boys…at least boys her own age. This was the bombshell she delivered the night following her high school graduation. Carol could still see her running down the stairs, much as she had outside just moments ago, eyes lit up like 4th of July sparklers. She might have been walking on air it was so obvious she was one summer night away from falling in love.

Feeling a little more adjusted now, she tried to catch Tanya's wavering gaze. Carol's smile broadened but not without a hint of melancholy. The innocence she'd caught glimpses of in her daughter even as recent as this past winter was gone now. It was high time. "You look absolutely radiant, honey, do you know that? You're glowing as if, as if—" Carol's head shook, opening the subject was just a bit difficult. "Well, let me put it this way. There's only ever been one man I know of capable of putting those stars in your eyes."

High color poured into Tanya's cheeks. Was it that obvious? She'd showered after Mick left, erasing his scent as well as the flush imprint his body left on hers in the kitchen. She'd used a moisturizer to sooth the scrapes made by his whiskers. She hadn't given her eyes a thought. Her lashes dipped down to veil them. "I…oh, Mom, I…"

"Relax, Tanya. The minute I saw you step outside, I knew Mick was back in your life."

"I wanted so badly to tell you over the phone, but I—" On the verge of tears, her voice broke.

Because it tore Carol up inside to see her daughter so distraught over something that now seemed so senseless, she immediately took hold of her shoulders. "Oh honey, it's all right. It's all right. We'll work it out this time. Don't worry."

The comment set frustration ablaze. "Work what out, Mom? Why does anything have to be worked out? Please, tell me what you and Dad have against him. I think it's about time I know, don't you?"

When her mother only held her gaze with troubled eyes and a loss for words, Tanya held out her hand, turning the ring right side up. "Well, it doesn't matter anyway because whether you and Dad like it or not, I'm going to marry him."

Looking down at the ring, Carol gasped, though it shouldn't have come as a shock, she supposed. The hand that flew to her heart folded and clenched. A sign of mixed emotions. "Well, perhaps that will help. And, oh my goodness Tanya, what a beautiful diamond! Just look at the clarity." She laughed, hugging her, blinking back tears. "I'm so happy for you. Believe it or not, I'd hoped it would work out this way."

Despite some sense of relief, Tanya chuckled derisively and dropped her head in her hands. She dragged her palms across her damp cheeks so hard her eyes began to slant. "Oh, Mom, Mom, Mom, you have me so confused. First of all, whatever possessed you to call Mick the night of the storm? Were you trying to—"

Carol quickly silenced her daughter with a raised hand. "Let's not get into that right now. Your father's waiting, and please, Tanya, until I say otherwise, that phone call stays between us."

She wanted to get into it now. Right now. She wanted this over and done with, off her mind for good. But rather than press on with her mother alone, she realized it would be more prudent to deal with both of them at the same time. Besides, as she half expected, her mother wasn't the problem.

Game on then, Daddy dearest. She refused to be browbeaten by her overbearing father any longer. That seventeen year old goody two-shoes was long gone, and she wasn't about to run away whimpering with her tail between her legs to do his bidding. Well, considering she'd lied and sneaked around that entire summer, that wasn't exactly the way it went down, but that was beside the point. This time things were going to be different. This time she was ready for him and fully prepared to do whatever it took to defend the honor of the man she loved. Oh no, this time he would be messing with the wrong chickadee.

Planting her hands on her hips, Tanya's jaw worked as she stepped out into the hallway and looked towards the staircase. She could hear him rummaging about the kitchen and knew he would be getting impatient by now. Twisting the band of her ring, she hid the diamond from view again. "How do you think he's going to take it?" Not that it mattered anymore, not in the least. Little did he know, the tenacity she'd inherited from him was about to be returned tenfold.

Carol stepped from the room to join her. The look she gave her didn't offer much hope. "I wish I knew, Tanya, but maybe you should wait and tell him after he's had his lunch. He's always more agreeable on a full stomach."

Hand in hand, the two women started down the hall, presenting a united front. At the top of the stairs, by unspoken agreement, they paused to mentally prepare themselves, each in their own way. A look passed between them as their fingers tightened.

"Just remember, I'm on your side this time," her mother promised.

Jim Morgan towered in the kitchen doorway, an impressive 6'2" with the shoulders of a linebacker. His face was boldly attractive for several reasons; good bone structure, olive skin tone with tight pores, even features and flat, perfectly formed ears. His thick-lashed eyes were a steely blue, darker than his wife's, lighter than his daughter's. A man with strong opinions and firm beliefs, his well-shaped lips tended to curl as often with distaste as they did with humor. There was nice body in his thick brown hair and so far no thinning at the crown. Feeling pretty lucky about that, he didn't let the gray sprinkles bother him much. His waistline wasn't exactly trim but he was content with the fact that one week shy of turning fifty-nine, he was able to look down and still see his belt buckle, especially when his two food vices were sweets and beer.

He occasionally wondered if his doctor made him choose one over the other—well, he wasn't about to let that happen anyway and figured as long as he consumed in moderation and played golf on a regular basis, the calories would burn well enough. It was early in the day for a beer but since he was on vacation, he decided to be on vacation from moderation as well. Turning the bottle in his hand, he checked the dietary info on the label. Not that he gave two figs but at the pace his ladies were crossing the living room, he had some time to kill. He looked up as they came walking around the leather chairs. "If you two move any slower, it will be time for supper."

"Sorry, we were just chatting," his wife explained, wondering if her voice sounded unusually high.

Tanya was trying not to over-react to the sight of Mick's beer in her father's hand. There had to be two six-packs in the refrigerator. She should have told him to take them home.

"I've never seen this beer before. It's good. What is it, one of those new fancy microbrews?"

"Actually, it is Dad. We serve it at the pub now. I thought you might like it."

"I do. I'd also like a sandwich to go with it if we could speed things up a bit here." He bent at the waist to lock eyes with his daughter. His were twinkling.

"Okay, okay," she shouldered past him. "You know you had to reach past the sandwiches to get to the beer," she couldn't resist chiding. "You could have helped yourself."

"Well, I was trying to be polite and wait for you two, but I'm wasting away as we speak."

"Sit. Eat." Tanya pushed the refrigerator door closed with her bare foot and placed the small platter of sandwiches in the middle of the table. She'd set the table before they arrived using the new summery placemats she'd purchased that came with matching napkins. "There's ham and cheddar for you, tuna for mom and turkey for me. but I cut them all in half in case we want to share. I already put the mustard on," she pointed out, seeing him lifting the edge of the roll to check.

"I made lemonade, Mom, if you're looking for something to drink," Tanya said to her from the other side of the open fridge door. "And, if you could hand me the pasta salad and pickles there on the middle shelf..."

Tanya took one large and one very small bowl from her mother and heard the diamond clink against glass. Their eyes met.

"What can I get you to drink, Tanya? Are you having lemonade too?" her mother wanted to know.

Tanya thought her attempt to sound normal sounded very abnormal. "Um, sure, yeah that's fine." She couldn't imagine her stomach being able to handle anything but she was going to have to try. Actually, it immediately started to churn at the thought of processing lemonade. "Ah, no, on second thought, Mom, I'm just going to stick with water. I have a glass. I'll just get it from the door.

"There, I guess that's everything." Tanya took her seat at the table. She knew she sounded unnecessarily winded but there was nothing she could do about it. She scooted in her chair. It would all be over soon, she kept telling herself. She smiled at her mother across the table. Her mother smiled back. Both cheerful expressions were as phony as a three-dollar bill—and then there was silence.

Jim Morgan heard the seconds tick by on the kitchen wall clock. He heard a drop of water hit the drain in the sink behind him. He heard a car pull into the Grayson's driveway next door, the door slam, and the Lavallette fire whistle go off. Usually, in the presence of these two, he was lucky to hear himself think, especially if they hadn't seen each other in awhile. He spooned another mound of pasta salad on his plate, lifted his sandwich and glanced from one quiet female to the other as he bit into the roll. He never saw such wooden faces. In the midst of chewing, he managed to squeeze a question out of the corner of his mouth. "Did somebody die or something?"

"No, no," Carol reached for some pickles and nearly knocked her lemonade over.

"No, Dad. Nobody died." Tanya glowered at the question and at the same time sent her napkin flying to the floor with a misplaced elbow.

Knowing something was up, Jim took another hefty bite of his sandwich and swerved his gaze between the two again.

"So, how is Nan doing? Is her ankle healing properly?" It seemed to take Tanya forever to think of a safe topic to discuss.

"She played all nine holes last week against doctor's orders," her father replied gruffly.

"And you let her?"

"No smarty-pants. I didn't let her. Your mother and I were out for the day. Lord only knows what she's up to now."

"She sends her love, Tanya, and said she hopes you are having a good summer and having great success with Paradise. She enjoyed the pictures you sent and said the pub looks beautiful. She especially loved the waterfall and those glazed pots you decided on for the palm trees."

"Oh, I'm glad. Mmm," Tanya nodded, swallowing. "I get a lot of compliments on those. I thought you guys might want to rest this afternoon and we'll go there for dinner. It looks especially pretty at night."

"Naturally," her father answered. "I want to see for myself if this Paradise was worth that major dent in my finances."

"Jim, that's unfair. Tanya invested the same amount from the money my mother left her."

"Did I say otherwise?"

"Well no, but you make it sound like somebody forced your decision to renovate the bar. I remember when Tanya proposed the idea, you agreed with her that it was time."

"I did, and I have no regrets. Particularly since the place is doing so well. Can't a man grumble a bit?" Sprinkling his eyes with humor, he looked to his daughter for support. "Boy, I make one wrong move and she's on me like a snapping turtle."

Watching him fork up the last of his salad, Tanya managed a limp smile. "I can't wait for you to see the pub, Dad. I think you'll be pleased."

"Well, if that critique was anything to go by, I'll be more than pleased. *The Morgan's create Paradise in Seaside,*" he stated aloud, quoting the headline of the article. "How was business this past week? I've been out of touch."

"Steady. Good actually," Tanya answered. "Last weekend we broke our record. I was going to call you but wanted to give you the good news in person."

Impressed, it showed on his face as he picked up his beer.

"Well, it is peak season," she reminded him. Her nerves were ready to snap, crackle or pop. She could hear the strain coming from her own voice and could no longer sit still in agonizing suspense. "So, how about some of that cinnamon cake?" She rose to start clearing the table.

Her father latched onto her hand. "What's the hurry? I was just thinking about having the other half of your turkey—" he stopped there, brows gathering, and raised her hand palm side up to see why something sharp should be poking the pad of his finger. Seeing the diamond, his gaze flew to her face. "What is this, Tanya? This looks like an engagement ring." Jim Morgan eyed his daughter who for some reason remained speechless. His attention veered swiftly to his wife. "What's going on here? What do you know about this, Carol?"

"I...I didn't know. Not until..."

"Mick Leighton and I are engaged to be married, Dad." There, she said it and was sorry she allowed herself to glimpse his reaction before walking over to the counter with the platter of leftover sandwiches. Initially, his expression wiped clean as a slate then began to alter in a hideous display of outrage. She thought she could hear his emotions roar while the news settled. Blinded by tears, she felt for the knife and poised it above his favorite cinnamon cake.

"Over my dead body will this marriage ever take place!" Slapping his hands on the table, he rose with such force the chair toppled over and banged onto the floor with a sharp crack.

The knife fell from Tanya's trembling hand and clattered on the counter. Spinning around, she cried out. She never believed his anger would turn violent but looking at him now, she couldn't be sure. "Oh God! Mom, please!"

Quickly, Carol rounded the table and took her husband's arms in a firm grasp. They were stiff with rage. "Jim, get hold of yourself. You're scaring the life out of her." She watched his breath labor in and out while Tanya remained the target of his unyielding glare.

Suddenly, Jim's fiery gaze jumped to incriminate his wife. "You knew about this, didn't you?"

"Not until we arrived."

By sheer force of will, Tanya stopped her tears from falling. Father or no father, she refused to allow him to do this to her again. She was a good daughter. The best of daughters! He had no right. But it was just as she feared, no worse than she feared. "Will someone please explain to me why I mention Mick's name and you act as if I've committed some kind of crime? I want to know and I want to know now!"

"He's scum! Just like his father! There's your answer!"

"Jim! Stop it!"

"Marry him and you'll be making the biggest mistake of your life!"

"If you think that, then you don't know him at all. He's a wonderful man, and he's wonderful to me. If you would just—"

"Are you sleeping with him?" her father bellowed. "Here? In my house?"

"Jim!" Carol tried to steer him out of the room and found his taut structure as deep-rooted as a California redwood.

"Yes! Yes! I'm sleeping with him! We love each other! For God sakes, Dad, I'm twenty-six years old!"

He barked a loud laugh. "It makes no difference how old you are if you're naïve as you can be! As soon as he tires of you, he'll be on to some other sweet thing. That's the way the Leighton's operate!"

"You're wrong. He loves me! We've been in love for years!"

"The Leighton men love women, plural, not singular! How can you live in this town and not know that?"

"Stop it you two! Stop it! There will be no more screaming in this house. Do you understand?" Carol's eyes bored steadily into her husband's. "Tanya, will you leave us alone please."

More than eager to abide, she gave her father one last baleful look and fled from the room.

"You're going to lose her, Jim. You can't control her feelings and she loves him. You're going to force her to make a choice and mark my words, it won't be you."

His anguished gaze raced over her features. "This is your fault." Tearing away from her, he strode to the sink and stared out of the window. All he could see was red.

His words found their mark, but she'd done nothing wrong and her only regret was for Tanya's sake. Carol walked to the kitchen doorway, stepped through and looked around the living room to make sure she wasn't within earshot.

Chilled, her arms folded for warmth. When her body turned, her gaze landed outside the patio door. All the colors of summer were there basking in the sunlight; blue sky, green leaves, red geraniums. A breeze flirted with the ruffled edge of the yellow and white striped patio umbrella. Someone was running a lawn mower. Carol envied all who were out there enjoying this beautiful summer day. Wishing she were one of them, she walked over to stand beside her husband.

"If you're going to throw stones, you're aiming in the wrong direction. I realize I'm only wasting my breath by repeating this, but I was never unfaithful to you. Michael and I shared one meal together and that was merely by coincidence."

"So you've said. Sorry, but I find that impossible to believe."

To ease his own guilt, he chose to doubt her just as he had twelve years ago. If that's how he wanted it, fine, but under no circumstances would she allow him to shovel the blame her way. Hurt dulled her blue eyes and burned her throat raw. "You should be sorry! Sorry for having a fling with that cheap floozy. Don't!" she grated, seeing he was about to deny it again. She had no idea if he'd ever slept with that bleached, overblown, bubblehead bartender he'd hired but it didn't matter. Carol had walked in on them just before closing one night and saw the look on Jim's face, the smile the woman was using to warm him up as they stood closely together behind the bar. He'd been growing distant, and Carol sensed something was going on between them. Her surprise appearance that night had been intentional, to catch them unaware. He swore it hadn't gone any further than a flirtation. To this day, she wasn't sure if she believed him, but their relationship had suffered for it as if it had. The next day the woman quit or he fired her. Carol was never sure. The damage had already been done.

One night, a few months later, their relationship still strained, she was in desperate need of a shoulder to cry on and arranged to meet a girlfriend for dinner and pour out her troubles. The mix up in dates left Carol dining alone until Mick's father, Michael walked in. They knew each other, of course, but not well. They exchanged a cordial greeting and he took a seat at a nearby table. It had been a stormy November weeknight, and they turned out to be the only two people dining in the Point Pleasant restaurant. Michael had caught her eye and made a few jokes about that, making her smile against her mood and will. Eventually, it became awkward trying to avoid each other. After a short time, Michael pointed that out and asked if he could join her. The evening turned out to be surprisingly pleasant and perfectly innocent except for the sharing of secrets. They opened up to each other quite naturally, two lost souls in the midst of marital misery, pining for their partners. That's all there was to it. In parting, he'd kissed her on the cheek, wished her luck and each thanked the other for listening. She had no idea Jim knew the owner of that restaurant and that the next day the man would run to him with the news.

At times throughout that following year, Carol was often tempted to call Michael and thank him for inadvertently saving their marriage. Turning the tables on Jim's alleged affair, certainly had revived it. Jim was so jealous, he walked around the house for months, half the time growling like a bear with a sore paw, the other half, showering her with love and affection.

They'd managed to work their way back from those crossroads without ever mentioning them again, until that night Tanya came running down the stairs all aglow, sighing the name *Leighton* as if she'd already fallen under his spell. Though Jim forbade the relationship, deep down Carol had always known it was just a matter of time.

Thinking it was time they got past the past, Carol picked up a cranberry dishtowel, folded it neatly on the glossy granite and gave it a pat. "You know this isn't about us anymore, Jim. It's about two young people who love each other very much and have waited a long time to be together."

He gave her a sneer under eyes rich with scorn. "Of course, you would say that. You're as blind as she is, blinded by a cocky smile and a swagger. I can't believe you want that type of husband for our daughter. I've known all three Leighton men and they're all alike. Their actions have been the main source of gossip around here as far back as I can remember. Michael senior and junior were both divorced by their wives because they couldn't keep their hands off other women—and other men's wives." He shot her a meaningful glare.

Fed up with his incessant high-handedness and closed-mindedness, his judgmental jargon based on nothing but rumor, she gave him a look of disgust. "Sometimes you have absolutely no idea what you blabber about. Mick's grandmother died quite young from complications with pneumonia. Perhaps after that, his grandfather dated but you certainly can't fault him for that. And, for your information, Michael was not the only guilty party in their marriage. Did you know Joanna was engaged before she even met Michael? Her fiancé stood her up at the alter. Obviously distraught, she left California to come to New Jersey and stay with a cousin who had a summer home in the Park. She met Michael, and they fell in love, but it wasn't until her ex came looking for her that he found out she'd married him on the rebound. As it turned out, she was already expecting Mick, but Michael never felt sure she wouldn't have gone back to him if she hadn't been pregnant. The whole thing ended up driving a wedge between them that just kept widening over the years. You know it might help if you actually knew the facts about that family before condemning them."

"Fine, then what about what I saw with my own eyes? You can't discount that! By the time Mick turned sixteen, he was running wild. Booze parties, girls hot to trot for him no matter which way he turned. Some of the stories that crossed the boards, you wouldn't want to know about. When Tanya started working with me up there, I used to cringe every time he came near her. Forget about you and me. It has nothing to do with that. The daughter we raised is way out of his league and mark my words, Carol, I will do everything in my power to make her see that."

"Oh, for heaven's sake, Jim. Listen to yourself. I seem to recall some pretty eye opening tales about you in your heyday, and I still married you!"

"What tales? When?" He reared back, scowling thickly.

"Actually, it was the night of our engagement party. Heavy drinking started a few of your old high school buddies' tongues wagging, and they began a trip down memory lane about all the pranks you guys pulled and the fun times you all had. Apparently, they thought this one particular story was old enough news and just too funny not to share. According to them, you once made two dates on the same night and both girls found out about it. After a roll in the hay with the first one, supposedly your steady, she ran off with your clothes and drove to the other girl's house and dumped them on her front lawn." Carol stopped when he closed his eyes and turned his head. Her brows lifted. "Need I go on?"

"It's not the same!" His gaze started to return to hers but his pride would only take him halfway. "When I fell in love with you, that was it for me. You were everything. That's what I want for her."

Carol raised her hands in supplication. "I believe that's how Mick feels about Tanya, and they are both old enough now to be sure what they want. Why don't you give him a chance? Get to know him. Trust Tanya's judgment. If it's still Michael you're mad at, whether you want to believe this or not, he was nothing but kind and comforting to me. I was hurt and vulnerable, but not once did he try to take advantage."

Blanching, Jim shoved away from the counter. "If he was so wonderful, why didn't you leave me for him after his divorce. Check with your daughter, maybe he's still available."

"Jim, where are you going?" Carol rushed after his hard, heavy strides through the living room. She'd come to Michael's defense strictly to make a point and in the process bruised her husband's ego and only made matters worse. Planting another seed of doubt was the last thing she'd intended. "Jim, wait!"

"I need some air."

At the front door, she caught his arm.

"Leave me be, Carol!" he shrugged her off.

"Jim, I…please, you misunderstood."

"Do you think he's going to look for Mick?"

Carol spun around. Tanya was standing on the landing. Her pale, tear streaked face was nearly her undoing. "I—oh, Tanya." Hearing a car motor rev, she spun around again and watched the Cadillac reverse out of the driveway. "I don't know," she looked back, forth, then back again. "Maybe that would be for the best. Don't you think?"

"I agree," Tanya replied but still gave a negligent shrug. "Whatever. I'm packing." Turning, she went back up to her room.

"What? Oh dear. No, no packing." Carol rushed to follow her, feeling like a peace activist caught between enemy lines. Coming to an abrupt halt as she entered her daughter's bedroom, she formed a steeple with her fingers and raised them to her chin. A suitcase lay open upon the bed, and it wasn't the size of a weekender. She watched Tanya stride about the room in controlled fury, gathering and tossing.

"I have a lot of my things at Mick's house already but not enough to last as long as you'll be here."

Carol closed her eyes, feeling them burn. "Oh honey, please don't do this. At least give your father time to get used to the idea. You've only just told him."

Tanya gave her mother a long-suffering look. With one big lump of hurt lodged in her throat, it was hard to even speak. "Mother, his opinion has not wavered in eight years. What makes you think a miracle will suddenly occur to make him have a change of heart?" Her mouth curved with disdain as she folded over a stack of camis and placed them in her suitcase. "Mick is scum?" She looked at her mother again but this time her tormented gaze had hardened, clearly stating she meant business. "That is unforgivable to me and I won't stand for it."

Carol wrung her hands and came further into the room. "Honey, I know. I understand, but—"

"Do you remember this mother?" Tanya pulled the long silver chain out from beneath her top and walked over to her. She dangled the heart in front of her mother's eyes. Tanya half smiled. "The chain isn't the original, obviously. It's mine. Mick gets a little embarrassed if anyone sees the heart. He wants to buy me a new one, you know something nice from a jeweler to replace this one, but I keep warning him I won't wear it. This is the heart from the grab bag barrel that I picked out when I was five years old. Do you remember? From his grandfather's shop?"

Her mother reached out, letting it rest against her fingertips. Looking at the little scarred and weathered charm with its tiny floral impression in the center, the years rolled back. "My goodness, Tanya, I do remember. I had no idea you still had this." Carol also remembered how Mick used to join them nearly every afternoon on the boardwalk, acting as though their appearance, or rather Tanya's appearance, was the highlight of his day. She didn't know much about young boys but thought it was a little unusual, yet quite endearing, that he should be so taken with her. He'd always treated her like a little princess. Neither had any siblings. It made sense when she thought of it that way.

She knew they remained boardwalk friends of sorts through the years but part of what Jim said was true. Working in his grandfather's shop at such a young age and roaming about all day in an atmosphere that attracted all types of characters, some with questionable morals, Mick matured on a faster track, always seeming a bit wiser to the world than most boys his age. Then there was the Marines. Four years. Carol never imagined he'd come back and be interested in a seventeen-year-old girl, even if it was Tanya. Obviously she'd been living under a rock with a bag over her head.

"Are you trying to tell me, you've been in love with Mick since you were five years old?"

"I know that sounds crazy but sometimes I do feel that way. And I know he feels the same. What we have is so strong, so…I don't know… amazingly intense. At least, it seems that way." She shook her head. "Maybe I am a little naïve. Maybe everyone in love feels like this, but I don't think so, Mom. I'm so incredibly happy that losing what we have now absolutely terrifies me. It hasn't been easy to get where we are, and I won't let Dad ruin it for us. You might want to tell him that." Tanya slid the heart back into place.

"I already have, Tanya. You know he only wants what's best for you. He's your Dad. It's a father's job to protect his daughter." No doubt because they have first-hand knowledge of what they're protecting their daughter from, Carol paused to consider the amusing irony. Still, even though she was on Tanya's side, she knew all too well the risks of marrying a handsome man.

"You know yourself that Mick is extremely attractive. His looks have always lured women." Carol thought back on that evening with Michael. Yes, there certainly was something about the Leighton men—that smile, those shoulders, definitely something about those shoulders. Carol caught herself, tripping over her untoward thoughts in an effort to get back to her point. Just because she'd honored her marriage vows that night didn't mean she was blind to Michael's charms. "Your father—" she paused again, this time with a huff of impatience, waiting for Tanya to stop chuckling.

"And what am I, chopped liver? My father what—doesn't think I have what it takes to hold on to him? Keep him from straying? Gee thanks for the vote of confidence, Dad." Punctuating each question with the pull and slam of a drawer, she posed another. "Doesn't he think I'm smart enough to know when a man is really sincere, or when he's just mouthing platitudes and using me for a good time in bed?"

Oh, heavens to Betsy. Carol's gaze bounced around the pretty pale lavender walls of her daughter's bedroom. Where was a good distraction when you needed one? She liked to think she and Tanya had developed an almost *best friend* relationship over the past few years. Sex was a topic they steered clear of though. With her own mother, she avoided the subject like the plague. She just assumed Tanya would continue to do the same. So this is how it's going to be. Young people today, they were entirely too uninhibited and then had the nerve to speak about it.

Collecting her favorite perfumes and lotions from the top of her dresser, Tanya caught her mother's eye in the mirror. "I'm fully aware that Mick is no saint. I know he's had lovers. Many...and I'd be lying if I said it doesn't matter. I'm only human—and so is Mick. He'll be thirty-three in October for heaven's sake. I'd find the reverse rather suspect, wouldn't you? What does Dad think Dan Wakefield is a virgin? If so, I believe he's operating under a huge misconception." It was a silly notion but it made for good argument. She made a mental note to raise the issue. That is, if she ever spoke to her father again.

The mention of Dan Wakefield had Carol seeking the nearest resting place. She slumped onto the chaise, burying her face in her hands. That's all they needed was Dan showing up.

"Oh, Mom," Tanya sighed and dropped an armful of clothing on the bed to go to her. She knelt down. "I'm sorry. I don't want to upset you or put you in the middle. I know Dad would rather have someone like Dan for a son-in-law. He's got that slick CEO thing going on, he plays a good game of golf, he's a great conversationalist, if you like hearing him brag about all his worldly adventures. That night we went out for dinner, he treated the waiter like a second class citizen and kept talking about buying his own jet and flying me to Dubai, like I was supposed to be impressed or something. I'm sorry but I found him to be a pompous jerk."

"You know what impresses me? Do you know that Mick puts on a free Thanksgiving dinner at The Cove for all the senior citizens in the Park and the Heights every year? And he didn't even tell me. I heard about it from his manager. He said he started it in memory of his grandfather. Do you know how important it is for him to support local farmers and how much he cares about the environment and the island. He gives back to the community in so many ways without expecting or wanting any recognition. Do you know he donates leftover food twice a week to a shelter in Toms River and more often than not delivers it himself? Do you know why the AC is working here today and why the front yard looks so nice?" Emotion gripped her throat and filled her eyes. "I'm so proud of him and proud to be with him, Mom. I feel like he's making me a better person. You and Dad don't know the man he's become. Mick and I parted ways for many years, and I didn't even really know him until these past few months." Tanya covered her mother's hands with her own and smiled. "You'll see."

"Come in." Hoping the tap on his office door was Tanya, Mick looked up at it expectantly and started to rise. Seeing one of his employees poke her head inside, he gave his pants a quick hike and sat back down, all the while doing a good job hiding his disappointment. "What can I do for you, Becca?"

"Sorry to bother you Mick, but I haven't seen Jack today. Will he be coming in?"

"He'll be in at four. Is there a problem?" God he hoped not. He wasn't up to dealing with anyone's problems but his own at the moment. They would have been there for hours by now. Why the hell didn't she call?"

"Not a problem exactly, but I do have a question. Do you have a minute?"

Mick held back a sigh and indicated the chair opposite his desk. "Sure, c'mon in." At least the interruption would take his mind off the blasted silence of his phone.

The waitress left the door partly open since it was nothing personal nor would it take long. She sat down across from her boss and sensing he might not be in the best of moods, got straight to the point. "I was wondering if it would be okay if I take tomorrow off? I know it's a Saturday, but I've already arranged coverage. Dylan said he would work my shift. Classes start up again in a few weeks, and I have all this stuff to do. My mom doesn't want me to wait until the last minute so…"

"That's fine, Becca. I'll let Jack know I've approved it." He didn't know why she couldn't have asked him that from the doorway. Raising his eyes from his computer screen where he'd been monitoring his inbox in case Tanya emailed, he saw Becca's crestfallen expression and realized he'd been unintentionally curt. Knowing she had a tendency to be overly sensitive, he took a breath and willed himself to lighten up. He closed the lid to the laptop, relaxed his shoulders and let his spine conform to the back of the chair. Resting his elbows on the arms, he folded his hands across his midsection. "So, what's your uncle been up to these days? Is he still playing racquetball?"

"Yes, he still plays. I think on Friday mornings and sometimes Sundays. He told me he misses the workouts you used to give him."

Responding to her timid smile, Mick tilted his lips. Now that he knew he never touched Tanya, he supposed he could stand the sight of him again. "Tell him if he's ever looking for a partner to give me a call." The slow swing of his office door drew another hopeful gaze. Once it fully opened, it framed a big man with a score to settle.

Mick's smile leveled. Well, apparently he needn't wait for a phone call. The outcome was being delivered first-hand and Jim Morgan's stark, uncompromising features presented the first clue that the news of their engagement hadn't gone favorably.

"Becca, will you excuse us please?"

The waitress looked over her shoulder to find a rather intimidating figure filling the doorway. The look on the man's face made her gulp. *What was up with this guy*, she wondered, shifting her eyes back to her boss only to find his gaze glued to his imposing visitor, as if he didn't dare let his guard down. “Um, of course,” she murmured, feeling a bit like they were actors playing out a scene. Rising, she walked to the door and said excuse me and thank you to the tall, unsmiling man as he crossed the threshold into the office and stepped to one side to give her room to pass. With a shiver dancing up her spine and an urge to call her uncle, one of Seaside’s finest, Becca hurried back to her customers.

A sitting duck rarely had a chance when a hunter had it in for him. Warily, Mick came to his feet. No greetings or handshakes were exchanged. Tapping the eraser end of a #2 pencil on his desk, he watched Tanya’s father walk across the room giving the lackadaisical appearance of someone out for a Sunday stroll, albeit with a lot on his mind.

Jim Morgan retraced his steps in the same manner. Before closing the door, he peered down the hall. He aimed his thumb in that direction as he returned his attention to the man he’d come to see. “Pretty little thing, that one.” The slant of his mouth boded ill for the onlooker. “Hope I didn’t interrupt anything…important.”

The pause was rife with meaning. Mick’s lashes dropped to shutter his eyes. His blood temperature, chilled from the moment he’d entered, plunged to deep freeze. “She’s the niece of a friend.”

“Is that so? Well, that’s very kind of you to give her a job and all. But then I suppose it’s no hardship having a sweet piece like that under you.”

The #2 pencil flipped into Mick’s fist and snapped in half. “Is that what you came here to talk to me about?”

Pondering the question, Jim reached up to scratch the back of his head. “Well, you know I suppose in a way it is, but there is just this one thing that’s about to drive me nutty, and I’d like to clear that up first if you don’t mind.” The chair the waitress had just vacated was given a ruthless shove. With fists at the ready, he braced them on the edge of the desk. “I’ve got one question for you loverboy and you better start praying to your maker you have the right answer. Have you been tested for AIDS?”

During his stint in the service, Mick had gotten into a couple of brawls overseas. On one occasion, the guy in front of him ducked and a meaty fist plowed between his eyes, making the room spin and blur. Mick thought if he ever had the choice of reliving that painful experience or hear Tanya's father ask him that question again, he'd choose the plowing fist.

"I had the test done last January," Mick answered. "It was negative. Tanya knows. You could have asked her." Somehow he knew his voice was going to dredge up the hell he'd gone through waiting for that phone call.

Jim used the riveting effect of his steely blue eyes to verify the truth of that statement. Satisfied, he hung his head and let relief wash through him.

With his mind spewing obscenities, Mick took a turn around the narrow space behind him. He couldn't say he blamed the man one stinking bit for wanting to make sure Tanya was safe. If he had a daughter—still it sailed the wind right out of him and gave him a pretty good indication what he was up against. When he stopped his pacing, the back of his leather chair was used as a means to steady his hands, and to keep them from doing something he was bound to regret.

"You're a lucky man, Leighton." Jim straightened and filled his broad chest with air. "Now we can get down to the business of this engagement, which is nothing but a farce the way I see it."

Mick's jaw visibly clenched. His gut did the same, as if it had taken a hard blow. The man hadn't laid a finger on him, and he felt all bruised and bloodied. Only because it mattered so much. If it didn't, he'd tell him to go take a flying fuck and kiss his ass on the way back. Mick swallowed the words before it was too late to stop them and forced himself to stay focused. "Tanya means the world to me, and I believe the feeling is mutual. I'd like to know why that's a problem for you."

The pasted on sneer deepened. "C'mon, Mick. I know you've been hot on my daughter's trail for years. I'm only surprised you had the decency to wait until she finished high school to go after her the first time. But I threw a hitch in your plans back then, didn't I? I managed to get her off to college safe and sound, and now I suppose I have only myself to blame. I allowed her to stay up here on her own and left you a clear field to make your move. So, you finally got what you wanted, but don't insult my intelligence or hers by pretending you know anything about commitment." His index finger jabbed the airspace between them. "I guarantee you'll be screwing around before the ink dries on your marriage license."

He wanted to deck him. His fingers actually itched to wipe that high and mighty smirk off his face. More than likely the man had done a number on Tanya before coming here and convinced her she was making a mistake. That's probably why she hadn't called. Without her… without her…he couldn't get beyond the black void. If her father destroyed what he'd finally managed to build between them, he was afraid he might kill him with his bare hands.

Keeping a tight reign on the hostility charging through his system, he came around the desk and looked him dead in the eye. "You're absolutely right about one thing. I have been hot on her trail for years because that's how long I've been in love with her. I don't know how, or when or why you've formed this opinion of me, but that's where you're wrong. Tanya happens to mean more to me than anyone or anything on this earth, and I swear that is not a load of bullshit. There isn't a man alive who could love her more or take better care of her. If you'd left us the hell alone eight years ago, you would have seen that by now."

They were profound words, fervently stated. They gave Jim pause for a brief moment, but that's all. "You can stand there and make pledges and vows until your well runs dry, but it won't do you a damn bit of good. Let me just cut straight to the chase here, Leighton, and wrap this up all neat and tidy for you. In my book, you're just not good enough for my daughter, and there is no doubt in my mind she'll come to her senses and realize that when Dan Wakefield arrives. In case she neglected to tell you, and I can see by the look on your face that she has, they've been seeing each other when she comes home to Florida every winter. Dan happens to own a very successful international firm. He's smart, rich, and has friends in high places—unlike the places where you and your tattooed losers hang out, if you get my drift. He not only thinks the world of Tanya, he can give her the world. You'll never measure up, Leighton, so why don't you just let her go now and save yourself from looking like a fool." With one fierce, final glare, Jim pushed the chair out of his way and strode towards the door.

When the latch clicked behind him, Mick let out a roar and cleared his desk with one swipe.

Chapter 13

All of the windows were dark except the one in the den where the TV created flickering illumination. Tanya slowed the Jeep to a stop in front of the house and hurried out. Running up the porch steps, she felt the vibration of loud music thumping through the walls. The hard pounding of her heart in her ears blended in until she could no longer distinguish between the two. The door was unlocked. She let herself in and proceeded to the rear of the first floor.

She assumed he had on a music video station or something. Not so. Oddly, he was watching a baseball game. The sound was set on mute while classic Stones blared through the stereo speakers. The next thing she noticed was the glowing tip of a cigarette. The sight of it was no surprise. She'd smelled it the minute she walked in the door. Her gaze rushed to take in the rest.

He was wearing his two favorite things. A pair of worn out jeans and a NY Yankees cap, parked backwards. There was a bottle of liquor on the end table and an ounce or two in the tumbler dangling over an upraised knee. He didn't budge from his slouched comfort on the couch when she walked over to the wall unit to turn off the music.

Simultaneously, the remote clicked, killing the picture as well as their only source of light. Into the darkness came a low-pitched slur, thick with insolence. "Well, well, well, if it isn't daddy's little girl sneaking out to visit the big bad wolf again."

Tanya felt for the switch on a nearby standing lamp and turned it on. More atmosphere than watts escaped through the oatmeal shade, but it didn't really matter. She'd already seen enough to know his day hadn't gone any better than hers. Taking in the whole sorry scene, she approached the couch, imagining the awful things her father must have said to him.

"No, I did not sneak out," she stated for the record. "I had dinner with my mother at the pub then I took her home. I told her I was coming over here to see you. I've been trying to reach you for hours. I left you several messages." His cell was sitting on the end table next to the whiskey bottle. She picked it up and saw that he'd received all of them. "Why haven't you been answering your phone?"

"Didn't hear it." Bleary eyes raked her body. A snicker followed. She looked sexy. Classy sexy. So what the frig else was new. Sometimes he wanted to hate her for growing up to look like something guys conjured up to jerk off in their dreams.

Tanya watched the last of his drink slide down his throat and vowed her father would pay dearly for this. The pint of whiskey was nearly gone. It couldn't have been full when he started, could it? "Oh Mick, what are you doing?"

He flicked the cigarette over a nearby ashtray and appeared to be giving the question some thought. When he spoke, it was with alcohol-drenched arrogance. "Let's see, what am I doing?" Tossing some answers around, Mick took one last satisfying drag on the butt, relaxed back and sent smoke rings rising to the ceiling. By the time he'd finished the exhale, he realized the truth of it all just might be staring him smack dab in the face. Seemed like it was going to be his destiny, so why fight it? "Oh, the things I like best I guess," he admitted, and went on to list them. "Having a smoke, getting high, thinking about you—this morning in particular."

It felt like a week had passed since then. Tanya tiredly rubbed her brow, dragged her hand down her cheek and shrugged. "Okay, I give, what about this morning?"

"When you let me screw you in the kitchen."

She stiffened, watching him reach up to tap the bill of the cap. It fell forward into his waiting palm. He tossed it aside with one hand while the other reached out to wrap her thigh and pull her forward. His strength was surprising considering the condition he appeared to be in.

The smile he wore was pure Mick at his brazen best. Conveniently, the juncture of her thighs met him at eye level. Cupping his hands around her bottom, he drew her close and groaned as his face pressed against her belly. He raised her shirt to french kiss her navel.

"Hot damn you were good, baby," he drawled. "You're always good. Best *I* ever had. So tell me," he tilted his head back to look up at her, "You ever let this Dan Wakefield hump you against a kitchen wall?"

She was reminded of a wounded animal, stripped of pride and looking for someone to finish him off. She was about to oblige. Clutching his arms, she steered them away from her hips and drove him against the back of the couch. "I did not come over here to listen to this. If I want to be harassed and badgered, I can get plenty of that at home." She stepped around his legs to leave. "Give me a call after you've cleaned up your act," she threw over her shoulder.

Mick shot off the couch. Snaking an arm around her waist, he caught her from behind. "Answer me."

The tortured depth of the demand softened her instantly. Wearily, she rested her head against his shoulder. Dan is one of his golf buddies. My father pressured me into going out with him, so I did, once. Twice actually but we were with my parents the first time. There was no chemistry between us. I felt nothing and that's exactly what happened, nothing. My father is only using him to cause trouble between us. Clearly it's working."

Mick rubbed his face in her curls wanting to lock all the doors and throw away the keys. "Your father doesn't think I'm good enough for you. I started drinking when I realized he's right. You deserve better."

"What?" Tanya twisted around. The mask of false bravado was beginning to slip, unveiling a pair of heavy-lidded, bloodshot, eyes dulled by defeat. His face bore all the signs of a disheartened man who'd finally given up a long hard fight. She took it between her hands. "Oh Mick." She'd never seen him like this. Knowing him the way she did, she wouldn't have thought it possible for another man to break his spirit, his pride. It made her realize just how important it was to him to have her father's approval, his blessing. All these years, it must have been weighing on his mind. Damn her father was going to pay. "Don't you dare go there after I have been singing your praises to my mother all day."

"Really?"

Tanya bore some of his weight, steadied him and pressed her lips together to keep from smiling. He looked so drunkenly, adorably, skeptically pleased. Poor man, he was desperate for the smallest crumb. "Yeah, and you're very lucky I didn't bring her here with me tonight. I was so anxious to see if you were okay, I nearly did. You would have ruined all my hard work."

He leaned on her heavily, held her so tightly she wanted to cry. "I'm sorry."

"Oh Mick, no, no. I'm sorry. I swear I don't know why my father has it in for you. What happened? Will you tell me?" She felt rather than saw the slight shake of his head.

"I have to kiss you," he slurred and took her head between his hands. "I know I smell like an ashtray but I have to."

"Yes," she nodded.

His hand glided up beneath her hair to cup the base of her skull. Anticipating one of his hot, mind-blowing kisses, Tanya raised her lips, but when his mouth descended, the impact was in direct contrast to the steely bands locking her against him. There was the lightest pressure, a rubbing sensation and then pow. It wasn't the whisky or smoke she tasted but every last ounce of soul-deep love pouring from him into her. It went on and on and on, exposing feelings down to the raw.

Mick finally lost his staggering balance and dragging her with him, they fell as one onto the couch. "Stay with me," he whispered, molding her against him with sweeping hands too needy to be called rough.

"I want to Mick, but…"

"Just for an hour."

"It's late. I told my mother I wouldn't be long."

"A half hour then. Please." His fingers located a button and slipped it through.

Upstairs, after the loving, Tanya lay on her stomach in the crook of his arm. His eyes were closed but she knew he was awake by the lazy circles being drawn on her back. She turned into him, resting her chin on his chest. Her fingers played in the soft whorls of hair. "Are you going to tell me what he said to you?"

"I'll sum it up for you. He hates my guts. I told him how much I love you and he didn't bat an eye. I wanted to slug him for not believing me."

"He seems to be dwelling on your reputation."

"I know, I know," he sighed. "I suppose I had one at one time. You were just a kid. I can't believe he'd still be holding that against me. To me it seems like another lifetime."

She came up slightly on an elbow. "Mick, you're sure there's nothing he could have heard about? Anything you did, even years ago to make him so…to make him feel this way?"

He raised his head off the pillow an inch to give her a look that said he wasn't happy with the question. "The worst thing I ever did in my life was what I did to you." Mick closed his eyes and ran a hand over his forehead when the room took a spin. "He wouldn't know about that since I'm assuming he never knew we were dating that summer. Unless you told him."

"No, no of course I didn't tell him. That's the last thing he needs to know. Nothing else you can think of?"

Grudgingly, he walked his conscience down memory lane, his tone resentful as he checked off the only things he could think of that might have given her father a bad impression, if he'd heard about them. "I got stoned one night when I was about seventeen but that's as far as I got into drugs. I had a few parties and there was probably a lot of shit going on that shouldn't have been. Yea, and I have a healthy sex drive and had my share over the years. Other than that, I don't know, Tanya," his tone grew more and more agitated as he searched to find the answer. "I guess he could give a rat's ass that I served in the Marines." His head came off the pillow again. "He does know I served, doesn't he? And that I went back and finished college? Maybe I can get a few Brownie points there."

Tanya sensed he was being facetious, or at least somewhat facetious. "He knows you served, and I'll make sure he knows you have your degree, but—"

Just from her tone he could tell she didn't believe any of that would help. "Right, like I said, he could give two shits," he finished her sentence for her. "It doesn't matter. Sounds like he wants Prince Charming Wakefield to give you the fairy tale life anyway. Trips around the world. A house on the Riviera. I don't know. I can't give you anything like that, but I'm doing well, Tanya, and my grandfather left me in good shape. I want to go over everything with you someday. We haven't done that yet, but I'll show you. You have nothing to worry about. We're good Tanya, I promise you, we're good."

"Mick, Mick, stop." To make him, she pressed her index finger against his lips. "None of that concerns me, and I find it hard to believe it would drive my father to this extreme, especially when he knows you are the sole owner of The Cove and Leighton's and that they are both in a class by themselves. Trust me, he still reads the local papers and knows what's going on up here. No, it didn't seem to be about money or success when he blew—when he objected to our engagement."

Mick peered down at her, having heard what she started to say. "Yeah, well who knows, maybe he could read my mind every time I looked at you on the boardwalk, and he just hates me for that reason alone."

"Mmm," Tanya smiled in response. "You do say a lot with those eyes."

His jaw finally pulled up with a smile. A dimple appeared. "Okay, so what were my eyes saying when you drove your bike between my legs."

She chuckled deeply. "You mean other than *son of a bitch!*"

"You did that good." Wishing he hadn't poured that last drink, his grinned turned into a grimace.

"You took me by surprise that day. You came out of nowhere and you looked so different in your camouflage with your cropped hair. I think it had been a couple of years since I'd seen you. I wasn't even sure it was you at first. I'm so glad I didn't do any lasting damage." Lightly, she scraped her nails down that pinstripe of hair, smiling wickedly when she felt a muscle jump.

"Oh, you did some lasting damage all right, with these." Feeling better with his eyes closed he kept them that way and used the hand of the arm beneath her to blindly feel for her lips. His thumb brushed across them. "The last time I'd seen you, you were about four inches shorter, all long brown legs with crazy curls down to your butt. It was a shock to see the grown up version. When I grabbed the handlebars and we ended up nose to nose, I took one look at these lips and that was the beginning of the end for me. What were you fifteen?"

"Fourteen, almost fifteen." Once again, the idea that they'd entertained secret fantasies about each other so long ago left her feeling all warm and tingly inside. Anxious to share her thoughts of him that day, Tanya scooted up higher to see his face better. "Do you know, after that happened, I kept dreaming about your arms."

"My arms?" He frowned. "What kind of dreams can you have about arms?"

Supporting her head with her hand, Tanya reached across his chest and smoothed her palm down the far one. "Oh, I don't know," she mused, drifting back to that time of her life. "They looked so muscular, so strong and impressive. I remember watching an old Rambo movie with Lisa and her little brother one night and thinking about you, thinking how his arms reminded me of yours."

The comment made him laugh out loud. "Stallone's arms are like machines. He raised his free arm, and they both gave a look. I fail to see the comparison, but thanks. My ego can use some boosting after the beating I took from your father."

Tanya only half heard him and half smiled. She was still locked into those moments long ago that stood out in her mind. "I think I started to feel a little nervous around you after that day but a little excited at the same time. Of course, I didn't see you again until the following summer."

"Is that why you took off like a scared rabbit and rudely ignored me when I called out to you?"

She gave another husky chuckle. "Probably."

He pulled her head down to meet his lips. "I dream about her mouth and she dreams about my arms. I suppose that's better than nothing." His hand tickled her where it rested above her hip bone. Enjoying the sound of her laughter while she tried to fight him off, he flipped her onto her back and got lost in her smiling eyes. Tracing a finger along her jawline, he looked his fill of her beautiful face and remembered something her father had said. The one and only thing he'd gotten right. *You're a lucky man, Leighton.* It was hardly the way he meant it but truer words were never spoken.

On his way to a kiss, he got another head rush and was forced to detour. Face first, he collapsed into her pillow and made a muffled admission. "I feel like crap. Don't move babe. Just let me lie here for a minute."

Obliging, Tanya removed her hand that was in the process of sliding up and down his spine. She could just imagine the peace and comfort he longed for after a run-in with her father, and she could certainly benefit from the same. What a dreadful day it had been, she thought, yawning

His legs were off to the side but his torso lay heavy across her own. It was a bit of an effort for her to breathe but she would have stayed like this forever if he needed her to. She wanted to run her nails across his scalp as she often did. It relaxed him, but if he was fighting back nausea, he probably didn't want to be touched.

Turning her head, Tanya gazed out at the sky and watched the blinking lights of a jet flying high above the coastline. The sliding door was open to the night sounds. There weren't many at the moment. An occasional bark from the Jack Russell next door. They'd had some good soaking rains throughout the week and the bay was high and active. She could hear the boat rocking, the water lapping. A breeze suddenly drew the drapes against the screen, making them rustle a bit.

They'd rearranged the furniture recently and redecorated the bedroom; new spread and drapes, new wall-to-wall carpet and lamps. They decided against changing the color of the walls. They were Benjamin Moore Navajo white Mick told her and the lack of color, they concluded, was just too easy to work with. With all the new accessories, the décor, at least, looked nothing like it did eight years ago. Regardless, she was afraid that movement of drape against screen would always stir the memory.

Unable to stop herself, Tanya began to envision herself at seventeen on the other side of the door, looking in. In another month, it would be nine years. She did a spot check. There was nothing left of the pain, just a twinge of heartache that might never go away—kind of like the white mark beneath her wrist bone where she'd burned herself on the sheet pan making chocolate chip cookies for her first sleepover. By no means did that minor incident compare, and unless from this day forward, she was destined to live a charmed life, there would be more scars acquired throughout the journey. Some would be visible, some wouldn't. For most people, she imagined the scars within developed from a deeper grief and anguish.

He came up slowly, dropping a kiss on the curve of her breast. "So what are we going to do about this?" He sat on the edge of the bed and looked back at her.

"Mick, do you know more than fifty percent of marriages fail?"

"I did read that, but didn't you see the disclaimer?" Raising his arm, his fingers created a visual for her by forming the blocks of text he pretended to have read. "It said, *This statistic does not apply to anyone who marries in 2013. Couples marrying this year are going to be given a lifetime guarantee of love and happiness.*" His hand lowered as his gaze returned to hers. "It even went so far as to list all the names, and Mick and Tanya Leighton were definitely among them. I saw it with my own eyes."

"Oh my God." Her lips trembled, eyes glittered. Digging in her heels, she shimmied up against the headboard. His pillow came with her, clutched in her arms. "I think that's the most beautiful thing you've ever said to me."

He chuckled and reached back to squeeze her leg. "Well, where the hell were you going with that anyway? Because I know, after all we've been through, you weren't referring to us ending up in the fail category."

Seeing her tuck her thumbnail between her teeth was answer enough. She had a habit of doing that when she was working up the nerve to talk to him about something. "No," he shook his head warningly, looking away from her then back again. "Don't, Tanya. You see, you *are* starting to buy into all his bullshit."

"No, no, I'm not Mick, but I do think it's worth exploring one more time before we take the final step." Her eyes closed beseechingly. "I just want you to be one hundred, no a thousand percent sure that you are ready for a monogamous relationship for the rest of your life. I mean, I know we have this great history between us, and we're so in love, and good in bed and everything, but if you think there's any chance at all that someday—"

Tanya swallowed with difficulty and plucked at the corner of the pillowcase. She couldn't bring herself to finish, though she was sure she didn't need to spell it out for him. It had taken every last ounce of courage to even raise the subject again, but she felt it important to give him one last out before they made a legal, lifetime commitment to each other.

Maybe he was thinking about it. He'd dropped his head, ran his hand through his hair and let it rest on the back of his neck. It seemed like a good position to think in, so maybe he was thinking about it.

Sweeping his jeans off the floor, Mick gave them a snap and stepped into them. "You know what the irony is here, Tanya?"

When she didn't answer, he looked back over his shoulder and zipped. "I know," he stated, turning to face her. "Between the two of us, I'm the one that knows for sure," he repeated, thumping his chest. "So that's the grade you would give us here, huh?" He threw his arm out over the mattress. "Good? You would say we're *good* in bed?"

Wow. Between her father and the whiskey, his response dial was set on hypersensitive tonight. It was just a figure of speech she'd used to make a point. Tanya looked up at him wanting to tell him that but he didn't give her a chance.

"I know the difference, Tanya," he carried on, the heat turning up under his proverbial collar. "You don't and never will. One night, one guy and under the influence? You can't know. You've got nothing to compare me to. And if *good* is the best you could come up with for us, then maybe I'm the one that needs to worry about you. Maybe you'd better start asking yourself if you're ready for this." He lifted her left hand off the pillow and gave it a shake. The diamond sparkled in the dimly lit room.

Because of her limited experience, she would never understand the vast difference between making love with the one you love and merely satisfying a physical urge. Though he wouldn't have it any other way, there was a sadness in that thought that made him feel worse than he had before she arrived. "It's been well past an hour. You'd better get home before he comes looking for you."

Tanya watched him go out onto the deck and hurriedly dressed to join him. Now she'd really done it. Why was she so easily influenced by others when the truth couldn't be any clearer if it jumped up and bit her? What was that saying? *Yesterday is history. Tomorrow's a mystery. Today is a gift. That's why they call it the present.* Well, she was about to take the gift of his love and run with it. No more doubts. No more fear of their future.

Fidgeting with her wrap style shirt to get her boobs in where they belonged, she came up short in the doorway. It was way past time for her to leave but, my oh my, she just had to take a second and enjoy the view—and not the view that added a good quarter mil to the price of the houses on this side of the street.

No, at the moment she was much more riveted to the scenery at close range, most especially the sturdy spread of those arms and the way his biceps swelled from the push of his weight against the railing. Maybe they didn't quite have Rambo's superhero bulk but to her they couldn't be more perfect. He had a beautiful back, flawless. The light from the bedroom, along with a little help from the moon gave his smooth bronze flesh a polished gleam. The Levis hung low on his lean hips. How blessed was she to have the love of this gorgeous, wonderful, sweet, complex man.

Coming up behind the arch of his right shoulder, she ran her fingertips through his hair. He would need a trim soon, though she loved it when it grew out long enough for her to play with. It reminded her of a time when he'd worn it long and kind of shaggy, before the Marines buzzed it all off.

Tanya ran her other hand over the hills and plains of his muscles, caressing them. "Would you feel better if I'd said that when we make love we come close to setting the sheets on fire. That when our bodies join, you reach so far into me, it's as if we begin to share the same pulse and it gives me the strength I need to sate you. That when I climax, it feels like you're filling me up with energy until I'm so full of you, of your love that I shatter into a million beautiful stars. And when it's over, I just want to lock my legs around you, hold you inside of me forever and never let you go."

For an answer, she was given lengthy consideration from a pair of simmering green eyes that Tanya was sure had melted just as many hearts as his dimples. Returning his steady gaze, her brows wiggled playfully. She saw that little hollow in his throat flutter. There was a heat wave rising up under her palms.

Mick hung his head to play back the words. His breath expelled in a whoosh. Better? Yeah, that made him feel better—about ten feet tall better. Growling, he pushed off from the rail and swept her up in his arms. "Do you make it your business to drive me crazy or does it just come naturally?"

Tucking her face against his neck, she whispered, "No more doubts. I promise." Soaking him up, getting her fix until they saw each other again, she hugged him tightly. "Will you walk me out?" she asked, hating that she had to leave him.

He sighed deeply. "If I have to." He left one arm around her as they headed inside.

"Oh wait, I just thought of something I wanted to ask you," she turned to face him. "You don't have to share this with me. I mean if you don't want to, I completely understand, but will you tell me why your parents divorced?"

Mick frowned down at her. "What does that have to do with anything?"

Tanya grimaced. "My father mentioned your father…and I…well, I believe…you know…"

"No, I don't know. My father what?"

Tanya shrugged. "You know," she pressed. "He alluded to the fact that he fooled around on your mother and that's why she divorced him. So he was sorting of lumping the two of you in the same category. If you know what I mean."

Mick stared at her, digesting this new piece of information. "Hell, I'm even guilty by association."

"It's true then?"

"C'mon, I'll give you the short version while I walk you to your car. The whole story will take too long. My mother was about twenty-two when my father met her for the first time up on the beach here. She'd just graduated from the University of San Diego. She told my father she was here visiting a cousin for the summer, which was true enough. What she didn't tell him was that she had been engaged and her fiancé stood her up at the alter. The only reason she came here was to lick her wounds, so to speak.

Things got pretty serious between them as that summer went by and just before she was due to fly home, they ran off and got married. A few months later my father found out everything when the guy came looking for my mother, wanting her back. Apparently, they had been high school sweethearts and were together a long time.

My father just couldn't handle the fact that he'd been her second choice. He felt she'd married him on the rebound, and things just went downhill from there. I know my father had other women eventually, but I don't think it started until my mother moved out of their bedroom. I was about thirteen I guess when that happened. As soon as I graduated from high school, she filed for divorce. He loved her, still does I believe. My mother's feelings have always been harder to gauge. Living with them was a fun time let me tell you."

"How sad. That must have been awful for all of you." Standing beside her car door, Tanya leaned into him, finding a resting place for her hands in the back pockets of his jeans. Exhaustion was beginning to set in. "Let's not think about my father anymore tonight. Maybe by tomorrow he'll have calmed down a little."

Mick spread his fingers through her hair, holding her against him. "So when is Prince Wakefield suppose to arrive and rescue you from my evil clutches?"

Tanya chuckled against his chest. "Hopefully, my father will call him and discourage him from coming, although he wasn't just coming to see me. His main objective, I'm sure, would be to acquire some land that my grandmother owns. He thinks my father can persuade her to sell it to his company."

"So he's not strictly coming to acquire you? Maybe I'll let him live then."

She tipped back her head to look up at him. "That would be decent of you."

"And if he does show up, and I hear you were walking around in your underwear—"

"Tanya slid her hands up the middle of his bare sexy back. "Like I would do that."

He smiled teasingly, intent on giving her a hard time. "I don't know. How would I know? As much as you love clothes, I think you sometimes have an aversion to them. Or do you just like getting me all hot and bothered?"

"Oh, that's always my plan." Tanya smiled seductively while her hands came back down the slope of his spine, circled his waistline then slid up his chest to grasp the back of his neck. Her sigh was heartfelt. "God, I wish I didn't have to say this but kiss me good-bye, and make it a good one. It may have to last me a long time."

Mick watched the red tail lights disappear around the corner and knew he was already sulking. *Four weeks. Give me a break.* Scraping his mood off the pavement, he dragged it with him as he strolled up the sidewalk and sat on the porch steps. He gave his burning eyes a rub then included the rest of his face. Coming down from the high, his skull was beginning to pound. The Jack Russell barking at him through the open window next door wasn't helping. Mick looked over his left shoulder, relaying a silent message.

Sensing now wasn't a good time to bother the nice man that always gave her a good scratch behind the ear, Genevieve, cocked her head with mewl of disappointment, dropped her paws from the sill and disappeared.

Resting his elbows on his knees, Mick hunched forward and folded his hands together. His head swung to the right for no particular reason. He eyed the company van sitting in the driveway. It could use a tune-up and new tires. The boat could use some work too, but he'd been thinking about selling it, getting a new one. Maybe an end of season bargain. If not this year, then next. Hard to find time to take it out anymore though. He'd see what Tanya thought.

A long cool breeze came along rustling the leaves of the lone tree in his front yard. The drop in temperature and humidity was a welcomed relief from the day's heat index. Mick assumed the winds must have shifted. A comfortable Friday night like this, the boardwalk would be packed. Last he saw of the forecast, they were headed into a nice stretch of weather. Should be a profitable weekend. There weren't many left. It was August already. It didn't seem possible. A few more weeks and another summer would come to a close, fall would set in, then the holiday season. Brisk autumn nights with Tanya. Christmas with Tanya. New Year's Eve with Tanya. How many of them had he spent wondering where she was, who she was with. Wishing. This year she would be with him. There was a God.

He remembered her saying how she'd always wanted to spend a few days in New York during the holidays. Done. He'd get tickets to a show, take her for one of those horse-drawn carriage rides around Manhattan if that's what she wanted. See the tree at Rockefeller Center. He'd research the best restaurants. They'd do some shopping. He looked forward to buying her Christmas presents. He'd buy her the moon.

Thinking about going in but too lazy to follow through, Mick changed his position from forward to backward and braced his elbows on the step behind him. He relaxed his neck, letting his head rest between his shoulder blades. He stretched out his legs and stared up at the sky. A million beautiful stars stared back. So that's how she felt when they made love. Me too babe, he thought. Me too. Then he heard the explosion.

His heart stopped while his muscles reacted and sprung him from the steps. He charged down the walk looking north in the direction Tanya had taken. A cloud of black smoke was rising into the sky. "No, no, no." Over and over again he repeated the plea as he raced into house. Grabbing the keys out of the ashtray, he tore into the garage, smacking the garage door opener on his way. There was a small part of him giving him that small shred of hope, reminding him it could be anything—a gas explosion, stupid kids playing with fireworks. It could be anything…anything.

Dear God, whatever it was, please don't let it be Tanya.

Forced to steady one hand with the other to get the key into the ignition, he wracked his brain trying to remember if he'd heard the sound of an impact first. He thought he might have but he wasn't sure. Tires squealing, he reversed out of the garage. He left a stretch of rubber on the pavement as he shifted gears and followed the route he knew she would have taken. Rounding the bend in the road he'd watched her take just moments ago, he heard the sirens. Sweat ran down his temple. Goosebumps broke out on his arms.

He came upon the accident on Central. Traffic was at a standstill, preventing him from getting close enough to see anything but red and blue swirling lights. First responders and people in general were running from all directions. Black smoke was still billowing into the sky.

He jumped a curb to park the Jag in the lot of a grocery mart where he and Tanya occasionally stopped to buy milk and bread, eggs, staples, that kind of thing. The last time they were in there, they'd run into Maggie and Sam. In the blink of an eye, she had that baby in her arms, sweet talking him, cuddling. He loved to watch her with Sam and Jennifer. Tanya was a natural with kids. She was going to make a wonderful mother. He'd never told her that. He should probably give her a call and tell her that now before he forgot again. She'd be home about now. If not, he could leave her a message. She wouldn't answer if she was driving but she'd call him back later.

Lacking shoes and a shirt, he walked up the middle of the street. He didn't know why he couldn't run. He'd taken off from the house like a bat outa hell and now he could barely move his legs. He walked alongside several stopped cars. Some of the drivers and passengers had gotten out to see what they could see. They were milling about, talking to each other, sharing information whether it was fact or speculation. It was so cold here. He knew it seemed chilly when he was sitting on the porch but here it was freezing. A sweat sheen covered his forehead and the center of his back.

Nearly sick with relief, he saw that it was the front end of an old pickup on fire. The police were controlling spectators, making sure everyone kept a safe distance away. They were stretching out the yellow tape for the assembling crowd to stay behind. A fire truck was trying to get through from the other direction. Two ambulances had already arrived. Police cruisers were stacked up as far as the eye could see. The pushed in nose of what looked like a shiny black sports car faced him as he got a better view of the scene. Both the driver and passenger doors were wide open, giving it the appearance of a strange looking aircraft ready for take-off. The driver was being pulled out onto the ground.

There was a lot of commotion going on, all of it still a good half block away, when like a moving jigsaw puzzle, everything began to shift and come together in slow motion. Two police officers appeared out of the melee. It was weird because all he could see of anyone else was their backs as they faced the scene, but these two cops…these two old friends in uniform were walking towards him. Mick thought he would be able to ask them what happened, get the news from someone who actually had first-hand information. If they ever reached him. Like him, they were walking so slow, through some kind of haze. They were saying his name, he thought, and though he couldn't hear them, he had no trouble reading the looks on their faces. He was going down. They weren't going to reach him. Not in time.

As the life in him began to drain, Mick saw the third car involved, it's dark underbelly with its four wide tires face up. He could see the mangled vehicle they belonged to, leaning precariously against a telephone pole. He could also see that the body of the vehicle was white. His legs were buckling as the two uniformed men caught him under the arms. Bile shot up into his throat. His chest caved then heaved. A wild cry screamed inside his head but found no exit. He surged, struggling frantically to move forward.

"Mick, Mick." Richie and Vince held on to him tight. It was like trying to hold back a train. "You can't go up there, buddy. I'm sorry man, we can't let you go there."

"Get the fuck out of my way. Let go! Jesus, let go of me. I have to help her!"

"Mick, hold on, hold on." The two officers struggled to restrain him. "There's nothing you can do. They can't get her out. They're getting the jaws. Listen to me! Listen!" Vince gave him a shake and stared into his eyes. In them was a fury and a fear he prayed never to see again. "She's alive. Benny and Lance are with her. They've got a pulse but she's unconscious, Mick. They'll take good care of her. You know they will. She's one of our own, buddy. She's not alone. They're with her, okay? Just hang on."

Both officers ushered Mick to their patrol car. They urged him to get inside but he refused and just stood leaning against it, staring across the intersection at the upside down jeep.

Richie drew Vince aside. "This is going to be pure hell for him. I'm not sure how long he's going to hold up. His skin feels like ice. I'll stay with him. Why don't you get him something to drink, hot coffee or maybe a shot of something? And see if you can find Garrett. Tell him to get here A-SAP and bring a shirt and some shoes."

He was in denial. He told himself it was only a nightmare. His mind could not accept this reality, therefore it chose to believe he'd gone up to bed, fallen asleep and was trapped in a nightmare. That's all this was. That's all it could be. This was not real. Not the emergency lights circling Central Ave. or the staticy voice coming across the police car radios, or the bystanders looking on with worry. They were all players in the theater of his mind. It was his fear of losing her today that brought it on. That's all it was. Tanya wasn't in that mangled pile of metal. She was home, or maybe lying right beside him. All he had to do was wake himself up and she'd be there. She'd roll over and wrap an arm or a leg around him just like she always did. He'd reach out and touch her silky skin. Their eyes would open and meet. Magnet to steel, their bodies would join.

Kiss me good-bye. I shatter into a million beautiful stars. Stay with me. I want to, but… Please stay. I can't Mick, it's late. Kiss me good-bye. It will have to last me until…I shatter into a million beautiful stars.

After running three blocks from where he'd had to park his car, Garrett paused on the sidewalk, panting heavily. He hadn't done much running since the Army. Man, did it show. He looked around. It was like a frigging scene out of a movie. He wasn't even sure what was going on here. He'd heard the phone ring while he was in the bathroom. Maggie had answered and told him the call had been an Officer Messina. The message was that there had been an accident on Central. Bring Mick a shirt and some shoes—and hurry. Maggie hadn't been given the opportunity to ask any questions.

Seemed like a strange request. Garrett tried to imagine what kind of accident would cause Mick to lose his shirt and shoes? And besides that, he'd just run past his Jag in the parking lot of the market. So, if it was a car accident, had he been driving the van?

Kelly McDonald was the first officer he saw standing several yards up. Catching his breath as he walked up the sidewalk, Garrett remembered about twenty some years back when the man was just a rookie. He'd come to his home one evening, around the time Rusty died. Scared the crap out of Garrett when he looked through the screen door and saw a policeman standing there. He thought maybe the neighbors had called the cops about Mick stealing their sickly pine tree, but it was about a different neighbor across the street who'd been robbed of a few high-end bikes and some other outdoor items. Officer McDonald just wondered if they'd seen anything.

"Kelly," Now on a first name basis with the man, Garrett called out to him over the crowd.

The stocky officer turned. "Garrett, jeez," he waved him through, sending him around the onlookers and under the yellow tape. "Jeez, I'm glad you're here. Mick's over there," he pointed to the patrol car at the corner. "Richie's with him but man I feel so bad for the guy. For both of them. Just engaged and all. Nobody can get a word out of him. I tried. You know, just to help the time pass for him, but nothing. It's like he's carved from stone."

Garrett opened his arms. A plastic bag hung from one hand, containing a sweatshirt and a pair of sandals. "Kelly, I just got here. I don't even know what's going on. What the hell happened? Where's Tanya?" A sick feeling was already creeping in.

The officer looked at him with glassy eyes and raised his arm again, this time pointing to the other side of the intersection where the jaws were working.

Garrett turned to look across the street. "Oh hell no. No, no, no, no." Shaking his head, he did a full turn then collapsed at the waist, his features wrenched with emotion. Coming up, he took a few steps for a better view and immediately turned back around. He hung his head. It was a moment before he could speak. "Have you seen her? Do you know anything yet?"

Kelly nodded gravely. It was times like this he hated his job. Tragedies stayed with you for a time but when it was someone near and dear, you were haunted forever. Richie and I checked her out when it first happened. She's twisted up in there like a pretzel. There appears to be quite a lot of blood. The windshield shattered but she didn't go through it. She was wearing her seatbelt and the airbag deployed, thankfully. She was unconscious but Richie felt a pulse. Hard to tell if anything we saw is life threatening. That had to be twenty minutes ago now, maybe more."

Garrett began to pant again, now more from fear. Every oath he knew kept going round and round inside his head. "Has anyone notified her parents?"

"No." Kelly frowned, giving him a strange look. No need to alarm them yet until we know more. There's no point in worrying them all the way down in Florida."

"I agree with you, except they're not in Florida. They're here in Lavallette. They just arrived today."

Kelly's rather fleshy, normally jolly, features blanched at the news. "Damn." Placing his hands on his broadening hips, he stared down the sharp crease of his pants at the shine on his shoes. "What a welcome home." Raising his head, he let a curse fly with quiet vehemence and asked that age old question no earthly being could answer. "Why? Why Tanya? Everybody in town adores that kid. She doesn't deserve this. Neither does Mick, her folks."

Choking up, the officer shuffled a few steps away. He had a daughter. She'd just turned sixteen. She kept pestering him to teach her how to drive. He and his wife were dreading the day she got behind the wheel and backed out of their driveway on her own.

Garrett's thoughts were running parallel with Mick's. He too wondered if he wasn't having a nightmare. He rubbed a hand over his face, hoping that when he uncovered his eyes, he'd find himself in bed with Maggie, but the horrible scene before him remained the same. He transferred his gaze from the crew working on the Cherokee to focus on his still and silent friend. Passing behind Kelly to go to him, he said, "I'll tell you one thing, Mick lives for that girl. If they pull her out and she… and she's…" he couldn't even bring himself to say it. "That will be it for him. Just so you're prepared. I may need some help."

Kelly clasped Garrett's shoulder. "Let's just keep praying for the best. When the squad leaves, I'll go over and get the parents. Richie and Vince will take Mick to the hospital. You might want to ride along with him."

Beside a store mannequin, Mick would have appeared the less lifelike. His complexion, stretched tight like a rubber mask over bones, had no color. Garrett figured there was a river of tears damned up behind his eyes. The strain of holding them back was taking its toll. He looked like he'd aged ten years. There was no physical or verbal communication between them. Garrett tried but to no avail. He couldn't get him to put the sweatshirt on so he threw it across his shoulders. He'd brought him a pair of leather flip flops, knowing his regular shoes would be too big for him, but no luck with those either. Garrett wasn't even sure he was aware of his presence. He worried that he might be going into shock.

Finally, the seemingly endless task of extricating Tanya appeared to be over and further activity was taking place. The paramedics were on the move. The stretcher was wheeled in closer. Mick came alive and started forward but after only a few steps, Richie and Vince appeared out of nowhere to stop him. Blocking his way, they had a brief conversation with him. Garrett heard most of it. They were doing their job, reciting their handbook, section 41.B, how to deal with loved ones in times of crisis. They threw in a few personal touches since they were all old friends.

They were right about one thing. In situations like this, time could be of the essence, a matter of life and death. By going over there, Mick would only create more of a delay and it had already taken precious time to remove her from the wreckage. As the three walked back to the patrol car, Garrett could see that the only thing holding Mick up was his pride.

Maggie was inside the emergency room lobby when they arrived. Garrett's mum heard about the accident through the Seaside grapevine and called the house to see if they knew. Immediately, Maggie took her up on her offer to come and stay with Sam. She arrived at the hospital ahead of the ambulance and was standing nearby when they wheeled Tanya in. Much of her hair was matted with blood. Dried streaks of red ran down her face. Her eyes weren't open. She wasn't sure if that was a good thing or bad. Her body was covered with a blanket.

Maggie rushed into her husband's arms when she saw the four men entering through the automated doors. Mick was walking beside Garrett looking dazed and haggard. She reached out a hand to him but there was no reaction. Simply putting one foot in front of the other seemed to require all of his concentration. Rife with meaning, her eyes raised to her husband's.

Returning her somber gaze, Garrett shook his head. "He's in another world."

They were all ushered into a nearby waiting room. Maggie immediately opened the bag she'd packed for Garrett earlier. She pulled the gray sweatshirt over Mick's head and guided his arms through the sleeves. She lifted each foot and slipped on the sandals. He didn't object to her dressing him, if he was even cognizant of the fact. When she was finished, she sat beside him, patted his back and prayed.

A short time later, Jim Morgan charged into the waiting room and found the person he was sure was at fault. In a fit of rage, he hauled Mick up out of his seat. "I want you to tell me how this happened. Where was she going? Where was she coming from?"

Yes. This was what he needed, Mick thought. This is what he wanted, what he welcomed and deserved. Not sympathy or compassion and comforting pats on the back, but somebody who'd land him a hard right hook. Better yet, beat him to a pulp. With his features pinched with torment and self-loathing, he began to purge the guilt bottled up inside of him. By the sound of his voice, the fires of hell had burned it to smoke and ash. "She was with me, and she would have been home hours ago if I hadn't begged her to stay. So go ahead you bastard, hit me. You were aching to do it this afternoon. Now you've got a reason." Mick brought up the heels of his hands and gave him a hard shove.

Jim stepped back to catch himself and lost his grip on the sweatshirt.

Mick's hands reached out again, pulling Jim back by grabbing his shirtfront. "Don't you hear what I'm telling you, bastard? She said she had to leave but I wouldn't let her go. I wanted her first. You get *my* drift?"

"Take it easy, Mick," Garrett stepped in to try and break them up.

"Stay out of it!" Mick's voice rose to a level that carried into the hallway, alarming Richie and Vince who'd been standing outside the waiting room doorway. They rushed in but were practically mowed down from behind by a tearful, distraught mother who latched onto them, pleading desperately for help in obtaining information about her daughter's condition.

"Didn't you hear me you son of a bitch?" Determined to get what he wanted, Mick's voice continued to taunt the man. "I seduced her into staying. That doesn't surprise you, does it?"

Jim took another hard shove with Mick breathing fire as he came after him again. "It's my fault she's here! Can't you get that through your thick skull, Morgan? C'mon you son of a bitch, hit me!"

The hands of both police officers reached out, coming within inches of stopping the meaty fist that shot out like a cannonball and plowed into

Mick's jaw. There was a flying spurt of blood as his head jerked. A high-pitched scream erupted from Maggie and Carol. His body landed hard, bounced and slid another two feet across the waxed linoleum.

"What in the sweet petunias is going on in here?"

All heads turned towards the pint sized, white haired, spectacled doctor. Advancing hastily with a short rocking stride, his gaze lighted on each face in the group. He continued past them to inspect the body splayed out on the floor.

Mick blotted his split lip with the back of his hand and followed the lab coat up to a pair of bright green eyes twinkling behind rimless lenses.

"You must be the fiancé." The doctor raised his head with its wispy fine, snow white cap of hair, to seek assistance from the pony-tailed, tattooed man facing him from the other side of the body. He eyed the double pierced earlobe. Since one of his earrings was a shamrock, he felt an immediate rapport. "Help the lad up, will you? I'd do it myself but that child has me tuckered out. Giving me orders left and right. Bossy as my wife," he muttered and moved over to the eldest man in the room besides himself. "You must be the father. A pleasure, Mr. Morgan," he held out his hand and waited patiently for the return gesture. Understandably, they were all in a state of shock and slow to respond. "Dr. Smally," he introduced himself. "I'm sure you'll all have a laugh about that later. Oh, and here's mum," again he reached out his hand. "I can certainly see the resemblance. You have a lovely daughter. Truly lovely. Though I'm going to assume she gets her spunk from Dad. That's quite a weapon you have there," he said, pointing a clipboard at his fist. "I tend to believe your daughter uses her tongue."

Dr. Smally counted seven open mouths. "Well, I'm sure you're all anxious to hear how the child is fairing. If you'd care to take a seat, I'll fill you in on her condition." There wasn't a flicker of movement. "Very well then, if you're comfortable. First of all let me assure you she is doing remarkably well for such a serious accident. I am waiting for some test results, however from what I see so far, I do not anticipate anything major developing. She is in excellent physical condition, which is always an advantage. We do know her left arm is broken, neat and tidy. A closed fracture as we call it, which if you're going to break an arm—" he tilted his head, leaving the rest implied. "We have an excellent Orthopedic on call. He will review the x-rays and undoubtedly apply some type of cast as soon as possible. She's obviously in a considerable amount of pain with that but I've given her something to make her comfortable. She does have a mild concussion and several abrasions. No doubt there will be many bruises making an appearance by tomorrow. As we speak, she's being stitched up quite nicely in three places. Two near her hairline. Well, actually they've just used a butterfly there. But, in the soft area here on the side of her hand, I estimate she will take six, possibly twelve here in the back of her right arm and a good five across her left knee." As he spoke, Dr. Smally demonstrated by pointing to the areas on his own body where she would receive the stitches. The injury here," he added, indicating his upper arm, "is smarting her a bit. The gash is quite deep."

He paused there, looking down at his clipboard to make sure he hadn't forgotten anything. He hadn't, except one thing. He dropped his chin to lift his gaze above his reading glasses. His merry green eyes swerved to the left, then to the right until he was sure he had included everyone. "I have to tell you though that she seems less concerned about herself and more concerned about what might be going on out here. Having seen this young man take flight a few minutes ago, I can certainly see why.

"I don't wish to minimize the extent of her injuries by any means," he continued. "She took a major tumble in that vehicle and will be feeling the effects for several weeks. She is most definitely suffering the consequences, therefore I feel it would be in her best interest if I keep her here for a day, possibly two, for observation. And, let me be clear, I do not want this young lady upset in any way during her convalescence." A pointed look was given to two individuals in particular, one with a swelling lip and the other with a smarting hand, or so he would imagine. "Now, I'd be happy to answer any questions."

None were raised, though there would be questions, he was sure, after the joyful hugs and tears. Dr. Smally was, however, concerned about the beau and doubted much of what he'd said even penetrated. Sometimes too much information at once. Perhaps when he saw her with his own eyes. Poor lad, he looked like he could use a bed for the night as well. That lip would need ice, possibly a stitch. The doctor gave them all a moment while he helped himself to a free cup of tea. He hoped they'd replenished the sugar since earlier in the evening. Ah yes, there it was.

"Mr. Leighton." Dr. Smally addressed the man with the vacant stare who sat forward on the edge of his seat. There was no response. Not even a blink. Aye, love could sure bring a body to the heights and the depths. He checked his clipboard to confirm the spelling the lass had given him. Not having far to go, he bent over. "Mr. Leighton." Nothing. The doctor turned to the redhead beside him. "Am I pronouncing it correctly?"

Maggie nodded and putting her hand on Mick's back, gave it a rub. "Mick, the doctor is speaking to you."

At last, a flicker. "Mr. Leighton, I have strict orders to bring you to her immediately." Once again, he turned to the friend beside him. "Take him down to emergency, will you? The nurse will show you where she is and give him an icepack. I'll bring mom and dad down in a moment."

Receiving a nod of agreement from the woman, Dr. Smally grinned at her with a smile that gave him an almost angelic persona. "If I may miss, do you still have family there?"

"I beg your pardon?" Thrown by the change in subject, Maggie turned an ear to hear the question again.

"In Ireland," he clarified. "Do you still have family there?"

"Oh," Maggie smiled, expelling a breath. She looked through the spectacles at a pair of eyes that were as green as the rolling hills she'd been born to, green as her own. "Yes, yes," she nodded. "I do. Hoards of them, actually."

"Excellent," he patted her hand. "We'll talk at the wedding. The Mrs. and I have been invited."

"Maybe he got lost. Maybe someone is stopping him from coming in here. Could you please go and check?" Tanya asked the nurse who didn't seem to be particularly enamored with her profession. Either that or she'd left her bedside manner at home today. She wasn't very friendly or helpful. Tanya thought if she were a nurse, she definitely would have been friendly and helpful to someone who'd just cheated death by the skin of her teeth.

"He'll be along. I'm sure Dr. Smally will bring him in shortly." Penciled brows furrowed. That should have been funny, the nurse supposed, but after seven hectic hours on her feet, she wasn't exactly in a *ha ha hee hee* mood. God, Friday nights. Everybody she knew lived for them. They didn't work the night shift in an ER.

Tanya closed her eyes beginning to float. "But I'm getting groggy and I think I'm going to be sick." She was having difficulty forming her words. She was feeling fuzzy and spacey too. The doctor said she might. "You don't understand. I need to see him." Oh no, she was getting weepy too. Why doesn't anybody understand?

His fingertip lightly grazed her cheek, catching the tear. Her eyes opened and instantly overflowed. Damn, she didn't want to cry. She wanted to see him clearly. See his handsome face. She'd been waiting and waiting and waiting and now he was all blurry. Tanya lifted her right hand and weakly clutched his shirt. She'd run out of strength and could only whisper his name. She attempted a smile but her lips were trembling too much.

She had been so brave for the doctor. For a short span of time, almost euphoric. Regaining consciousness, her thoughts had immediately turned to Mick and her parents and the agony they must be going through. Poor Dr. Smally. She'd hardly taken a breath during the exam, burdening him with her life story about Mick and her father. After she'd said everything that seemed determined to come out, and he left her to report her condition to those in the waiting room, she'd crashed like a lead balloon, finally becoming aware of all her aches and pains and injuries—right down to her pinky toe, which hurt like a son of a gun.

Seeing Mick now, touching him, brought everything back in a head rush. They'd kissed good-bye. The first mile had been uneventful, the traffic busy as usual for a Friday night. Approaching a red light, she was about to brake when it turned green. Instead of slowing down, she accelerated through the intersection. She remembered the radio station she was listening to began playing the same Rolling Stones song that had been playing from Mick's stereo when she walked into his house earlier. The Stones were one of his favorite groups and feeling a surge of love for him, she'd reached out to turn up the volume when bam, she was struck broadside with a force that nearly knocked her head off her shoulders.

The nurse said there had been three cars involved. She didn't know. All she remembered was the one hit, the world turning upside down then her final thoughts of Mick when it turned black. "So fast," her voice slurred, looking up at him. "He was flying. I was afraid I would never see you again. I was going to die." The flood filling her eyes gushed over her cheeks and down her temples. "Hold me," she cried. "Please, hold me." Feeling his body press gently into hers, she sobbed and sobbed and sobbed.

Mindful of her injuries, Mick held her as best he could and buried his face against her neck. Using extreme care, he placed his hand on top of her head.

Her good arm came around him and feeling that strip of bare skin where his shirt and jeans parted, she hungered for more of him. She took her hand higher, beneath the hem and stroked his back where the shudders raced. His shoulders tucked in around her and Tanya knew he was crying too.

It was a moving scene to witness. Quietly, the nurse walked around to the other side of the bed and started to pull the privacy curtain before she left to check on the broken nose in unit three.

"You can leave it open, Sara," Dr. Smally advised, coming upon them accompanied by Jim and Carol Morgan.

"I was going to give them a few minutes," she whispered after six footsteps shuffled to a halt. Unable to resist, she gazed back at the couple with envy. "It must be wonderful to be loved that much." Recently divorced, she too went in search of a shoulder to cry on.

Voices penetrated. Mick brought himself under control, uncomfortable with the fact he had lost it. Not so much in front of Tanya, but specifically her parents. He sensed they were behind him, and the little leprechaun doctor as well. Raising his head, he rubbed her cheek with his own, feeling their tears blend. Pressing his lips there, he kissed them away then framed her face to kiss her properly. "I love you," he told her. Afraid the doctor had missed something, he didn't want to leave her. He repeated those three little words again, frustrated with how ordinary and overused they sounded. He wanted to say something new, something different, something that would come closer to describing what he felt for her. Squeezing a fist full of her curls, he eyed the bandage at her temple, the mixed smear of yellow disinfectant and dried blood surrounding it. Her hair on that side was caked with it. One last shudder shook him. Gently he touched his lips to hers. "I'll be right outside."

Tanya clung to his shirtsleeve before letting him go.

Running a hand over his damp face, Mick turned and walked out under her parents' watchful gaze. He chose to look elsewhere.

"He's been like that all night," the petite blond nurse with the short ponytail and tiny voice whispered. "I offered to bring in a cot for him but he refused. He dozes off and on, but mostly he just sits and stares at her. Look at the way he has his hand wrapped around her wrist. I think he's constantly checking her pulse."

The sturdy brunette with the no nonsense attitude consulted the patient's digital chart. While she brought herself up to speed, she unclipped her damp hair, swept her fingers through it, gave it a twist and threw it back up. Another crazy morning. She hoped Cody remembered to let Max back in before they left the house and made a mental note to call him at her in-laws. "She came out in pretty good shape for rolling her jeep into a telephone pole I hear. What's he afraid she's suddenly going to snuff out on him?"

"Looks that way."

Silent soft-soled shoes padded from the foot of the bed to the head on the same side the visitor was seated. Her purpose, to get a better look at the guy the night nurses were all gaga over. According to them he was the next best thing since Cunningham's bread pudding. He'd even gotten into a fist fight with someone in the ER, and they'd given him an ice pack and some Advil and wasn't it romantic the way he refused to leave her side, and bla bla- bla bla- bla bla bla.

The man was zonked, softly snoring, his head pillowed on his folded arms. The rest of his body formed a Z around the visitor's chair. She took a closer look. "Holy cannoli, I know this guy," she said over his head to the other nurse, her voice so low, the statement was practically mouthed. "He was a few years ahead of me in high school," she said further, retracing her steps to the other end of the bed. She went to say more and luckily was smart enough to pop a cork in it. She and her best friend had the biggest crush on Mick Leighton. God forbid she let that one loose. Her co-workers would have a field day. She wasn't exactly known on the floor for her softer side. Still fixed on his zigzagged form, her eyes lost focus for a moment. Seeing him after all this time took her back to those fun-filled, carefree times before three kids, a dog, a hamster and a hefty mortgage. "Hmmph," she shook her head and let out a sigh. Kiss those glory days goodbye. Her eyes shifted right to her sleeping patient. "So, this chick finally hooked him, huh?"

"They're engaged."

"I can see. That's some bling, but it will have to come off. It should have before they applied the cast. What idiot could have missed that rock?" She checked her chart to see. "Look how her fingers are swelling." Yes, she heard that little somethin somethin in her tone, but it wasn't intentional. Just doing her job.

The blond walked over to the bed to see for herself. "I noticed that too, after the fact. I thought maybe the patient talked them out of removing it. Jodi assisted, I'll ask her." She tossed her colleague a look. "Glad I won't be here when you break the news, especially if it has to be cut off. Well, I'm going to hit the road. It's been a long night. Oh, just so you know, her father is on his way. He called to check on her condition and asked if there would be a problem getting in this early. I don't know which one of them is paying extra for the private room, but I assumed it would be fine."

"Okay, hasta manana," the day nurse replied absently as she took one long last look at the nice stretch of skin visible between Mick's shirt and jeans. Tilting her head, she did a full body scan of whatever else she could see. Damn, that was still one good lookin dude.

"Whenever you're finished ogling the visitors, Mr. Garswicki needs to pee."

"Shhhhut your pie hole, Restivo!" The brunette pulled a pair of surgical gloves from the dispenser on her way out. "Big mouth. He might have heard you."

The sun shining through the half opened blinds warmed his face where the stripes crossed him. It felt good. Like life. Like the pulse beating sure and steady beneath his fingertips. He woke gradually, sadly aware of his surroundings, yet considering what might have been? God, it didn't bear thinking about it. Releasing her wrist, he came up on his elbows. Both hands tunneled through his hair and continued down the back of his neck. Leaving them there, he worked on the kinks.

She looked better this morning, but not perfect. He wouldn't be satisfied until then. Her night had been restless. Around dawn she fell into a peaceful sleep. They both had, apparently. Bruises were showing up. Two that he could see. One on her cheekbone and one bigger than an old silver dollar on her right hand. What he couldn't see, again he couldn't bear thinking about. Placing a kiss on her forearm, he thought it felt cool to the touch. He took the edge of the blanket and folded it up and over her arm, tucking it around with the meticulous care of a collector wrapping a priceless object d'art. Becoming conscious of the ache in his back, he straightened his spine then let it roll into the armchair. Jim Morgan entered his line of vision.

"Morning."

Mick had the urge to look behind him to see if the greeting was meant for someone else.

"I brought you coffee." With a nod, Jim indicated the bedside table on Mick's side of his daughter's bed. "Hospital brew is usually for the birds so I stopped along the way."

After giving the man a deeply suspicious once over, Mick turned his head and saw the Dunkin Donuts cup, packets of sugar, two creamers and a stirrer. For someone who made coffee a number one priority every morning, it was a tempting sight, but he was no fool.

"It's not laced with arsenic, if that's what you're thinking."

Was that a ghost of a smile on his face or the morning light playing tricks on him? Or maybe he was smiling because he *had* laced the coffee with poison. It always paid to view things from every angle, he thought, wanting to remind the bastard he wasn't born yesterday.

Mick watched Tanya's father take a sip from his own cup and knew he wanted coffee so bad he was just about ready to die for it anyway. Figuring he was safe enough in a hospital, he decided to go for it. If he didn't keel over by the time the drink was gone, he might even start believing this was some sort of peace offering. He reached over and lifted the cup off the high table. He removed the lid. "Thanks," he muttered before he took a swallow. Unfortunately the anticipation didn't quite live up to the reality. Immediately, Mick winced when the coffee and the rim of the cup touched his swollen lip.

Jim had been watching—just as he'd watched for the past half hour, just as he'd watched last night. He was convinced now beyond a shadow of a doubt. The poor guy had it so bad he almost felt sorry for him. "You asked for that."

Using his knuckle, Mick checked his lip for size. It was a little puffy, damn sore. They'd dabbed some stuff on it in the ER but it hadn't called for a stitch. He was lucky the hit hadn't loosened any teeth. "I know," he finally said after the self-exam. "Believe it or not, it felt good at the time." He took another sip of coffee, keeping to the healthy side of his mouth.

"Same here," Jim flexed his hand where it rested on the arm of the chair. Yeah, it was going to be a few days before it was back to normal, but for just a moment when his fist connected, he felt thirty years younger. Yup, he still had it and was grateful for the opportunity to prove he still had it. Things like that meant a lot when life was pushing you around the bases faster than you wanted to go.

Purely by chance, they happened to catch each other's eye. Grins began to take shape with neither giving up more than a dent in their cheeks. It was a fight to the finish but soon their lips were inching their way into full-blown smiles, accompanied by deep chest laughter.

What the heck were they talking about? Tanya woke up and started to open her eyes when she heard her father's voice. He'd brought Mick coffee that wasn't laced with arsenic? Oh my gosh, how sweet. She would have been hard pressed not to smile if her body hadn't felt like it plunged off Mount Everest and bounced its way into a rocky ravine. But what was it Mick had asked for that felt good at the time? And what the devil was this—they were actually laughing together? Under the cover of her lashes, Tanya shifted her gaze from one man to the other. Seeing Mick's dimple was like getting a shot of pure nirvana, until he turned his head a bit.

Her eyes flew open. "Oh my God, Dad, you hit him?" Struggling up on her right arm, she glared at one, then the other.

Both faces fell blank and guilty. "He asked for it."

"I did Tanya. I really did."

"He shoved me and called me names."

"He's right. I did. Really bad names."

With her position putting pressure on the stitches in the back of her arm, she grimaced in pain and lay flat again. "You two are a couple of babies. Raise the bed Mick, please. I can't see anything."

"Top o'the mornin to ya and what a fine mornin it is." Dr. Smally entered with his comical jaunty gate. Oh, how he loved to whip out his Irish when the mood was upon him. He shook hands with the da, keeping half an eye on his patient whose body was dipping and rising like the tide.

"Will you please show him how to work this thing before I get seasick?"

Dr. Smally rounded the end of the bed and squatted down beside the beau. "Here laddie, let me show you." He did so, then out of the corner of his mouth. "You've got your hands full with this one. She'll keep your blood rushing. Reminds me of my Deirdre. Bold and sassy. Wouldn't have her any other way."

"I heard that."

Dr. Smally popped up wearing his angelic grin. The blanket caught onto his hair, sprouting an alfalfa. He patted it back down as he walked around to the other side of the bed again. "Well, let's take a look at this gem first of all. The nurse tells me your fingers are swelling." He raised her hand carefully to see for himself. He tried turning the band and gave it a gentle tug. He couldn't imagine why they hadn't made her remove it before applying the cast. "We could try some lotion or good old fashioned soap and water but lass by the looks of it, I'm afraid it may have to be cut off at this point."

Stunned by the unexpected announcement, Tanya looked down at her fingers and saw that they were swollen. But she didn't care. "No," she stated adamantly. Just the thought of it made her heart ache. Cutting her ring off was unacceptable. She wouldn't stand for it. Out of the question. "No," she repeated, plainly. What else, her mind screamed. What else!

Mick stood beside the bed, holding his breath. Of course the ring should come off if that's what the doctor decided. The band could be fixed or replaced. Tanya's finger couldn't. It was a no-brainer, but damned if he didn't feel like shedding a tear right along with her. Didn't they have enough strikes against them for Pete's sake. He didn't know where he could touch her that wouldn't hurt so he stroked her hair. Looking up at him for a moment with the saddest eyes, she dropped her head against his chest.

"The ring stays." To Mick and Tanya's amazement, it was her father who made the decision. He rose from the chair to join the doctor in his examination. "We'll keep a close eye on it to make sure it's not cutting her circulation."

Dr. Smally gave one last look behind him before leaving the room. A touching scene. Yes, yes, quite moving. He remembered the punch the lad had taken last night, as well as the boundary line between family and friends. According to her story, there'd been quite a conflict between father and fiancé prior to the accident. Aye, the Lord works in mysterious ways, he thought with a twinkle in his eye and if possible, an added spring to his step. He'd come back later to check her condition. Right now she was getting the best kind of medicine.

Chapter 14

Tanya scooped up a dollop of vegetable dip with a cucumber wedge and rose from the table. Leaving her mother, Lisa and Maggie behind, she walked over to the lawn chair to stretch her legs out under the sun. For what seemed like the tenth time, her mother ran down the wedding checklist. Tanya didn't know why hearing it again made her want to scream.

Of course she knew why. It was just hard to admit she wasn't feeling like the happy bride-to-be. The accident had changed everything. More to the point, it had changed Mick.

Carol Morgan read from her spiral bound notebook. "Let's see, we've finished the guest list and I've notified all family members. Dana is in the process of calling everyone else. Jack will be in charge of all the food and the menu has been finalized. We have until Friday to order the flowers. Garrett has arranged for his band members to play later that night. We've booked the church with Father Dimitri performing the ceremony at five, reception to follow with the cocktail hour at Paradise and dinner at The Cove. Is that right, Tanya? Has that been decided?"

"Mmm," she nodded without elaborating.

"Think about what kind of entertainment you'd like to have during the cocktail hour then, Tanya. Just something light. They can perform on the patio if we're lucky enough to have a warm sunny day like today."

Again, Tanya bobbed her head. "Okay."

"Good, good," Carol gave her daughter a second look, this one a bit bewildered as she applied an appropriate wax smile drawn from the collection all mothers kept on hand in lieu of a real one. "Well then, now let's see, what else? I'm sure we're forgetting something." She tapped her pen against the pad, thinking.

"Has Mick been able to reach his mom and dad yet, Tanya," Maggie asked, reaching for a slice of fresh pineapple.

"Not that I'm aware of." The listless response discouraged further questioning.

"My gosh, I'd forgotten all about them. Where are they living now anyway?" Lisa asked Maggie since she had raised the subject, and Tanya was being about as communicative as the trees.

"His mother lives out in San Diego and his father is up in Lake George."

Listening to the exchange, Carol wasn't the least bit fazed, aside from hoping for Mick's sake that both his parents would be able to attend. Jim had finally accepted Mick and in so doing had accepted the fact that Michael would most likely attend the ceremony, and from that day forward would, in a sense, become family.

The day her husband gave Mick and Tanya his blessing had been a turning point for them as well. Strangely, it breathed new life into their own marriage, and they were able to find that romantic love again that had faded since those difficult times. They felt like giddy teenagers trying to make love quietly so Tanya wouldn't hear them. They also talked for hours, openly, honestly, banishing old scars and secret fears. Jim had, and even without her prodding, called Dan Wakefield, tactfully informing him that his daughter, as well as the land, were no longer available.

In a macabre way, the accident had been the miracle Tanya thought it would take to bring her father around, but oh, the price had been much too dear. The memory of Kelly arriving on their doorstep that night with the dreadful news…Carol choked up every time she thought of it. She decided to return to the much more pleasant task at hand.

"Tanya, don't forget, after your cast is removed Wednesday," she held up crossed fingers, since her Ortho doctor hadn't made any promises, and it would all depend on the x-ray, "we'll need to go dress shopping." Carol glanced over at the lawn chair. "Tanya?"

"Hmm?" Her mind elsewhere, Tanya opened her eyes and tuned into her mother.

"Your dress, dear. Have you thought about what style you would like or where we should begin our search? I thought I saw you looking on the computer the other day. Did you have any luck?"

"No, I didn't, not really."

"Well, have you decided on formal or semi-formal? You know since you'll have to buy off the rack, your options will be limited. If you get a formal gown, Mick will need a tux. He'll need to see about that soon, if that's the case. All of the men will. Don't forget, the wedding is only two weeks from Saturday."

Carol turned her attention back to the girls at the table and gave a light laugh. "Can you imagine the four of us walking into a bridal salon and telling them we all need dresses that quickly?"

"I'll probably just wear a short dress or something. Mick won't need a tux."

She might as well have said...*Any old thing will do.* Troubled by Tanya's growing indifference regarding one of the most wonderful days of her life, Carol's smile slowly faded into a frown as she continued to peruse her. It had been almost five weeks since the accident. On the surface, she'd been recovering beautifully. Other than the cast and the fresh scars from the stitches, she was beginning to look the picture of health. The bruises were long gone. Days of rest and relaxation and basking outdoors on the deck had added a new golden luster to her skin. In her denim shorts and pretty blue flowered halter top, she was perhaps revealing a little more than Carol considered proper, but then as Mother Morgan would say, *If you've got it, flaunt it.* She and Tanya were so much alike. Carol stretched out her arm to touch her daughter's ankle. "Tired, dear?"

Tanya looked up from her engagement ring on her right hand. "No mother, I'm not tired at all." She lowered her gaze to her diamond again. She knew they were going to remove it. Before discharging her from the hospital, the doctor insisted upon it. Of course she and Mick were having problems now. What did they expect after the symbol of their love was destroyed, the band mangled beyond repair? With Mick's arm wrapped around her, she'd wept silently while the mini saw buzzed, severing her beautiful ring.

Carol watched her daughter studying her engagement ring. She knew Tanya had been very upset about it initially, but after a good cry, she appeared to move past it. Mick was able to pay extra and expedite the purchase. Within a week the ring was back on her finger, looking as flawless as before. No, there was something else bothering her, she was sure. A kind of quiet sadness had been growing day by day. It was evident in her eyes, the only thing about her that didn't shine. Yes, something was definitely wrong, but what? Carol turned back to their guests with a shrug and a tremulous smile. She kept her voice low. "Delayed reaction from the accident maybe. I think I'll call the doctor and see if this is typical behavior."

"So, what's up wich you kid?" Lisa dropped down beside her best friend.

Tanya scooted her hips over to give her room then sat up and peered around her.

"Maggie went upstairs to check on Sam, and your mother is in the kitchen worrying her little heart out."

Tanya sighed, reclining. "I was afraid of that. I suppose I should have shown more interest."

"Yeah, a little enthusiasm would be nice. This is your wedding we're planning, you know, not your funer—" Lisa slid one hand over her mouth, her other grasped Tanya's and held tight. "Oh dear God, I can't believe I nearly said that." She inhaled deeply and raised her eyes to the sky. Neither could help but recall how close it had come to that. The hand she still held was given a squeeze. "So, c'mon tell me what's going on. I can't get a read on you today."

"Nothing is going on, Lisa. That's the problem."

"Well, doctor's orders, no? Take it while you can get it I say."

"Mmm, I wish I was getting it. I'm long past that stage of my recovery."

"Come again?"

"Funny you should say that."

"I'm lost."

"I'm— Don't make me say it, Lisa. You know I hate that word."

"Ooooh." Catching on, Lisa locked her hands around her knee and leaned back." Still uncertain though, her nose wrinkled. "Horny?"

"Do you know that word is in the traditional Merriam-Webster dictionary? I never knew that before. I always thought it was slang."

Chuckling, Lisa asked, "Is that what you've been doing with all this free time, looking up dirty words in the dictionary? No wonder you're horny."

"I might as well. It's good for a cheap thrill since I'm not getting them anywhere else. I feel like I'm about to marry a boy scout."

"Mick? A boy scout?" Lisa felt her brow. "Oh yeah, you've been out in this sun too much."

"I'm serious, Lisa. He's changed since the accident. All we do is play cards, watch TV, go for walks. And if he brings me one more container of custard or ice cream— If it's in the house, I'll eat it. Mostly out of boredom. I bet I've gained five pounds. Anyway, that's no big deal, and in the beginning when I couldn't do much of anything, it was nice of him to come over and sit with me and help pass the time, but I'm all better now and he's still treating me like a porcelain doll or something. When we're alone he doesn't sit close to me or want to cuddle like we used to. I know he's deliberately avoiding touching me. He'll hold my hand when we walk and give me a little peck on the lips when he leaves at night. But that's it. I know something is wrong. Very wrong. It's not just the intimacy either. He's quiet and distant. I just want to shake him and say, who are you and what have you done with my Mick?"

Lisa patted Tanya's good arm. "Well, don't be reading too much into it. You two have been through a traumatic experience. He knows you've been recuperating. Plus, you're getting married soon. Maybe he just wants to wait for your wedding night. You know, make it more meaningful. Something to really look forward to."

Tanya gave her a look through her lashes. "No," her head shook. "No," she stated again and couldn't have disagreed more. "Before the accident, I would have said this man could not even go five days without it, never mind five weeks. Mick is the real deal you know. He's not just eye candy. He completely lives up to his looks. I could barely get in the front door and he would be all over me. He's just a very physical person. He strips you naked with his eyes before he even gets his hands on you. He's got this off the charts libido and this raw, lusty sensuality that just… just…you just know he's about ready to…to…"

Lips parting, body humming, Lisa listened with rapt attention. "Go on."

Tanya ran out of steam trying to say what she meant. Her shoulders collapsed. She semi grinned, giving her friend a swat. "You get the idea."

"Thank you very much, now you've made me horny and John's away."

Tanya chuckled and tipping forward, she gathered up as much hair as she could with one hand, piled it high and leaned back again. The sun had shifted, making her close her eyes until she removed her sunglasses from the top of her head and put them on. She exhaled with feeling, all the way down to the bottom of her diaphragm. "Will you listen to me? You'd think I'd be on top of the world. Mick and I are finally getting married. He and my father are practically becoming bosom buddies. It was something of a miracle I survived that accident, and all I can do is find something else to complain about." Her head rocked to the side as she looked up into her friend's face from behind dark lenses. "I want my old Mick back, Lisa. I just don't know where to find him."

Lisa rested her jaw in her hand and ran her gaze over the Cover Girl face, the centerfold body stretched out on the lawn chair. *I should have such problems*, she thought, then immediately felt bad…and ashamed for even thinking such a thing. Here she was with the most wonderful husband and sweet little Jennifer. Her problems compared to others were one big fat goose egg. She considered herself a very blessed individual, never having to face the emotional upheavals her friend had been through between Mick and her parents and now the accident. She wished she could tell her she was getting this beautiful vision of her upcoming wedding, but unfortunately she was a blank. It wasn't something you could force. "Are you going to see him today?"

"He's coming over later."

"Well," Lisa flicked the hem of Tanya's shorts before standing up. "This outfit ought to light a fire under him, and if it doesn't, then I'd say you've got something to worry about."

~

"Hi." Tanya offered her lips and received a kiss on the cheek. Another time he would have lifted her by the fanny and made a meal of her mouth. She shut the front door and turned the lock.

"I passed your parents at the corner. Where are they headed?"

"Spring Lake. Dinner with friends. They'll be gone for awhile."

"Oh." He looked halfway over his shoulder. "They'll probably stay ahead of the storm then. It's coming up the coast."

The old Mick would have said...*Alone at last*...and pinned her against the nearest wall. "Mmm, I thought I heard thunder."

"Mind if I grab a beer?" Mick threw back another quick look.

"Help yourself. It's your beer." A dramatic swing of her arm indicated the kitchen. When he turned his back, it slapped against her thigh. She could have been dressed like a bag lady for all he noticed. Another time his eyes would have burned three holes in her clothes.

Tanya positioned herself in the doorway. Leaning a shoulder there, she cocked her hip. "Hungry?"

"I ate at The Cove." He twisted the cap off and tossed it in the garbage on his way to gaze out the sliders. "I would have brought you something if I'd known your parents were going out."

He was exhibiting a rapt interest in the coming storm. Envying the sky, she replied softly, "You did bring me something."

"Hmm?"

The glance he threw back at her fell short, only reaching as far as the light switch. The mis-connection appeared to have been intentional, a deliberate effort *not* to look at her.

"Nothing," her head shook. "So what do you want to do tonight?"

"There's a game on. Yankees are still hanging onto first place. They're playing the Sox. They're one game behind. You like to watch the games, don't you?"

"Yeah, sure, love'em." A loud clap of thunder rolled over the sarcasm, drowning it out. Fat raindrops began to hit the deck. "Oh, I just remembered, my windows are open upstairs. You know how that one sticks. Would you mind?" Tanya waved her *poor little ol' me* broken arm when he turned around.

Mick set his beer on the counter and walked towards her.

Tanya turned sideways but remained in the doorway. Her look dared him to get by without brushing against her body. "Thanks," she gave him a smile full of innuendo when her breasts made contact with his shirt and the hard body beneath it.

When he reached the landing, she dashed to the sliders and locked them then ran back across the kitchen, across the living room and up the stairs. He was on the second window when she entered. Quietly, she closed the door and locked it behind her. Her heart was racing. She hadn't had that much cardio since the accident.

Mick turned around. "Unless you want to turn the air on, we should watch the game downstairs. It's going to get like an oven in here with the windows closed."

Tanya slumped against the door. They had the house to themselves, and he was trying to get her *out* of the bedroom? Didn't he want her anymore? Was he having second thoughts? They'd finally set a date because her parents needed to get back to Florida now that she was better and could handle Paradise on her own again. Was he getting cold feet now that the wedding was about to become fact instead of fantasy? Had her father been right about him after all? The bastard, she'd kill him!

"What's wrong, don't you feel well? Mick noticed her breath quickening, her color heightening. "You should have stayed downstairs." He started towards her. "Where's your sling? Why aren't you wearing it?"

Pushing off from the door, she started towards him. "I feel fine, Mick. Other than being extremely baffled by your behavior, I feel great. How do you think I look? Do you think I look all right?"

"You look…better."

"Do I Mick?" Her head tilted sending chestnut waves swaying across her bare back and over her shoulder. "Do I really look better? Because I don't think you've really looked at me since I came home from the hospital." Tanya reached out and took a fistful of creamy yellow cotton. "Look at me, damn you!"

Mick covered her hand with his and drawing her against him, tucked her head beneath his chin. "Okay, okay, calm down. Don't get upset. I'm getting all the signals. It's just easier if I don't look at you. Especially when you're dressed like this."

"I dressed like this on purpose. What's easier?" She was near tears from the scare he was giving her.

"It's easier to keep myself under control."

"I don't understand. Why? Why all of a sudden do you want to keep yourself under control?"

Dropping his hands, he turned around and walked over to the chaise. He sat down on the end and bowed his head. All ten fingers rubbed at the pressure hammering at his brow, as if he could erase the image that haunted his dreams.

"Every time I look at you, I see the blood and bruises, the stitches, your arm. Sometimes I see worse. I see you like that when I'm trying to fall asleep at night. I wake up in the same cold sweat every morning. I can't get that night out of my head. You were there in that intersection at that moment in time because of me. You wanted to leave and I wanted—" With a rueful slant to his lips, his eyes traveled up her legs. His head shook. "If I'd let you go when you wanted to go…God, if only I'd let you go, you never would have been there at that time. You would have been home, safe and sound. I might as well have broken your arm and cut you up myself. It makes me sick."

Tanya's bottom dropped down on the bed. She was stunned he'd been harboring so much guilt. The thought never crossed her mind. "I don't believe this! I had no idea you were blaming yourself. That's ridiculous, Mick. I hardly put up a fight. If I'd really wanted to leave, I would have."

"But that wasn't the case. You stayed for one reason, to please me."

In a way that was true but— Flustered by her attempt to think of the right thing to say here, Tanya's mouth opened and closed a few times. "Mick, you can't go through life second guessing every move and what may or may not happen as a result of it. Who knows, if I had left earlier, I might have been in a fatal crash. It would have changed the traffic pattern. Maybe you saved my life. It makes just as much sense as your theory."

"Mine is not a theory, Tanya. It really happened. It's a fact. Do you have any idea what it was like for me to stand there and watch them work on that twisted pile of metal not knowing what kind of condition you were in, wondering if they were going to pull you out alive or…or dead. And all the time knowing that if I'd only had the decency—"

Tanya rushed forward and dropped down on her knees before him. "Stop it! Stop! This is insane, Mick and I won't listen to it!"

"No. No it isn't," he argued, adamantly. "You know what else is a fact? Your father has good instincts." He threw a hand towards her bedroom door, even though he wasn't in the house. "He's been right all along. All these years I hated him for it, and you know why? Because somewhere up here," he tapped the side of his head, "I knew he was right. I'm no good for you." Driven by what he believed and feared could be true, he took her face in her hands and stared deeply into her eyes. "You picked the wrong guy squirt. I'm not right for you. All I do is hurt you. Look what I did to you eight years ago. I hurt you emotionally, and now I've hurt you physically. Jesus, I nearly killed you."

He lifted her hand from his thigh. Folding her knuckles, he pressed them against his forehead and rubbed. His eyes closed tight. "That night I stayed with you in the hospital, I watched you sleeping and I promised myself that if I couldn't find the strength to let you go, then I would make it up to you by changing and treating you like the incredible lady I respect and admire."

Tanya felt the lightning strike overhead spear straight into her heart. "What? No, no. Nobody is going anywhere and nobody is changing. And when did I become a lady?" Her head shook swiftly. "No! There will be no changing. Feel free to treat me like that in about forty years maybe. Mick, I know you respect me. My God, do you think I would even be with you if I didn't get that from you? That has nothing to do with this. You've always made me feel loved and cherished and desired. The way we are with each other is the way it was meant to be, the way it's always been with us. It's passionate. It's powerful, the way we feel about each other. It's natural. You're trying to force yourself to behave in a way that's just not you. Besides, I don't like it and I can't believe you do either."

Running her hand into his hair and down the back of his neck, she touched her lips to his. "Don't. Please don't keep saying those things. Everything we've been through, we've been able to overcome because of how much we love each other. Now, we're finally in a good place. We've been through all the bad stuff, and now it's time for us to be together and be happy and plan our future and you're going to mess with that?"

"It doesn't feel like a good place, Tanya. How can you not blame me for this?" Mick ran his hand down her cast. "I can't forgive myself. Not this time."

She sat back on her heels. "Mick, do you remember that night the way I do? I didn't stay just to please you. I stayed because with you is where I belong. I hated to leave at all. If my parents weren't here, I wouldn't have had to drive home—so you can just as easily say the accident was their fault. Which is ridiculous. It was no one's fault except that asshole that ran the red light."

Tanya couldn't tell if she was getting through to him or not. He just stared downward, off to the side, locked in his own private hell. He needed something to help snap him out of it, something to *light the fire*, as Lisa put it.

"Look at me." She placed a finger beneath his chin, steered it straight then raised it. She gazed into his eyes. "The way I see it, you have two choices. I can either hit you or you can make love to me."

Mick chuckled faintly in spite of his low spirits.

Tanya ran her thumb across his amazingly soft lips. "And now that these are all healed and looking very kissable again, my guess would be that you're not in the market for another fat lip. Correct me if I'm wrong, but I think you might be leaning toward option two. It's your call, but to be perfectly honest, I could go either way. My palm has been itching to smack something all day, and I almost think I could be happy with either, but—"

On a fierce growl, Mick dove into the side of her neck. "Liar." In a flash she knew he was capable of, she was off the floor, in his arms and on the bed. His lips came down like a crushing machine then eased back to soft and gentle. "You want it so bad, I knew it the minute I walked in the door."

Tanya's lips parted for his tongue. It stayed just long enough to start her bones melting. "I do. I do. I can't believe *you've* lasted this long." She rushed to pull up his shirt to feel his smooth back. "I thought we would at least do a little something on the beach the other night."

"I told you, I've been trying to change. I wanted to prove to you it's not the sex between us that's most important to me."

"Mmm, that's very sweet," she panted, squirming, smiling weakly. "And not that I don't love you for it, but do you think you can help me get these off?" Tanya struggled with the denim shorts, using one hand to work them over her hips was proving difficult.

Mick laughed and grabbing a handful of blue flowered fabric, he threw her halter over the side of the bed.

"What?" Tanya watched it sail. "How…? I didn't even feel…"

"C'mon, those things are a piece a cake. That's why you wore it."

Dropping her lashes, she gave him a look that wasn't all pleasant, despite the fact the cocky comment was a good indication he was on his way back to true form, right where she wanted him.

"God, I've missed these." Even on her back her breasts rose full and lush, creamy white against her new tan. "Don't worry about the shorts," he pushed her hand aside. "I'll get to them."

Feeling the need and the greed taking over, Tanya guided one of his hands down to blue denim. Not that she wasn't enjoying the foreplay by any means but at the moment, it wasn't really necessary. "Mick?"

"Hmm?"

"I'm kind of in a hurry."

"Wow, maybe it was worth the wait," Tanya murmured languidly, once she was able.

Giving her room to breathe, Mick came up on his forearms but bore down on her mouth as if he needed it to break his fall. "God, I need you back in my bed. It's so frigging big and empty without you."

"I know, I know. Just two more weeks."

"I was thinking about waiting until our wedding night. Good thing we didn't or we might have done some serious damage to ourselves." The statement was made in all sincerity.

Their lips met and settled comfortably together this time, the tips of their noses touching. Blue eyes connected with green. Smiles began in the visual exchange then stretched across their sealed mouths at a tentative rate. Laughter followed, slow and silent, bubbling in their lungs until it burst free and filled the air.

Mick rolled them over on a chorus of loud sighs. "Forty years, huh? Does that mean you're expecting me to perform like this in my seventies?"

"I have tremendous faith in you."

"Yeah, well dream on baby." He clutched her rear and gave it a shake "You better get it while the gettin's good."

"I fully intend to." They laughed again, clinging tightly.

Mick nuzzled her cheek. “We should get out of here. I’d hate for your parents to come home and find us like this.”

“Mmm,” With the pad of her thumb, Tanya smoothed back sweat dampened hair at his temple. “You look like you’ve been hard at work.”

“Hard at work? You damn near killed me.” According to his flashing dimple, he hardly suffered through it.

“Well, if you hadn’t made me wait so long.”

His cell phone began to ring. Rolling into a seated position on the edge of the bed, Mick looked back and gave her a once-over as he swept his pants off the floor. “Yeah, you want me to tell you what you look like?” He dug the phone out of his front pocket and looked down at it to see if he wanted to answer. “You look like you’ve been royally—”

Afraid he was going to access the caller in mid raunchy sentence, Tanya gasped, laughing and tried to grab the phone out of his hand.

Switching it to his left hand and ear, he covered her face with an open hand and shoved her back onto the bed. “Hey Jack, what’s up?”

“Mick, sorry to bother you but you’ve got a few visitors over here.”

“Who?” He adjusted his position slightly to face Tanya. God, she was hard to look away from. He reached out and cupped one breast, thumbing the rosy nipple.

“Your parents.”

“My parents?”

“Mick?”

“Mom?” Mick’s surprised gaze leaped from Tanya’s chest to her widening eyes. He dropped his hand to her leg as she sat up to listen in. “What are you doing here?” Jack had said “*parents*,” plural. “Dad’s with you?”

“Actually, he is. If you’re not busy, we were hoping you and Tanya could join us here at The Cove?”

“What’s going on?” Even though his mother sounded in good spirits, there was a feeling of foreboding starting to build as to why they were here. What possible reason would they be together unless one of them was sick? That’s the only thing he could think of, although he couldn’t imagine either one of them turning to each other for emotional support in times of crisis. They never even spoke.

“Well, we’d really like to tell you in person. Is now a bad time?”

“We’ll be right there.”

Tanya got into the car and with a little jockeying of the strap was able to buckle the seat belt one-handed.

"Got it?" Mick asked her, sliding into the driver's seat.

"Mm hmm," Tanya nodded, hoping she was all put together properly. She adjusted her watchband, nudging it to a more comfortable position. It was the first time she'd put one on since the accident. It felt strange on her right wrist. Glancing down at it, she saw the time and couldn't believe it was going on seven. "Mick, it's been forty-five minutes since they called. I feel bad I held you up. I should have just let you go on your own and met them another time."

"Absolutely not. I can't wait for them to meet you."

She smiled in response and flipped down the visor to look in the mirror as he drove to the end of New York Ave. "Now you see what I've been going through, trying to shower with this stupid cast and get dressed." She checked her appearance from the square neckline up; hair, make up, earrings. She wasn't nervous she kept telling herself.

"Always happy to help in that department."

"Are you sure this dress is okay? It's a little summery for September, but it's hard to fit anything with sleeves over the cast."

Mick glanced down at the outside temperature gauge digitally displayed on the dashboard. The storm had kicked it up a notch. "Tanya, it's 76 degrees. Besides, officially, it is still summer." Stopping at a red light as he entered Seaside Heights, he turned his head towards her and looked over the dress with the bold black and white print. Her favorite silver hoop earrings shone brightly against her pretty slender neck in the dim interior of the car. If it wasn't for the blue sling, she could have stepped off the cover of a magazine. "Come here," he leaned towards her for a kiss.

The knock on the car window made them both jump. Police Officer Kelly McDonald stood at Mick's door peering in with a big smile. "Hey you two, don't you know you're holding up traffic?"

Mick depressed the appropriate button, glanced up at the green light then checked the rearview mirror. There was one car approaching from a distance but there wasn't anyone directly behind him. Already, the Heights was beginning to look like a ghost town.

"Let'm wait." Holding his hand out the window, he grinned up at the man.

Kelly grasped the offered hand tightly and gave it a good shake. "I don't blame you, buddy. I don't blame you. See you at the wedding."

Mick swung the Jaguar into its designated spot. It was Monday evening, Labor Day, and from the empty streets and number of cars in The Cove's parking lot, it was obvious most vacationers had packed up and headed home. The last holiday weekend of the season was coming to a close. The summer heat might be lingering, but the sky was changing, the sun setting earlier. Mick chose to think about that during the short drive rather than speculate on the reason his parents were here. Whatever it was, he was about to find out, he thought, cutting the engine. Stalling, he stared over the silver hood of his car at the *Reserved* sign hanging from ship's rope between two cedar pilings.

Tanya had one foot out the door before she realized Mick wasn't moving. She looked over her shoulder. "What's wrong?"

He shrugged. "What do you think they're doing here?"

Tanya told him her first instinct. "It is odd that neither of them have been reachable for a few days. Is it possible they could be back together?"

"That was my second thought. Yesterday, I would have said there'd be a better chance of pigs flying. If they are back together, I hope they don't expect me to celebrate." On that note, he opened his door.

Tanya shut hers and stood staring at him as he came around the car. "Why? Why wouldn't you be happy for them?"

Mick shook his head. "Let's see what they have to say first."

They were seated at the bar having cocktails. Pete was keeping them company. Tanya urged Mick to walk ahead of her and say his hello's first. He did so, but kept her hand in his until he nearly reached them. Standing off to one side gave Tanya the opportunity to form a quick first impression.

His mother was meticulously groomed wearing raw silk cropped pants the color of root beer and an oversized ivory shirt. Her long necklace and drop earrings were gorgeous, made with antique gold and amber stones. She was a much sought after interior designer in the San Diego area, Mick had told her. Tanya would have hired her on the spot just based on her appearance. She had chin length, blunt cut, natural blond hair and warm hazel eyes made up with an expert hand. Her high prominent cheekbones seemed to require no such artifice. They glowed with a youthful blush that Tanya considered might have something to do with the ruggedly attractive man at her side.

The natural aging process and perhaps some long suffering heartache had marked Michael Leighton's lean features with premature grooves and creases, but his eyes hadn't lost that Leighton charm, nor his smile that dimpled twist. Like his son, he was very nicely constructed, and though his father had more of the dark, they both had the same streaky golden brown hair.

His parents certainly made a striking couple, Tanya thought, broadening her gaze to picture them as such. She looked on while Mick hugged his mother and kissed her cheek soundly. He and his father exchanged back slapping hugs along with their hearty handshakes. There was a true show of affection all around. So what was his problem?

Suddenly, Mick reached back and drew her against his side. Tanya smiled at her future in-laws, knowing during that one-minute exchange with their son that they had been taking their own covert glances, sizing her up as well. No doubt they were as anxious as she was to meet.

"Mom, Dad, this is Tanya."

Joanna Leighton clasped the offered hand between both of her own. "Forgive me for staring. I've been so excited since Mick told me you two were together. I remember seeing you on the boardwalk with your mother when you were just a little girl. I was beginning to worry Mick would never meet someone only to find out it's been you all along."

Joanna kissed her cheek and it was clear to Tanya this was an emotion filled moment for her. Before she could say anything in response, his father chimed in and took her hand.

"Tanya, my pleasure. From what little my son finally tells me, I gather you've been a well-kept secret. We couldn't be happier for both of you. How are you feeling since the accident? We've been thinking about you."

"Thank you. And thank you so much for the beautiful flowers," she was glad she remembered to say. She'd received a fantastic summer bouquet from his father and get well wishes from his mother written on a lovely Claude Monet note card. "Other than this," she raised the sling a bit, "I'm fine now."

"Thank heaven. Pete was just telling us more about it. I can't imagine how frightening that must have been for you."

"It was…pretty bad," she nodded. "Definitely not a night we like to revisit. I was very fortunate." All eyes turned to Mick as he took a few steps beyond them to look across the bar at the far corner booth. He found it empty and coming back suggested they move there. He took everyone's drink order. Within ten minutes they were all settled comfortably, exchanging awkward glances over filled glasses—at least she and his parents were.

Mick got straight to the point. "Well? I assume you both got my message that Tanya and I are getting married on the twenty-fifth. Since that's still more than two weeks away, you must be here for some other reason."

It was plain to see his parents were both having trouble expressing whatever news they were there to impart. After a few tense moments of silence, his father reached over to take his mother's left hand, which had been clutching the stem of her wine glass. Whether it was his intention or not, Michael let their matching platinum wedding bands begin their story. Tanya's sidelong look at Mick caught him staring down at their hands. His expression was stark and grim. She wanted to touch him but he was on her left side.

"About a year ago your mother mailed me an envelope full of old pictures she found of Pop," his father finally began. "I wrote her a letter to thank her and told her it would be nice to hear from her from time to time. I never thought I would, of course, but a few months later, to my surprise and delight, I received a letter. Soon after, we began corresponding via email, then the phone. I flew out to see her in March on a whim. She didn't know I was coming. I had to see her." He squeezed her hand and the loving look they exchanged was filled with words unspoken.

"Since then, we've been somewhat enjoying a long distance relationship. I say *somewhat* because we both knew we wanted to be together again, but where? You know how I love Lake George, and my work is there, although I've taken on a partner which will certainly help. Your mother is, of course, partial to the west, so we're just going to have to compromise and see what happens." He chuckled deeply.

"I've been told the log cabin is in desperate need of a good decorator, so we'll be spending the next few months there while she gives it the Midas touch."

While Tanya's eyes turned to blue glass, Mick had been tapping his fingers on the table with an unmistakable show of indifference. Knowing he was about to say something unpleasant, she took more than a delicate sip of her wine.

Michael cleared his throat as Joanna slipped her hand from his for a sip of her Bordeaux. "We re-married Friday in..."

The drumming rhythm ceased. Mick raised his hand. "Okay, okay, hold on, Dad. You know, I really appreciate you two coming here to fill me in on all the romantic details but to tell you the truth, I'm really not interested."

He left. Tanya couldn't believe it. He just picked up and left her there sitting in the booth facing two people she just met who were trying to contain themselves in front of a complete stranger. It soon became too much for his mother, and she burst into tears.

"I knew he was going be mad at us. I was a terrible mother to him Tanya. He has every right to be upset."

Mick's father closed his eyes and rested his head against the back of the booth. Tanya saw his arm move and knew he had placed a hand on his wife's thigh to comfort. "Mrs. Leighton, I...I can't speak to this situation obviously but I can tell you that Mick's had, we've both had, a pretty rough few weeks since the accident. I know he's ultra-sensitive right now. I'm sure you took him by surprise and he just needs a little time. I'll go and talk to him."

Tanya found him in his office propped against the desk, arms folded, staring down at his shoes. Something about his expression made her swallow the *thanks a lot* ready to bounce off her tongue. Instead, she walked over to him, stood beside him and assumed the same position.

He gave her a quick look. "Sorry, I didn't mean to leave you stranded out there. I figured I better leave before saying something I'd regret."

"Will you tell me why this upsets you so much?"

"No. It's no big deal really."

"Evidently it is, or you wouldn't be in here and your parents out there."

Pushing off from the desk, his muscles rippled beneath his polo shirt. He was a man with a man's pride, a man's ego. He was a Marine for heaven's sake. This had to do with his childhood. It was a given he didn't like the vulnerable position he found himself in. "Mick please talk to me. When I'm upset about something, you don't give me a minute's peace until I tell you about it."

That earned her an over the shoulder glance. There was a hint of a smile riding the corner of his lips. He turned around shaking his head. "I just don't get it. When I was very young, I guess it wasn't so bad. We did family things, ate meals together, if I remember correctly. The memories are vague but at times it seemed like they were happy, or at least they worked at it, even though my father knew by then he wasn't her first choice. Then the fights started, then the silence. I hated that. I used to hang out in my room and blast my stereo and somehow I could still hear the silence. When I was old enough to leave the house on my own, I started spending most of my time with my grandfather up on the boardwalk, or at his house a few blocks away. They were so wrapped up in their own miserable little world, I think they were relieved to have someone else dealing with the responsibility. My mother would call over at his house or the shop to check on me sometimes but..."

On a deep breath, he raised his focus from the middle of his desk to the tree-shaded window overlooking the parking lot. He slid his hands in his pockets. "I let off a lot of steam in the Marines and developed a much better relationship with them as an adult. I'm actually pretty good friends with both of them. They're good people but as parents, they sucked. I have a hard time remembering anything worthwhile. My grandfather was more involved in my life, taught me more, was there for me more. I don't know," his head shook as he looked down at his shoes again. "Maybe I'm being too hard on them, but I remember watching some of my friends with their parents and seeing what it should have been like."

Tanya wiped the tear from her cheek and went to him. She wished she had two arms to hug him tight. She couldn't even get close enough with the stupid sling. "I'm so sorry Mick. I never knew."

He pressed his head against her own during the embrace and continued to stare out the window. "What the hell took them fifteen years to realize they really do love each other? And they've been communicating since last year? Why the hell didn't they tell me?"

Tanya reared back and gave him a look. "It's pretty obvious, isn't it? They must have known this is how you would react."

"Well, whether I did or didn't know, this absolutely blows my mind. Look at all the time they wasted. Now that I see them holding hands and making googly eyes at each other, it just pisses me off that they didn't realize it a long time ago. Then maybe I wouldn't have been so—"

"Lonely?"

He shrugged. "I wasn't lonely, I guess. I had my grandfather. I had Garrett. I had…you."

"Oh, Mick," she hugged him again, even tighter. Looking back up at him, she said, "When I left the booth, your mother was crying. She told me she'd been a terrible mother to you."

He harrumphed, peering down at her. "So what, now I'm the one that's suppose to feel bad?"

Tanya ran her palm across his soft shirt. "People make mistakes, Mick. You know if you stop and think about it, we're perfect examples. We made the same mistake as your parents, separated for eight years, still loving each other without being able to show it. I kept telling myself I hated you. Even if you had tried to force the issue, I wouldn't have been ready. Forgiving can be very difficult, Mick. Sometimes impossible."

His arms embraced her as hard as he could, as hard as he dared mindful of the cast. "I'll never forgive myself for that, Tanya. I swear I wouldn't know her if I passed her on the street. To think I might have lost you forever because of that night, scares the hell out of me."

She closed her eyes, letting his strong arms and words dissolve the last fragments of pain. "We're all human, Mick. We got a second chance. See if you can find it in your heart to give your parents one, too. I think they need your blessing to be really happy now, just like you needed my father's."

Mick kissed her brow, his hands gently caressing. "You're right. C'mon, let me try this again." Walking over to the door he held it wide and followed her out. "Man, this has been one helluva summer. Maybe I should go buy a lottery ticket or something."

"Feeling lucky," she grinned, glancing back.

Coming alongside her, he threw an arm over her shoulders. "Luckiest man alive."

Epilogue

"What color do you think mommy would like, hmm?" Mick gave the sheer fabric in his hand a toss as he studied the cut, color and fine lace trim. "Pink, blue, or wait here's black, although the pink is more transparent," he muttered to himself.

Ten-month-old Summer Reese Leighton, nestled in the crook of her daddy's left arm, reached out a dimpled hand towards the pink confection.

"Ah, ah, ah. I know it's pretty but this isn't for you, darlin. No, you are never going to be allowed to wear anything like this. Never ever ever." He used a soft lilting tone. The kind he used when he read to her from picture books.

As if she knew their effect, Summer batted her big blue eyes. Her face lit up with a slow smile. Jiggling happily, she patted both hands against her daddy's jaw then buried her face against his soft sweater. She turned her head, found her sweet spot and sighed contentedly.

Mick moved on to some other slip of nothing that caught his eye. He felt Summer's little fingers tapping his neck. "You can try buttering me up all you want but the answer is still no. I see how Sam's been hanging around, all protective, like he's some big brother or something. He's a sly one but I'm onto him. It takes one to know one, you know? He's a lit-tle too willing to share his toys if you ask me."

Summer tossed back her crown of wispy blond curls. Her button nose screwed up on a laugh and turned a bright pink.

Mick looked down at his daughter and chuckled back. "You think that's funny, huh? Well, Sam won't think it's so funny when Grandpa Morgan gets hold of him."

At the mention of the name of the really big man who had a nice wide shoulder to fall asleep on when she was up past her bedtime, Summer gave a little start of surprise and looked in one direction then the other.

"He's not here now, darlin. Tomorrow, you'll see him and Grandma CC."

Summer suddenly tilted her head back and studied her daddy's face as if she found it as fascinating as her favorite Baby Einstein video. She stared at him, eyes wide and lingering as she concentrated on each of his features. She patted his ears, pinched his nose, poked her finger inside one of his dimples.

Equally fascinated, Mick gazed back at the miracle he and Tanya had created. He was utterly wrapped around her little finger and terribly afraid she was already using it to her advantage. Sometimes he shuddered thinking about the future, envisioning his daughter a teenager, hanging out at the beach wearing a teeny bikini. Wherever she went, he was sure he wouldn't be far behind, hiding in the tall grass to make sure she stayed safe. He was definitely not looking forward to that. God, how he hated to admit it, but he could totally understand everything Tanya's father put him through now.

Mick cupped the back of Summer's head as she continued to inspect him like a bug on the wall. He saw Tanya in her eyes, her coloring, the plump cherry pink lips. Her hair might change, Tanya said, but right now she was pure blond. Though some people disagreed, Mick didn't see himself in his daughter and good God wouldn't want to. He saw his wife and his mother and that suited him just fine.

Mick pressed a kiss on his daughter's sweet smelling brow as emotion washed over him. If life got any better…

Tanya caught sight of them through the glass wall just as she began to bristle with frustration. She headed for the entrance to Victoria's Secret. She should have known she'd find him in here. She paused at a big table piled with scanty panties and went to raise her hand to gain his attention but he'd already turned the other way.

A high heeled, attractive, thirty something screaming of retail polish, sidled up to her. Tanya assumed she was going to ask her if she needed any help. *No,* was on the tip of her tongue when the woman instead said, "Do they belong to you?" Her head angled towards the rear of the store in the direction of the only male customer with the baby attached to his chest.

"Yes," Tanya sighed, keeping an eye on her husband. "Has he been any trouble?" When it came to intimate apparel, he was like a kid in a candy store. He wanted one of everything.

The black haired woman laughed throatily and crossed her arms. "I've been getting a kick out of watching them. He wouldn't have a brother on the loose, I suppose."

Tanya gave her a double-take as she made her getaway. "No, fraid not." He's an original and all mine, she thought but didn't say.

"Tell him not to forget his package," the woman called out.

Tanya threw her a smile and proceeded deeper into the store.

"Hello sweetheart," she greeted her daughter who looked back at her mother during a big wide yawn. "I know baby, you're tired. We're leaving now. Tanya rubbed her back and smiled into her sleepy eyes. All snuggled against her daddy's chest, she looked like she was going to go out any minute. Tanya felt terrible keeping her up this late but they had an early flight and she just had one more gift to purchase. Of course, they would have been gone by now if Mick had stayed where she left him. Tanya flicked his sleeve. "I was looking all over for you."

"And you found me." He was preoccupied with a black lace garter belt. "We were right across the way. I figured you'd see us in the window."

"Well, eventually I did. What are you doing in here?"

"Christmas shopping."

Sidetracked by a short scrap of lavender blue silk, Tanya held up the hanger. "But, we already exchanged gifts, except for the few things we shipped to Florida. Which reminds me. You didn't by any chance send anything like this, did you?"

Mick gave her a comical scowl as they headed towards the checkout counter. "What do you think I'm crazy? Your father would probably make us sleep in separate rooms. Every time we're down there and it gets near bedtime, he starts giving me the evil eye."

Tanya laughed. "He does not. You're imagining things."

"Am I? You watch him next time. It's like he's giving me this silent reminder that their room is right next to ours and he doesn't want to hear any funny business."

Tanya walked past something almost irresistible and paused to consider it. Her head tilted wondering if she was back in shape enough to wear something like that again. Soon, she hoped. A little more belly work. "Funny business?" She looked up at Mick, grinning and frowning at the same time. "Is that what we're calling it these days?"

To call his wife a smartass now, Mick had to rely on his expression. He'd been trying to clean up his language. Funny business had been one of his grandfather's frequent sayings and the older he got, the more often he found himself using them.

The same saleswoman included all of them in her generous smile. Handing over a pink and silver shopping bag, she wished them a happy holiday.

On their way to the car, Tanya linked arms with her husband. She drew his between the opening of her leather jacket and teased him with the press of her breasts.

"So, if you're not bringing my gift with you to Florida, when are you giving it to me?"

"Tonight."

"But, that's not fair. I don't have anything left to give you."

Shimmering green eyes turned her way. His lips lowered for an intimate brush with her own. "Don't worry about it," he murmured. "All I want is a thank you."

The End